THE ABDUCTION OF SEVEN* FORGERS

* plus one falsely accused

THE ABDUCTION of SEVEN FORGERS

PLUS ONE FALSELY ACCUSED

SEAN DIXON

Freehand Books acknowledges the financial support for its publishing program provided by the Canada Council for the Arts and the Alberta Media Fund, and by the Government of Canada through the Canada Book Fund. The author acknowledges the financial support of the Ontario Arts Council Recommender Grants.

Freehand Books
515 – 815 1st Street sw   Calgary, Alberta   T2P 1N3
www.freehand-books.com

Book orders: UTP Distribution
5201 Dufferin Street   Toronto, Ontario   M3H 5T8
Telephone: 1-800-565-9523   Fax: 1-800-221-9985
utpbooks@utpress.utoronto.ca   utpdistribution.com

Library and Archives Canada Cataloguing in Publication
Title: The abduction of seven forgers / Sean Dixon.
Names: Dixon, Sean, 1964– author.
Identifiers: Canadiana (print) 20230454178 | Canadiana (ebook) 20230454186 | ISBN 9781990601491 (softcover) | ISBN 9781990601507 (EPUB) | ISBN 9781990601514 (PDF)
Classification: LCC PS8557.I97 A73 2023 | DDC c813/.54—DC23

Edited by Liz Johnston
Book design by Natalie Olsen
Cover image: "The Parasol" by Francisco Goya, 1776–1778, oil on canvas, © INTERFOTO / Alamy Stock Photo
Printed on FSC® recycled paper and bound in Canada by Imprimerie Gauvin

Now use your silver tongue once more

There's one thing that I'd like to know

—LHASA DE SELA, "FOOL'S GOLD"

PART ONE

ASSEMBLAGE

*Term coined in the 1950s by Jean Dubuffet to
describe works of art made from fragments of natural
or preformed materials, such as household debris.
The term is not usually employed with any precision
and has been used to embrace photomontage at one
extreme and room environments at the other.*

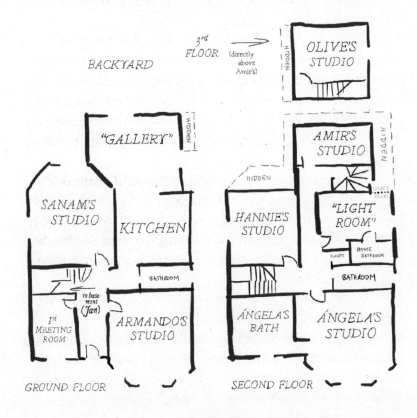

1. *A M P H A R O O L*

One day, not long ago, I was kidnapped by a bitter but fun-loving South Korean art collector named Mr. Jackie Lin who had been burned one too many times by art forgers and wanted a bit of revenge.

When I thought back on it later, it was so obvious. There I was, jumping at an invitation to London, "to be feted." But nobody ever gets feted without knowing the details in advance. Do they? Nobel Prize winners get the phone call without any warning, but the phone call itself is packed with information and everyone knows the day it's made. The caller doesn't just say, for example, "Come to Oslo; we've got a surprise for you!"

In my case the invitation didn't come in a phone call but rather an email — no, a private message on Facebook, in early January — from a woman named Ella Unton Bride, who looked very much like a Londoner to me, red-haired, with a tight white collar and bow tie, not to mention an address in Dollis Hill and the following postscript:

"Don't tell anyone just yet. We want it to be a surprise. Send measurements. And please, no children."

How could I have fallen for it? My only achievements, of which I was admittedly very proud, were hidden behind the names of far more renowned Canadian (and, in my single most successful case, American) artists. Under my own name I had accomplished nothing whatsoever. So why did I think I deserved to be rewarded? How could I not have smelled a rat?

Well, in my own defence, doesn't everyone feel they deserve to be rewarded? Do you, reader, not feel you deserve to be rewarded? Don't judge me for *that*.

That universal truth aside, I think I fell for it because I was looking to change my life.

2. DARA

The address was in an area of London near a big patch of green called Gladstone Park. I looked at Street View and saw a lot of beautiful old trees. I thought I remembered a children's story set there in which many of those trees were hollow, filing that information away in case it turned out to be a kidnapping trick and I had to find someplace to hide. Ha ha. Ha ha ha ha.

The house I was heading to was on Olive Road. Funny coincidence because Olive is also my name. I took the Heathrow Express downtown, bought an Oyster card (waste of money, as it turned out) and took the underground to Willesden Green Station. Came up just after two p.m. into a sunny, mild midwinter day and stopped for a roti. Somehow the small talk with the server turned to my hailing from Canada, and the man said, "I came here from Somalia last year. I was also accepted to Edmonton, Alberta. It's in your country, yes? I lie awake at night sometimes and wonder whether I made the right choice, coming here instead of going there." And then, more rhetorically: "How can I ever know if things are not better in Edmonton, Alberta?"

I had never been to Edmonton, Alberta. And the truth is I had always longed to visit and considered it a terrible flaw to my integrity as a Canadian that I had not. But that's not what I told him. I told him that I'd heard it was flat and cold in Edmonton, Alberta, and mostly populated with mistrustful people who would definitely look askance at someone from Somalia, that it was obscenely far away from the rest of the world, that you couldn't get any fresh fruit there and that people had been known to develop rickets and even scurvy, that residents heard loud, otherworldly sounds at night, as a result of which it had been named the most likely city to be used as a landing pad for an alien spaceship of colossal size.

I really don't know what came over me. I think I just saw his need. He laughed, and I hoped I would get my roti on the house, but I did not, I'm sure much to the relief of the Edmontonian reader. I'm sorry, Edmontonian reader: I was just trying to do the man a good turn. London is one of the great cities in the world, isn't it? It's absurd to think a Londoner might lie awake at night wondering if he should have chosen Edmonton, Alberta.

So, then I stepped out onto Walm Lane or Walm Line or whatever it is, walked up and left and up and left, past lawns that were green even though it was winter, found myself approaching a house that might have been from a nice area of my home city of Toronto. Only larger and probably older. It had two big bay windows, one on the ground floor and the other directly above it.

"You have arrived," I said, mimicking Google.

It was surprising: I'd been picturing an embassy-style neighbourhood, with tall black gates and intercoms. This street was purely residential, though, and seemed like it would normally be as quiet as a mole in one of those hollow trees of Gladstone Park.

Except there were a man and a woman standing in front of the house I was heading for, and they were screaming at each other in a language I did not understand.

The man was flourishing a white-cuffed hand through the sleeve of a woollen black overcoat and accusing the woman of something — I thought perhaps a domestic impropriety, assuming they were husband and wife. She yelled back, and then he, and then she, overlapping more and more until finally she said something that astonished him into hurt silence.

Both were in their fifties, silver haired and elegant. But whereas he was dressed in a tuxedo beneath the overcoat, she was all in black except a headscarf of bice blue, with pants beneath her skirt and an umbrella in her hand.

He continued to talk to her, summoning the universal sound of dignity and hurt, and she seemed to be ignoring him now, but I had no idea what he was trying to communicate until, a moment later, he turned away from her, as if in search of emotional support, and clapped his eyes on me.

If this scene were a picture you were standing before in a gallery somewhere, the two of them would be quarrelling in the top right corner. This is where the eye enters a picture: the upper right. In the brief amount of time the forger has to establish her con, this is essential information. Let all your genius flow into that corner; the rest can be more quotidian and mimetic.

So, first you would see the woman, and then you would see the man, and then your eye would swoop down and toward the left — this is how the eye travels through the image, in this case passing the pile of luggage, the bays, gables, shrubbery and the surprising green grass of Olive Road. A big ash tree. And then there would be me, somewhere on the lower left, tremulous and timid and out of place. Also, the man would be halfway turned toward me, but also turned back toward her, heading in two different directions at once in a bold painterly homage to the dynamic techniques of Greek sculpture as I have come to understand them. Specifically, he was displaying what is known to art historians as the *serpentine* pose, where the body is twisted almost all the way around itself — a detail I only mention because this pose is often subject to the claim that it would never happen in real life, and yet here it was, here it was!

When he came flying toward me, I'll admit I was scared. He told me later that I yelped, and since he's forgiven me, I won't deny it, gripped as I was with the conviction it was a domestic quarrel on the verge of becoming violent and that I was impending collateral damage. So imagine my surprise when he clapped his hand upon my shoulder and spoke calmly in perfect English. "This woman says she is not my sister. Can you believe it? After all we've been through together."

So they were arguing about whether or not she was his sister.

"Don't you bring this stranger into it," she said (in the other language, but I was pretty sure).

He, in English: "She is my sister—"

She, still in the unknown tongue: "I'm not your—"

He, carrying on: "But she has lost all respect for the artistic Persian traditions of our homeland." Glowering at her now, giving her a chance to stop him, which she didn't. And so he turned to me and dropped an octave to explain: "We are not related by blood, no, but as a child I was nursed at the breast of her mother. And so she is my *milk* sister. In the eyes of the law, we could never marry—"

"Oh, disgusting, why even bring that up?" (Approximate.)

"Because, sister, you know I am not that way inclined." (English.)

"I used to help my mother change your diapers," she said, switching, at last, to English.

He froze, coloured, cast a swift mortified glance my way before looking down. "You did not have to say that."

"No less true."

"I was a helpless infant!"

"You still are a helpless infant."

"Ha! As this person is my witness, I here attest that we have not seen each other in twenty years, you and I, yet here you are treating me abominably. I am merely expressing a bit of despair over this perpetual throwing over of your talent. First by marrying straight out of high school—"

"I did what was expected of me."

"Not by me!"

"By my family."

"I was your family. I thought you would go and be an artist and then I could follow in your footsteps! I thought you would pause on some high hill far ahead and then turn and signal to me with semaphores—"

Overlapping: "That's what you expected of me? Semaphores?"

"From my older sister, milk sister, yes. I hoped for semaphores, yes, telling me, This way, it's safe, careful of the falling rocks. And then, when that didn't happen, when instead you made that spectacularly bad decision only lessened by the fact that your husband died so young—"

"Well yes, I am an artist now."

"So very late—"

"It's been ten years."

"— and so very dubious in your choices."

"Why should your disapproval matter one iota to me?"

His voice started to quaver now as he turned to address me again: "My milk sister, Sanam, had a prodigious talent. When she was fourteen years old, she was asked to pen and illustrate a series of private invitations for the Shah of Iran. You remember the Shah of Iran."

I said I did.

"Lately, though, she has found common cause with men who, upon seeing an image of a horse, would try to walk around it. In short, she has become a Sunni."

"It's a small shift." She turned toward me now. "Madame, the differences my brother speaks of are minor, especially when compared to any religious views you yourself might profess—"

I tried to object that I professed no relig—

"The Sunni faith is all but indistinguishable from the Shiism I was raised in—"

He: "*We* didn't murder the third Imam."

She: "You're no less secular than me! Must we jump back to the seventh century?" And then, returning to me: "This new version of my habitual faith has a strong — and, to me, satisfying — proscription against images. I needed that. To get going again. I required the limitation. I am a calligrapher. Do you understand?"

A calligrapher seeks to work in a world without images. Yes, perhaps I did understand, since images had always oppressed me, or at least the beautiful ones had. But I didn't know what would happen if I nodded my head. So I suppose I just blinked at her sympathetically and she took it for assent. She turned in triumphant conclusion to her brother, her milk brother. "There, see? She understands."

"And what of your birthright?"

"Boro tu Koonam!" (whose meaning, I learned later and it simply cannot wait, was "crawl up my ass"). "I seek the best conditions in which to *write*, Amir. With the pen. That is my greatest priority. The lampblack line gathers on the page, swells to a crisis and then flows away just before the moment of catastrophe. Always wreaking order and beauty out of chaos, moment after moment. That's what the practice of calligraphy is. And Arabic is the appropri—"

"You see?" The brother pressed in toward me again, as I began to imagine myself walking away in search of some other house. "Arabic. There are traditions of calligraphy in Farsi, but no, no, no, no, no! She turns her back on her language, her culture. It's as if she wants to be covered up and tied down by these men who hate both images and women."

"They don't hate women!"

"And now, when I have come here, been invited here to receive some great honour, she has to come all this way to show me up."

"No, Amir," she said. "You have it wrong. I am here with an invitation of my own."

My eyes had been drawn to a beautiful satinwood box with ebony corners and a gold label on the lid in the hands of the milk sister. Arabic writing, I assumed, since Arabic seemed to have turned her head away from Farsi. The beauty of the box was better company than my own thoughts, so I was, I'll admit, fixated on it. For just a moment too long. When I found my focus again, I saw that the milk sister was looking back at me.

"Are you here for this too?" she asked. "The event?"

I: "I—"

She: "Are you an artist?"

"No."

"But you have an invitation!" she said, pressing me. "You're clutching it in your hand!"

It was true. I had pulled it out to check the address. "It's just a printout of—"

"Let me see."

And then she had the copy of my messenger text (curse my irrational attachment to paper) and there was no way out anymore. Not without some shameful desperate lying to cover my other lying. Why is that so hard? You entertain a bigger lie to avoid showing the world how out of control you are in your life.

And by your life I mean my life.

She took my arm — trying to distance herself from her brother. He fell in behind as she guided me smoothly up the walk toward the spectacular ash tree that grew close to the house.

I keep neglecting to mention — probably because I don't really want to — I have a few physical challenges that I felt at the time rendered me really rather, um, ugly, and so . . . Well, in the first case, when I was born, my frame was just a bit too large to come out of my mother with any grace, so my ribcage got all turned around and bungled up on one side, causing me to develop, over time, a bit of a hunchback. I also broke my nose, apparently, according to a doctor I went to see about a lifetime of sniffles. He told me I had a deviated septum from having broken it at birth, forceps probably (he said), and that I shouldn't mention any of this to my mother, as it would hurt her feelings. I found the information unhelpful as it did not relieve my sniffles and left me wondering whether I had injured my mother at birth.

I also have a terrible skin condition, on my scalp and my — well, also my face. Doctors can't identify it, but it looks sort of like a combination of eczema and a strange loss of pigment around my eyes that leaves me looking racoonish. I thought myself repugnant, both to look at and to listen to. I speak with a permanent glottal stop and nasal block . . .

Ahem. What I'm trying to say is, I was always a little surprised when someone was willing to touch me, even if it was only to take my arm in camaraderie. The woman who escorted me up the walk, she wasn't my friend and I had only heard her name, Sanam, in passing, but I was grateful. She had an ally in me from the moment she took my arm.

When we rang the bell, it was answered by a tall, round man in paint-stained coveralls, another artist, I supposed. He had a wide beefy face and transparently emotional bug eyes revealing an active play of surprise, curiosity, disappointment, annoyance — I read faces compulsively, especially handsome or charismatic faces. I love to see the things people can express when they do it freely, without shame. He looked at us for a moment, then over our heads to the street and back into the house, then back to us. He ran his hand through the brambles of his hair a couple of times — it stayed how he left it each time — then took a breath, presumably to say something, when a small voice behind us squeaked, "Do you have a bathroom I could use?"

The Persians and I turned around to see a very odd father-son pair. The kid — eleven or twelve, with square, almost cubist ears — had just spoken (London accent), and the sylphlike man next to him remarked, "This child appeared next to me and has been speaking of his emergency for the last three blocks, behaving as if he hoped I had a portable toilet in my pocket—" (Central Europe, north of the Alps. Perhaps Czech?)

The boy interrupted him, addressing the man in the doorway. "I just thought he lived close by. I'm just an optimist, I'm just desperate. Can I just go?"

"Listen to that," said the slender Czech. "Just desperate? *Merely* desperate? It's clear this child and his rhetorical diminutions are not going anywhere in life."

I looked at the Czech. My first impression was that he was tall, but I was eye to eye with him and could see it was only that his head was small enough to create the illusion of a tall man standing a short distance away. And he wore a sloppily tied cravat, as if he wanted his head to look like a bust on a plinth. I realized I was staring at him, terrible habit. He caught my eye just as I meant to look away. Shrugged. A moment before, he'd been imperious and judgmental. Now he seemed to be sharing a private joke with me.

The man in the doorway — our presumptive host — ran a hand through his hair again, frowned, finally, and then spoke at last, replying to the boy: "Yes," (resonant, not unkind, Spanish accent unmistakable) "down the hall, up the stairs. Don't use the main floor one please."

As the boy made his way, the rest of us (me, the Persian siblings and the unconfirmed Czech) were ushered inside by the clearly reluctant Spaniard, who guided us through a door to the immediate left into a small sitting room fronted by a large single-pane window. The room was bare walled and empty except for a couple of club chairs and a creased leather couch. There was a woman, dressed in green, perched on one of the chairs. Her colours detonated my vision as I turned into the doorway, bringing the terrible flush of shame I feel when confronted by beauty. Her eyes were green. Viridian (safe) not Schweinfurt (poison). If colours don't exist except on the surface of your eyes, then I wanted to close mine and keep her colour in. Maybe it would spread from there and set right all my deformities from within. Stranger things have happened, I thought.

I also thought, Well, no wonder the man in the doorway didn't want us to come in.

"Sit down, sit," he was saying to us, gesturing to the couch and the second chair. We sat. I took a spot on the couch beside the Persian milk sister, discovering too late that her brother had chosen to sit on the other side, the two of them hemming me in. The Czech, for his part, maintained his streak of odd behaviour by forgoing the empty chair and sitting cross-legged on the floor. There were several moments' silence, during which our host, who had not sat down, who in fact looked very much like he wanted to flee his own house, tried desperately to make eye contact with the woman he'd been alone with so recently. She seemed to take no notice. Finally he spoke up. "I'm sorry. It's a surprise. I wasn't expecting anyone for another half hour. This is Ángela Efrena Quintero. She's come all the way from Oaxaca, just got here five minutes ago. I wasn't expecting her either, although she's been here *just* long enough that we were in the middle of an — ahem — private — ahem . . . She even brought luggage. It's in the kitchen. Do you all have luggage? No."

That wasn't quite true. I had a knapsack and so did the sylph-like Czech. The Persians were definitely without luggage, though I recalled two separate piles of matching bags sitting on the lawn where they had been fighting, in which case they had arrived with more luggage than anyone.

Our host went on. "It's strange though, no? Perhaps you've all been given the wrong address." Then he made as if to introduce us to one another. "Ángela, these are . . . I don't know their names. I don't know why they are here." He turned back to us. "Ángela says she has a meeting with the same buyer I do. Perhaps so do you all. Perhaps that is the client's way of being efficient. Let's hope he doesn't expect us to collaborate, however. As I was just explaining to Ángela, these days I prefer to work alone."

Ángela looked up at him: "What makes you assume I would ever want to work with you?"

Our host, whose name I still didn't know, looked back at her. "I love you," he said, with disarming sincerity in what seemed to me at the time a non sequitur. Her eyes went hard for a moment, and then she looked away as I exchanged a glance with the Persian sister and the Persian brother guffawed.

I thought, At least it seems he could be a good host for a party.

"My primary condition for any collaborator," Ángela went on, "is that they do something I ask them to do from time to time." She looked at our host. "Clearly that's not you."

His mouth fell open as if she had just thrust a knife into his heart.

She looked around at us. "We are all artists, yes?"

We all nodded our heads. Even me, with no reputation of my own, I was nodding my head. The criss-cross Czech wasn't nodding, I suppose. He was sitting on the floor with his head down, listening perhaps to the strange sounds of construction that were rising in the street. A low rumble coming from somewhere.

The Persians on either side of me were ignoring each other. I was feeling restless, wondering, uneasily, about what our host had said about "a buyer." What if all these people had been given a different story — the Oaxacan and the Czech and the two Iranians? I was just starting to wonder what I had gotten myself into. And what about the kid? Where was the kid, anyway?

And again: was it not strange that our host had not been expecting us?

If this scene were a picture you were standing before in a gallery, you'd be lucky, because you would not, in the next moment, have been hit with the slivers of glass that flew everywhere when the front window exploded.

On the couch, Amir, Sanam, and I had had our backs to the window. When the explosion happened, the couch moved swiftly forward, as if pushed with great force, legs scraping against the hardwood across the room, pushing the club chairs and the diminutive Czech before it. I had curled up as small as I could, with my face pressed into a cushion, but when we stopped against the far wall, I first exchanged a look with the Czech — whose poker face was now alarmingly close to mine — and then peered over the back of the couch just in time to see the neat silhouette of a fit, elderly Asian man step lightly through the jagged window, backed up by a pair of construction workers holding small automatic rifles. Behind them, through the window, I saw the wide shovel of a backhoe pulling away and several more workers: they appeared to be assembling a scaffolding with lightning speed; upon completion of each level, they threw a tarp over the structure. Our window was darkening. We were being walled in. The last I saw of the outside world that afternoon was high above the top of the scaffold, when a small bird flew to the branch of the spectacular ash tree, perched there for a moment and then flew away.

The man who had stepped through and now stood in front of the steadily darkening window was impeccably dressed, with shiny black shoes, a navy-blue suit, and a white open-collar shirt. Even the lenses of his glasses shone. He held up his hand in a gesture known to fine art scholars as the *adlocutio* pose, reserved for Caesar or Napoleonic types, and said, "Well now. Time to get down to work."

A few minutes later, when the couch had been set right and all of us shell-shocked guests had checked ourselves for cuts and bruises, he spoke again.

"I am a proper man. Formal and polite. Just as you might expect, albeit not from someone who would introduce himself with an explosion. This was required to get your attention. You see, it is a hostage taking. Do not worry, however. I am not so reckless as I might appear. Already, outside there are English workmen, very well paid, with copies of the relevant permits, and a sign on the lawn that reads, 'Renovations in Progress.' Forgive me, Señor Matamoros" — he was now addressing our host — "for making a small post-sized hole in your front lawn. You should also know that these same workmen are quietly armed and have been instructed to detain anyone who seeks to escape. More important, I wish to say that none of you were in any danger from the flying glass. I cannot precisely explain why, though we have the skill of Jan Komárek to credit." Here he paused and gestured to the diminutive Czech, who had resumed his cross-legged position on the floor. "Not quite sugar glass — it was installed last week, during Señor Matamoros's trip to Barcelona. He is quite a magician, our Jan Komárek."

The slender Czech bowed slightly, uncomfortably from his position on the floor, as the mysterious and threatening stranger continued. "You must forgive him, though. He is not actually a collaborator in this hostage taking; he knew nothing about it and will perhaps be surprised to learn he is as much a hostage as the rest of you. Jan Komárek was simply led to believe I wished to give a demonstration of his skill for your entertainment. I am aware of the skills of each and every one of you, a great admirer of them, in fact, which is why you are all here. Thank you, Jan

Komárek. We have to wait a moment or two for my executive assistant, who has insisted on using the front door."

He stood silently for a moment or two, as if expecting something to happen on cue that didn't. His face darkened, and then there was the sound of a doorbell and he brightened again. "Oh, I see. She insists on being invited in; a semblance of propriety. Señor Matamoros, if you would be so kind."

Our host had been sitting on the arm of the chair occupied by the woman in green named Ángela. When the window had blown in, he had flung his body over hers in ecstatic protection. Then, over the course of the calm monologue that followed, he had gradually extracted himself, sliding back up onto the arm of the chair, registering expressions of alarm, embarrassment, confusion, despair, indignation. Now, he crossed his arms, refusing to get the door.

There followed a suspended moment where it seemed nothing would happen. I found myself rising from the couch and sidling over to the doorway, passing close enough to the Spaniard to sense him stiffen, as men tend to do in my vicinity. And then, as the others crowded in behind me, I looked out into the hallway just as the front door was being opened from the outside to reveal the bright day and two women.

The first was tall and grey haired in a high-collared blouse of shimmering grey with wood buttons: an exemplar of high fashion, except she also looked like she'd just recently put her finger in an electric socket. By which I mean to say her short hair was untamed. She was carrying a large, well-used sketchbook under her arm.

I could see that the woman behind her had just reached forward to open the door with a house key in a manner reminiscent of the contortions of Michelangelo's famously wingless angels in *The Last Judgement*, flexing all the muscles in her extended arm as well as her back. The artist was criticized for depicting muscular effort in his angels, thereby debasing them, i.e., allowing an onlooker like me to compare them to this woman in her crisp white shirt and bow tie. She had a face I recognized: hair of cadmium orange sweeping down over one eye. Ella Unton Bride, who sent me the invitation, looking like her profile picture and an angel.

Behind Ms. Bride, over her narrow shoulders in the doorway, several workers climbed up onto the scaffolding constructed around the massive canopy of the ash. Time to get to work indeed.

And then, the elegant woman with the high-collared blouse and electric-socket hair tripped, right in the doorway — sending a shockwave through the onlookers almost as severe as the window's shattering — and stumbled to her hands and knees. Mortifying. Her sketchbook landed on the floor, open to a portrait of an elderly woman. The artist snatched it up and closed it as Ella Unton Bride drew a sharp breath and said, "Oh Hannie, dear!" pulling her to her feet.

The one named Hannie allowed herself to be hauled up, looking at the floor as if there was some solace to be found there. Then she gave Ms. Bride a glance that would have turned me to stone. "We shall speak no more of this," she said. (Dutch accent, intrinsically upper-class to my ear, low alto, cigarettes.) "Let's get on with this mysterious meeting upon which you were so insistent."

We were all crowded back into the front room again. The impeccably dressed man who'd appeared in the window was now standing by the door with Ella Unton Bride at his shoulder, while the woman named Hannie had joined the rest of us. She sat in the empty club chair, looking back and forth from Ms. Bride to the broken window, slightly vexed, traces of her recent humiliation fading from her features.

The man spoke up, introduced himself as Mr. Jackie Lin, and then turned and introduced Ms. Bride, "formerly of Wallace Unton Gallery on the South Bank, defunct," before continuing with his prepared speech.

"Now, where was I? Oh yes: Your neighbours, Señor Matamoros, were given notice about the construction two weeks ago. And your brickwork will have had a thorough cleaning, while the trouble you've had with your roof will—"

"I don't have any trouble with my roof!" shouted our host.

"Señor Matamoros, there is no need to yell, but I can assure you there has been trouble with your roof tiles for some time now. The work was long overdue."

"I wish they wouldn't touch my roof."

"Ah, but they must. You see, they will be climbing all over it with some regularity. Soon, in a matter of minutes, the entire house will be encased in scaffolding, and then the crew will set to work."

"What work?"

"Ensuring your secure stay here, in this house. All of you. Moreover, you'll find by now that the internet has been cut off and satellite signals have been blocked."

I checked my phone, confirming no bars, as the woman named Hannie spoke up, looking more alarmed: "I beg your pardon?"

There was an alert sound, and Mr. Lin produced a small personal device to read the message. He'd fixed a solo satellite signal for himself, it seemed. I wondered what it must be like to be so organized, how you could suddenly have absolute power over seven people without even breaking a sweat.

"Right on schedule. Ms. Bride, would you be so kind as to answer the door?"

The doorbell rang right at that moment, presumably unnecessarily, though it caused me and the two Persians to jump in our seats. Ms. Bride disappeared into the hallway and a moment later directed six burly men carrying crates past our doorway to a room down the hall. This house was already proving to be larger than it appeared from the front, and Ms. Bride moved with a confidence that suggested she was familiar with the layout. We could hear the sound of creaking wood as the crates were disassembled in the other room, and then the six workers appeared again and filed back out through the front door. Ella Unton Bride rejoined us a moment later.

And then the woman she'd arrived with, Hannie, spoke up. "Ella, if I may ask, what is going on?"

"It will save time," said Mr. Lin, "if you allow me to complete my prepared statement. I have given it a lot of thought, and you may find your answers there."

He turned to his assistant. "Perhaps you should get yourself a chair."

Ms. Bride glanced over at Señor Matamoros, who sighed. "In the kitchen," he said wearily.

She went, as Mr. Lin said, "Yes, Señor Matamoros, your house goes on and on. It has proven quite useful to me. Thank you for not making too much of a fuss about the liberties I have taken so far."

"But I have made a fuss!" cried our erstwhile host, a hint of self-pity finally creeping into his voice.

"But not too much of a fuss."

"Yes too much of a fuss!"

"Very well, you have made a fuss."

Ms. Bride reappeared from the kitchen, carrying a chair whose addition made the room feel finally overcrowded. Whereupon I naturally began to panic.

And then she sat down, which made me feel suddenly better.

"Larceny," said Mr. Lin. "It's an old-fashioned word. You don't hear it often these days. It is the felonious taking away of the personal goods of another with intent to convert them to the taker's use. Something, I might add, you are all guilty of, though, paradoxi- cally, the shame of your actions has fallen upon me, over and over again, rather than any of you. I have come here today to restore the balance."

Hannie in the club chair spoke up again, indignation creep- ing into her tone as she nursed her bruised hands. "But we don't have a relationship. I've never met you before in my life."

"No, perhaps not," said Mr. Lin. "But if a work of art can be described as the most intimate expression of the artist's soul, then I have met you, in fact, Ms. Van der Roos. There were certain parties that went between you and me, of course: you used a bro- ker, and I used a buyer. In my case, the buyer was often Ms. Ella Unton Bride here. You all share the common distinction of hav- ing defrauded me with your talent, allowing me to believe that several works of art I have purchased over the years were by someone other than you."

"Pshaw," said Hannie.

"It is my sincere hope that you will all feel it is beneath your dignity to protest innocence, since I went to a lot of trouble and expense to identify you and I have ample proof in every instance."

Hannie Van der Roos turned back to the study of her finger- tips, as if they were the ones that had offended her. I noticed the backs of her hands had a fine webbing of craquelure, like what you see on the surface of old paintings, an effect you can fake with a bit of solvent, a bit of siccative and salt, and a lot of back and forth between the oven and the freezer (it being advisable to cultivate relationships in the restaurant business). Then, when it's dry, you apply a bit of watered-down umber to get the dirt in the cracks and wipe off the residue. Stay away from beeswax unless you want to get caught.

"Soon I will invite you into the next room," said Mr. Lin, "where you will have a chance to admire your own work and the work of your compatriots in this business. There is one exception, though, I'm afraid, a piece whose recent destruction has served as a catalyst to this action. You see, I have suffered many of these indignities in silence over the years. I am given to understand that I am viewed as a dupe because I am so far from the centre of the art market — the galleries of London and New York; the auction houses, Sotheby's and Christie's — living until very recently in Seoul, where I am perennially expected to keep quiet. And I have kept quiet. One does not like to be made a fool of on an international stage.

"And I confess, too, a certain admiration for the artistry of the mimic, especially when the work they are producing is not even a copy but rather a false original, signed with another's name. Over the years, as I've become aware of your deceptions, I consigned your work to a private room in my home in Seoul reserved for the bittersweet reflection of your skill and my shame.

"I was content with this, for many years. But then there came a day, quite recently, when a third party became involved.

"This concerned a piece I owned that I thought was the work of a certain Spanish artist and graphic designer, Javier [redacted], purchased on my behalf by Ms. Bride from a dealer who went by the name Armando Matamoros, which, it has augmented my shame to discover, was not even a false name."

Matamoros mumbled, "I needed ready cash. Anyway, one needs to be mostly truthful."

Mr. Lin went on.

"The work, which featured a mouse in a motorcar that I liked very much, was allegedly a cover design that had been submitted by Señor Javier [redacted] to *The New Yorker* magazine in 1997 and subsequently rejected. I came to learn it was a forgery through the aegis of *The New Yorker* itself, which publication sent a sympathetic lawyer to inquire after the veracity of some gossip being shared among the city's wealthy art collectors. Was it true? Had I been foolish enough to spend a large sum of money on an artwork that had included their magazine's nameplate? I had. Was I aware that cover art did not generally have the publication's nameplate already printed on it? I was not. 'These words are added later,' the lawyer said helpfully, with an expression of apologetic dismay.

"The news got worse. Those words, 'The New Yorker,' he said — printed with that particular typeface and kerning — could not be used 'for profit' without the express permission of Condé Nast.

"Anyway, the sympathetic lawyer asked, did I really want this evidence of my great folly to exist in the world?

"He compelled me to burn it, right then, before his eyes. Which I did with such violence a towering desire for revenge was born."

So this was an act of revenge unfolding . . .

He went on.

"The loss of this piece precipitated a crisis in me. I realized I was no longer in control of the fate of my own collection. There was no guarantee the demand for a given work's destruction would not happen again. And so I resolved to conduct the extensive research that brings you all here today, with the apparent exception of Mr. Ezra Coen, whom I do not see in this assembly but whose fake gouaches stand with the rest in the far room — high of quality; dishonest; deserving of their place. If you would all do me the kindness of accompanying me down the hall and through the kitchen to our little makeshift gallery, I would be much obliged."

Ms. Bride spoke up: "We call it the Matamoros Gallery. I believe Señor Matamoros knew it as the TV room."

She flashed a small smile, betraying full collaboration in this enterprise. But then she glanced at Hannie Van der Roos and the smile faded.

"Yes, indeed," said Mr. Lin. "The Matamoros Gallery. Come this way. On behalf of the curator Ms. Bride and myself, I sincerely hope you appreciate the exhibition."

When I was a child, every time I picked up a book I was hoping to read, I would flip through it first to see whether there was any-thing that broke the procession of prose from left to right across the page, page after page, from the beginning to the end. So, for example, I would check for drawings or photographs or maps, but I would also check for unfamiliar alphabets and even enlarged typefaces or the smaller typefaces you get when you see epi-graphs at the openings of chapters.

Every time I saw something like that, it cemented my com-mitment to the work.

By the time I came of age I was beginning to realize that seri-ous works rarely engaged in this visually playful practice and that the average reader considered it to be at best a distraction and at worst a sop to the kind of reader who followed the lines with their finger and moved their lips.

Still, I longed for these adornments, even if they indicated I was not a serious reader.

Maybe it was because I was afraid of all that unmitigated length, but I think it was more an indication that I had a visual imagination: those books were sending me the message that I was an artist, even if nothing else did and even if I went down a dubious (well, lawless) path to try to prove it to myself.

So now I find myself in charge of the compilation of a book. And I am here asserting – to myself and to you, the reader – that I have a visual, spatial imagination and will act accordingly.

Forewarned is forearmed. But also, if you feel the impulse to follow the words with your finger as you go or engage in a bit of whispering with its attendant ASMR, well, be my guest.

And so, without further ado, I present:

THE MATAMOROS GALLERY

ARMANDO MATAMOROS

34 Because the work in question had been destroyed, Mr. Lin represented Señor Matamoros in the Matamoros Gallery with a small ceramic bowl containing the charred remains of high-gloss paper, surrounded by prints of several *New Yorker* covers that were legitimately by the artist he had mimicked: a fellow Spaniard named Javier [redacted]. As far as I could tell from these, Señor Javier made quick, exuberant, haphazard cartoons depicting joyous play, food and drink, coastal living, a sun-kissed good life. And so did our Señor Matamoros, apparently. His current gloomy demeanour was, it seemed, out of character.

Next to Armando's I saw the work of the allegedly absent artist, whom I hypothesized to be the boy who had slipped down the hall to use the bathroom. Our host didn't know he was here and (assuming I was correct) seemed unaware that the forger was a child. There were eight gouaches that had been attributed to a young woman named Charlotte Salomon, who had perished eighty years before in the Holocaust. Although our host never specifically referred to Ezra Coen as an adult, it seemed excessive for him to want to punish a child for mimicking an artist, and it seemed unreasonable to believe a child could be responsible for slipping these gouaches into the art market. Someone else must have done that. Ezra Coen had been taken advantage of.

Also, I did recall an addendum to the invitation saying that there should be no children. So perhaps our Mr. Lin was not perfectly in control of every detail. The child Ezra Coen had my thanks for this comforting thought.

Amir painted ornate miniatures. His forgery — exhibited with a magnifying glass hanging beside it on a hook — purported to be a tenth-century rendering of Mohammad's Night Journey, with a veil placed discreetly over the Prophet's face. The compelling argument for its provenance, which Mr. Lin had believed, was that the proscription against bodily depictions of the Prophet meant that this masterpiece of a miniature had been created in secret and hidden in a locket behind a more quotidian portrait for eight hundred years.

SANAM HAGHIGHI

Amir's milk sister worked in calligraphy and, as I understood, exclusively lettered passages in Arabic from the Muslim holy book. Her forgery, as scandalous as her brother's, was a copy of Saddam Hussein's Qur'an, said to have been calligraphed using vials of the Iraqi tyrant's own blood, taken bit by bit. The amazing thing about Sanam's achievement — by which I mean the achievement of the forgery (which as a fellow forger I have a right to admire) — was that Mr. Lin had managed to secure a blood test and received a return that claimed the blood ink had a 97.5 percent chance of being from a close relative of the tyrant — leading one to speculate on who had commissioned the forgery from Sanam Haghighi.

Ms. Van der Roos's works were signed with the name of a recently deceased Canadian artist named Claire [redacted], who had not in fact made them. They were strange, morbid drawings of aging naked bodies and haggard faces, which I heard the milk sister describe in a whisper to her brother as "erotic." Although I did know what that word meant, where these drawings were concerned, I was beyond befuddled. As far as I knew, eroticism was supposed to involve young muscular bodies entwined in some kind of common cause. These drawings were not like that. They were solitary and bereft. They were scribbly and desperate and *emotional*, mimicking an artist I had never heard of (unsurprising since we were both Canadian). I'll confess I once caught a glimpse of what I thought erotic might mean when I perused a video of two snails being tender with one another. I know that does not speak well of me. Anyway, this work was not like that pair of snails. I'm not sure why I brought them up. In any case, when the milk sister leaned in and whispered that they were erotic, the milk brother leaned back and snorted, calling them punk rock.

"These are studies, merely," said Hannie Van der Roos, when presented with her exhibit. "Not forgeries."

"So you confess you made them," said Mr. Lin.

"I would hardly call it a confession."

"But they are signed by the artist."

"That," said Ms. Van der Roos, "is not my doing."

"The evidence," said Mr. Lin, "is conclusive."

"It would seem that as a repeat buyer of forgeries," said Hannie Van der Roos, "you would not recognize evidence if it took you by the ear and sliced it off."

ÁNGELA EFRENA QUINTERO

The work that Mr. Lin displayed from Ángela in the TV room gallery was represented a series of newspaper clippings.

    I've heard a lot of stories about art hoaxes in my time, but I had never heard of any forger other than Ángela Efrena Quintero actually standing in for the artist she was masquerading as. In 2015, she travelled to a protected section of the Black Forest in Germany, where she organized, publicized, fundraised for, and actually installed a light-based earthwork whose primary donor turned out to be none other than Mr. Lin. It was apparently so beautiful and so successful that the artist in question — Teresita [redacted] — took credit for it. No one does that. No one dares counterfeit a modern installation artist who relies entirely on the force of her personality, mobilizing an army of acolytes to get the job done. It doesn't happen. Ángela did it. And she didn't even get caught, except, somehow, by Mr. Lin, though he seemed to have kept that information from the world. The newspaper clippings all spoke of Teresita [redacted] and not Ángela Efrena Quintero.

    How did Mr. Lin catch her? I wondered.

    And then I began to wonder:

    How did Mr. Lin catch . . .

M E ?

40 I am too appalled to reveal the aesthetics of my imitations, to show how I lost my freedom for so little.

I was proud of it, don't get me wrong.

But I was also ashamed.

And it is barely relevant to the story.

(Redacted.)

Moving on.

JAN KOMÁREK

Ugh. This one is embarrassing. I'm tempted to just point to the explosion of the bay window. It demonstrates much of what Jan Komárek was all about. As you shall see.

Jan's forgery, according to Mr. Lin, had been of an early piece by Damien Hirst, the photographic self-portrait of the artist with the head of a cadaver. This was allegedly the highest-profile fake in the whole of Mr. Lin's collection. No savvy counterfeiter went after a living art star, but Jan presumably had his own reasons for doing things.

And there it was, hanging on the wall before us: a sheet of printer's paper, yellowing at the corners, with a photographic print in black and white of the young Damien Hirst flashing a worried grin, showing his tenacious baby teeth, holding his face close to the large bald head of the cadaver, who seemed to be grinning too, if somewhat more painfully. It was troubling to gaze upon, but as we stepped away, I found myself wanting to look back.

Believe it or not, when I clapped eyes on the forgery a second time, the grinning man in the photo no longer resembled a young Damien Hirst. Rather, he looked just like Jan Komárek. Amazingly, the cadaver was clearly Jan Komárek as well. The overall effect was of something so poorly executed I suddenly failed to understand how the others could ever have been fooled. I looked around to see if anyone else was seeing what I was seeing, but no one noticed me, they were all lost in contemplation of their own forgeries. Hannie looked equal parts alarmed and annoyed, and Armando looked ashamed; but Sanam, Ángela and Amir all seemed rather proud of themselves, as if they were gratified to see work under their own names, at long last, hanging in a gallery.

But then I caught the eye of Jan Komárek. He held my gaze for a moment, beetle browed.

And then he winked at me.

And then he looked away.

And then I looked back at the photo and saw that it once again depicted the famous artist and the anonymous cadaver.

Just as I was about to speak up, protest, demand to know what the hell was going on here, my thoughts were interrupted by Mr. Lin, who chose that moment to speak at last about our enforced commission. He declared that we would each be installed in a room in Armando Matamoros's house, that these would be our studios and sleeping quarters, and that he wanted us to fill the walls of these rooms with art. The task was for each of us to cover every inch of space, akin to what you might see (in my opinion, not his) in the cell of a Victorian sanatorium commandeered by an obsessive genius gone mad. *Art Brut* is, I believe, the term for that.

"Let me be clear," Mr. Lin said. "I don't want your rooms to come out looking like busy, inspiring, disorganized studios. I want them to forge fully realized works of art. I will be patient with your work, respectful. I will indulge all requests, but when the work is done, it will belong to me."

"But why?" asked Amir. "Why go to all this trouble? Why not just present your evidence and have us all arrested?"

By the kitchen doorway, I spied Ella Unton Bride shift uncomfortably. Did she have this question as well?

"It is true," said Mr. Lin, "that I do not wish the world to know how I have shamed myself by purchasing your heartless copies. But," he added, "my intent is also altruistic, for I would like to ensure that, once you leave this place, not one of you lies on canvas ever again."

"Har har," said Armando.

"Then I might as well leave now," said Hannie.

"Lying is at the very centre of my work," said Ángela. "So I guess I had better settle in."

"Can we lie on paper?" asked Armando. "Can we lie on the side of a building or an interior wall? Can we lie to a lover? Can we lie on a bed? Or will we be working twenty-four hours a day?"

"All punning aside," said Mr. Lin, "I plan to extract, from each one of you, in the final outcome, a sincere and solemn oath that you will never make a forgery again."

"You have it," said Hannie. "Since I never made one before."

"I don't believe it," said Mr. Lin.

"I do not care what you believe," said Hannie. "I have had quite enough of this charade."

And then she made her way resolutely toward the front door.

A large woman with round pillowy arms and a bulletproof vest appeared from the stairs. She swept Hannie up so fast that the artist's resolute stride transformed into furious scissoring. The security guard treated the struggle as if she were carrying a skittish colt across a shallow lake, except she was heading up the stairs and around the landing as Hannie Van der Roos chopped the air and shouted that it was only a matter of time before they would all be "thrown in the *doos!*"

"It seems I must remind you," said Mr. Lin, once the security guard had disappeared with Hannie onto the second floor and the rest of us stood agape at the foot of the stairs, "this is not a joke. You are my hostages. The embarrassment you all caused me is of a sort that is generally suffered in silence by collectors of my standing. Not me though. Not this time. You will all repair your wrongs to me with your work. I will collect my ransom. Make no mistake about that."

"How long will it take?" asked Amir Haghighi.

Mr. Lin shrugged. "Time has nothing to do with the matter."

"Oh, indeed!" said Armando Matamoros. "Time has nothing to do with it! Oh, well then: since time has nothing to do with it, I've decided that I have completed the work right now. Call it a minimalist explosion."

And then Armando elbowed his way from the back of our little group and strode toward the entrance, just exactly as Hannie Van der Roos had done before him, only to be blocked by a guard who appeared from the front room. The Spaniard raised his fist as if to strike the guard, but instead rounded on his heels, just as the guard's hands closed over thin air. Then, before arriving back with our little group, he dove instead for the stairs, thumping down toward the basement at alarming speed.

A moment later there were four security guards heading after him as Mr. Lin remarked, "I don't believe there is an exit down there. Señor Matamoros is merely putting on a show. Unless perhaps we missed something?" This last he addressed to Ella Unton Bride, who did not answer his query and seemed to be contemplating the floor, troubled. Mr. Lin went on: "That is your studio down there, Monsieur Komárek, for your information. I hope our host does not do any lasting damage."

From below us there came the sound of thumps and curses and thrown furniture.

My studio was on the third floor, right at the top of the house, at the back, with its own little squared spiral set of stairs, its own little landing and its own door. It was a simple white-walled room with an east-facing window looking out over the edge of a flat roof that currently had scaffolding clinging to it. There was a sink and a modest single bed with a table and a lamp whose zoetrope shade featured the illusion of tropical fish swimming around and around. I wondered if its kitschiness was intended to offend me. In truth, it reminded me of the lamp in the room I shared with my sister in the furnished cottage my family used to rent every year at a Lake Erie beach town, and this brought me unexpected comfort. I particularly recalled a night when my parents had gone to see a production of *Man of La Mancha*, leaving us alone for the evening, and a tornado roared through after dark, and I crawled into bed with my sister, who kept me distracted from my fear with stories of Van Gogh's life in Arles.

I should not neglect to add that my view through the window also featured the black-clad torso of a sentry standing so still it took a full minute of staring to ensure he was real. He held his weight mostly on one foot, in a casual stance known to art scholars as *contrapposto*, exemplified most famously by Michelangelo's *David*, where the hips tip one way and the shoulders tip another. I'll confess I thought for a moment that he *was* David, I mean a replica, until it occurred to me that he wasn't naked. And then I blushed. And then I realized I was staring. And then he sat down.

Our host had assured us that these sentries would eventually recede, once we settled into a rhythm, and that they were a preferable alternative to bugging all our rooms, something he considered to be an invasion of our privacy. Absurdly, I had credited his sincerity. Still, this more direct invasion of privacy was notable.

I was already exhausted.

There was a bench and a chair and a shelf with a series of artist tools, charcoal, and paints. Everything was ready for me. All my needs were apparently going to be seen to. Anything I asked for would be provided to me, within reasonable limits, though I could barely imagine what I might ask for, prisoner that I was. The caged bird desires only to be free, no?

It was nice here, though, I had to admit. But I felt no small dread about my "commission." What Mr. Lin failed to understand, about me at least if not the others, was that I was simply incapable of creating work under my own name. I supposed for some of the others, forgery was a criminal thrill ride or perhaps even a revenge project against the society that had been indifferent to the artwork that came from their legitimate selves. I had read about such forgers. Impassioned. Charismatic. Daring. Devil-may-care. Inspired by bitterness, they loved the thought of exposing all the experts as fools, even if only in their own minds. Perhaps Armando Matamoros was like that. Or Ángela Efrena Quintero. Or even Hannie Van der Roos, whose character was so strong she would never allow the mask of fakery to slip.

That was not my own story, though. There was no art that came from my self. My self was precisely the problem. Forgery was the way I could escape from my self. I barely even had a self. If I had to sit up here and contemplate my self, I was going to find my self squelched like a bug between a rock and a wall.

Lying now in my little bed, contemplating the fierce rebellion Armando had waged in his own basement, along with the disappearance of a protesting Hannie Van der Roos and, finally, the certainty of my entrapment, I grasped the textured edges of my comforter and pulled it up past my chin, wondering how I would ever achieve atonement for something I had only ever pursued to distract myself from hastening my own demise.

I was just falling asleep, eyes closed, light off, zoetrope fish still, when I had the distinct sensation of getting paffed on the tip of the nose by what felt and sounded like a small crumpled piece of paper whose trajectory continued with a soft baff baff baff-baffbaff off the pillow and down onto the floor. Surely I could not have imagined it. When I switched on the light, my eye was abruptly drawn away from the fish resuming their travels, up to the white ceiling, where I thought I had caught a sound and the sway of a shadow.

Nothing. There was a trap door up there, a square hemmed in by moulding, but no access to it, and its edges appeared to have been painted over since whenever it had last been opened. A quick perusal of the floor yielded no tiny missile, and a glance at the window revealed a crouching sentry, arm hanging casually over a diagonal piece of scaffold in the dark, head bent and backlit, eyes peering in at me and my switched-on light. I couldn't look at the ceiling again for fear the sentry would follow my eyes. So I rolled back, switched off the light, pulled the soft white comforter up around my ears, retook the privacy of darkness, and wondered what to do next.

The brief slide of wood against wood from the ceiling. Then another missile: baff baff baffbaffbaff.

And another: baff baffbaffbaff.

And yet another: baff baff baffbaff.

One more: baff baff baffbaffbaff.

And then, after a long pause, one last, perhaps larger than the rest: baff baff baff baffbaffbaffbaff.

I did not turn on the light again, though I knew it would be several hours before I slept. If I was going to sleep at all.

PART TWO

ACADEMY

An association of artists, scholars, etc., arranged in a professional institution. The original Academy was an olive grove outside Athens where Plato and his successors taught philosophy, and his school of philosophy was therefore known as "The Academy." In the Italian Renaissance the word began to be applied to almost any philosophical or literary circle and was sometimes employed of groups of artists who discussed theoretical as well as practical problems.

In the morning, the sentry was gone. Coffee break perhaps? Shift change? I climbed out of bed, got down on my knees, lifted up the skirt of the box spring, and saw the five bits of crumpled paper,

just there beneath the bed.

The missives were composed in efficient, tiny handwriting. I assemble them here in the order in which I imagine they were written:

> *Help my name is Ezra Coen. Was in upstairs bathroom when heard explosion. Found my way into existing crawl space behind wall. Not first time I've done this. Have studied diaries of Anne Frank.*

> *overheard accusations. Will explain how. Am innocent of the intent if not the act.*

> *Hard to tell how much trouble am in, though? can someone advise?*

> *Need food, water, more paper, pencil, sweater, blanket. Pillow. Toilet paper?*

And the larger scrap:

> *info that might be important: remember how I arrived with that Czech man who called me 'mere'? Well, I had walked with him for a few blocks, and though he maintained a sour expression the whole time, he suddenly pulled four rabbits out of his shirt and let them go into the bushes. All while glaring at me. One of those funny people who pretend to be mean, I think. A real magician. Maybe he can help?*

I was being tasked with determining how a magician might be called upon to assist in a hostage situation.

After wondering for a moment what I might do, I heard a knock at the door. I wadded the final scrap into a ball and was about to pop it into my mouth to chew it up and swallow it, when I looked to the window again and realized my sentry was back, crouching out on the scaffold, peering right in at me with an expression of exaggerated concentration that would have reminded me of sixteenth-century Mannerist portraiture if I had not been so alarmed. Furthermore, he was still on the job, even after a whole night. How was this possible? Did he never sleep?

Trembling with faux nonchalance, I checked the door. Nobody there, despite the knock. Then, instead of chewing up and swallowing the wad, I casually tossed it to the floor, trying to project the idea that this was the beginning of my art practice. Then, as casual as could be, I approached my notebook, by the bed, grabbed a pen, tore out a page and sat down to —

Write something

— in as accurate a mimicry I could muster of the handwriting I'd just seen. Crumpled it casually and tossed it to the floor. Then I tore out another sheet and wrote —

Is he still looking at me?

— and, once again, crumpled and tossed. My ruse had taken less than a minute, at the end of which I learned the source of the knocking: something had bounced down from the top of the scaffold — a loose bolt or a squirrel's nut — and been caught by the sentry who'd actually been examining it the whole time I thought he'd been peering at me. When he finished, he tossed it over his shoulder, a gesture that caught my startled eye, and the little thing went knock-knock-knocking again, all the rest of the way down to the ground.

And so, after this frenzy of activity, I made the decision to venture out of my room. I had slept in my clothes, as was my usual practice, and so was appropriately dressed to go downstairs.

12. *D U M A*

I padded out on cat feet onto the small private third-floor landing and stepped carefully down the noisy wooden spiral staircase toward the (much larger) second-floor hallway. Trying to be silent. Creak. Creak. Creeeeaak. Creak creak creak creak. At first there was no sign of anyone. I tiptoed (creakcreakcreakcreak) past a closed door just at the bottom of the stairs to my right. I thought I could hear someone moving furniture inside. Turned into a hallway and saw another door up ahead on my left. I couldn't tell whether there was anyone in there, but considering there were several hostages, the rooms had to be in use. Past that door, the hallway widened, and I couldn't see anything up till the far end, where another door faced me.

As I passed into the wider hallway, I saw there was another, smaller door to my left, maybe a utility closet, and beyond that, opposite the second-floor landing, a possible bathroom, whose door was also closed. And then, as I rounded the landing, I saw on my right yet another closed door, perched at the top of the stairs.

As I descended, I felt the dread of realization that I needed some private time in a bathroom and didn't have a strategy in place. I should have gone back and knocked lightly on that second-floor door, but the very idea sent a chill up my spine. It had been so long since I had to share a living space with anyone. In the house where I'd grown up, there were two bathrooms: an upper floor one for my parents and a basement one — damp, with a constant dehumidifier hum — for my sister and me to fight over. I had adopted a strategy of crawling out of bed at six in the morning so I could luxuriantly use up all the hot water and give it time to reheat so she would not yell at me. Here, now, in this enforced London confinement, I could already hear that most everyone had risen before me.

Then, as I came to the bottom of the main stairs, my eyes were drawn to a bright glare spilling noisily out of that front-room study where we'd all first met. They must have been repairing the window in there. Our kidnapper was standing in the doorway, turned away so I could not see his face, and his right hand was resting benignly in the grip of a small girl, who appeared by her size to be ten or eleven years old. She was wearing a blue blazer and a stiff skirt that went down to her knees. Her face, like his, was turned away.

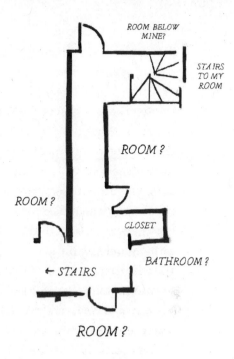

The presence of a (presumptive) daughter was an immediate balm on my anxiety, suggesting for better or worse that a status quo would be maintained, at least for the time being. There would be no more explosions, no police battering on the door, and a level of control that would brook no rebellion. We were stuck here, but we were safe. That's what the small shoulders of a child communicated to me in that moment.

Then the bodyguard who stood behind them swivelled his head and looked at me with bullet eyes and my heart jumped again as I rounded the curtail step and headed down the hall, past the bathroom (door closed, water running) and into the kitchen.

Imagine you are in a gallery, standing before a hyperrealist painting of a kinetic, overcrowded mess hall on a film set for something big and action-packed. On the oak-countered island, a large catered breakfast was spread, incongruous in its beneficence: lox, Montreal-style bagels (!), cream cheese, muesli, fresh strawberries and blackberries, a cut-up and reassembled pineapple, milk, cream, coffee, hot plates with scrambled eggs, bacon, sausages, pancakes, waffles, assorted juices and large thermoses of coffee and tea. Burly bodyguards and construction workers in safety vests were reaching across each other to fill up Armando Matamoros's brightly coloured plates. The caterers were just packing up their bags. I couldn't help but notice they all wore something akin to horse blinders, presumably to keep them from looking at anything but their work. Or do I misremember?

On a counter off to the side stood a machine whose vintage-taillight lines, white, chrome and powder blue, were shielded by the broad body of an apparently unhurt Armando. Despite all his efforts to mask what was clearly the flagship luxury item of his household, the audible and olfactory arrival of two espresso shots in a flourish of steam and crema could not be prevented. It inspired a rush of hope, desire and courage in me, thwarted only by the sudden swelling of my bowels. I fled the kitchen just as our erstwhile host turned with the small cups in his beefy digits and presented one to Ángela, who sat in a silk air-blue robe by the island and took it into her surprisingly large hands.

I arrived back at the bathroom door just as it opened. Hannie Van der Roos emerged, looking embarrassed but unbruised, still defiant, wearing earbuds blasting something loud, refusing to meet my eye. I didn't care. I had my miniature kingdom with its tiny porcelain sink.

I realized I would need coffee before I could ever hope to broach the subject of the hidden Ezra.

When I returned to the kitchen, trying to locate the courage to ask someone to make an espresso for me, the workers and bodyguards had departed. Armando and Ángela still huddled by their cups. Ms. Van der Roos stood brittle in a corner, cultivating stillness while raising small spoonfuls of muesli and milk to her lips.

I was about to ask after the machine, clearing my throat at the volume of a moth flutter, when my attention was drawn to a tuft of hair that sprouted like wheat on the other side of the island, and I saw that Jan Komárek was there, sitting cross-legged once again on the floor, eating yoghurt, dabbing his lips with the tip of his cravat and gesturing with a spoon that was bending in the middle, all by itself.

"You see?" he said, to someone, I couldn't tell who. "I manipulate the real world, not like your lot who dabble in pigment to create ghosts."

From the doorway, a decisive riposte from Sanam Haghighi, sporting a headscarf patterned with pale shades of yellow, orange, green and two different blues: "You can call me many things. But you cannot say I am a creator of ghosts. There is no angel walking among us who would shun *my* work."

And then she left the kitchen as Jan continued to demonstrate the prestidigitation that Ezra Coen had claimed to witness. "Ah yes," he said, dismissively. "Your famous Sunni admonishment against images. I myself have *never* seen an angel turn away from the image of a portrait. Quite the contrary, they seem to adore them, far more than I do. Just my personal experience, you understand," he added. And then he called, so Sanam might hear him even though she was out of sight: "No offence intended!"

"None taken!" she called back from down the hall.

As I fiddled with the espresso machine, trying to dismiss the subject of angels and images, I could not help but overhear Armando and Ángela engaged in a quiet little spat, in English. "Don't judge me!" Armando was saying. "You bankrupted an entire town! I chose a simple afternoon's work on a cloudy day because it gave me pleasure to undertake, that is all!"

"And the magazine logo: did drawing that give you pleasure too?"

"The magazine logo, the magazine logo! Who cares about that magazine logo! I thought we cared for each other, you and I!"

"You overstate our relationship."

"Oh, stop trying to embarrass me."

"You're embarrassing yourself. Just because I came to your door yesterday, does not mean—"

"You came to me, all the way from Oax—"

"By invitation of Mr. Lin."

"Yes, it seems I was the only one who did not receive such an invitation to my own house. So there you were, and so, for the hundredth time, my life was ended and begun again."

"Grow up."

I don't know why I chose this moment, still bereft of coffee, to speak.

I ahem'd.

The quarrellers looked up at me.

"Excuse me," I said, almost in a whisper. "I have to tell someone. I've been contacted by the boy who came in yesterday to use the bathroom. He is hiding in the house."

The pair blinked, once, twice.

I said again, "He's hiding in the house."

Just as I started to wonder whether I was wrong about the language they'd been speaking and the language I was speaking, Ángela spoke up. "Oh my God," she said. "How did he contact you?"

"He threw some crumpled notes at my face. I believe he's hiding in some kind of attic crawl space above my room."

I looked up and was shocked to note that all my fellow hostages had moved into a little scrum around me. Hannie Van der Roos was standing by my shoulder, an expression of appalled concern on her face. The Persians were behind her, Sanam having returned to the kitchen with her brother. Jan Komárek, while sitting no closer than he'd been before, had produced a vintage ear horn out of nowhere.

We were, for all our differences, in that moment, as one.

"What did he write?" asked Ángela.

"He said he needed food and water and paper and a pen. And I'm worried . . ." Here I paused to collect my thoughts. "I'm worried that everything he's done so far makes him already guilty of a serious attempt to escape. He's worried about that too. Mr. Lin said the punishment for that would be severe ... so maybe we should help him really escape, truly escape ... but he can't escape ... Even though he's hidden, he can't escape because there are guards outside, all around the perimeter!"

"Calm down," said Jan Komárek, who finally saw fit to stand up.

"Yes," I said. "Thank you. I only mean to say ... I don't know what to do. He seemed to think you could help."

"Me?" Jan was indicating himself with the point of his ear horn.

"Yes, you. He wrote that you were a clever magician."

"I have never been so flattered in all my life," he deadpanned.

Amir said, "Why don't we just let him come out?"

Ángela said, "No! It would show up our kidnapper. For a mere child to have tricked him? No. We have to keep that boy hidden."

"Do you think?" I said, feeling now a shortness of breath. "Maybe we do. Maybe we do need to keep him hidden. Because he can't escape, but he's sort of in a ... mid-escape. So, um, how can we help him? I mean, what a task! What if we get caught?"

"Calm down," said Jan again, now pointing his ear horn at me.

And then, almost as if the Czech knew it was going to happen, Mr. Lin entered the kitchen, accompanied by his daughter and a bodyguard. Our scrum blew apart like a murmur of starlings, everyone becoming interested in their breakfast. If Mr. Lin noticed the flutter, he did not comment. Perhaps he was preoccupied, seeming to be engaged in a minor *sotto voce* spat with his daughter.

I put my hands on the espresso machine to steady myself and tried to think only of the coffee I so abjectly desired.

"My friends," said Mr. Lin, "I feel since it is a bright beautiful morning and you have availed yourselves of the fine repast that has been offered to you, it is a good time for me to introduce the second iteration of my undertaking. This is my daughter. Her name is Esther. She has long expressed to me her desire to one day join the company of artists. In the spirit of avoiding pretension and the various little shams and hams and frauds of the teaching profession, I have, after some reflection, decided I should like her to witness and assist in these labours of yours. However they turn out, I anticipate a worthy struggle and can vouch for your high level of skill. May we presume?"

He paused. After a few awkward moments, it became clear that we were meant to extend our permissions and that room was being provided for us to do so. Or no? Were we allowed to say no?

Armando Matamoros was the first to speak. "Are you being serious at this moment?"

"Quite serious," said Mr. Lin.

The Spaniard stared wide eyed as he huffed a breath. "What makes you think your daughter would be safe in our hands? What makes you think we would not make another hostage situation inside this hostage situation?"

"Can you be more specific?" asked Mr. Lin. "Can you say precisely what you mean by 'another hostage situation'?"

"Well..." said Armando, glancing with alarm at the child who was looking at him now with a poker face. "Well, I mean..."

"I am all ears," said Mr. Lin. "I'm trying to determine whether I should modify my behaviour to ensure the safety of my daughter. I'm trying to determine whether you are uttering a threat. My daughter is my light, my life. Should anything happen to her, the expiation I seek would, to put it mildly, cease to be aesthetic or rehabilitative; my revenge would no longer demand something of an artistic nature; I would stop looking for the virtuous, the creative, the spark of originality inside you all; in other words, I would cease to make of this hostage situation a grand experiment in *elevating* the most base, craven, selfish, miserable impulses of human nature — your human nature, Señor Matamoros. No, instead I would seek to bring fire and misery down upon your—"

I should note that at this point I don't know what Armando was feeling, but I was so scared I was ready to volunteer myself as the daughter's mentor even though taking on an apprentice would have been, for me, a fate worse than death. Fear is worse than death. However, it was just at this moment that his speech, directed calmly at Armando, was interrupted by Ángela Efrena Quintero, who was either being heroic or genuinely welcoming, it was impossible to say.

"I feel that there is no company more inspiring," she said, "than a child who is not my responsibility. So I will invite your lovely daughter into my studio. And the rest of you are welcome to visit any time. After all, we are a sort of club, no?"

At last, Mr. Lin removed his gaze from Armando and smiled at Ángela. Then he picked up a slice of crispy bacon, leaned against the counter and began chatting combatively with his daughter.

It appeared our planning session to save the hidden boy was going to have to be postponed.

Not for long, though. When I returned that first morning to my studio, so called, just after nine-thirty, I was startled to find Jan Komárek there waiting for me, sitting cross-legged on the floor with his back to the wall beneath the window, below the eye line of my sentry.

"Please carry on as if I were not here," he said, in that humourless vein of his that suddenly struck me as giddily funny. "Give no indication that you can hear anything I'm saying. If you understand, walk to your desk and tap it twice as if in search of something and forgetting what it is."

I did as I was told, grateful for the motivation, even though it didn't make sense to me. It wasn't easy.

"What's so funny? Don't answer that, never mind. I do like it up here. A private room you have, surrounded by sky. Closer to the tops of the trees. Much nicer than my dark cellar deep in the bowels of this house . . . What on earth is so funny?"

It was mortifying. I had no idea what had come over me. At least I didn't have to look at him.

"Very well," he went on. "Have you heard again from the boy? Tap once for no, twice for yes."

I tapped once, regaining composure.

"Do you think he can hear us? Tap once for no, twice for yes."

I had no idea and did nothing. After a moment, though, I was shocked to hear a tap and then another tap coming from the ceiling above my head. It took everything within my power not to look.

"Good," said Jan Komárek. "Excellent, I hear you loud and clear. A boy is up in a ceiling. Did I not predict this? Yesterday in the doorway? Did I not assert that a boy was going nowhere in life? May I point out, then, that stuck above a ceiling is the very essence of 'nowhere.' On the other hand, perhaps there is a garret up there, and he is settled nicely among the eaves."

I had no idea how I should react, so I busied myself with tearing pages out of my notebook, writing little messages, twisting them up and tossing them to the floor.

A man in my room is a magician.

Jokes about a boy going nowhere in life.

Jan went on. "We are correct to fear the wrath that our kidnapper, Mr. Lin, will unleash if he discovers this hidden boy. The man clearly feels a strong need for control over us."

Here he ducked his head, as if fearing to be overheard.

"As you have no doubt inferred, I've had dealings with him already and managed to conduct some background research. It is not pretty. Well, some of it is, admittedly, pretty, but most of it is not. Here, in brief, is what I have learned about our Mr. Lin: he comes out of the Korean culture of the chaebol, the family businesses that rebuilt his country after the war. Most of these families are honourable, if perhaps a little too mired in a medieval tradition of social hierarchy. But his family is not like the rest of them. His family is not called Lin but rather [redacted] — and this is the pretty part: another thing I learned about him is that he changed his surname to Lin. There was a woman he loved who, my sources tell me, disappeared. Lin was *her* surname. He is said to have looked high and low for her, searching the world over, and when at last he returned, empty handed, he had become a harder man, a more brutal man, bitterly aware of the price one pays to be part of a family such as his."

I wondered what Jan was implying about Mr. Lin's family. Well, presumably that it was a criminal family. But what had happened to the woman? Was it her disappearance itself that made him a more brutal man? Or was it rather the details surrounding her disappearance? Was she —? I couldn't even bring myself to imagine the question, except that it involved criminality and . . . and perhaps revenge? Had Mr. Lin's criminal family done a criminal thing to another criminal family? Had that other criminal family retaliated by enacting some kind of brutal revenge involving innocent parties, like . . . ?

My imagination was not equipped for this.

Jan went on: "So that story was pretty but also not so pretty.

"But as for the family: his actual family, the [redacted] family, had already managed to reinvent its prewar criminal self, transforming into a modest manufacturer of small cars. The scrappy street smarts they worked so hard to leave behind turned out to be more beneficial than they first knew, allowing them, for example, to avoid a bribery and corruption scandal that reached so high it brought down the country's president. Paradoxically, they stayed clean because everyone had assumed they were dirty and consequently never accepted their bribes.

"But I have heard it whispered that when this family cannot avoid moments of stress, the old criminal practices come to the fore, skillfully hidden, highly professional. So a boy who has crossed them might end up, for example, dangling upside down from one of the many bridges that grace the Thames."

I thought I saw, out of the corner of my eye, the ceiling tremble.

"Oh," I said quietly.

"Yes," he said. "A very dangerous man, obviously."

"So Ezra Coen . . ."

"By virtue of being uncaptured in this house, young Ezra Coen is in danger, yes. And if he tries to escape, he will surely be captured by the security roaming the perimeter. But I have an idea how I might bring this boy out of the walls and allow him to hide in plain sight, comfortable but away from danger. It is an audacious plan. You should not underestimate me, however, though that may well be your inclination. I have every confidence that my plan will work."

I must here confess I had no idea what Jan Komárek meant by saying it might be my inclination to underestimate him.

The very idea that I might underestimate anyone — that I would even be capable of underestimating anyone or that my opinion mattered one iota in this regard — was mystifying.

He went on.

"My plan involves the age-old tools of the magician's trade. Yes, it's true, I can produce rabbits aplenty. But there are far more serious tools in my box, and if my plan works, it will allow the boy to move with more freedom in the confines of this house than he can at the moment, perhaps even with more freedom than all the rest of us. Would that not be something to see?"

I murmured at my table, asking what Jan Komárek needed from me.

"Well, for my plan to work, I will need to have some time to consult with the boy face to face. And since it would be inadvisable for him to come out, then perforce I must go in."

Here he raised his voice ever so slightly: "Is there room for me up there? A boy might tap once for no and twice for yes."

There was a tap. After a suitable duration, it became clear to us that there was no room for Jan in the crawl space above my ceiling.

"Fine. Good. Not a garret then. Can he move around the house?"

Two taps in quick succession.

"Is this an improvised set-up involving water pipes and wall studs, or does a boy have access to actual secret passageways?"

There was a pause.

"Ah, yes, how stupid of me: improvised?"

A single tap.

"Secret passageways, then?"

Two taps.

"Within narrow, hollow walls?"

Two taps.

"Ropes?"

One tap.

"Stairs?"

One tap.

"Ladders?"

Two taps.

"Well," said Jan. "Well, well, well. Ladders. *Dobře*. So there is, presumably, another location within the house where I might meet him?"

Two taps.

"Good. Now all we have to do is find it. I grow tired of this binary line of inquiry. And I fear my growing excitement might cause me to be discovered by the sentry. So, I propose that my new friend Olive here will make a perambulation with me around this fine manse, to all the rooms. And we shall linger just long enough in each one to perceive a knocking. We will commence in twenty minutes, starting on the ground floor, giving a boy perhaps enough time to find a way to his more spacious confinement. And I shall have food for him. I hope he can eat rabbit. I hope he can eat venison and wild roots."

After a moment, two knocks, as I wondered where Jan Komárek was going to get venison and rabbit.

"And so," said Jan, presumably to me now, "you will join me?"

I tapped distractedly upon the desk, twice.

"Good. Good. You know, you're an interesting character. I don't really know what to make of you."

It was only later that I realized what an immensely flattering statement this was meant to be.

"Just remember: do not underestimate me. I will prove just as capable as you, if not more."

And then, with this utterly baffling remark, Jan drew me to my door. I opened it, and he slipped away like a cat.

14. S O T H I S

The magician said I lived in the tops of trees

There are things too scary to write will just have to remember

Magician has a practical plan for

once for no twice for yes

going house exploring

Twenty minutes later, I found myself in the first-floor living room — not the front room where we had all first met, now off limits, but a larger room across the checker-floor hallway from it. A charming feature of this house was how narrow hallways opened into spacious rooms. The architect practised a kind of sleight of hand: constraint followed by liberation. Your shoulder blades squeezed together as you slipped down the hall and then flew open like wings as you passed through into the broader spaces, from forest to field.

But I'm overstating my feelings in the matter.

This room was wider than the room where we'd first met: instead of a single pane, there were three, the bay window allowing me to see several layers of green-veiled scaffolding barring any view of the street. A colourful, oddly shaped daybed sofa had a rumpled comforter thrown over it, indicating that someone had slept there. The daybed was designed to look like a cartoon: angled off-kilter and painted in complementary colours. There was another couch too, along with two large, soft throw cushions, all of a similar eccentric design. In the middle of the room was a drafting table covered with scribbled drawings. And a pile of old painted canvases on the floor, worthless in and of themselves, presumably being stripped for future forgery. Armando was standing on a stepladder beside the wall opposite the front window, carefully removing a top layer of colourful doodles on buckling paper that had been affixed to other work beneath it, a chaotic studio palimpsest. The under layer was covered in trace bits of sticky-tack that he was sullenly picking off with his fingernails. So, this room had once been covered with art atop art, and it was all being taken down and carted away to make room for the new art Mr. Lin had demanded. The old pieces had an energetic, joyful, doodley quality: a sunny disposition, dashed-off, full of light and bathing suits and humour and food and small animals behaving like people. In marked contrast to the man himself, who was piled atop his stepladder like a mound of earth on a plank, with a single grey cloud drizzling dull rain down upon it.

He glanced down at me with cultivated disinterest and a droopy eye. "Why are you here?"

Before I could answer, Jan Komárek spoke up, having appeared almost as if by magic, in the doorway. "Did our host not say we could visit one another?"

"I am your host," said the sullen mound of Matamoros. "And I did not say you could visit me."

Jan slipped past me and entered the room.

"We are here," said Jan, "on a rather important errand. But before we get to it, I was hoping I could convince you to exchange studios with me."

"Ha!" said Armando, still on his stepladder, removing the bottom layer of artwork. "There's little chance of that."

"But I'm in the cellar," said Jan. "Correct me if I'm wrong, but is the cellar not your best chance of digging your way out of here?"

"I have no intention of ceding my home to anyone. I will remain captain of this ship no matter how many pirates climb over the side. And this room has always been my studio. It has not been arbitrarily chosen; it is not makeshift; it did not have a wholly different purpose up until yesterday's hostile occupation. Forced to choose between a glorious bedroom and a beloved studio, I will be shifted no further. What's more, I do not trust you."

It was true. Everyone was suspicious of the part Jan Komárek had played in the shattered window, if not his weird image-shifting photograph, which had only been noticed by me.

"All right, all right," said Jan. "And an impressive speech. I am excited by the prospect of bearing witness to this so-called glorious bedroom, as my companion and I," indicating me, "are planning to make a visit, on the same errand that has brought us to your door. But while I have your ear and before we come to our reason for being here, I would like to first commend you on your taste in houses. This one is" — here Jan gave a chef's kiss — "just a little bit off alignment; the floors are not level, the corners do not quite meet so much as slide past each other with a sidelong wink. And it has hidden ladders! More secrets too, I imagine . . ." He cocked his ear for a moment's hesitation and then continued. "Even now I think I hear a knocking, a knock-knock-knocking, coming from within the walls. But I suspect what I hear is not the particular knocking I have been listening for. Oh no, it is not a knocking of *human* intent but rather a mocking mimicry of what I wish to hear, performed, I believe, by the house itself."

I found myself remembering the dropped bolt or nut from that morning that had startled me and made me think someone was knocking on my door.

Jan continued.

"You see, I have been studying this house for almost a full day now, and I don't know what it was like before, but I can assert that it is itself in possession of a sense of humour. I suspect this sense of humour has been taken from you and is being held for safe keeping. I'm not sure when you lost this sense of humour — whether it was yesterday when you lost possession of your house or whether it was sometime before that and had something to do with your relationship with Ángela Efrena Quintero. But I have the powerful sense that the humour is being safely kept for you, nestled within these walls."

Armando Matamoros was regarding his guest dryly. Jan went on undeterred, warming to his subject. I was beginning to wonder whether he would ever bring up our real — and to my mind rather urgent — reason for being here.

"What's more," Jan continued, "if this is the truth, then I can think of no safer place to keep your sense of humour until you seek to have it back. For if the behaviour of this house is any indication, the sense of humour you have lost is prodigious and wide ranging. I'll go so far as to speculate that it must have been, at times, of the flatulent variety. Yes? Am I warm? You must have been in the habit of seeking, time from time, an inexpensive laugh from those around you by, for example, screwing your face up into a clownish balloon and then slowly releasing the air through a series of ripples of the lips in what is known as a 'raspberry.' Have I got that right?"

Armando yet stared.

"Because I must tell you I have perceived, down in the darkness of my basement studio, all through the night, a patterned, almost musical series of hilarious belchings, each one more outrageous than the last, as if this house were seeking to remind me that the institution of the cellar — though normally a place that conceals the sinister projects of diabolical men — can also be a refuge of joyous and flatulent celebration."

And then, by way of example, Jan produced a long series of raspberries, fricatives, uvulars, trills and squeaks, all the while holding Armando's eye, whose expression, in an awe-inspiring performance of stillness, affected no change whatsoever, not even a ripple.

I realized in that moment that I was in the presence of masters.

"But," Jan went on, "I digress. And I suspect that my speculative theories as to your character will not be confirmed on this day."

"Nor perhaps," said Armando, turning back to his ladder, "on any other day."

"No," said Jan. "Though I am delighted to hear that you have been paying attention. So I will complete my dissertation by declaring appreciation for the fact of your cellar having no electricity, lit as it is by candlelight, and then I will, at long and dear last, get to the rather serious reason for our visit. Look at our friend here. She has been so patient."

This last was with reference to me. Jan turned and poked his head back out into the hall, checking for any sign that our host might be lurking, and then popped back to his purpose, affecting now a raspy, heightened whisper.

"As you may recall, this humourious house of yours contains a single hidden and hopeful child, believed by our host to be a grown man, a forger like the rest of us, but no, no: just a boy."

Armando: "He is not our host."

Jan: "Granted. Not our host. My apologies. You are our host. Still, this does not change the current reality with respect to the boy. My mysterious companion and I are currently on the trail of this boy. He seems to have located the walls behind the walls and the ceilings above the ceilings, which the house may or may not have afforded him through the power of a recently acquired sense of humour, who knows? Do I know? I do not know. Who can know? All I know is that this boy is currently attempting to lead us to a place in this house where I might be able to squeeze myself in beside him for a conference. We have alerted him to our intent to visit all the rooms, and, when we arrive in the place of proximity to him, he will attempt to communicate with us via a subtle knocking. However, I chose the knocking without thinking, and now I have a sinking feeling that this humourious house might interfere with our efforts at communicating by indulging in a bit of knocking of its own, along with some belching and sighing. And so I imagine the boy will have to resort to scratching, scraping, jabbing and dragging himself around before his presence will be perceived by us; such are the playful intentions of this house."

Armando, earnestly: "I can't speak for the rest of the house, but there are no hidden crevices in this room. The only thing above our heads is the floor of the master bedroom, though I suspect—"

Jan: "You mean the glorious bedroom, so called?"

Armando: "I am saying it is possible that the room above my head, with its slanted ceiling and private bathroom, could have more than its share of nooks and crannies and nests where a little bird might work its way in."

Jan: "By little bird, I have the suspicion you perhaps might mean a little boy?"

Armando: "Your suspicion is correct."

Jan: "We are much obliged to you then, captain. We shall make our way there in short order."

Armando nodded. Despite his annoyance, it was clear he liked being called captain. After a moment's hesitation, he asked, "And you have a plan for this boy?"

"I do," said Jan. "Indeed I do. It is a good plan too."

"How is it a good plan?"

Jan leaned in conspiratorially, his loud whisper becoming a quiet whisper. "It is a good plan in the sense that it will undermine the brutal authority a certain Mr. Lin has imposed over your household."

Now Armando brightened, visibly, if only for a moment. "How?" he asked. "No, wait: don't tell me. I don't want to know. I want to imagine it for myself." He went on. "If you can make a fool out of that man, if together we can humiliate him, even in some small way, even if he never even knows how he has been brought low, that would make me so happy: helping the boy is simply icing on that cake."

"I had hoped you would be of this opinion," said the slender Czech with a small bow. He was indicating that we were finally going to depart and leave the large man to his own company, but Armando Matamoros did something I did not expect. He shifted his earthwork self down the ladder with a sigh and said, "I'm coming too."

Jan's face lit up, not quite into a smile, but his eyes seemed to spread apart, impossibly, conveying an openness that made me blush.

"You understand, though," he said, "that we must be methodical. Ground-floor studios come first."

"What about your basement?" asked Armando.

"I have already made a thorough investigation of my basement," said Jan. "If the boy had interior access to it, then I would have found it by now."

"Very well," said Armando. "Lead the way."

And so we repaired to the foot of the stairs. I was momentarily distracted by the persimmon-and-white polka-dot wallpaper that covered most of the front hallway (above a raised-panel wainscoting). In the house where I grew up, the paint job in our suburban basement only went as high in the stairwell as the painter could reach with a short-handled roller and then stopped with a jagged edge, exposing the primer beneath. Design in that house was unserious; here beauty was a necessary part of living.

When I came back to myself, Jan was asking us to remove our shoes. Armando was objecting.

Jan: "It is customary and polite, when entering the abode of a Mus—"

Armando: "This is my abode. My abode."

Jan: "Should I expect you to harp upon this theme forever?"

Armando, with a face: "Only for as long as it irritates you."

Still, he did it: he slipped off his shoes, and we were preparing to knock. But then Jan produced a small shiny parcel tied up with a ribbon. This surprised me, since the Czech had not left my side since he had concocted the plan to visit everyone. But if I was surprised, Armando was affronted.

"A gift now?" he said.

"It is indeed a gift! A customary—"

"How come you are giving her a gift and yet you did not bring me a gift?"

"You did not expect a gift!"

"Does it matter? I am wounded that you did not bring me a gift!"

"In my country, and in this woman's country, it is customary to arrive for a first visit bearing a gift."

(I was still wondering how Jan had come to possess the gift.)

"I am offended by you. I am offended by your gift," said Armando.

"As long as you remain sympathetic to the boy, I do not care what you feel for me."

"You are a cold-hearted Slav."

"I beg your pardon, I am not a Slav. I am a Czech."

"And I am standing in a hallway of my own home without shoes."

"I remove my shoes when I enter my own home. I dare say you are becoming civilized."

Their exchange played out, Jan stepped up to the door and gave it three firm raps.

A voice called, "Come in!" and the door opened to the arresting scene of the milk sister already hard at work, with her brother (this was a surprise) assisting her as if they had never fought, helping her to prime the walls of the room. The two of them were clothed in paint-bespattered coveralls, Sanam having exchanged her multicoloured headscarf for one of slate gray. Armando sallied forth into his former dining room, pointing back at the diminutive Czech and declaring, "We brought a gift."

Amir looked up, surprised, and Sanam rose from her plastic-covered chair and invited us to find someplace to sit. "There are six free chairs," she said.

Jan stepped forward with his gift. Sanam put out her hand to accept it. I thought it might get squirrelled away; that's what I would have done with a gift, embarrassed as I would have been for having been placed at the centre of attention. But no: Sanam made a great show of interest in the shiny parcel, trying to guess what it might contain before she finally settled down, donned a pair of reading specs and opened it up.

Inside the small box was a little plastic sack full of ash. Sanam held it up to the light coming in from the bay doors (which were open, by the way, and led directly into the backyard, allowing the clear-honey light of morning to come in along with fresh air and the eyes of a sentry who stood so still you might forget he was there). Then she placed it on the table and carefully unknotted the top of the bag, producing a pair of tweezers from somewhere and delicately combing through the ash.

"What is it?" she asked.

"Can't you guess?" said Jan.

"I would guess it was ash that came from the drip tray of an oil lamp, but only if the gift-giver were a person of my profession."

"It is indeed ash that came from the drip tray of an oil lamp. But not just any oil lamp."

"Well," said Sanam, "if, again, I were to be receiving this from a person in the same profession as mine, and that person had just coyly spoken your words, I would venture to guess that this ash was scraped from the drip tray of the oil lamps in the Süleymaniye Mosque of Istanbul, Turkey, said to be the most prized for bringing blessings to the ink of an Islamic scribe."

"And you'd be correct," said Jan, "for that is what it is."

"But how?" asked Sanam, even as Amir came down from his chair to peer at the small plastic bag.

"I collect things," said Jan with a shrug. "More to the point, I collect ash. Many varieties of ash. I have a library back in my studio in Hradčany."

"An ash library," said Amir, hovering by his sister's shoulder. "I'm curious about what other examples of highfalutin ash you have there."

"The nice thing," said Jan, "about collecting ash is you don't have to worry about losing it in a fire."

"That's true in theory," said Amir. "But what if it became contaminated with mere bedside-bureau ash or even neighbouring-busybody ash?"

Jan gave the impression that this possibility had not occurred to him.

"Ha," said Amir, smiling with satisfaction as he returned to his work.

"I might ask," said Armando, "how this little Czech came to know he would have a reason to give away some ash in my house, but I'm too busy wondering how you already found rollers and cans of primer."

"Forgive me," said Sanam.

"There is nothing to forgive," said Armando, blushing at the woman's solicitousness. "I never really used this dining room, even if it does share a wall with the kitchen, and anyway we all are doing what we must here. I just wonder how you found it."

"I can answer that," said Jan.

"I might have guessed," said Armando.

"I made a full inventory last evening of the artistic supplies that were to be found in the cellar, posting a list to the cellar door. These items were among them. Madame Sanam here seemed to need them most, given the darkened pallor of this abandoned room."

"You speak as if these walls would have a brighter hue if I'd used this room more."

"That just may be true," said Jan.

Armando sighed.

The floor was covered with newspapers, as were the table and all the chairs surrounding it, except two that Sanam and her brother were using for their painting. These were covered with a layer of plastic. Beneath the table was a comforter and rumpled pillow. Had she spent the night under there?

"We can move the dining-room table out of here for you," said Armando.

"Where to put it though, eh?" called Amir from his perch. "In the hallway?"

"No need," said Sanam. "Truly. I tell you, kind sir: I feel like a six-year-old girl down there among the chair legs. I have my comforter and a thin foam mattress just narrow enough to fit. And, if I may add, that childlike feeling is something I will need to hold onto if I am going to get any sleep in this room, given my plans for it. Better for me to lie beneath a table."

Jan smiled approvingly. Amir was nodding with admiration. Armando declared himself convinced.

"I would appreciate, however," Sanam said, "if you took away the dusty old wine bottles."

"By all means," said Armando.

"And you can move these too, if you would be so kind," Sanam added, gesturing to the two large paintings leaning by the door with their faces turned away. "They cannot stay here if I hope to summon angels."

I'll confess I did not understand that remark, though it seemed significant. Was this the "famous Sunni admonishment against images" that Jan had mentioned in his breakfast argument with Sanam?

I may not have understood the remark, but Amir seemed to, as he rolled his eyes.

Another thing that confused me was the deference Sanam was showing Armando, given the force of her personality that I had witnessed the day before. But then she broached a topic that must have been weighing on her.

"I would like to make an apology, sir, to you specifically, for what I am about to undertake in this room. It troubles me, as a student of history."

Armando said, "By all means, Señora, you must speak your mind."

Amir put down his brush and sat cross-legged on the floor to listen, indicating that Sanam was about to launch into a disquisition that required his full concentration. I could see now how he was her little brother, how he doted on her and looked up to her and was genuinely excited to hear her speak.

And disquire she did, placing her relationship with Armando's house into a historical context that spanned over a thousand years, comparing her position within our ranks to that of an anonymous engineer from fifteenth-century Istanbul who was commissioned, under duress, by Mehmed the Conqueror (presumably

Mr. Lin in her scenario) to undertake the architectural transformation of the Hagia Sophia from a centuries-old Christian cathedral into the first domed mosque in the world. The engineer was said to have discreetly pulled aside a Christian priest found begging in the street and asked him how he might construct a small Christian place of worship so that he might make his apology directly to the God of this church he was destroying. "This request," Sanam continued, "precipitated a debate between the priest and the engineer on the subject of whether the God of the Muslims and the God of the Christians was indeed (or not) the same God, and whether perhaps the problem of redesign in a place of worship was something more akin to rearranging the deck chairs on the *Titanic* if the *Titanic* were the larger community of faith and the iceberg were the shock of temporal existence."

"Of course," added Amir from his place at his sister's feet, "they were not actually discussing the *Titanic* and the iceberg—"

"No, I suppose not," said Sanam, playfully cuffing her brother's hair, "though such debates have a way of stepping directly outside the flow of time.

"But the point I am struggling to convey is that, under similar duress, I am going to have to transform this truffle-brown dining room belonging to our new friend Armando Matamoros into something fully immersed within my Islamic artistic tradition. I am uncomfortable with this idea, and I am hoping to find some way to honour the room's original function."

"That's not necessary," said Armando. "It is merely an unused dining—"

Sanam went on. "I hope to take some inspiration from another anonymous architect, this one from Spain."

"Oh, really?" said Armando. He had a look in his eye. I felt perhaps he was falling in love with this woman, though I am constitutionally incapable of identifying such chemical interactions.

"This architect was asked to transform the mosque of Córdoba into a cathedral, the opposite of the Hagia Sophia's fate.

In doing so, he allowed the mihrab in the wall of the original mosque to stay."

"I don't think they know what that is," said Amir.

"It is the niche in the wall that points to Mecca," said Sanam. "His preservation of it allowed all the secret Andalusian Muslims to know where to turn when they spoke their secret prayers in that Christian church. I pledge, hereby, to retain some aspect of this dining room's original aspect. I don't know how yet: some indication toward living in the moment, since dining was the prehistoric form of prayer, its pagan power stolen by the saying of grace."

"This is really not—" Armando began to reply.

"And yet I must insist," said the woman. "We make our rebellions as we can, even as we hurl ourselves into the abyss of officially sanctioned art practice."

"Do what you must," said Armando. "But I will tell you that my forebears knew the *duende* of Andalusia. We are connected, you and I, in some small way. I never used this dining room, always ate in the kitchen."

Amir said, "How can you really be sympathetic to Muslims? Your surname means Moor-slayer."

Sanam tsked. "Amir, honestly. A man cannot help his name."

"Sure he can," said Amir. He had returned to his perch on a plastic-covered dining-room chair, was now hesitating over a brushstroke as if he were applying something more sublime than primer.

"I apologize for my name," said Armando, "and I have no objections to the work that will be done in this room."

The house did not emit any knocks or belches during Sanam's history lesson or Armando's response or Amir's objections. And neither, it seems, did the boy. I found it hard to believe I was standing in the same building as Armando's studio. We had shifted our perspective so completely from a room where we were asked to consider the scatological sense of humour of the house itself to this one where a thousand years of history was standing plain before us like a naked model adopting an *adlocutio* pose for a life studies class.

The five of us were standing now, waiting for Jan to say why we were really here.

He finally spoke up, so quietly I wasn't sure it wasn't my own conscience speaking to me.

"We need a holiness to surround our task," he said. "So I am glad for the serendipity that brought that small sack of ash with me from the Castle District in Prague, because . . ." He paused before leaning in close to Sanam and speaking even more quietly. " . . . we are here in search of the hidden boy."

"The boy," said Sanam, also quiet, hushed. "Where is he? Has he revealed himself?"

"He wishes to reveal the most capacious of his hiding places by knocking," said Jan. "We simply have to locate the place where he will knock. And then I will squeeze in and join him and explain how I will give him the disguise that will allow him to emerge, time from time. I had hoped it might be your room, but I suppose it was unlikely for it to be on the ground floor. Let us venture up to the one above."

"I will accompany you," said Sanam.

"As will I," said Amir.

Our pilgrimage had grown.

Our trip up the stairs to the second floor*was cut short when the front door opened and Mr. Lin walked in, holding Esther by the hand. The pair were followed by a resplendent Ella Unton Bride, sporting her enigmatic bowtie, along with a pair of women wearing mushroom chef's hats who were carrying an oversized black duffle bag with a handle at each end.

"Ah," said Mr. Lin, waving his hand at us on the way by. "All present, save two. It is good to see the development of community. I come bearing gifts. If we could convene in the Matamoros Gallery, that might be best."

And then, turning to Ms. Bride just before he entered the kitchen, he added, "Could you summon the missing two?"

Ms. Bride nodded and slipped past us like the breeze through a silk curtain, heading upstairs.

"Follow me," said Mr. Lin, ushering the two Korean chefs through the kitchen and then gesturing for the five of us to follow.

The meeting turned out to be about wardrobe. We had all arrived without much more than a change of clothes. Mr. Lin intended to remedy that. I recalled that Ms. Bride had requested measurements in that original Facebook message. I had thought nothing of it at the time, perhaps having believed I was going to be awarded a ceremonial robe; I don't know. Vanity is ridiculous. I hate to think about it. I have it obviously, in spades clearly. Let's move on.

Everyone was being given coveralls for painting, as well as five complete suits of clothing. The surprising thing was how

---

* During my time in the house, I learned that the second floor is known as the first floor in the UK, whereas the first floor is referred to as the ground floor. But I've already begun with the Canadian terminology, and so I should stick with it.

appropriate to the wearer these garments turned out to be, both in tailoring (they all fit) and style.

Hannie Van der Roos was the first of the second-floor dwellers to arrive. As she walked into the gallery room, she pronounced, "You know, I was working. I had assumed that was the goal of our time here. When I work, I generally do not like to be interrupted. I have a reputation to uphold, despite having been accused of something I would never do. Your professional handler, Ms. Bride, would be able to convey the absolute truth of this fact if only she were ever to transform back into a human being."

Ella Unton Bride, whose blush was deepening from a Spanish pink to a cameo pink, said, "I think we should allow Hannie to go first so she can get back to her work. I do think she will be pleased with what I've brought for her."

"It's doubtful," said Hannie.

However, I couldn't help but register Hannie's reluctant expressions of approval as Ms. Bride, keeping her own eyes down, presented sartorial variants of silver and grey, especially with the tour de force: a fine, shimmering, culturally neutral variant on a Tang suit, complete with high collar and cedar toggles. Ella Unton Bride asked her if she wished to try any of them on. Hannie demurred, said she was certain they would fit. Ms. Bride's blush darkened to crimson, eyes still down. I confess I must have stared, not knowing what was being communicated between these two women, who, I recalled, had arrived together.

Finally, I had to look away. I decided to make a study of Mr. Lin's daughter.

The girl was dressed as if for Catholic school, shiny black shoes, argyle stockings, starched navy skirt and a blazer buttoned over a crisp white shirt. But the notable thing about her was how the blazer breast pocket was stuffed with coloured and conté pencils, how she clutched a medium-sized Moleskine with a black cover, how her eyes darted from person to person, resting on each face and studying it. She seemed accustomed to being ignored in the context of a large group, and so I watched her rest her gaze first on Hannie Van der Roos, then Sanam, then Armando. When she finally cast her gaze upon me and found me looking back at her, her eyes widened for a moment, and then she looked away.

I mean, at least, I think she looked away, because I'll admit I was just as startled as she was, having neglected to consider that I might be an option for study. So I looked away too. And when I finally summoned the courage to look back, she was looking down, had her notebook open a crack and her hand tucked inside it, wrist bobbing ever so slightly. Trying to draw without calling attention to herself! I used to do that! She knew I was watching her, I think, but she also knew I was the only one, and her expression betrayed a certain annoyance as she was forced to prioritize her drawing over her privacy. So I gave an imperceptible nod to no one in particular and turned away to watch more wardrobe revelations. Hannie Van der Roos had already withdrawn in sartorial splendour, but I did notice that Ella Unton Bride appeared blushless and spent. And there was much else for the eyes to feast upon, even as the idea of hungry eyes got me thinking of poor, presumably famished Ezra Coen, ready in his upper-floor spot to knock and feast upon Jan's promised rabbit:

Armando was examining a herringbone suit.

Jan was making a line on the floor with ten new cravats.

Amir was all in black, including a turtleneck. He looked like an extra from *An American in Paris*.

Ángela Efrena Quintero got a red ruched dress, though she chose to keep wearing the jeans and T-shirt she already had on.

Sanam had two standouts: a thaub in black and gold that looked like evening dress and a peach-and-yellow salwar suit that seemed best for morning. Also several headscarves with the words *Hermès Paris* written on them in elegant coloured script.

Ella Unton Bride, though trying to conceal it, clearly counted herself pleased, while Mr. Lin stood by patiently, nodding his approval. If it had not already become clear that this was not a conventional hostage situation, it was becoming so now.

"I want you all to feel comfortable," he said. "I want you to feel that you have been given an opportunity to be your best selves. I speculate that we could all be here for somewhere in the vicinity of a hundred days, but I have made provisions for up to seven months, so your comfort is important to me."

He was very well organized, our kidnapper.

"Now, on the subject of my daughter's first visit to a studio—"

"I thought we had determined that I would take her," said Ángela, interrupting. "As I said before, I'd be delighted. All I've got in there at the moment is an unmade bed, but perhaps this girl can assist me in listing the materials I'm going to need. And there is a sentry standing outside my window who continues to look discreetly away no matter my efforts to get his attention. Perhaps she can help me with that."

Mr. Lin said, "These guardians have been instructed to give you your privacy and not engage with you."

Ángela said, "Yes, but what if there are butterflies outside? I will need them."

"But it is winter," said Mr. Lin.

"Yes, but it is pupae I seek. Eleven species hibernate in this country. They could be under the eaves. And, to me, there is no better assistant than the man who spends his whole day out there, communing with the flowers and the trees."

"Be that as it may," said Mr. Lin.

"But I must insist," said Ángela. "I make do with the inspiration at hand. That man is already part of my project."

Mr. Lin started to object again, but Esther suddenly pivoted and whispered in his ear. He listened for a moment, then straightened up and addressed Ángela again.

"My daughter has agreed to assist you."

"Excellent," said Ángela. And then, casting a rueful eye at Armando: "Now I have someone to visit me."

Armando scowled back.

The gallery conference had come to its natural end. The chefs in the kitchen had begun to sear the sashimi-grade salmon steaks they were planning to serve with spinach and steamed asparagus. I worried about the boy, hidden somewhere in this house, waiting to make his knock. Was he hungry too? Like me? Surely yes. There must have been another forty-five minutes or so before we would be expected to assemble again for lunch. Would that be enough time to locate him?

DRAWING - Redacted.

Everyone got up to leave. But then Ella Unton Bride called our attention back as she gestured to a pile of unclaimed attire and then looked up at me.

Oh no. No, no, no.

If you are expecting me to describe what happened next, or what I came to be wearing . . .

No, no, no, no. No.

I was clothed. Let's move on.

No, I'm not going to describe it. Let's move on.

All right, I will say it was pleasing, but let's move on.

To me. It was pleasing *to me*. This is not to say it would have been pleasing to anyone else.

It had a bit of a stimulating effect, but . . . let's move on.

All right. I still won't describe it, but here is a drawing. A scribble. Drawn years later, it is important to understand. Influenced by the style of Hannie Van der Roos. Perhaps I should sign her name to it?

It turned out, in the end, that when we finally arrived at Ezra Coen, we almost didn't hear the knock.

Everyone had come upstairs, escorting the young Esther for a preview of Ángela's luxurious suite. Everyone except Hannie, I should say, since she had taken her leave from the group just after her fitting. And Ms. Bride, who had withdrawn to the front meeting room, now office. But even Mr. Lin had come, along with his daughter, making the continued search for Ezra Coen somewhat tricky. So we cooled our heels and did our best (Armando, Sanam, Amir, etc.) to quell the envy we felt to see the quality of light, the glorious south-facing windows, the size of the bed, the private bathroom with its clawfoot tub and marble sink and, also, a bidet. This turned out to be too much for Sanam Haghighi. When she saw the bidet, she said, "Señorita Ángela, if you were to switch rooms with me, I would present you with a fifteenth-century Timurid Qur'an copied on Ming Dynasty gold-painted paper, one of only four in existence, with an estimated value of 1.5 million American dollars. Very beautiful. It's a fake, of course, with materials and labour giving it an actual value closer to nine or ten thousand dollars, itself nothing to sneeze at. But I would give it up in exchange for this room or really just for this bidet and you could take your chances with it at Christie's when at last we get out of here."

I thought Mr. Lin might speak up, but he said nothing.

"I am sorry," said Ángela. "I prize my bidet."

"No one values the written word anymore," said Sanam.

Having put off Sanam, Ángela now took the opportunity to show Mr. Lin how the sentry was ignoring her. She walked up to the window and did a controlled handstand in which her toes came up and gently touched the window as her T-shirt fell over her face, revealing her breasts. I looked away, but the sentry was already looking away, so he remained as a stone. Armando however, I could not help but notice, pushed his chin into his chest and blushed as red as Ella Unton Bride. Then Ángela stood up again, adjusted her shirt and indicated with a large gesture that the sentry had done nothing.

Mr. Lin nodded approvingly at his sentry's discipline.

After that, somehow, Ángela convinced everyone to partici- pate in an improvisational exercise where each guest was asked to step up to the window and make an extreme gesture to catch the sentry's attention. Everyone participated. Not me. I did not participate. How could I? I find it almost too mortifying even to relate what the others did, and I really only mention it because I believe it was due to the particular nature of Ángela Quintero's talent, perhaps even the reason she chose forgery as a profession: convincing people to do things for her that they would never do for anyone else.

Now that I've written that down, I realize that the best illustration of her talent is to admit that I've just now lied. She convinced me too. I did do something. But even though I did it, I find I cannot bring myself to relive it here, despite how far I've come. That's why I wrote that I didn't do anything, even though I did. But be assured, I did. I performed.

All right, all right. I twirled.

By which I mean: I performed a pirouette. A single one. Well, three quarters. And did not fall down. In front of the assembled group and also the sentry. There, I've done it. That's enough writing for today. I'm exhausted. The next paragraph will be written tomorrow, a fact that will remain true even if I decide to delete this entire sordid tale about my pirouette. I've read a few instruction manuals on writing, and I can't find much about whether you're allowed to relate how writing makes you feel while you're doing it. I thought it was important to read up on how to write because I've read a few books by artists, and they don't seem successful to me: the writer-artist gets distracted by the feeling of their fingertips on the typewriter keys and so devotes a page to it. If I end up doing that — which, all right, I concede I am doing right now — I'll never reach the end of my story. Rest assured, I intend to hone this new craft. Until tomorrow, then.

Ángela next convinced Amir to lick the windowpane.

Then Sanam stepped up and made several piercing bird calls.

Armando refused at first, huffing his objection to being one of Ángela's playthings, but she looked so genuinely put out that he finally relented, stepping up to the window and pounding on the glass so hard I thought it might break.

But the sentry did not flinch and neither did Mr. Lin.

Jan Komárek leapt up onto the sill, which was only wide enough to hold a cat, whereupon he stretched and preened and then leapt lightly down again.

Finally, Mr. Lin's daughter stepped forward and performed a routine that she later explained was from her favourite κ-pop group. She was indignant that the sentry did not turn to look at her, so Mr. Lin finally pulled out his cellphone and punched a number. Outside the window, the sentry pulled something out of a pocket and put it up to his ear. By the time we took our leave from that sunlit room, Ángela was standing at the window, Esther Lin by her side, talking with the sentry and presumably giving him a detailed set of instructions.

His business finished, Mr. Lin made his way back downstairs while the rest of us let out a slow collective breath and resumed our task, leaving Ángela (and, of course, Esther) unaware of our search for the boy.

We lingered for another minute in the hallway before turning to face the door opposite Ángela's, taking up the search again, but then —

"May we take a look?" asked Jan, to Hannie Van der Roos.

"No."

"Why not?"

"I have my work," said Hannie. "And I have no interest in letting any of you see it."

"No one is interested in stealing your work, I can assure you," said Armando.

"Oh, I am quite assured," said Hannie.

Armando lowered his voice. "The boy might be hiding in there. Behind your walls."

"I'll be sure to let you know," Hannie whispered back, "if I hear him."

"You think you're too good for us," said Sanam.

"I try not to think of you at all," said Hannie. "But I can assure you, if the boy is scurrying around behind my walls, I will hear him. My hearing is very good."

"Is that right?" said Sanam. "Can you hear this?"

There was a pause, and I didn't hear anything, so I looked at Sanam and saw that her lips were moving at a rapid pace, though she didn't appear to be making any sound, all the while holding Hannie's calm gaze.

When she finally broke off her performance, Hannie said, "Are you finished?"

"Did you make it out?"

"I did," said Hannie.

"What did I say?"

Hannie sighed. "You named a place," she said, "and said that it calls to you. You said the place glitters and that it laps at your feet, so presumably you are speaking of a lake or a river . . . Then you said that someone you love calls to you. It is a poem you are reciting, I think, not a memory, so not your own lover but rather the poet's lover. You describe the sand being like silk against your toes — river sand; so, yes, you are imagining yourself standing by a river. You want to return to this place. Then you wade across the river and approach the green hills. You remember the horses up there. Someone up there is crying and calling for you. Quite a beautiful poem, which you were gracious enough to translate into

English for me, though I suspect you must know it in your native Farsi. I suspect it must be quite old. Being a forger, you might feel tempted to publish your English rendering of it under your own name. And there is nothing stopping you, given that Iran is not a signatory of the International Copyright Agreement. You Persians can pillage from the art world as you please within your borders and presumably pillage from your compatriots outside them."

"I would never do that," said Sanam. "It's quite a famous poem. I simply like to recall it."

"I appreciate that. But I feel compelled to add that I'm a lip reader, since my mother was quite deaf and taught me the skill. So your recitation did nothing to prove the acuity of my hearing. It did, however, make me miss my home."

"Me too," said Sanam. "It was originally commissioned by a collection of homesick courtiers to help convince the emir of Bokhara to pick up and go home."

"Did it work?"

"History does not say."

"Well, it worked for me," said Hannie. "I long to go home. At the moment, however, I'd settle for being left alone."

So we moved on, the five of us, leaving Hannie standing sentry at her own door, solitary as a stylite and (I believe) harbouring a newfound respect for Sanam Haghighi.

As we headed down the hall, I whispered to Amir, asking him if what Hannie had said about copyright agreements was true.

"Oh yes," he said. "We protect our own intellectual property within our borders, but everyone else is fair game. And our work is fair game too, I suppose, anywhere else in the world."

"So then how can you be in trouble with Mr. Lin?"

"Because, my friend, like you, it was a *name* I stole, not an artwork. Not even a real name. A fake, a name that had been lost to the mists of time. I stole *Anonymous*."

We checked Amir's room next. It was very small, perhaps the smallest in the house, even smaller than mine. Still, since Amir was a miniaturist and, like the rest of us, expected to cover every inch of space in the room, I could only suppose he preferred it that way.

I wondered for a moment if I had perhaps only dreamed up the boy, to delay the contemplation of this strange captivity.

But no, Jan had heard him too, had spoken to him, had interpreted his responses.

We began to feel exhausted and despondent as a group. Everyone was hungry, everyone was carrying five sets of clothes in sweat-inducing polybags.

But we lingered and hesitated and fretted just long enough for Armando to recall that, just back down the narrowed hallway that led to Amir's room and my own private stairwell, there was yet another door, which was unlocked and which opened up into yet another room, unoccupied, though the late-morning light through its east-facingwindow made the emptiness feel fitting. Like a Christopher Pratt painting.* This "light" room, of course — the sound of five foreheads getting slapped in unison — must have been intended for Ezra Coen.

The most shocking thing about this unoccupied and nearly forgotten room was that it *also* had its own private bathroom, just like Ángela's. Nothing to sneeze at, that, and I could see the wheels turning in Amir's head. Perhaps the two of us could try to keep this bathroom a secret from Hannie. Although, on the other hand, would that not mean we ended up sharing this one and leaving the other to Hannie's private use? No, if we kept it a secret from her, then we still had two options whereas she only ever had one. The sharing of two spaces among three people has long been a troublesome affair in the world of diplomacy and statecraft.

As it happens, this bedroom shared a wall, north-facing, with the square turning stairwell that led up to my room. It was here,

---

* I feel compelled to assert, because both I and Christopher Pratt are Canadian, that I have never attempted a forgery of this man's work.

in the space behind this wall and above a turn in the stairwell, that the knocking was being attempted. The boy had resorted to scratching, scraping, jabbing, pushing and dragging himself around behind the section of drywall before we finally heard him. Well, that's not quite true. Only Jan heard him at first. He'd kept his ears cocked. It was the rest of us who had become distracted by the beauty of the light and the contemplation of a private bathroom.

Until we stopped. Because Jan was standing by the northern wall. And his eyes were spread apart in that strange smile of his. And his finger was in the air. And then we listened. And then we heard.

PART THREE

POUNCING

A method of transferring a drawing or design to another surface (typically a cartoon to a wall for fresco painting) by dabbing pounce (a fine powder of charcoal or similar substance) through a series of pinpricks in the outlines of the drawing, thus creating a "join up the dots" replica of it on the surface below.

19. JALUHA

I don't know for sure whether you, the reader, have the experience of being confined to one place for months on end, hardly ever going outside, having food and amenities delivered to you. If you have, you might know what I'm speaking about when I say that the sense of time passing in a conventional way begins to get away from you, like a slipstream, like trying to maintain your equilibrium in a room full of Rothkos, until you can't tell the difference between above and below or, more to the point, you can't tell a weekend from Wednesday. And if you're a compulsively creative sort, then the things you make bloom up in front of you as if out of nowhere, perhaps not beautiful things but things nonetheless: monstrous companions that burgeon and breathe beside you until you have to ask, Where did they come from? Well, ma'am, that's the work you've been doing during all this . . . time.

And then there are the people you share your space with. No matter how strange they started, they're not so much strangers anymore. Armando Matamoros and Hannie Van der Roos and Ángela Efrena Quintero, Amir and Sanam Haghighi, the hidden Ezra Coen, and Jan Komárek; even the unsettling Mr. Lin and his daughter, Esther. They all begin to feel like working parts in a single familiar mechanism, a silent running spaceship or a Saint-Exupéry planet with its tight gravitational pull, blanketed in a bed of unique flowers and surrounded by forbidding space.

Well, except the Little Prince did not have such dinners. In the end, the way to recognize the reality of the passage of time was to tally the dinners:

Vichyssoise, followed by fresh artichokes peeled in layers and dipped in butter.

Martinis and oysters.

Grilled squid with a garlic aioli and hot sauce.

Pan-seared scallops with lemongrass.

Mango pickle that stains a snowy bed of rice and homemade yoghurt.

Roast beef with Yorkshire pudding.

Whole steamed lobster.

Prime rib rare, au jus, with garlic mashed potatoes and Brussels sprouts, roasted.

Omakase by an expert sushi master.

Black tonkatsu with gyoza on the side and matcha ice cream dessert.

Chicken liver.

Spring pea soup.

Takeout from Casa do Frango.

Duck breast and then a pina colada and a Ziggy Stardust Disco Egg for dessert.

Hamburger and a root-beer shake.

Charcuterie and Four Roses.

Crispy beef.

Grilled sea bream with paella on the side and a Greek salad.

Bangers and baked beans.

Spinach-and-gruyere crepes.

Balsamic-fig pork tenderloin.

Pecan-crusted roasted salmon with maple sweet potato mash.

Pan-fried salmon and bok choy with sriracha mayo and ginger jasmine rice [We had this dish more than once, and I eventually learned how to prepare it myself.]

Lemon-pepper roasted salmon with warm orzo and spinach salad.

[Et cetera.]

I wrote these dinners down on the little scraps of paper that I threw on my floor. They piled up, burying the original crumpled messages from Ezra Coen. And so time went by.

Hannie Van der Roos tried to escape several more times, perhaps as many as eleven. I was invested in these escapes at first, wanting desperately for her to succeed, but I suppose I lost hope. I particularly remember rooting for her the time she tried to go through the back. She pulled open the sliding door in the gallery and sprinted out over the dull winter grass, rounding the bend of the long yard, security guards in hot pursuit. I had not yet seen the back of the yard at that point, but I believed at the time, erroneously, that it bordered Gladstone Park, and I imagined there must be a high stone wall that Hannie might vault over like a builderer, and then I imagined her hiding out inside one of the ancient hollow trees until darkness fell. And then I imagined her strolling safely out into the world, head held high, dressed in one of the shimmering gowns she would have stashed in her handbag for the occasion and a bright silver choker.

In reality, though, I don't think she made it to the end of the yard.

As her efforts proliferated, it became harder to stay invested, but this also meant I could observe certain details that had earlier escaped my notice. After her first few attempts, for example, I began to notice she always had a passionately scribbled drawing of a face taped to her chest while making her escape. It was never the same drawing. I'm not even sure it was ever the same face; certainly, the expression went through subtle transformations: haughty indignation, surprised indignation, judgmental indignation, etc. Sometimes she wrote on it: *CECI N'EST PAS UNE FAKE.* Sometimes she used green edging tape and sometimes she used masking tape. She was consistently excellent with the drawing, no matter how haphazard the approach.

The ritual puzzled me because it telegraphed her intent. Everyone would be heading for their studios for the day, and then

Hannie Van der Roos would appear in the hallway with a drawing taped to her chest. And so we would step out of the way because the guards were already on the move, and then we would see, for example, the expression of appalled indignation on the face of the drawing mirrored by Hannie's own expression of appalled indignation as she was carried back upstairs by security.

I started to wonder whether it was all being staged as a protest. By which I suppose I mean art. I started to wonder whether it was protest art. Like, some kind of performance protest art. After all, Hannie wasn't a peddler of fakes like the rest of us. So went her claim, and perhaps this action certified it: perhaps she had dreamt this up, right out of thin air. Right out of her imagination! Perhaps she staged these attempts to escape, framed them as a sort of artwork, to make us think about why she would go to all the trouble despite getting caught and to make us wonder about our own choices in that regard and also what it meant to have your struggle borne witness to by a face that was taped to your chest.

I found it exciting to contemplate: this was what it was like to be a primary creator, to dream up art that was new, without seeking permission, without waiting to see whether, absurdly, the universe would give you a sign that you should do it or, equally absurd, whether someone else was going to do it first. She just — went ahead and did it. Like a *punk*. Amir had called her *punk*.

I know it sounds silly. I had not always been like this, standing on the outside of everything, pushing up onto the tips of my toes trying to look in over the sill, like the handsome Bruno Ganz in that movie *Wings of Desire*: watching, listening, longing without knowing what I was longing for.

Protest art. I thought: when I get out of here, I'm definitely going to look that up.

A telling detail in revealing Hannie's intent was that, during these efforts, she always left her studio door locked with her work inside. It would seem she had a key. It would seem Mr. Lin allowed her to have a key that she was able to keep even when she was making a break for it. The reason I know this about the key is because, I will confess, there was this one time — maybe her sixth try? — when instead of standing and gawping as she tried to fight off the padded security, I rushed to her studio door to get a peek inside. Alas, no. Key required. And then, when I turned back to the action, I saw that they were already on their way up the stairs — the guard with the artist in her military arms — and they were both looking at me with the same shocked and contemptuous expression on their faces. And the drawing too: the drawing was looking at me with a shocked and contemptuous expression.

So I stepped away, with a familiar feeling of mortification, and watched from around the corner as the guard told Hannie that if she didn't give her the key, then she was going to have to kick the door down. Hannie made the guard promise that when the door was open she would not look, she would turn away and would block the view of anyone else who might be looking — and here they once again looked pointedly at me, and so I slunk away in shame as Hannie was set down and the door unlocked and opened and closed again.

And then I turned around from the back end of the hallway and saw that Ángela Efrena Quintero was also standing there, in her studio doorway opposite Hannie's, also admiring the end of the latest performative escape effort.

Within the hour after any one of her performances, Hannie was always back out and about within the household as if nothing irregular had taken place.

I believe it got to be that Hannie and the guard were on a first-name basis.

The earliest risers were Ángela, Sanam and myself, with Armando not far behind. I sensed that our erstwhile host did not relish the idea of getting up so early, but also did not like the thought of stumbling woozily into a kitchen full of people, yellow housecoat falling open to reveal childish striped pyjamas. He was also perhaps seeking to spend as much time as possible in the company of the woman whose floor lay on top of his ceiling.

Oh! Was that a double-entendre? I did not mean to do that! Thank god I didn't add an immodest adverb. The floor did not lay *gently* on top of the ceiling, for example, or, you know, *lasciviously*. It just lay there, on top of his ceiling.

There was undeniable tension between those two, apparent to even me. She always seemed to be ignoring him, and he always seemed to be indignant about her lack of attention. I suppose I would have found his behaviour inappropriate, were it not for her occasional taunts like when she told him how she was happy that Esther was coming to visit her. It was as if she was saying she wished Armando would come and visit her. Except, to me it was fairly clear that she did not want Armando to come and visit her, that she would have rebuffed him if he had come to visit her. The object for her in these exchanges seemed to be to watch how her remarks could transform the expression on his broad face, like clouds moving across a darkening sky: rain squalls, tornadoes, that alarming yellow tint in the grey that augurs electricity. She really seemed to enjoy the weather.

And then there was Sanam Haghighi. I had the impression that Sanam was comfortable here because she would have been comfortable anywhere. By all appearances, she worked as hard as Hannie Van der Roos, but she didn't try to hide her work, and she didn't try to pretend she was anywhere but here. I suppose she had the advantage of working in a medium and a language no one else understood, apparently not even her brother. He was a Farsi speaker, and she was working in Arabic. Still, she was easy with herself and with everyone.

I wondered whether it was the convictions of her Sunni faith that gave her such equanimity.

I asked her one day, in the kitchen, mid-morning – just to make conversation while she was sitting down with some leftover rosewater pudding – whether there were any inspiring sayings in the Qu'ran about living the way we were, in a kind of prison.

"Why?" she asked. "Are you looking to convert?"

"No!" I replied, with an enthusiasm I realized too late was probably insulting.

She thought for a minute, and then she said, "You know, it so happens, since we've been here, I have given some thought to an old folk tale I remember called the Seven Sleepers. It concerns a group of young radical Christians in late antiquity who were being persecuted by the Romans, and so they fled to the country-side and found refuge in a cave. I can't recall now whether they were shut into the cave by their persecutors or whether they found their own way to hide in there, but in any case, they were so exhausted that when night fell, they went to sleep, and, to make a long story short, they slept for a few hundred years. When at last they awoke, they were hungry, so they gave one of their number a coin and told him to run to the nearby town and get some food. The man showed his coin to the merchants, and everyone was amazed because they did not know his coin. It was an old coin; of course it was an old coin; I've already spoiled that part of the story for you. Anyway, the long and the short of it was there weren't any Romans anymore. There weren't any old Roman gods anymore. And so they rejoiced, these men. They were glad, for they were not going to be persecuted any longer. But here's the kicker: when they pulled out their crucifixes and began to rejoice and pray, the townspeople explained to them that no, no, no, they weren't *Christians* either, not Christians, oh no.

That religion was gone too. No, they explained joyfully: we're all Muslims now, and we're going to tell your story too, albeit with a few modifications."

Sanam finished her story, and then she laughed and laughed. I was confused.

She said, "You think I'm religious, my friend, but I'm really not. I just like to have some imposed limitations. Islam is the ultimate postmodern religion in the sense that it's easy to perform the duties and not think too hard about whether you believe in them or not. Sunniism is even better for that than Shiism. I like imposed limitations, in my life as well as my art. It stops the abyss from yawning at me: that great black cavern we all dangle over. Don't you feel it?"

I allowed that I did not, except perhaps now that she had mentioned it.

"This here," she gestured broadly, "is a pretty severe imposed limitation, don't you think?"

I allowed it was. But I said I still didn't understand her story.

"Don't wait to start your life, my friend. That's all. The only time we have is now. If you go to sleep for several hundred years, things might not be the way you want them to be when you wake up."

I said, "So you think we're going to be here for several hundred years?"

"You know, that is a very good question. Honestly, I haven't given it any thought. But consider this: even now, the world outside might not be the garden of earthly delights we long for."

Just as I started to ask what Sanam meant about the outside world, we were interrupted by Amir coming into the kitchen.

"Did I overhear you telling Olive all about your philosophy of limitations? Your theory of Sunniism as the great postmodern religion?"

"Amir has his own self-imposed limitations," said Sanam, to me. "He is a miniaturist."

"That's not why I do it," said Amir, hopping up onto a chair. "Miniaturism is hardly a limitation."

"Oh yes it is," said Sanam.

"My sister is mocking me," said Amir. "She knows I believe that the only reason life grew beyond the purview of the very small was to provide a big enough palette for beauty to fully express itself, whether it be in a peacock's tail, a sunset over the ocean, or the Orion nebula."

"But Orion comes by its beauty dishonestly!" said Sanam. "That's the absurd thing my brother believes."

"Exactly," said Amir. "At that scale, it's just too easy."

"Ha!"

"And so I aspire to introduce beauty to the realm of the very small." Amir was pinching his thumb and finger in front of his eye like a funny drunk.

"Your limitation," said Sanam.

"My vocation," said Amir, spreading his hands wide. "I go where I know my work will be appreciated."

"By whom? The tardigrades?"

"That is exactly right. I aspire to be appreciated by tardigrades."

I wanted to ask what tardigrades were, assuming — not entirely inaccurately — that they were creatures smaller than ants but bigger than amoebas. But Amir went on. "I'm such an accomplished miniaturist I can masquerade the signature of carbon dating with a bit of misdirection. My eye for detail is so fine I can insert the tree rings you need to fool the experts. Sister, why don't you come take a look? You know the door to my studio is always open to you, my first inspiration and mentor."

"No angel will enter your room, no matter how small your images," said Sanam, "and so neither will I."

I'll confess they were now capturing my attention away from the subject of tardi —

"That doesn't sound like some postmodern attitude toward Sunniism," said Amir. "It sounds like true belief."

Sanam shrugged. "Rules are rules."

"I dispute your rules: angels are way more likely to have a drink with a bum like me." Amir was bobbing up and down on his chair, and indeed he suddenly looked like he had been drinking. An expression of alarmed concern flashed over Sanam's face for a moment, as if she thought he was going to lose his balance, and then she wiped it away with a gesture.

"And why, dear brother, would angels ever want to have a drink with you?"

"Because, sister, I would give them a good time. Don't they dance upon the heads of pins? Well, I'm the one who can decorate their ballrooms for them, painting microscopic Dada Vinci fakes."

"Dada Vinci? Pick a period, little brother! Are you doing Dada or da Vinci in your pinhead ballrooms?"

"So I slur my words now and again." Amir was hurt. "Go ahead and mock me, you *ableist*."

"But why?" asked Sanam. "Why are you suddenly slurring your words?"

"Don't change the subject! Anyway, you don't care."

"No, I really don't," she said, with unconcealed insincerity.

"All I'm saying is maybe the angels like my studio better than yours, keeping me company through my lonely days feeling unsupported by my big sister."

"Oh, they already keep you company?"

"Why? Would it make you jealous to learn they feel out of place flitting among your drab, colourless, repetitive wordblots?"

Sanam stood up. Amir slipped off his perch. Sanam was holding a cup of black coffee. I thought she might hurl it at him. They approached each other.

"No one can rip the veil off the face of truth like me!" said Amir.

"*I'm* the one," said Sanam, "who combs the tresses of truth with my pen!"

Mr. Lin appeared in the doorway. "Please do not fight."

The brother and sister surveyed each other up and down, and then they took their leave. But Amir seemed happy and Sanam seemed satisfied too, so there may have been more to their sparring than met the eye.

Jan was constantly on the move, and it was hard to tell what he was up to at any given moment. And he ate like a bird. He came to all the aforementioned dinners, even dressed up for them — choosing from what appeared to be an endless assortment of cravats — but he never seemed to partake. Perhaps he dined on things he found mouldering in the cellar.

You know when a storm's passed and you've just closed your umbrella and you're walking down a laneway somewhere and you come across an old green wine bottle, standing up and containing a season or two of sludge stirred up by newly fallen rain? Any one of us would leave that wine bottle where it stands, yes? Unless compelled by a punctilious desire to clean, in which case we might, you know, pinch the neck between thumb and forefinger and run-walk it to the nearest recycling bin.

Jan was not like that. He would sweep that bottle up with a widening smile of the eyes. And then he would dig around in one of those deep pockets of his until he located an ornate stopper so that he could cork the bottle and stow it in his sack. I never witnessed this activity, of course, but he did show me the collection of stoppers he kept in his pocket for such a purpose.

Sometimes, he claimed, he would even venture to take a sip from the bottle: swish it around and spit it out. So as to ascertain the contents.

If I had witnessed that, I would have fainted straight away.

In short, Jan's captivity in an aging, sagging, mouldy, and apparently "humourious" house did not bother him any more than it did Sanam. He sensed a whole world there, of moulds and spores and spiders and pill bugs; and how could he be captive within a whole world? He divided his time between the cellar and the unoccupied room on the second floor. He called himself an alchemist, by the way: not a magician, but an alchemist.

This is not to say Jan did not have his more quotidian interests. He was, against all odds, a hockey fan. Of course, there was no television or radio or internet in our enforced situation, so the only reason I learned he was a hockey fan was because he assumed, since I hailed from Canada, that I was a hockey fan too.

I would go further in my assertion: he implied that he played the game, with some prowess, and seemed to assume that I too played the game, also with prowess. He assumed such a strong interest and ability on my part that he was sensitive to the idea I might "underestimate" him, with regard to both the hockey and also, it seemed, everything else.

It happened like this: I wasn't even doing anything. I was in the kitchen (these kinds of stories always take place in the kitchen) trying to make some oatmeal as a treatment for anxiety-induced stomach upset, and Jan came in having just crumpled up a sheet of paper, presumably a rejected spell. He balled it up, tossed it onto the floor, produced his ear horn from somewhere, and, swinging it like a hockey stick, smacked the paper ball toward the wastebasket, and missed. I didn't even notice he missed. I most certainly would have missed. Of course he missed: the opening of the basket was two feet off the ground and pointing at the ceiling, not like a hockey net at all. Really, I never would have even tried. I would have walked over and dropped my balled-up sheet of paper into the wastebasket. In fact, that's precisely what I did: without even thinking, I went over, picked up his crumpled paper and, as a favour to him, placed it in the wastebasket.

Jan watched me, and then he said, "You know you can't assume we're not good players. Because we are. We are every bit the excellent players you are."

"I'm sorry?" I asked, because what he'd just said sounded to me like a whole string of nonsense words.

"You may not realize it," he went on, "but we take the game very seriously. You would underestimate us at your peril."

"I . . . would never," I said, hoping that was the correct reply.

"You think because you defeated the Russians in 1972, with one single goal, that you're the best players in the world. But you must understand that we too have defeated the Russians. That goal in 1972 was a thrilling moment for us, an iconic moment, to see how the Soviets could be defeated by the players of a small country. It is no exaggeration to say our entire nation celebrated the triumph of that goal with you, after holding our hearts in our mouths for the entire game. And while we have elevated your player Paul Henderson to the level of sainthood, you must understand that we have, since that time, trained ourselves, and we have risen to your level. We can defeat you. We have defeated you. We defeated you at the Nagano Winter Olympics in Japan in 1998. We defeated your Wayne Gretzky. We defeated your Eric Lindros. We defeated all you Canadians, huzzah!"

I must confess that it was only here, this late in the conversation, that I finally realized he was speaking to me in my position as a Canadian. And that he himself was representing the Czech Republic. I confess as well that I did not yet know that we were discussing the sport of hockey.

He went on.

"We were able to put you behind us and then go on to defeat the Russians. It was a glorious moment in a glorious time."

"I don't know what to say," I said.

"Say you will not underestimate me."

"I will not underestimate you."

". . . with specific reference to the hockey."

"With specific reference to the hockey," I repeated, happy to receive the last piece of the puzzle.

"You think I'm joking. But I tell you, I am very serious."

"I believe you are serious."

"You know, there is even an *opera* about this victory. Composed by the great Martin Smolka. It is called *Nagano*. It had its world premiere in the famous Estates Theatre in Prague, where Mozart first presented *Don Giovanni*."

Absurd as it felt to be characterized as an athletic person, I was grateful to finally understand Jan Komárek's sensitivity around me. Even if I merely reached higher in the cupboard to grab a cereal box, he would wave a finger at me and say, "Don't underestimate me, my friend!"

But after this story was finally told, he was more likely to refer to me as his *Canadian* friend and would sometimes go so far as to sing a few bars of operatic Czech, in a soft tenor, smiling his eyes-apart smile. And I was more confident and successful at reassuring him that, no, I would never, ever, underestimate him. Because, although people are always a vast mystery to me, I had, in this singular case, been enlightened.

No matter our personal habits, everyone drew consolation and stimulation and structure from the project of keeping Ezra Coen alive inside the walls while Jan Komárek readied his plan to get him out. Jan explained to us that his plan ("Don't underestimate me!") was complicated and needed to go in stages. He also assured us that Ezra was as comfortable as could be expected living like a mouse within the walls. Ángela and Hannie were eventually apprised of his movements, and everyone was steadily working up the habit of leaving a portion of food on their plates.

For me, unfortunately, this practice of holding back food turned out to be more difficult than I imagined. It was a revelation to discover I liked eating. I'd had no idea. This might sound a bit strange, but it was gratifying to be given evidence that I loved something about life. I had always assumed food was just the intake of fuel, but I genuinely liked the sustenance I was given during our confinement and felt a real tug of regret having to leave some on my plate only to see it get scooped up by Jan in a masterful feat of misdirection, sometimes right under the nose of Mr. Lin, by (for example) encouraging Ángela to impart her knowledge of a winter moth he'd just spotted and directing us all to look outside the kitchen window or prompting Hannie to fret about a mould stain that was appearing up in the high corner of the kitchen wall in the image of a long-skirted babushka, going so far as to call for a ladder and climbing up it to scrape some samples into a beaker and then sniffing the beaker.

All the while consolidating Ezra's next meal in plain sight, in a plastic tub tied to his waist.

But speaking of ceilings and walls and their hidden secrets — their crawl spaces and their gaps — it turned out the passageways only covered the back of the house. According to Jan, Ezra had little difficulty navigating from my perch on the third floor all the way down to the first, and where the second floor was concerned, he managed to venture as far as Hannie's studio, a fact that led me to wonder whether he had any idea what took place in there. Perhaps one day he could fill us in.

Also, according to Jan, the boy was managing to bathe himself. It seems that certain portions of the secret passage had been constructed outside what had once been an exterior wall. Ezra had apparently found a working tap at ground level, at the back east side of the TV room, the kind that services a watering hose. There was dirt beneath his feet. All behind the wall. He did all his washing at one end and dug himself a modest outhouse hole at the other, for which he requested a pair of rubber gloves, goggles, a face mask, and ten kilograms of lime.

We also finally learned Ezra's own story, conveyed in whispers, bit by bit.

Apparently, he was twelve years old, and he had done it all for love.

Jan said that the boy said that he didn't know anything about art. He just knew what he liked. And what he liked, he copied. He was a bit obsessive about it and better at it than he realized, but, as he put it, it wasn't like he was faking Dürer or Leonardo or anything like that.

Ezra had set out to copy the work of a young artist named Charlotte Salomon, who made a kind of graphic novel in the early 1940s while she was hiding from the Nazis in the South of France. He had discovered the book soon after moving to London with his father, all the way from Washington, D.C., in the middle of a school year in which he had had to leave all his friends and start over in a new place where everyone made fun of his accent. His father, as far as Jan could determine, was some kind of low-level analytics man who had been drawn to London during the heady times in the immediate wake of the Brexit vote. Once they were there, Ezra hardly ever saw him, so he started skipping school and spending more and more time at the public library. Then one day his father lost his job and started hanging around their apartment a little too much for Ezra's liking, sleeping late into the day and inquiring about his comings and goings. To avoid him, Ezra started finding all the nooks and hidden places in the building and spent a lot of his time first studying the pictures in the Salomon book and then trying to copy them.

As he worked, he fell in love with her. She painted a thousand gouaches as an antidote to her desire to commit suicide and then got taken by the Nazis to Auschwitz and died there. Jan said that Ezra set out to copy Charlotte's paintings as a way of feeling close to her. He thought she was a teenager, not in her twenties, and therefore attainable according to the peculiar logic of embracing stories from the past. He often had fantasies of Samuel Beckett coming from Roussillon to rescue her. Or Franz Kafka coming from Prague to rescue her, even though Kafka was already dead. Or Marc Chagall coming from Paris with a forged visa for prominent artists and bringing her with him to America as his adopted daughter. And then after the war they would visit London, where she would meet Ezra even though Ezra wasn't born yet.

Ezra was not imagining himself as Charlotte Salomon as he painted, Jan told us, so much as one of those three men, setting out to rescue her with all the power and stick-to-itiveness of their adulthood. That's why he made occasional departures from his copies to create original work in the style of Charlotte Salomon, depicting her relationships with Samuel Beckett or Marc Chagall or Franz Kafka. It was the Kafka one that Mr. Lin bought first, apparently, and then the other two. Lucky for Ezra's forging career, he wasn't very good with likenesses. His Beckett didn't look like Beckett; his Chagall didn't look like Chagall. But they didn't have to because he wasn't a forger. He was twelve years old, and he was in love, and he was trying to extend Charlotte Salomon's biography. He didn't think it was ever going to fool anyone. He was only doing it because he could, and he was not entirely sure how Mr. Lin got his hands on the three gouaches or what he paid for them. When pressed by Jan, he did reveal that he had made the mistake of leaving the finished drawings in his bedroom rather than creating a filing system within the building's walls. But Jan said that Ezra didn't want to get any more specific than that, presumably, in Jan's words, "because it heavily implicates a boy's father in the crime of being uncaring, unloving and a thief."

Jan said that he knew what it felt like to be betrayed by a father, revealing how he himself had been sold by his parents to an alchemist in Prague named Fulcanelli, who had been on the run from the SVR, the CIA and MI6 and needed someone to run errands for him in the city.

So the man and the boy who had arrived together at Armando's front door turned out to have a few things in common.

After his mealtime sleight of hand, Jan would head upstairs into the otherwise unoccupied "light" room, having explained to Mr. Lin that, though he cherished his cellar laboratory, he needed to collect a certain substance — scaly and white — which task he said he could only accomplish by "sifting through" the sunlight that was coming through the window of that upstairs room. I think he might have been referring to salt? Though how an alchemist can collect salt from sunlight is beyond my capacity to explain. This work, he said, would also cause him to vanish for up to forty-five minutes at a time. "Do not be alarmed if I disappear," he said, "for the sifting of the light requires great concentration." Remarkably, Mr. Lin accepted this explanation.

It should have been clear to me that the story of disappearing to sift light was entirely a ruse to buy time and slip behind the wall with Ezra Coen to make plans for his emergence into the house.

But I could never rule out the possibility that Jan Komárek was multitasking: that he was, indeed, occasionally, truly, making himself invisible and sifting salt out of light. The room did, admittedly, have a special quality of light. Like that Vermeer painting where the girl is playing a grand piano and you can see that the artist has painted the entire underside of the propped-up lid. The light in that room does feel like something you could sift.

I went into that room once and stood very still.

If it were an installation in an art gallery and you happened to be standing beside me, you would hear a whispering, very low, that, when I heard it, gave me such a longing, reminding me of the times when, as a scared-of-the-dark five-year-old, I would crawl into my big sister's bed and we would talk about the origins of modern and postmodern art deep into the night, giving the darkness, to me, a sort of shimmer that I sought to invoke with my forgeries, leading to a lifetime's commitment to seeking out the paintings that recreated this unique feeling in me and then setting out to copy them — a task that was especially difficult because, of course, the works had to be by second- or third-tier painters whose forgeries were not so easily identified so that I could make a little bit of money and not get caught.

So I suppose I had something in common with Ezra too. Mine was also a labour of love. You can't counterfeit something without loving it. But I also needed the money and had few illusions about my status beyond the absurd openness to "being feted" that got me into this debacle.

Whatever Jan was planning during his alleged vanishings, it involved consultations with each of us about our practices and intentions within the sanctuaries of our studios. He started with me, but I failed to pass muster. My clear minimalist aesthetic — conceived only as a coverup for Ezra's crumpled notes on that first night — was at odds with the sort of chaotic junkyard frenzy he seemed to require.

He didn't spend much time consulting with Amir either, since Amir had placed a small wooden chair in one corner of his studio, facing the wall, and this seemed to have been all he'd done. Hannie was so tight-lipped and lock-doored about her projects that Jan didn't even bother with her, while Ángela was out of the question, apparently, because of the expected daily attendance of Esther in her studio.

That left Sanam and Armando. Jan spent a little more time with Sanam, which surprised me because she was not cultivating anything that resembled a junkyard frenzy. I thought I had grasped her intentions immediately: she was going to cover her walls with one particular passage from the Qu'ran, written in ornate calligraphy, with black ink presumably mixed with the ash Jan had gifted her. How could this task possibly contribute to a chaotic studio environment?

Contemplating Sanam's work always led me to the question of what we hostages could possibly all have in common. Aside from being forgers, I mean. We were required to cover our walls, Mr. Lin said. But what on earth was his bigger project? Did he have a bigger project?

(And was it possible Jan knew what his bigger project was?)

Jan left his consultation with Armando for last. The talk left Jan looking satisfied and our erstwhile host annoyed and uncomfortable, committed to something he did not like. But neither he nor Jan would tell me what it was. It was certainly true that Armando cultivated a chaotic environment in his studio. He had divided the walls into two separate rows of panels — bottom and top — that traversed around the room, and he'd begun to fill in the bottom section, slapping up cartoons depicting a perky-eared mouse on a road trip through landscapes and cityscapes by the sea. The journey began with the little fellow operating a solo traincar in a heavy windstorm, like something out of a Buster Keaton short. Then, heading right to left along the walls,*

---

* I have been getting some resistance from my editor about this. Surely, she asked, Armando must have painted his narrative panels from left to right? As in a comic strip? The artwork in question no longer exists (spoiler alert) so I cannot provide visual evidence. Armando himself claims to not recall. Still, I haughtily dismissed my editor's concerns with the argument that her expertise is in the realm of *books*: the narrative of a *book* generally moves from left to right, whereas the reader may recall my earlier assertion that the eye enters a painting at the top right and then swoops down toward the left.

However, I have just looked it up and am surprised to find that prevailing wisdom is not on my side. The first example I saw used the famous Andrew Wyeth painting *Christina's World*, arguing that the viewer looks first at the figure of Christina, in her pale pink dress, with her back to us, on the left, looking up towards the house in the upper right corner.

But I'm certain I saw the house first. *What is that house? It's so far away. Do we know who lives there? Oh, look . . .*

Is it possible I'm wrong about this? This is going to come up again. All I can say, in my own defence, is that Armando Matamoros and myself are both left-handed. Sanam Haghighi is also left-handed. Amir Haghighi, Hannie Van der Roos and Ángela Quintero are all right-handed, but none of them pursue narrative preoccupations in their work. The narrative scroll paintings that have come down to us from centuries of Chinese tradition move demonstratively from right to left, my favourite example being Gong Kai's *Zhong Kui Travelling with his Sister* from the Song Dynasty. This fact is more important than it may sound . . .

What's more, every instance of narrative painting in this account moves from right to left. Right-handed readers are going to have to see the world like a southpaw, for once, instead of the other way around.

you or I would arrive at a sketched-out image of two more little creatures, similar to the first, sitting upright in a small shell of a boat; then, just past that, there was another creature riding a dune buggy through sand hills.

After Jan's consultation, however, I couldn't help but notice a small transformation in the character Armando was depicting in the world of his studio:

Continuing farther toward the left from the images I've already described, the mouse started to look a little less mouse-ish and a lot more boyish. I saw a standard mouse figure trudging through those same sand dunes I mentioned before. But just beyond that, Armando had left an empty place in the dunes where there seemed to be room for a character to sit in a deck chair in the shade of an umbrella and read a book. He'd painted the umbrella and the deck chair, along with a stack of books, but there was no one sitting there — neither person nor mouse. He even included a little dog now, sitting by the chair and pre-sumably waiting for a master. And I noticed he went back and sketched the dog into his earlier panels.

Other details were sketched in too. And I wondered: how did these two men think they could get a real boy into a painting? I mean, it was one thing for Jan to make claims about sifting salt out of sunlight or resort to sleight of hand to make himself disappear, but the inherent three-dimensionality of a twelve-year-old boy was, as far as I understood it at least, a dealbreaker.

I've always followed the adage that curiosity does, indeed, kill the cat. But I was undoubtedly curious. And yes, it's true, when my curiosity was finally sated and I found out how it was all going to unfold, how it was *meant* to unfold, and then later how it all went wrong, I did discover, belatedly, that I was much like the cat in that construct. It very nearly killed me. And even though it didn't kill me, it changed the course of my life and my work forever.

I have always been clumsy. In my life, I perpetually find myself in precisely the place I do not want to be. And so, in this house, I was cursed to find myself again and again in the company of Mr. Lin. I'd come into the kitchen, and he would be there. I'd sit down for a private moment on the stairs, and he would appear in front of me, ascending. I'd make my way to the back of the house to gaze through panes of glass and scaffolding at the greenery of the backyard, and a moment later he would be there. He was not seeking me out. In fact he didn't always register my presence during these encounters. But I still felt I had to wait a suitable amount of time before I could take my leave.

Once, I caught him in the late afternoon as he walked into the kitchen reading a letter. He finished it, emitted a cry of frustration, and tried to rip it in half, managing only to tear a measly strip. Then, more enraged, he tore the rest successfully in two, threw the whole thing into the garbage and left the kitchen. The two bigger pieces didn't even land in the wastebasket. Sitting right there, right there on the floor, right out in the open, was something that had hurt him, something not within his control.

Yes, I was curious.

Yes, of course, I went and picked up the fragments.

r. Lin,

* ind enclosed the results of our apprais   f the artwork*
ntitled Autumn Colours of the Moun   ins, allegedly by
*   e Chinese master Zhao Mengfu. W   egret to inform you*
* hat this torn fragment is a forge   printed on an ancient*
*   rap of hand-scroll sometime   thin the last ten years.*
urs,

* erine Foster Edison*
theby's,
ndon

So we weren't the only ones who had tormented him with our forgeries. It seemed, further, that we were all somehow embroiled in this man's curse.

Another time, I accidentally encountered him bent over and gazing through the magnifying glass at Amir's fake miniature in the gallery room, talking to himself with tears running down his face. When he saw me, he looked abashed, straightened up, hung the magnifying glass back on its hook and left the room, muttering something about the intoxicating depth of the landscape behind the veiled prophet.

As soon as I heard the front door close and determined that he had in fact left the house, I rushed to look at the painting. I must confess I did not see much depth in it. There were some buildings in the background, to be sure. One of them had an impressive staircase that wound around its exterior. And behind the buildings there was a forest. Mountains in the distance. And clouds in the azure sky. But the perspective was implied more than it was felt. I can't say I had any impulse to step into the painting. Which is of course something you will feel sometimes. Perhaps I had misunderstood the man when he spoke of depth. Still, I felt it was a great compliment, especially in regards to such a tiny work, so I told Amir at my first opportunity, which happened to be while we were waiting for the upstairs bathroom during a period when Jan had barred us from the hidden one.

"He praised your landscape the other day," I said.

"Who?"

"Mr. Lin. I heard him mutter something about its depth."

"Oh," said Amir. "It doesn't really have any depth. Too much gilding for there to be depth."

"That's what I said."

"To him?"

"No, to myself. I said that to myself. I didn't speak to him."

"Then who was he talking to?"

"He was talking to himself."

"We're clearly a madhouse," said Amir.

The bathroom door opened, and Hannie came out, rolling her eyes to see us standing there. And there was a drawing of the face of an elderly woman taped to her chest. So the conversation was quickly dropped.

Despite not seeking or wanting these encounters with Mr. Lin, they had the effect of cultivating my curiosity about him. When he had first stepped through the broken window, he had presented himself as a terrifying spectre. These days he continued to terrify me, of course, but with all the unwanted encounters, I found myself becoming intrigued by a loneliness and mystery that gathered around him, especially the detail Jan had once told me about how he had loved a woman who had disappeared, or had been disappeared, possibly as an act of revenge against some horrible thing he'd done. This small fact coloured my fear with curiosity. Who was this woman? How had he come to love her? What had her loss done to him? This detail of shattered love made Mr. Lin an interesting monster to me. An iconic monster, like Frankenstein's, a creature you both fear and pity.

And then there was his daughter. Who was his daughter? Was his daughter the daughter of the woman he had lost? If so, was his daughter aware of the fate of the mother? Did the scheme he had going here have anything to do with the fate of the mother? Did we forgers have anything to do with the fate of the mother?

That was not possible. How could that be possible? We forgers could not have anything to do with the fate of the mother.

Within a few days of Esther beginning her apprenticeship in the studio of Ángela Efrena Quintero, the two of them, artist and apprentice, began to appear in matching outfits — blue jeans and a T-shirt one day, herringbone dress the next. I could only assume the apprenticeship was going well. You would see their heads bent over a Taschen catalogue in the gallery room or over a pair of complementary-coloured sodas in the kitchen.

I had the impression that all this annoyed Mr. Lin and that he disapproved of the sartorial choices his daughter was making under the sway of the Oaxacan artist, though he was reticent to speak of it. Still, one morning, just as he was about to take his leave for the day, he turned and asked if Esther was really going to be comfortable working all day in that "squeaky leather skirt."

His daughter waved him away, saying, "You're just my father. You wouldn't understand."

To which he responded, "I am father and mother to you, and the mother in me does not approve of that skirt. But I will allow it today."

I wish he had provided more detail, amending that statement with, for example, "since your mother died tragically at the hands of my worst enemy." But no such luck.

Ángela, who was also wearing a version of the offending skirt, said, "I asked her to bring a pair of sweatpants this morning. I'm sure we'll change into them before too long. She's using me as a bit of a mirror: experimenting; you understand."

"Yes," he said. "I suppose I do understand."

It made me wonder: was Esther looking to Ángela for a sort of surrogate mother? She certainly hung on the artist's every word. Indeed there were occasions when I felt Ángela might better have held her tongue. One morning over breakfast, for example, I overheard her describe to the girl the frankly intimate story of how she got her start as an environmental artist: "I'm a fake, yes," she said. "The point, as I saw it, was exactly to be a fake. A profligate fake. Ostentatiously a fake. I wanted the world to know I was a fake. I wanted to say 'fuck you' to the world, so fake, and pay homage to . . . well, to someone. Perhaps I will tell you one day. It is too early in the morning."

"Who were you paying homage to?" asked Esther. And I leaned in too, wondering what the story was that justified using such bad language to a young person.

"Oh very well, twist my arm," said Ángela: "to my beloved, beloved papá."

After some discussion about how early in the morning was too early to discuss tragic matters, the story that Ángela told went like this: her beloved papá, Benicio Quintero — one of her two fathers, *papá* and *papi* — had been, for all her life, presumably all *his* life, a straitlaced, soft-spoken, clean-cut, well-groomed, sartorially appropriate computer programmer, very much in control of every aspect of how the world saw him. As far as she understood it, he had never hidden who he was from anyone, though she was aware that her grandparents were strict conservative Catholics who could not have been much fun to come out to. Still, Ángela's papá had come out to them, firmly, had expressed his intention to live his life and follow his heart with or without their blessing. And the grandparents had most assiduously not withheld their blessing. And that was the end of that.

But they were not generous. They did not give love. The grandfather in particular did not give love. And he carried an air of ungiven love.

Still, Benicio Quintero strove to be a good son, was always socially impeccable and modest. He stubbornly behaved as if the withheld love was nothing more than redundant shreds of an old cocoon that would one day be pierced through and cast off.

Ángela's grandfather died when she was about fourteen years old. If she thought this would be a release for her papá, it proved to be too much so. He managed to make it through the funeral and then a day or two following before the transformation began.

He began to emerge as a far more ostentatious person than he had ever been before: started buying exuberant and colourful clothes, booked trips at the spur of the moment, brought home new friends he'd met while purchasing the clothes or booking the tickets, or while perusing vegetables at the market or sitting at the bar or standing at the bus stop or lingering at the corner.

His transformation had a joyous, celebratory aspect to it. But there was a darker side too. One day he flew into a rage in the middle of an argument with Ángela's papi over nothing in particular, and he ended up smashing every single breakable object in their home. Ángela had to sleep over at a friend's house for several days as her papi tried to figure out how to react, how to clean up, what to do next.

But the event that finally pulled Ángela into her papá's mania happened after he had been voluntarily institutionalized. No institution could hold him, however, and the moment he arrived back home, he made the spontaneous decision to reforest all the urban planters in a six-block radius. He emptied the family's bank account and enlisted Ángela's help in buying up all the flora available for sale anywhere he could find. Then, when he saw the planters were neither big enough nor plentiful enough, he decided to replace them, heading out again to buy several clay urns that were uncompromising in their capaciousness. "Vamos a lo grande," he said to his daughter. Over the course of four days, the two of them worked continuously to create eye-popping colour schemes that that were themselves outstanding ephemeral works of art. Gloriosa superbas and saffron crocuses surrounded by feather finger grass; black dahlias and agave azuls and cacti and sweetgrass; poinsettias and Aztec marigolds, pitayas and white laelia orchids, plus a host of other orchids whose names she could not remember, fringed with tufts of feathertop grass and bougainvillea. All these were arranged in fourteen gargantuan explosions of colour for the enjoyment of passersby. They lasted for about a week before wilting and fading away. Benicio Quintero waited for a moment when his husband and daughter were out of the house, and then he ingested some of the essence of the gloriosa superba and died.

"I spent a long time thinking about what my papá did," said Ángela, "and why he did it. I think that though he had been brave enough in his life to declare himself to his father, he was not strong enough to live without all the love the *viejo patriarca* had withheld: an unlimited, unconditional love that he had imagined but never felt. So while his father was alive, he had painted himself into a silhouette of what his father wished him to be. He spent his life that way. And he was a wonderful father to me. He had grown to be a beautiful, outstanding, loving man, and I loved him eternally; but I could not put my love in a time machine and send it all the way back to where he needed it most.

"And so a part of him, a *critico* part of him, always remained hidden, stunted, falsified, faked.

"When his father died, when the patriarch died, he knew he could release the painted silhouette, let go of it all.

"But the painted silhouette had become his shadow. And your shadow is a part of you, yes? It cannot be torn away. His shadow was a part of him, so he did not know what not to let go of or even how to hold on to any part of himself at all. As he released these pieces, these bits and facets and fragments of a battened-down life, they blew off him like a seismic event creating a vast *cordillera* in the Pacific sea. An explosive chain of beauties that disappeared immediately under the waves as soon as they were born.

"How many people in the world must be like that? Are you like that?"

She was asking Esther.

"No," said Esther. "I am not like that. I know I have love." She looked around as if to confirm her father did not hear.

"Are you like that?" Asking Sanam now, since she was also present.

"No, I am not like that. Nor is Amir, though it would perhaps be better for me if he were. A more buttoned-down, subdued Amir would be less annoying for me."

"And what about you? Are you like that?"

It took me a moment to look around and then back at Ángela and realize she was addressing me.

I shrank away. Slipped out of the kitchen and into the stair-well and then continued to listen to Ángela Efrena Quintero's forger's manifesto:

"I honour the memory of my papá every day," she said. "I honour him when I approach a work, trying to determine whether it should be undertaken. I ask if it is an explosion of complete commitment. But I also ask, How can I get away with it without destroying myself? The real world no more deserves to see the real me than Papá's father deserved to see him. Only the artificial world deserves that, the made-up world, the fake. I will present myself as a fake, just as he did, but I will show how he can win. I will commit to the explosion and then jump out of the way. And so I ask, always, of a project: Is this beautiful? Is this uncompromising? Would this kill me if I was paying for it? Will it express a hunger deep within myself? Can I present myself as someone other than myself while creating it? With someone else's name? With someone else's money? Will I be caught? Will I live? Will it bring him back to life? Will it matter, in the end, to anyone other than me? If the answer is yes, yes, yes, yes, yes, yes, yes, no, maybe, maybe, no, then I do it! And damn the torpedoes!"

I'm still not sure what it was about Ángela's story that hurt me so much. I fled up the stairs to my room after that, not hearing anything else she might have said, and wept for inexplicable reasons. It was days before I could get out of my own way and become curious about Mr. Lin and his daughter Esther again.

27. TAFTIAN

It turned out that Esther was not the daughter of the woman Mr. Lin had once lost. I discovered this one morning when I was coming down the stairs. He was hesitating in the front entrance-way, I could not understand why, but then realized it was because he and Esther were in the middle of a quarrel. They were speaking Korean, and I could not understand them, but it seemed pretty clear his daughter was winning.

Hannie Van der Roos appeared behind me, making me jump as she remarked, "You seem to be very adept at *spying*." Oddly, I felt like she said it with affection. I really did not understand her at all. And then she breezed past and rounded the hallway toward the kitchen. She was wearing her earbuds. I blushed, experiencing a jumble of conflicting feelings, and then stepped out to follow her just as Esther was breaking away from the argument. Seeing me, she switched to English as she shot back, "You're not my real father anyway. You're more like a *step*father." And then she began to run up the stairs.

"An adoptive father is not the same as a stepfather!" he replied, also in English. "Which is not to say the stepfather is not an honourable position!" And then, yelling because she had reached the top: "Adopting you was the proudest moment of my life!"

To block her father out, just before she disappeared on the upper landing, Esther emitted a loud, piercing scream, shocking in its violence. I plunged my fingers into my ears, ducked, did not dare to look back, and made my way to the kitchen.

But Mr. Lin appeared a moment later. To my embarrassment, I saw that he wanted to explain. Which had the added awkward-ness of being witnessed by a bodyguard, just behind him, who was evaluating my every reaction and expression.

"My daughter has ADHD," Mr. Lin said. "It can make her impul-sive and quick to anger, and I often fail to temper my response as

I should. She loves the moment of the fight and the flight. I can't seem to take away her taste for it, no matter how hard I try. And in truth I love her all the more for it. And I realize now I am describing it all incorrectly. It's not that she *loves* her impulses. But it is more difficult for her than most not to give over to them. I never used to believe in such modern diagnoses as attention deficit hyperactivity disorder, because I was a foolish, old-fashioned man and set in my ways. But a doctor finally convinced me that it is a true thing. May I tell you how he did that?"

I nodded my head, shocked that this conversation was taking place.

Mr. Lin continued. "The doctor told me that you will find ADHD prevalent among adopted children because the birth mother likely also had ADHD. It is a commonly inherited condition. And it can make life extremely difficult for a person, especially if left undiagnosed; personal relationships can blow apart, which can leave a woman alone with a child, and then the ADHD can make it very difficult to look after the child. A person might hear me tell this story and retort: 'Why, she should pull herself together!' But these are the words of a person without ADHD who has come to expect her own brain to function a certain way and believes it should be the same for everyone else. But it simply cannot be, especially when the mother has no support and, crucially, when she has no knowledge of her condition. She comes to believe she deserves all the hardship, all the pain, all the fallout from behaviour that was almost entirely beyond her control. It is heartbreaking, and then the child ends up as ward to the state.

"This doctor said all this to me, and I will confess it was a bit of an aha moment for me. In Esther's case the mother did not give her up to the state, though she was most certainly alone and gave birth in less than ideal circumstances. Her heroism was remarkable, she had travelled over land and sea in search of a better life for her child. The idea that she may have also been burdened by such difficulties fills me with admiration and wonder. I had always believed I was an intelligent, intuitive man. Alas, I am a fool. And so I was finally convinced to pursue medical interventions for my daughter.

"Recently, however, she asked me to allow her to forego her medication and to pursue only matters of education that inspire her, matters she feels passionate about. This is a known cause of fulfillment for many people who grapple with such challenges as these.

"And so I have taken her out of school and agreed to allow her to be an artist's apprentice. But professional artists are so arrogant generally, I find. Don't you find? I find your type of artist to be far more humble. Workmanlike. Artisanal. Better suited for company with a person of her temperament.

"But here I am betraying a private matter and also interfering with your breakfast. I will leave you to it."

And then, as swiftly as he had come, he was gone, followed by his bodyguard. I turned around and met the startled eyes of the normally haughty Hannie, who had witnessed the conversation and seemed no more capable of evaluating what had just taken place than I.

I wanted to ask her: did she think Mr. Lin had kidnapped us all in order to give his daughter an education? And was it because he felt that counterfeiters were more humble and therefore better teachers? No, that could not be right. That could not have been the reason. That could not be right.

He had said his daughter loved the fight and the flight.

But he also said he was trying to discourage her taste for the fight and the flight. Why then toss her into the middle of a quixotic kidnapping revenge scheme surrounded by burly guards armed to the teeth and padded with two inches of memory foam?

Because he also said he loved her for it . . .

I realized I was still staring at Hannie Van der Roos, my mouth opening and closing like the mouth of a drowning person whose lungs are already full of water. I thought for a moment she might say something. And then she did. She said, "That man seems to like you."

And then, amused by her own remark, she returned to poaching her egg. And . . . and if this had been a drawing you were looking at on an art-gallery wall, well, that would have been impossible because it could only have been drawn by me, and I could not draw such things, and my subject would have been Hannie Van der Roos poaching an egg, which was not something I could ever do: draw her. And this impossible theoretical drawing would have been infused with all my longing and loneliness, my perplexity about Mr. Lin, curiosity about his daughter, and mostly, in that moment, confusion about Hannie the punk and protest artist's amused regard for me.

After that, I became even more curious about the daughter Esther. I was frightened of her, though. I was frightened of that scream. I have sensitive ears. So I proceeded with caution. A morning came when I saw her through Ángela's open door as I arrived at the top of the stairs from my breakfast. It had not been my intention to look. I was keeping my eyes down in a habitual practice of minding my own business. But I heard the twitter of a bird, very close, except it was not quite like a bird. It sounded, to my ear, like a kind of hybrid between a human and a bird, not like a human whistle but rather like a human communicating with a bird.

Anyway, I looked.

And I saw the child, Esther, already engaged in her work with Ángela, leaning out the window and taking a small object from the hand of the bald and burly sentry. If that image were a painting you were standing before, it would be an instant classic, like cover art by Norman Rockwell: you would see the tired sympathy and mild confusion in the eyes of the sentry, unsure whether he was supposed to be doing this thing he was doing. My curiosity was awakened even though I didn't know what Esther had in her hand and even as, behind me, I could hear, through Hannie's closed door, a groan, followed by a cry, and then a sob and finally a howl of startling intensity, breaking my reverie and causing me to exchange a startled glance with, of all people, Mr. Lin, who had lingered, *just like me,* to watch the object pass from the hand of the sentry to the girl and who was now taking his leave.

Despite all our previous awkward encounters, I had never before managed to look him right in the eye. This unprecedented contact startled me nearly as much as the explosion that had disrupted the living room on the first day, and it sent me scurrying away and up to my room.

Where I found Jan Komárek standing by my pile of twisted notes, waiting for me.

"It's time," Jan said. "Right now. We're going to bring Ezra down just as Mr. Lin is saying farewell for the day to his daughter. Ángela Quintero has been asked to detain our host for just a moment, whereby wherein where*upon* he will commence his careful steps on the stairwell. We'll follow close behind with our precious cargo, adhering to the adage that you keep your friends close and your enemies closer, and then we shall bustle the boy into Armando's studio just as Mr. Lin is turning into the front room. Stop. I see you are trying to object. Do not object. Believe me, this is the best time. And the best path. Do *not* underestimate me."

131

Dear god, he was bringing up the hockey again. I dared not object. So the plan was to ensconce the boy in Armando's studio. But how was that going to work? And why were we starting all the way up here? And why now, just at this moment, with Mr. Lin not only in the house, but actually on the stairs?

Jan had said not to object, but, forgive me, I objected.

"Why not go through your light room?" I asked.

"That light room door always catches his eye," he said. "And its hinges squeak. He is far too curious about it. Now, I've noticed that your floorboards here are rather flimsy. So: I will be attempting to catch the boy when he drops from above, but I must keep a wide stance if we are not going to crash through into Monsieur Amir's studio below."

Worse and worse. We were going to either get killed or get caught.

"Why don't we just wait until Mr. Lin leaves the house? Shouldn't we wait until Mr. Lin leaves the house?"

"You may not realize it," said Jan, "but there is a sentry standing guard just inside the door of that front room where we first met. And since that door faces Armando's door, that sentry sees everything that comes through Armando's door at all times.

The only time he moves out of the way is when he steps aside to allow Mr. Lin past on his way into the room. That's our chance to manoeuvre the boy from the third step of the stairwell down the short hall and into the studio."

"But there's a sentry outside Armando's window too!" I yelled, *sotto voce*. "Won't he see the boy?"

"Don't worry about him," said Jan.

"How can I not worry about him?"

"I don't have time to explain."

"And what about *my* sentry? What about him?"

"Oh, him. He won't see anything."

"Why not?"

"I have been making a study of your sentry. He is already deeply troubled by this constant surveillance. He clearly admires you and senses your discomfort with his presence. He spends half his time blushing, and he keeps his eyes averted."

What?

"He brings a different book to every shift," Jan continued. "The books get thicker and thicker. He hopes to get absorbed by something, but mostly he reads the same first two pages again and again, thus neutralizing the book in his hand. And so the next day he brings a new book. Today he has the first volume of Proust's *La Recherche*. Truly, there is no hope for the man."

This could not be. I felt the swelling of a blush accompanied by far too much heat. I thought I might faint.

"*That* is not possible," I said, even as I heard some scurrying above. Jan had already timed his assignation with Ezra, and it was all about to unfold right here, in my room. I was not ready. I was not worthy and I was not ready. I was not worthy because clearly I was not ready. And then I looked out the window and saw my sentry, sitting a bit stiffly on his scaffolding, looking muscular of torso. He was reading a finely bound paperback volume of at least three hundred pages. And his brow was furrowed, indicating (if he were a painting you were standing before) too much concentration.

And I thought, *I am being made a fool of in this house.*

And then a number of things happened in very quick succession:

Ezra came down through the trap, leaping into the space below the ceiling, and was, miraculously, caught like a medicine ball by the diminutive, bent-kneed Jan, causing the floor to buckle alarmingly, almost like a trampoline, sending all my little papers flying.

I checked my sentry; his eye had been drawn to the quick movement of Jan, but, oddly, he immediately returned to his book, having seen nothing untoward. And, yes, he seemed to be blushing.

I looked back into the room. I saw Ezra as Jan set him on his feet. I gaped: the boy was covered in a coat of black and white paint, the same pigments covering both his clothes and his skin, giving him the appearance of a two-dimensional thing against my northern wall, an optical illusion rendered in the style of Javier [redacted], or rather, I should say, in the style of Armando Matamoros's forgeries of Javier [redacted] or his originals clearly influenced by the free-flowing Javier [redacted].

It was true, it was really true.

Jan stepped back to take a good look at the boy, presumably to admire his mastery, to show off his artistry.

And then:

our host, Mr. Lin, who had climbed the stairs, silent as a thief, looked in through the door, which had inexplicably been left open, and

he

cleared

his

throat;

Ezra had already frozen, just against the beige of the wall, standing well apart from Jan and myself;

I saw Ezra's eyes move, I heard the throat clear, I saw Mr. Lin, I was horrified.

I yelled,

"PRIVACY!"

or something to that effect, shrill, embarrassing, surprisingly effective.

Mr. Lin's eyes widened, and he silently withdrew, closing the door behind him.

And then I heard a voice speaking through the door, explaining, calmly, that he had earlier perceived fear in my eyes when he exchanged glances with me outside Ángela's studio, and he was simply now seeking to ascertain whether that fear had been a fear of him.

He then explained how he himself had been startled by the groan coming from inside Hannie Van der Roos's door, and this was why he had caught my eye, in case that was not clear, and that I had nothing to fear from him and that I must forgive him for this invasion of privacy.

He furthermore wished to express his appreciation for the other day when I had heard him out, with no judgement, as he confided in me with reference to his struggles with his daughter.

Finally, at the risk of offending me further, he wished to express admiration for the fact that I had decided to step outside my artistic comfort zone during my time here, indeed, that my new experimentation with figurative art in a grey-scale palette was the most gratifying thing he had witnessed so far during this period of what he sometimes liked to call our "retreat" but which he mostly preferred to think of as our time of collective work, though he was, again, sorry to have witnessed it since this act of witnessing had constituted an invasion of my deeply cherished privacy.

Inside the door, I exchanged glances with Jan, and then we both looked at Ezra, who was looking back at us. Figurative art? Grey-scale? What was he talking about? What could he possibly mean by grey-scale figurative art?

And then the three of us came to the same realization at the same horrifying moment:

Mr. Lin had seen Ezra.

Mr. Lin had mistaken Ezra for figurative art.

Mr. Lin had mistaken Ezra for *my* figurative art.

Mr. Lin had specifically mistaken Ezra for my first foray into figurative art.

Which meant, to keep up a ruse that had only just begun, wherein Ezra Coen walked freely within the hostage household, I had to take up the terrifying practice of figurative art.

I sank to the floor, settling into my dusty pile of crumpled paper scraps.

"You people don't understand," I said, to no one in particular. "I don't do faces. I don't do bodies. I don't do bodies or faces looking at me or away from me or anything like that."

Jan blinked at me, not smiling.

"But surely you *can* do it when the safety of the boy is at stake?"

"I can't, no . . . Medusa . . ." I said, barely coherent now.

And then I looked out the window and caught the eye, for a brief moment, of the sentry, before he turned away.

I started to feel dizzy.

"You can't draw faces," Jan was saying.

Dizzier. "No." I was fortunate to be sitting down. "I can't . . ."

"Listen," said Jan. "Armando makes lighthearted doodles. Cartoons. Surely, you can mimic that easily."

And then I must have just . . . fainted.

When I came to, I was downstairs, in Armando's studio, in the middle of a *sotto voce* argument between Jan and Armando.

Jan, *sotto voce*: "All I said was that you do cartoons. That's all I said."

Armando, *sotto voce*: "You say *cartoons* as if to dismiss them, but I sit firmly in the tradition of Goya and Picasso. Would you say those titans drew *cartoons?* And yes, sure, *bueno*, you might say I have a weakness for exploring the good life, but all it would take is the stroke of a brush and then my poor whimsical creatures would be swept away in the storm, cut down by the scythe, blighted by the bug. They are vulnerable; beautifully vulnerable."

I said, "How did I get down here?"

"Oh," said Jan, dismissively. "Everybody helped."

I didn't know what he meant by that. All I saw were his and Armando's faces, up close.

Armando whispered, "I hear you have to begin mimicking my work. I suppose that was inevitable in this household, but I offer my sincerest condolences. To copy a copyist, horrible to contemplate. Still, there are worse fates."

My eye was drawn through the detritus of the studio, straight to the window and through it, where I saw Armando's sentry peering in at me like a western screech owl, complete with ruffled feathers.

I sat up, embarrassed, thinking of my own sentry, realizing suddenly what it was like to be observed by these great unfeeling, unblinking eyes outside this window, understanding the truth of what Jan had told me: my sentry was bending over backwards to make the best of a bad situation for both of us, and I was better off with him than the brute I just saw seeing me.

Oh my god. Oh my god. I was practically in love. I mean, obviously I don't know the meaning of the word. But I was. Practically.

I looked around. Sanam was standing in the doorway. And just by her shoulder I caught a glimpse of Mr. Lin himself, an expression of concern in his eyes. But he withdrew as soon as he saw me.

"Ah," I thought. "Ezra must still be up in my room."

But I was mistaken. Just then, I caught sight of Ezra, sitting beneath a tree and eating a sandwich. By which I mean eating a real sandwich beneath a painted tree on Armando's wall. Ezra was sitting and moving freely beneath the painted tree, his chin bobbing up and down as he took his bites. I realized that I could only see him because I had seen him before and knew what to look for. The chaos of Armando's studio was already so complete that Ezra was blending into it and the sentry, for all his vigilance, simply could not see him.

My eyes lingered on him for a moment. I must not have been out for long because he had clearly just begun to eat, was clearly ravenous. I had to tear myself away from this moment of gastronomic bliss.

Since Ezra was here, it meant that my upstairs wall was bereft, now simply a blank wall.

I looked away. Braced a hand on the floor and started to lift myself to my feet. Jan and Armando leaned in but did not touch me, perhaps due to my repugnance or —

Who was I kidding? They had obviously carried me down here. These people were being kind to me. And they must have gone through with their plan to spirit Ezra down here just behind Mr. Lin, only they used me as a distraction. Which meant that Mr. Lin himself must have helped to carry me down here. It would have been the only way such a distraction would have worked.

Sanam moved in and took my arm, steadying me on my feet.

"Well," I said. "Thank you all for your assistance, but if you'll excuse me, I know what I must do, and there is no cause for delay."

"And what is that?" asked Sanam, amused by my pale resolve. "What must you do?"

"Work," I said, in a dreadful tone. "Paint eyes. Paint mouths. Paint bodies."

"Oh," she said. "You go to your work as a revolutionary goes to her execution. It is admirable. But you must first come to the kitchen and take a glass of water."

And so she led me out into the hall, where I was startled to see the others: Amir was right there. Even Hannie was perched upon the stairs looking clear eyed and concerned. And the beautiful Ángela Efrena Quintero was there, once again in the green dress she had worn on the first day. And there too was the child Esther standing just behind Ángela, a few stairs up, and looking over her shoulder, not at me like everyone else; it was so clear as to have been fixed forever in the plastic image of a painting: Esther's eyes were rather fixed on the open doorway to Armando's studio — focused on something inside, something on the wall.

The kitchen happened. The glass of water happened. A bowl of clear broth from the chefs.

But my new path was not to be avoided. I mounted the stairs like a climber, sans Sherpa, taking the first steps up Everest.

PART FOUR

GROUND

The surface or support on which a painting or drawing is executed, for example the paper on which a watercolour is done or the plaster under a fresco; or, more specifically, the prepared surface on which the colours are laid and which is applied to the panel, canvas, or other support before the picture is begun. The purpose of the ground in the second, more technical, sense is to isolate the paint from the support so as to prevent chemical interaction, to render the support less absorbent, to provide a satisfactory surface for painting or drawing on, and to heighten the brilliance of the colours.

So after that I withdrew from the public life of the house to spend some time in my high perch, solitary but for the sentry who held me in corner-of-the-eye contemplation of his torso, not the face he kept turned away, beyond contrapposto, tending toward the serpentine.

The sentry's torso and four bare walls.

This anxiety regarding figurative art was because of my sister: the one whose bed I would crawl into from an early age of nightmares reaching toward me in the dark. There we would discuss postmodernism or Walter Benjamin and the angel of history or Plato's *Republic*, which introduced to her the idea of the "artless world." My sister liked the idea of an artless world. But only because she imagined herself stepping into an artless world and introducing art to it like an explosion. That was how she was. She knew her limitations: she had somehow come to realize she wasn't the smartest or most talented person, and so she said that the only way to succeed was through guile. Remove all the art and then reintroduce it. Boom. That's what she told me. She wanted her art to have an effect on the world like magic. But that could only happen, she said, in an artless world.

I didn't love that idea, but I did love her, very much, and I looked up to her, I suppose in the way Amir looked up to his milk sister. If I'm not entirely mistaken, being no expert on the subject, she was the last person I ever loved before coming to the house on Olive Road. And that might have been enough — I was never greedy — except that my sister did not love me back. She had discovered criticism, and she saved all her love for that. I guess she had studied the essays of an American critic named Dave Hickey and mimicked him while at the same time (as far as I could tell) inverting his intent: rather than elevating works of art, she sought to destroy them and then recreate them as beautiful critical texts.

She called it *ekphrasis*: taking a work of art and making it into another work of art. Only I'm pretty sure the original impulse of ekphrasis did not include the destroying part. Ha ha. Not one hundred percent sure, because it's an old word and most of the original examples of ekphrasis make reference to art that is dead and gone. But pretty sure. Pretty pretty sure.

The reader may recall a story I told early on about a doctor I once encountered as an adult who explained to me that my deviated septum and hunched back were the result of my own traumatic birth. This revelation had shocked me because I already knew I'd had a traumatic birth, but with the significant difference that I had always believed the trauma had not been mine but rather my mother's.

One day, when I was eleven years old, my sister appeared in my doorway and said, "There is something Mum never told you, in order to protect you, that is nonetheless true and very dangerous."

I said, "Dangerous for who?"

She said, "Dangerous for Mum."

I said, "What do you mean?"

She said, "It can happen, you know. Have you ever heard of pemphigoid gestationis?"

I said, "No."

She said, "It's a disease where the mother is allergic to the baby, even when it's in her tummy. It gives her a rash. I just saw it in a book, and I looked it up."

"Oh," I said.

"This isn't that, though," she said.

"Okay," I said.

"This one has more to do with your blood type," she said. "Do you know anything about blood type?"

I allowed that I did not, which lack of knowledge allowed my sister to expand the breadth of her canvas.

She said, "I remember when you were born. They said that you and Mum had incompatible blood types."

"Who said?" I said.

"The doctors said. They said that Mum was blood type A and you were blood type Zed." My sister did not even bother to use a real blood type. Did I know that? No, I did not. "Blood type Zed, Olive. Do you know how serious that is? She nearly died because of it when you were born, but the doctors managed to save her with a blood transfusion."

I think I must have gaped. My sister carried on. "The doctors warned Mum that it would never stop being dangerous for her to live with you and that, if she were wise, she should palm you off on a relative who shares your blood type.

"They said that just nursing you or washing your dishes or giving you a hug or stroking your hair could send her into ana-fantastic shock." Yes, my sister said *anafantastic*, not *anaphylactic*, I remember it like it was yesterday. I was unfamiliar with the word, it not being a term of art in my field. "Such a shock," she went on, "leads inevitably to a swift and painful death. An anafantastic death."

"An anafantastic death," I repeated, near catatonic with fear.

"They said this risk will never be mitigated, this risk will never cease."

Her monologue continued, rising now to a level worthy of Eleonora Duse, the great Victorian tragedian: "Mum replied hero-ically to the doctors, 'Hear my words, you craven collection of quacks: you will not keep me from my most beloved youngest.' And she marched out of the hospital, trailing the umbilical cord and holding you at her breast, dragging me, almost as an after-thought, by the hand."

It only occurred to me when I learned the true story of my traumatic birth that my sister must have seen my mother express some concern for me, having seen me twisted and broken in my little birthing bed. And so she must have believed that our mother loved me more than her. It helped me to realize that. It helped me to contemplate that she may have been motivated by nothing more insidious than simple jealousy. It wasn't my fault.

"But the doctors were not quacks," she went on. "Her self-less, heroic love notwithstanding, Mum has always been at risk because of you. She always will be at risk. Now you are eleven years old, I believe it's right and good to equip you with this information so you might act accordingly, maturely, responsibly. What do you think you should do?"

I said, "Should I go talk to her about it?"

My sister said, "She will claim it's lies, lies, lies, all lies."

"Why?"

"To protect you, silly."

"Oh."

"You need to decide for yourself what to do. I am available for consultation."

Then she held up her little instant-print camera and took my picture. The photo slid out. My pale and horrified expression. And then she turned to leave the room.

"How much time do I have to think about this?" I asked.

"As long as you like," said my sister, "with the understanding that your presence here is a clear and present danger to our mother."

Instead of screaming and crying myself, I retreated to our mother's library and pulled down all the art images I could find of people screaming and crying. Picasso was front and centre with his Minotaurs and weeping women. I found myself identifying with all of them, first the weeping women, with their volcanoes of tears, and then the more immovable and monstrous Minotaurs, sitting in their labyrinths. How fortunate to be a monster trapped in a maze, I thought. Even if he wanted to, he could not go anywhere. There was no choice in the matter. Because where was he going to go? Where was I going to go? This was the only place I knew; it was the only place that gave me comfort. If I left, I would die of fright and loneliness and misery before I had walked two blocks.

As I sat there on the floor of my mother's library, surrounded by openly weeping art books, I imagined the house transforming into a labyrinth where everyone would be safe from me but I could still stay and be safe myself. The only fate I could manage for myself: to be the Minotaur, banished internally in a place where no one could touch me and no one could even find me except perhaps to kill me.

Reader, I was not heroic. I retreated to my room and stayed there, enduring the occasional instant-print photo taken by my sister, and willed myself into the state of that Minotaur, eating my own innocence daily like the virgins that were left for him. Eventually someone was going to come to cut off my head, and then, once the toxic cleaners had made their way through to mop up the type-Zed blood, my mother would finally be safe. And I would never have to face the terrifying prospect of leaving home.

In the end, my sister revealed her "true agenda" to me. She said we had collaborated on an art project whose thesis was to show the difference between the nice and the good, explaining it thusly:

"You are nice enough to worry about our mother, but you will never be good enough to do the right thing. People," she added, "think that they are good because they have no claws. You and I have created an art project together to prove this adage, driving a wedge between the nice and the good."

Her art project was a manila envelope comprising twenty-five portraits of me alongside a month's worth of school absence slips and a prescription for Paxil that was only finally withdrawn after I counterfeited a return to normal. Also, an artist's statement. Her teacher did not conduct any research beyond what my sister herself reported. He assumed I was a willing collaborator and gave her an A.

I remember asking her why she had embarked on an art project in a world that was still full of art. She asked whether art still had any meaning for me after what we had accomplished together. I said probably not.

She said, "And that's good enough for me."

So then I guess I waited for her to reintroduce art to me, like an explosion. I think that would have almost made the trick she had played on me worthwhile. I still loved her. She was my big sister. Guiding me with semaphores. I longed for her to do that. But she never did.

It was arranged that the chefs would bring me all my meals, giving a discreet knock and opening the door just enough to slide the plate quietly in. The private washroom in the empty room on the floor below, the light room, was prepared for my exclusive use. It was requested that Amir keep his door closed. I had no idea why Mr. Lin was so indulgent of my sudden desire for solitude. He couldn't have known what trauma it was for me to have decided to pursue figurative art. Must have rather drawn some conclusion about his invasion of my privacy. In any case, the tyrant's instructions were that I was to be left alone until I chose not to be.

I did not lift a brush though, not yet, nor a crayon, much as I felt I should. Instead I continued my fake project of twisting paper with written messages. Paper after paper after paper after paper, messages in a bottle, imagining telling the story of my sister and me to the sentry.

This room is not like that room was.

My sister's name was Lise-Anne.

My sister's name is Lise-Anne. She is an art-history professor in Edmonton, Alberta.

My name is Olive. I never liked my name, not even before.

The street with the house I'm being kept in is also called Olive. Olive Road. This is an odd coincidence.

What is the difference between a street and a road?

I wonder if I'll ever be able to put these paper scraps in their proper order?

My father used to say he never understood why Olive was a girl's name.

The olive tree is native to the Mediterranean coast.

The olive tree is evergreen. I have always known this. Did you know this?

I long mistook my father's puzzlement over my name for criticism of me as a person.

My mother loved the green ones with the pimentos.

It has been proven that I am nice but not good. QED. No claws.

And so on. Any time I used the word *you*, I was addressing the sentry. I imagined that at some point his job would require coming in and making a thorough study of my messages. There was never any sign, however, that he would ever actually do this. Sometimes, I'll admit, I found his discretion contemptible; I mean, was he not aware of the power he had over me?

But other times I was as appreciative as should be appropriate under the circumstances.

Enough about the sentry. My task was to start drawing figurative images and by so doing protect the free movement of a boy along the walls of Armando's studio. And the only way, I believed, for me to start drawing figurative images was to somehow remember how I was figurative myself: not a blob or a smear or a stain but a *figure* in space. Not outer space, but . . .

I had to remember how I once had been corporeal and had form. I had to be a body to put a body on the wall.

The question was: how could I achieve this?

As it turns out, I did achieve it, entirely by accident. Through a hapless pratfall, like a Keystone Cop who goes down as a Keystone Cop and somehow rises up as Charlie Chaplin. How does that happen? Is it that when you are at your most vulnerable, you might . . . ? I can't finish the question.

I don't know how I'm going to be able to tell this story. I will have to be swift, or else I'll lose my nerve.

The sentry was there, outside the window, on his scaffolding, in the weather.

What did he want? What was his desire? Look at him: callously presenting himself with his head turned away. A surreptitious feast for my fearful eyes. Beyond contrapposto. Undeniably serpentine. The snake in the garden, yes, but also *figura serpentinata*, the artistic term for a subject who is still graceful despite being contorted. Aesthetically pleasing in a manner that troubled me, disgusted me, made me feel ashamed. Why had he taken his shirt off? Oh! No. I had completely imagined that. He had not taken his shirt off. It was winter, for god's sake! Spring was coming, but it was still cold, and the sentry was shirted. And padded. Still, his padding followed the contours of his body, like Ricardo Montalbán as Khan in *Star Trek*. Maybe that's a bad example. I have a terrible sense of the erotic, I should apologize right away. For me to contemplate form is like asking a ghost to mould some clay.

Desperately, at last, feverish with an embarrassed sensuality, I drew a figure on the wall.

My swiftly rendered image was hideous, twisting both toward me and away. Gruesomely naked, with painful pink pimples and sprouting hairs. In an impulse of loathing, I grabbed a bucket of primer with the intent of throwing it at the wall, meaning to clothe that garish nudity with a white sheet of paint. I caught the wire handle in my fingers and swung the bucket up, managing to guide it with the heel of my other hand underneath. All was going well. But then, unluckily, I tripped just as I started to swing the pot sideways in the direction of the wall. I keeled forward, and alas the trajectory of the bucket changed. The primer flew out and created a thick glob of puddle on the floor that in the next moment became a target for the falling me. I landed with a sort of splat and a bounce of the flimsy floorboards, and then, boy, everything just flew. I was blinded. I tried to leap to my feet, but I slipped in the spilled paint, and the force of my slippage created a primer tsunami that I fell back into.

Instead of obscuring the art, I had made a mess of myself. I tried to get up, but I slipped again, this time on my own paint-sogged crumpled notes — somehow finding a moment to realize it was going to require an art forensics technique like infrared reflectography if anyone was ever going to read them — and slid into the ever-so-slightly sagging centre of the room. Paint was still in my eyes, still blinding me. I was plucking blobs of paper off my shirt. For a few crucial moments, I lost all sense of how I might appear from the outside.

I needed to get out of my clothes. The little sink was my only option for mitigating the disaster if I didn't want to leave the room. I stripped to the waist and tried to feel my way. Just as I got there, I realized the paint had dried enough on my face that I could open my gloppy eyes. I was shocked to see the sentry looking straight at me. And then he turned away, embarrassed, just as I slipped again, clonked my chin on the edge of the sink on the way down, and was out.

In truth, the clonk on my chin did not cause a concussion. What happened instead was approximately eight hours of amnesia, albeit not a kind of amnesia I have ever seen described in a book or movie. When I came back to myself finally, at about three a.m., having apparently slept a bit, I was completely naked, still partly covered with the primer, though it was dry now, crimping and crinkling as I moved; there was a gash on my chin, and my walls . . . my walls were covered. And the work was mostly dry.

Bodies that were scribbles and bodies that were dots and bodies that were smudges, rough hewn, overlapping and climbing over each other like caterpillar pillars; there were bodies carrying pigeons and releasing pigeons and kissing pigeons and bodies with wings like a heavenly host, cherubim and seraphim singing hallelujah: bodies that fell like autumn leaves crumpling and bodies that themselves formed a single body of a bird of prey with the body of a tiny Minotaur in its claws. They were bodies that were neither nice nor good. But they asserted themselves nonetheless. In the roll call of existence, they raised their delicate little hands and said, "Present!" before rolling back into bliss.

I gaped at what I'd started. It was a cornerstone for real work.

When I've thought about it — and I've thought about it a lot — when I've tried to get some of those hours back, I find that there are moments, here and there, isolated and random, that I can reclaim: there's one where I believe I had just stood up and made my first mark, with charcoal or — I must have stepped back to look at it, and I kicked the primer bucket with my heel. There was a crash behind me, it scared me, and I turned to look, swift as a thought, and I remember that. It was like my flight instinct woke up a different part of the brain with its own rules for memory. My "spine," perhaps. *Remember, creature, loud noises are bad.*

I remember, too, being spooked by a sudden puzzling burst of light outside the window.

I remember a few white feathers — maybe pigeon feathers? — drifting to the floor in late-morning light.

I remember the sentry looking at me from his scaffold, startled, at some point. And then, after I returned to myself, I remember the sentry being gone. I was alone.

Alone, I looked at the wall and carried on.

Time went by in there. The gash on my chin healed and left a scar. I started to like my room. I filled in details, left a note outside the door requesting a divan, which was delivered. I continued to sketch more bodies. Some of the bodies were trampled and bruised and broken, near the floor; others cared for them, strove to lift them up. I was allowing Armando to influence me. And through Armando, Javier [redacted].

A morning came when I realized some time had passed and the sentry had never returned. Some part of me had been expecting him, like there had been something I wanted to tell him, though I could no longer remember what it was. Through the bright window I saw that his bit of scaffolding was empty. Perhaps I had done something to drive him away. What had he witnessed? I did not want to contemplate it. This too was a new sensation: holding off feelings of shame or guilt rather than diving right in. Still, would I ever find out where he had gone?

I became curious about outside. The weather had warmed a bit. I don't know what possessed me. The sash rose easily. I climbed out and onto the scaffolding. Outside. Sun pinching my pores. Barefoot. Little breezes enticed my cheeks, making me blush. I felt deep excitement, perching above the comical house, seeing all, unseen by any.

I discovered the sentry's stash: a large tin box strapped to the scaffold with zip ties. Inside were plastic tubs stuffed with protein bars and fruit. There were books there too, each wrapped within its own plastic shopping bag. *The Old Man and the Sea; Moby-Dick;* the *Epic of Gilgamesh;* the poems of Yamabe no Akahito.

Why had he left all this behind?

I couldn't shake the uneasy feeling that something had spooked him. Something I had done.

My third-floor room sat like an isolated cardboard box atop the rest of the house, with the backyard scaffolding clinging to its northeast corner. I looked up from my place and saw that I could step straight onto the roof. I drew a breath and took the step. Then I looked around for the trees of Gladstone Park, which wasn't to the north where I expected it to be, butting up against our backyard, but rather a block or so to the southwest. Oh well. I had never been brilliant at navigation. The day was sunny. Temperate. What month was it? Trees were beginning to sprout. Everything was becoming a little bit green. I wanted to respond to the beauty of the world. I had never known how to do it.

There was a structure in front of me, also sitting like a some-what larger box atop the house. It was some sort of addition converted from an attic, maybe? A loft, clad in aluminum siding that gave it the veneer of a high-school portable. There was no door that I could see. Perhaps around front?

Between the structure and me was a simple area of flat roof. This was not surprising. Neither was the layer of gravel that covered it. What was surprising was the spot where the layer of gravel had been swept to one side, leaving bare roof and a sym-bol, painted fairly recently in what appeared to be thick gobs of arterial red:

I should add that the real thing was rigorously symmetrical, whereas my drawing is not. It also had a five-pointed star inside it, something I don't think I can render easily. I'd be stuck here all day, unable to move on with my story. Really, it could only have been created by our resident ~~magician~~ alchemist, Jan Komárek. I can't claim to know much about the symbols of alchemy, but I guess I know them when I see them.

Then I noticed there was a window on the loft structure in front of me. I stepped carefully around the seven-pointed-star and approached it. Peeked inside.

Ducked.

It was set up as a break room for the sentries. Four of them were sitting on folding chairs drinking from coffee cups. I had moved too fast to see if one of them was my own sentry. I steeled my resolve and peeked again. My man was not there. They looked pretty relaxed, as if they had become accustomed to spending a lot of time up here. It seemed to me they must have had a ladder set against the front of the house to get up without being seen by any of us. One of them had his own art project going on an easel. I couldn't see what it was. Things were so casual I began to imagine that Mr. Lin must have been in the process of letting some of them go. These sentries had nothing to do, clearly. I mean, were we not the most docile crowd of hostages ever assembled? Was my sentry even now reporting to the unemployment office? Also, why was I concerned about him? What had he seen? What terrors had he witnessed, looking through that eastern window into my little room?

Then I heard the crunch of a footfall in the gravel. Oh. Oh. Oh oh oh. Someone was walking across the roof from the other side of the break room. I was not going to have time to scrabble back to the scaffolding and in through my window. So I ducked and eased my way silently over the pebbles to hide around the opposite corner of the structure from the approaching footsteps. If I were to have fallen through the roof here, I would have come through Hannie's ceiling and landed in her arms.

When the steps came to a stop, I slowly pivoted, trying not to mash the pebbles, and peeked back at the spot where I'd just been.

It was Jan. How could he have gotten up here? If he had come via the sentries' route, then he could only be up here with Mr. Lin's blessing.

Jan had a rucksack slung over his shoulder, and he walked over to the seven-pointed star and then stopped and looked over his shoulder at the window in the portable, peering through it for a good two minutes before becoming satisfied with whatever he saw there. He tossed his backpack to the gravel, affected a wide stance over the star, spread his hands in an open gesture of supplication, threw his head back, and then thrust out his tongue with eyes closed. He held this position with arms outstretched for a couple of minutes and then relaxed, then spoke aloud:

"I speak plainly! In the language of this country! None of this business about how the wings of the wind understand voices of wonder! Do you understand, angels? I speak plainly!"

Then he assumed the position again, head thrust back, tongue out, eyes closed. This time he held the pose, adding a bit of commentary every thirty seconds or so.

It sounded as if he was . . . naming tastes?

"Sugar . . .

"Salt . . .

"Honey?

. . . (mumbled) . . .

"Asphalt?

"Cloves?

"Coffee . . .

"Mmmm."

I could not quite believe what I was seeing. I could not claim I had ever seen a conjuring before, but I guess I knew one when I saw it.

Out on the roof, he still had his tongue in the air, still pausing to name, in English, the tastes he claimed to be experiencing . . .

"Something fetid . . . something burning . . . burning a lot — ow, ow, ow; honey again . . . salt . . ."

It occurred to me to wonder whether the sentries could see him through their window.

As soon as I had that thought, as if on cue, Jan dropped the words and started into a toneless humming sound, still with his head thrust back, like a transformer about to blow, into which he tossed the occasional call of the word *gong*. Why *gong?* I wondered. It sounded like he was performing the part of a big church bell: "Hmmmmmmmmmmmmmmmmmmmmmmmmmmmmmmmmmmm gong gong gong hmmmmmmmmmmmm gong gong gong gong." It was pretty clear the sentries could see him.

He hummed for a long time, throwing in the gongs once every twenty or thirty seconds. I needed to put an end to my spying and get out of there. His eyes were still closed, and he was making a lot of noise, so I decided to take my chances and bolt, on the tips of my barefoot toes, across the roof, keeping my crunching of the pebbles as quiet as I could make them. It hurt. But I made it.

Once on the scaffolding, I had to twist myself around to climb into my window, and I managed that too, or, I was in the middle of it, halfway inside, when I realized Jan had ceased his clamour, so I twisted back around toward the roof and saw him looking at me with that unnerving eyes-widespread gaze of his.

I froze. He looked like he was pleased to see me. As if I were a protégé who was measuring up. Then he thrust his head again to the heavens and continued the humming and the gonging. I didn't budge for another couple of minutes, until it became clear he had moved on from noticing me, and then I pulled myself the rest of the way into the room and closed the window.

I stood there for a long time. The sun went down.

Was Jan Komárek trying to conjure celestial beings? Angels? I had distinctly heard him say the word. Had used the plural, no less. Angels.

Was this . . . his art project?

I looked at my own painted walls and thought, I'm doing the impossible. Maybe he is too?

Then I saw a detail that cried out to be changed and jumped back into the work.

When finally I came out of that high-perch room, I found that some things in the house had changed.

The first thing I noticed when I ventured down the squared spiral of my staircase was that the door to Amir's studio was open, though he had agreed to keep it closed. He was not inside.

I'd always been puzzled by the nature of Amir's work. He always sat in a chair facing one corner with all his implements gathered around him, but he never seemed to be doing anything. Now, with nobody present, I had the brief opportunity to venture a few steps inside and take a closer look. Despite all the time that had passed, there still didn't seem to be anything on the wall, though I did note that his chair had moved a degree or two to the left of the corner. Perhaps I was imagining that. Or perhaps it had only shifted as he got up.

I wondered whether the tardigrades had anything new to see.

As I continued down the hall, I found myself wondering what had become of the boy Ezra with his life of camouflage in the wilderness of art. Had he made it? Was he getting by? Or had he incurred the wrath of Mr. Lin for trying to stay out of his clutches?

I was feeling some dread about that.

Ángela's door was closed. But then, rounding the corner, I saw that the door to Hannie's room was ajar, as if it had not been latched properly and had drifted open. As with Amir's, this was unprecedented. Hannie usually locked her door, whether she was in there or not. I briefly considered that the house had been abandoned and I was alone. Lingering in that feeling, I felt suspended between relief and disappointment. Would my fellow kidnappees really have left me to my solitary upper room?

I lingered further. That landing between Hannie's and Ángela's doors always felt to me like the point of convergence for the whole house, its beating heart, suspended between the haughty one and the one with open arms.

I looked through the crack in the door.

There was Hannie. I saw her. Her head was thrown back, lips slightly parted, eyes closed, i.e., an ecstatic expression on her face like the one on Bernini's famous statue of Teresa d'Avila. I know I am being too technical in my description of something that was frankly, stunningly erotic. Her white painter's frock was open and pulled over bare shoulders as she thrust her sternum toward a light coming from the ceiling. She was all angles. Her arms were behind her and in her left hand I saw, clutched there, a large hunk of charcoal. Her hair was, as usual, standing on end.

Behind and before her were many stretched canvases, every one of them turned toward the wall.

I averted my eyes, naturally, downward.

And then I saw that her toes were not touching the ground.

They were, rather, floating an inch or two *above* the ground. Hannie Van der Roos was suspended, mid-air.

And then the door was closed. By an unseen hand.

I stood there between those two doors for a long time. Ángela's door stayed closed. Hannie's door stayed closed. The second floor stayed quiet.

I had just seen Hannie Van der Roos, bathed in light, expression of ecstasy, feet off the ground, artwork facing the wall.

All her artwork facing the wall.

An image of Sanam filled my head, suddenly remembered from some time ago, admonishing Amir: *I will never enter your room!* asserting that angels do not enter rooms where there are depictions of the living, according to ancient Islamic tenets she believed but he did not.

Like Amir's miniatures, Hannie Van der Roos's work was figurative: all human faces and bodies.

Her artworks were all turned to face the wall.

And I had recently seen Jan, up on the roof, calling out to angels. QED.

Well, hold on, not QED. I categorically did not believe in angels: neither angels who loved figurative art nor angels who shunned figurative art, and I certainly did not believe in angels who engaged in sexual consort with humans, invisibly, behind a door left ajar. I did not believe in that!

My sister, who ended up leaving her Machiavellian tendencies behind to study art history, had once told me a story she'd learned in class about angels involved in sexual consort with humans. It might seem like an odd thing to learn in art class, but it made sense to me that teachers wanted their students to know some of the arcana concerning a perennial subject matter for figurative painters.

In other words, there was a weird sort of precedent for the idea that was now lodged in my head, the one that presumably caused Hannie to turn her canvases to face the wall.

But, on the other hand, could angels — assuming they exist (I thought), which they don't (I thought), and laying aside the idea that they might ever engage in, um, sexual consort with humans — could they really have an aversion to depictions of the living in art? It didn't seem likely. I mean no disrespect to Sanam, but consider the evidence:

KNEELING ANGEL, *single-page painting mounted on a detached album folio, Anonymous Bukhara school (Calligrapher: Mahmud), Persia circa 1555, British Museum.*

ANGELS–*fresco, Giotto Bondone 1304-06, Arena Chapel, Padua.*

DIE ORDNUNG DER ENGEL, *paint, clay, ash, chalk, iron, cotton & linen dresses on panel, Anselm Kiefer, 2007, Private Collection.*

UNTITLED, *Acrylic paint on canvas,*
Frantz Lamothe, 2011, Private Collection.

PARADISO CANTO XXXI - *engraving,*
Gustav Doré, for Dante's Divine Comedy:
"in the shape of that white Rose, the holy legion"

DER WÄCHTER DES PARADIESES,
oil on canvas, Franz Stuck, 1889,
Museum Villa Stuck, Munich.

THE ASSUMPTION OF THE VIRGIN,
Francesco Botticini, 1475-6, National Gallery, London.

BACK, BEFORE, WHEN ME AND
LEONARDO DICAPRIO WERE HOMELESS
Margaux Williamson, 2006, private collection.

WINGLESS ANGEL, *oil on canvas, Oluwole Omofemi,*
2020, Private Collection.

ANGEL ICON, *Silkscreen ink on embossed Arches*
Cover paper, Keith Haring, 1990,

MESSENGERS, *graphite & acrylic on plaster wall,*
Bridget Riley, 2019, National Gallery.

TAIFENG , Bamboo, Silk, Ai Weiwei , 2015, Niemeyer Museum.

THE INSPIRATION OF ST. MATTHEW-
oil on canvas Caravaggio, 1599-1600,
Contarelli Chapel, Rome.

SAINT MICHAEL TRIUMPHANT
OVER THE DEVIL
WITH THE DONOR ANTON JOAN,
Bartolomé Bermejo, 1468, National Gallery.

THE ANGEL STANDING IN THE SUN-
oil on canvas,
Joseph Mallord William Turner, 1846,
Tate Gallery, London

CLONEX #13134, NFT,
Takashi Murakami and RTFKT, 2021,
FT3a2l Collection

THE WOUNDED ANGEL
- oil on canvas, Hugo Simberg, 1903, Ateneum Art
Museum, Ahlström collection.

IN ANGELS CARE - watercolour and coloured inks on
paper, Paul Klee, 1931, Guggenheim Museum, New York.

THE FALL OF THE REBEL ANGELS.
-panel painting, Bruegel the Elder, 1562,
Royal Museums of Fine Arts of Belgium, Brussels.

BUTLER-BOWDON COPE - cope, unknown, 1335/1345,
The Victoria & Albert Museum, London.

And so on. How can you have an aversion to something that adores you as a subject?

So maybe the averted canvases weren't evidence of anything. Maybe Hannie was floating a few inches above the ground while bathed in an unearthly light for reasons other than . . . what I was imagining.

On the other hand, even if it was nonsense that angels had an aversion to images, still, perhaps like me, Hannie had overheard Sanam and Amir arguing about it and simply took precautions because she didn't have time to ask before she set out . . . to engage in . . . sexual consort with —

This was ridiculous. Clearly, I had been spending too much time by myself.

My mind jumped back to the time of my amnesia and the disappeared sentry. I found myself wondering, troubled, once again, whether something he had witnessed had caused him to . . . flee.

No. No no no. Why was that even in my head? Banish the thought. Banish. It was one thing to imagine Hannie Van der Roos engaged in sexual consort with angels. It was quite another to imagine . . .

Banish.

Still, I was afraid of what I might encounter on the floor below. I wondered: Should I just . . . go back to my room?

But Ezra? What of Ezra? I was worried about the fate of Ezra. I ventured on.

As I came down the main stairs, I heard what sounded like the scream of a monkey coming from within the open door of Sanam's studio, which was illuminated by bright light from within. First angels, now monkeys. What had I missed?

Getting closer, I could see directional lights just inside her room pointing toward the wall above the doorway. And then I arrived and saw a tall stepladder set up there too and Sanam's feet, in running shoes — PRO-Ked high tops — just at my eye level. High in the air, but not floating.

"Hello?" I said.

Sanam's face appeared from above, poking upside down into the frame (of the door, not a painting I was looking at). Her paint-bespattered headscarf had once been the colour of Van Gogh sunflowers. She was bright and brown and round and warm, detonating a small explosion of happiness in my breast.

Then the monkey screamed behind her again, and I heard a chitter — from a cockatoo maybe. When she saw me, Sanam averted the lights and said, "Back to the world, stranger!" with a familiarity that made me blush just like I did on the first day when she had taken my arm on the walkway up to the house.

I didn't know what to say. I blurted, "Are we all working with open doors now?"

"Just while I'm in front of it," she said. "I was scared someone might barge in and knock me over."

She climbed off the tall stepladder, moved it aside, tossed her belt full of brushes onto the dining-room table and came out into the hall, pulling the door closed as I caught a glimpse of her work. The room did not look like she had said it would. Unless I had misunderstood? The walls were covered not with beautiful ornate Arabic text, but rather a menagerie of stylistically painted animals in brilliant colours. Did that mean Sanam had set aside the Sunni proscription against images? Or had I misunderstood that too?

She took my arm, giving me yet another surge of the pleasure of human contact as we walked down the hall toward the kitchen. Who needs art when you can have happiness?

The shrieks and chitters were finally explained as she told me she had requested a sound palette of Amazon fauna. "For inspiration," she said. "Does it bother you?"

Mr. Lin had indulged her request beyond any reasonable expectation, arranging for a series of stereo speakers to be set up for her. Thus the shrieks and cries and calls that could be pleasantly heard muffled through the walls.

No, it did not bother me. I was ecstatic to get a quotidian explanation. It occurred to me with a rush of relief that Hannie's defiance of gravity probably had a similar rationale. Yes, likely she had requested a climber's harness and rigging and was simply dangling from a permanent anchor in the ceiling. And the light was just a work light. And the expression was because . . . the work was going well.

Still, I kept wondering about the door being closed by an unseen hand.

As we passed through the kitchen, I saw that Armando had befriended the chefs and was currently cajoling them to whip up a trio of Spanish desserts for him: quesillos and churros and crema catalanas.

He looked large handed and swirly of hair, more relaxed than when I had last seen him.

Sanam and I walked past the TV room and then through the sliding veranda doors, underneath the feet of the scaffolding and out into the beautiful expanding greenery of Armando's backyard.

This was new. We were allowed outside. I had caught so many glimpses of this backyard I had endowed it with what I supposed was a very English folkloric quality, populating it with a country of bug-sized warring tribes straight out of Cicely Barker's *Book of the Flower Fairies* (beloved of me but dismissed as kitsch by my sister), clinging to the petals of lilies as they thrust their barbed spears across the cut grass at one another.

There was no sign of warring fairies, though. No sign of angels either.

The yard was huge. In front of us, the first thing I saw was a breezy badminton net. Jan was there with a racquet and had found a willing partner in Amir, who had acquired old-fashioned tennis attire for the occasion: long flannel pants, a sweater vest, a white fedora. They were hopping around now.

Amir looked a little strange; I couldn't put my finger on what had changed since the last time I saw him. He seemed off balance somehow, though it was not reflected in the pleasure he took in the game. Their bright birdie play seemed to have attracted a fair number of chickadees and butterflies to the yard. I was surprised to see Mr. Lin and Esther there too, both with butterfly nets, attempting to catch a small clouded yellow. The wind was rising, carrying birdies and butterflies inconveniently over the high fence to the neighbouring yard. I imagined and dismissed the notion of a sentry being sent to recover them. Anyway, there were no sentries that I could see. I recalled Mr. Lin promising they would withdraw eventually.

Was that what had happened to my David-torsoed sentry? Not a flight out of fear from witnessing something untoward in my studio, but rather a promised reduction of work hours?

Farther toward the back of the long garden, in view of a beautiful stone wall that I used to think peeked over into Gladstone Park, Sanam greeted Ángela, who was waiting for her, having spread a blanket out on the grass for a round of backgammon. She smiled at me warmly, as if I were a stranger who had just arrived.

I ate my lunch outside, watching the backgammon and the badminton as clouds rolled over the house. I can't recall the savoury part of the lunch, but I do remember the quesillo and the churro and the crema catalana. The wind was moving the pieces on the backgammon board. Despite my self-assurances about rigging, I could not quite shake the image of Hannie's feet, the possibility of summoned angels. Also, I had definitive questions about the status of Ezra. The wind became even more insistent. The clouds lowered and darkened. Amir and Jan finally decided to take the net down. Amir fell, laughed as he got up, then fell again. They saw me and waved. I wondered whether I would be able to gather the nerve to speak with Jan about what I had seen on the roof. Questions were welling up within me, building pressure in my belly.

With the wind picking up and the men packing up, Sanam and Ángela decided to move their game into the kitchen. I followed them and watched for a few more minutes as the world outside transformed from the uncomplicated brightness of springtime into a combination of light and dark of the sort that swept over the fields and barns back home in Ontario to tell you a big storm was coming.

I thought, I'd better go up and close my window.

Ángela was right behind me. I paused at the ground-floor stairs, and she swept me by as I stole a glance through Armando's open door into his unoccupied studio, where I was greeted by a colossus of clutter and colour and line, his walls covered with a thousand distractions so you never quite wanted to linger over any particular detail.

I wondered: Was Ezra still in there? I believed he must have been, though I should probably say here for the sake of clarity that I was wrong. He wasn't there. But he was safe. Safely hidden somewhere else. If he had been taken and punished by Mr. Lin, surely life in this house would not have the kind of balance I was seeing. Surely there would be no badminton or backgammon or quesillo or churro or crema catalana. Surely the sentries would still be standing sentinel everywhere with their bullet eyes.

When I arrived at the top of the stairs, I felt the wind rushing through walls and a knocking against the side of the house.

The power of the storm was rising. I was back on the landing between Hannie's and Ángela's doors. Of course, all my attention was focused on Hannie's — now closed and quiet — and my heart was beating its own storm in my chest.

But then I felt a huge gust of wind catch me from behind, and I turned and looked through the open studio door of Ángela Efrena Quintero, where, I was surprised to see, there had been a renovation.

HERE FOLLOWS

EVERY✳THING

that happened in the

MATAMOROS HOUSE

while I was upstairs[*]

[COMPRISING 18 PAGES]

reconstructed via interviews with

JAN KOMÁREK

ÁNGELA EFRENA QUINTERO

SANAM & AMIR HAGHIGHI

ARMANDO MATAMOROS

EZRA COEN

MR. JACKIE LIN & MS. ESTHER LIN

(but not Hannie Van der Roos)

---

[*] including frequent reminders that I was not present despite what will likely be the occasional lapse

Ángela had become dissatisfied with conventional light sources in the creation of her studio project, and so she had put in a request to Mr. Lin to have her second-floor bay window removed and replaced with, well, nothing, in order to allow everything that was outside to come in: birds, bees, butterflies, squirrels, bats, etc. It was not just one window either: her request proposed that all three windowpanes projecting out from the main wall be removed. The top portion of the scaffolding had to be removed, with Ángela's sentry, when he was present, moved into the ash tree. The hardwood floor had to be given an exterior finish, and the walls had to be stuffed with the appropriate insulation to protect the rest of the house from caving in around this weak spot that was to be given over to the elements. Armando's studio, just below, would be particularly vulnerable.

According to all later reports, Ángela's request had given Mr. Lin pause, not so much because of the gaping hole it was going put in the second floor of his prison fortress, but rather because he was painfully aware of the debacle that had brought Ángela here in the first place. One of the details he had failed to mention about her forgery in the Black Forest was that after it had stood for only two weeks, it had caused a near environmental disaster by crumbling into the Mummelsee lake just as the earthwork was also found to be attracting thousands of Canada geese, who had diverted their flight path to make a permanent home around it: honking, displaying their impressive big bellies, and covering all the trails of the Schwarzwälder Genießerpfade with green guano that got picked up under the shoes of the tourists and tracked everywhere in the country. The cleanup had been embarrassing and expensive. The impersonated artist (Teresita [redacted]) had rescinded her credit, claiming to have confused the Black Forest with the Divoká Šárka in Prague. Mr. Lin had footed most of the bill for the cleanup and removal of the geese back to Canada, where everyone thought they belonged.

In short, Mr. Lin had evidence that Ángela could be reckless. Still, he had committed to her presence here; he had his own reasons, which sometimes seemed to us to extend beyond the conventional rules of vengeance.

And so, I am told, he allowed the removal of the bay window, and as a result of the impending second-floor chaos, it was decided that Esther would spend her days in a different studio. A meeting was convened in the gallery room to discuss the move, presided over by Mr. Lin, at three o'clock on a Wednesday afternoon. Finger foods were served on small plates. I do recall an early afternoon when there had been a discreet knock on my door and I opened it to find a plate with

miniature grilled cheese sandwiches,

breaded coconut shrimp,

latkes with sour cream,

palm-sized tourtières,

a small bottle of mineral water

and a paper cup.

I recall wondering what the occasion was. The occasion was deciding who would take Esther next.

Posed with the question of where she would like to go, Esther immediately chose Armando: Amir told me she chose him so fast that no one thought they had heard right, and she had to say it again and then a third time.

This was inevitable, of course. They all knew that Esther would eventually make her way around the house. But she was pointed in her desire to go to Armando, and she would brook no offers from anyone other than Armando:

"I think something very interesting and very *friendly* happens in there," she said.

In the end, Armando gave a broad, welcoming smile and said, "Of course, kid. I would be delighted. Also, yes, my work is very friendly."

Esther did not smile back.

The move was to take place two days after the meeting, in advance of the work crew commencing the transformation of Ángela's studio. Jan didn't have a lot of time. Two days to both find a new refuge for Ezra and camouflage him anew.

Inside Sanam's studio, Jan looked up at the walls, which already shimmered with the strategic blot and flow of her brush-laid calligraphy, spreading like a thousand black comforters thrown willy-nilly over a thousand white beds. All calligraphic words at that time. All black on white. There was as yet no trace of the animals I would later see.

Here follows a transcript of their conversation, as related to me by Jan, albeit with several strikethroughs proffered by Sanam, along with her brief commentary. I chose not to delete, as it was clear she did not consider the affected passages to be inaccurate, merely in bad taste:

"How should we do this?" he asked.

"Leave it to me," she said ~~imperiously~~.

"I cannot 'leave it to you.' Alchemy cannot be left to the non-practitioner."

Sanam: "Nor can calligraphy."

Jan: "Calligraphy cannot be left to the non-practitioner?"

Sanam: "Precisely."

Jan: "But I'm not — I need to do the work, which is not so simple as to cover the boy with an Arabic camouflage."

"This Qu'ranic passage flows like a river," said Sanam. "Slowly but inexorably. *La ilaha illallah.* It makes the eye move along with it. If a passage flows over one small boy, he will be as a minnow never spotted by the bear. There is, then, no need for magic, though one must be careful with the words."

"It's not magic," said Jan, indignant.

"It is magic."

"It is applied art," said Jan. "And I am an atheist. I prefer my alchemy to be bereft of theology."

"The language may be divinely inspired, but its aesthetics are earthly," said Sanam.

"Still, I insist upon the undertaking of this project," said Jan.

"Tell me: What would you write on the boy?"

"What else? The same as you have written over and over: *La ilaha illallah*. There is no God but God."

"See? You cannot do that. ~~Would you never expect the boy to visit the bathroom?~~"

~~"As we did with Armando, you will have to set up a pot for him."~~

~~"This is out of the question. He cannot have the name of God written upon him at such a time as he sits upon a chamber pot."~~

inappropriate

"Then what would you do?" asked Jan.

"I would write something that flows up and down like that particular sentence but would really be, essentially, gibberish."

"Well, I could do that just as easily."

"You could not do that. You would fuck it up. You would write a part of God's name accidentally, bringing all manner of trouble down on the boy and on me. I will not allow my calligraphic practice to be sullied, not by you nor by anyone."

"You speak of some strange standard of purity ~~even though you are a fabricator.~~"

~~"My art was sincere; it was only its origin that was disputed."~~

~~"Thomas Jefferson's Qu'ran."~~

~~"Saddam Hussein's!"~~

~~"That's right. A commission, I gather."~~

~~"As was my work on Thomas Jefferson's, though I do wonder how you know about that."~~

~~"You have made fakes of many Qu'rans."~~

~~"I ask you: how can the uncreated word belong to anyone?"~~

~~"Tell that to the judge."~~

irrelevant

~~"I already did, if by *judge* you mean Mr. Lin."~~

There followed a stalemate. They drank Sanam's tea. Sanam opened Jan's gift. A small sack of saffron from Kashmir. Thoughtful, if not as impressive as ash from the Süleymaniye Mosque.

176

Eventually, they resumed their sacred/secular debate for the sake of a boy:

"Is there anything I, Jan Komárek, could do to make it possible to spirit the boy into your studio?"

"Not in the form of calligraphy, not from you."

~~"What if I painted him as an angelic figure wandering through your calligraphic landscape?"~~

~~"What?"~~

~~"You believe, do you not, that an angel will not enter a household that has pictures? Your studio has no pictures; therefore we can bring in an angel."~~

~~"You are proposing a picture of an angel?"~~

~~"It is not a picture; it is the boy!"~~

~~"The boy depicted as an angel! Oh, you are impossible! You think we allow dramatic presentations in Islam? And so you propose that I allow him to wander around my studio with a pair of ragged wings dragging behind him?"~~

~~"I had thought that was possible, yes."~~

~~"You are more of an idiot than I would have thought for someone who brought me ash from the Süleymaniye Mosque.~~ Here is an idea, though, ~~since you won't stop bothering me,~~ since we two are on the same side, like Süleyman and Francis I in their alliance again the Holy Roman Emperor: I know how to render calligraphy into a figure. It is what you might call a loophole in the Islamic proscription of images. Some even create calligraphs of the human figure, but I draw the line at animals. I can transform calligraphy into animals."

"May I see?"

Sanam rose, dipped her brush in black, and drew it across the wall. The way Jan described it, her hand moved swift as a bird, and the text was a lion. Then the text was a rabbit; the same text again was a fish; and then again a camel; and then again another lion; then a great blue whale awesome to behold; then a warbler. "Magic," is how he described it to me later, though he pressed his finger to his lips when he said it and smiled his eyes-wide-apart smile.

In the room with Sanam, he held his own: "So you're saying that if I brought you the boy as a bird, you could still render him as text? But would he not be a picture and thus turn away angels?"

"He would not be a picture, no," said Sanam. "He would be himself. Himself as a sheet of blank paper. Flattened. I would merely add the words."

"I think this is how we could work together," said Jan.

"Agreed," said Sanam. "You do whatever it is you must do to flatten him into a sheet of paper, and in the meantime, I will write several of these what we call calligrams so he might blend right in. It is far from my original intent for the room, but I can do it."

"Thank you," said Jan. "You are good. Your God is good. We are agreed. I will bring you the boy as a bird."

"You will bring the boy as a sheet of paper."

"I will bring the boy as a sheet of paper."

So Jan moved Ezra from Armando's studio to Sanam's, and then, later that same morning, Armando welcomed Esther. And then the renovation of Ángela's studio began.

But Armando reported to Jan and Sanam (and me, later) that as soon as Esther arrived in his studio, she began to lobby for a transfer to Sanam's. Mr. Lin said he would inquire but warned it might take a few days, adding, "You might take the time to learn things from Señor Matamoros."

And, according to Armando, she did take the time. If only, he complained to anyone who would listen (though only Jan took notes), to learn how to push his buttons.

Armando said that on the very first morning of her apprenticeship with him, Esther effectively flipped their relative status by saying, "I have a message for you from Ángela Efrena Quintero."

His jaw dropped, and she went on (Jan, editorializing: "with that level of smugness that can be displayed so effectively by a child").

Esther: "She told me to tell you to be a man and do that thing you promised to do."

Armando, described by Jan as gazing quietly at his sock feet: "While I am grateful to you, Esther, for relaying this message to me, the 'thing' I promised has turned out to be impossible for a man of his word to fulfill. I am bound in a double bind."

"I disagree," Esther said. "I think you can do it."

Armando: "Are you telling me that you know what it is I promised?"

"I do know," said Esther.

"You know, then, that some three years ago I asked Señorita Ángela Efrena Quintero for her hand in marriage?"

(I confess that, when I heard this detail from Jan, I gasped, like a —)

"I do know that," said Esther.

"And you know she said yes, with one single caveat?"

"I know the caveat," said Esther.

"That we should get married in the Catholic Church?"

"Not just any Catholic Church," said Esther. "The specific Catholic Church that stands in the centre of Oaxaca City, the one with a window that draws in the evening sun to set ablaze an altarpiece made of solid gold stolen five hundred years ago from the sacred Zapotec site of Monte Alban. I forget what it is called."

"I forget what it is called too," said Armando. "But—"

"She was planning to transform your wedding into an art project — an original one, under her own name."

"Yes, I know, though I am rather amazed that she told you all tha—"

"She was planning to borrow the statuary from quaint little churches in the countryside surrounding Oaxaca City, the ones that are adorned with human hair and look so real you can have conversations with them."

"I did not know that detail," said Armando. "But it seems like it would be disrespectful to the local communities if she were to—"

"She was going to design costumes for the wedding party that would be evocative of Zapotec royalty, and she would force the guests, congregants and passersby to consider that perhaps the Church is not so much the assimilator of culture as the assimilated."

"Sure," said Armando, "sure."

"You agreed to do this," said Esther. "You agreed to get married in the Catholic Church."

"I did," said Armando. "I confess I did."

"You swore to do it."

"Well, I promised."

"You swore."

"It amounts to the same thing. But I did not realize what it involved."

"But you promised."

"Look, kid. I intended to. I very much intended to. But I had spoken too soon. What did I know about the requirements that have to be met in order to be married within that church? I knew nothing. She had extracted a promise from me that I could not fulfill!"

"You were married before."

"Because I have been married bef—! I see, she told you that too. I was married very young to a fellow student of *la Universitat de Barcelona*. Twenty-five years ago! We thought it would be funny and charming to get married in the church. And we eventually had an amicable split that coincided with the end of our schooling."

"You were required to get an annulment."

"Yes, exactly: if I wished to marry a second time at the altar of a church, I was obliged to obtain a written assertion, from the Vatican, that my previous marriage had never taken place. That it had not been consummated. That it was a sham, a farce, a fake. And let me tell you right now that I was very much willing to do that: I was willing to cross my fingers behind my back and say that my first marriage had not been a real marriage. It was going to be easy! Am I not, after all, an expert at the sham, the farce, the fake? It was a long process too: we began almost three years ago now. The wheels of the Church grind ever so slowly. But I was committed. And the fee demanded by the Vatican, of course, was quite large. But I gathered it. I had recently sunk all my savings into this house, but I managed it! In fact, the funds came directly from the sale of that notorious *New Yorker* cover, now reduced to ashes, to Señor Lin. And the money itself might as well have been burnt along with it, for all the good it did.

"I had my own interview a year ago. Passed it with flying colours. I painted a picture for them of a pair of destitute students so blinkered we were forced to eat paint, suffering from a number of delusion-inducing toxins. It was not far from the truth. We had propped each other up and prodded one another through those formative years. *Mi primer amor* has since become quite an accomplished artist in her own right; I'm really proud of her. So all I had to do was call her up and say, 'Look, you are going to get a visit from a pair of Roman clerics. They are going to ask you some very personal questions. I am wondering if you could do me the favour of lying to them?' That is all I had to do. And I was planning to do it. Though I did . . . put it off . . .

"When I did finally call her, it had been quite some time since we had last spoken. And I . . . well, time was of the essence, the clerics were clamouring to mark up their day-timers. So I called her. And I asked if we could meet at the Mesón del Cafè in Barcelona. When she arrived, she was wearing mourning black, complete with the veil. I asked her what had happened. As it turned out, her current *amor* — the man she loved and had lived with for most of the years we had been apart — he had died in a motorcycle accident. Just the day before."

"Yes, I know," said Esther.

"Yes, of course you know," said Armando. "And, like Ángela Efrena Quintero, you are unimpressed."

"You need the annulment. You promised to marry in the Church. This woman will understand."

"Well, sure, that is simple enough to say. And there I sat at that café table, looking across at the grieving woman who had been my first great love, with every intention of going through with it. Tell me, kid, if you had been in my shoes, would you have been able to say what you had come to say? That, within a day or two, there would be a pair of pale, bloodless, rubber-faced clerics knocking on her door to ask her if she had ever really been married to me? And that, as a great favour to you, she would be obliged to say, 'No, sirs, no?'"

Armando told Jan that he had expected young Esther to continue to berate him like he deserved.

And Esther told me later that she wanted to nod and say that, yes, in his shoes she would have secured the annulment.

But she suddenly found she could not.

"I couldn't do it," he told her, after a pause. "I could not erase the past we shared, especially given the true erasure she was currently experiencing. I could not do it. And there has been hell to pay."

"You can still do it," said Esther.

"I cannot do it. And, on the one hand, it is deeply unfair that Ángela has revealed all this to you. But on the other hand, it's nice that someone in this house finally can see how she has been gaslighting me."

"You are gaslighting her."

"She is gaslighting me!"

"Hardly," said Esther.

(In the margin of his transcript, Jan has helpfully scribbled a definition of the term *gaslighting*, presumably for his own edification and also mine.)

"Look, kid," Armando went on. "Here is something you probably don't know: we haven't even had a chance to really speak about my annulment failure, she and I. I was just breaking the news to her in the very moment all these other people came to my door."

Armando had finally told Esther something she didn't know.

"Do you understand," he asked, "how hard that is? I thought I would have time to prepare: fly down to see her, show up at her door bearing the gift of a rare butterfly still sleeping snug in its little sac. I thought I would have the time to cultivate my words, to paint a picture in her mind about how the past is prologue, that the way you treat your former lover is the way you will treat your present one. But then she suddenly just showed up, invited into this infernal carnival by your tyrant of a father. And so I found myself stammering and pleading. And then the carnival arrived at the door, and this horrible business began. Kid, I have misplaced my humour, my eloquence, my romance. Who would not in my shoes? Can you not see how hard that is?"

Somehow Esther gave her assent without saying anything. It was enough. Armando wept. Esther patted him on the back, once, twice: and so the apprenticeship began.

That was their first morning together. Ezra had only been in Sanam's for a few hours.

Presumably because of the way Armando confided in her, Esther began to confide in him as well. Everyone told me later how surprising this friendship was between the big shambling man and the trim private kid. Most notably, she told him that her birth mother had been born in Hanoi, Vietnam, and had gone to Seoul on a visa through the Employment Permit System to work a repetitive job in one of Mr. Lin's family's automobile factories. She had been pregnant when she arrived.

Mr. Lin had recently resumed interest in his father's business after a long period of playing the prodigal. His father had tested his long-in-the-tooth adult son's new commitment by putting him to work on the floor of the factory, answerable to the foreman without any special privileges.

And so he was present the day Esther's birth mother went into labour on the production line. He witnessed her distress. He witnessed the mistreatment she received at the hands of the foreman when she requested to be permitted to step away from her work. Eventually, he stopped being a witness and instead became a participant. He defied his father's order, reasserted his privilege, carried the woman a few yards away from the line and assisted her with the birth. It turned out he was surprisingly capable, but his skills were not enough. He was holding the baby to her breast with bloody hands as she was dying. The mother had looked into his eyes and made him swear that he would ensure a life for her child, even if he had to raise her himself. All the workers from the line were present to hear him swear that she could count on him, that he would do it. Once, later, Esther met one of them who told her that when her father swore in that moment, he used a voice that came out of nowhere and seemed to resound across continents and centuries. All the workers had dropped to their knees then and pledged to the mother that they would hold this boss's son to his promise and help him when they could. All spoke except the foreman, who had stolen away.

Esther told Armando that not even her father's father could undo what had been done.

He tried, though, the father: Esther was taken and put in an orphanage. Because her new caregivers looked askance at Mr. Jackie Lin's unmarried status, it took three years for him to secure her adoption. But he did it. He secured it. And when he did, at long last, his first act was to book a flight for the pair of them to Hanoi, Vietnam, so she could see with her own eyes where she came from: he wished for her to always have the tools to hold her own culture rather than just having his.

Mr. Lin had never been to Vietnam before. He chose to take her sightseeing among the streets of the old quarter in the ancient city.

There, among those thirty-six streets, Esther twisted her hand out of his and skipped away, down Hang Ma Street, her hands flapping wildly, asymmetrically, as she ran, sending hundreds of paper votive offerings flying up into the air as she shrieked with all the exuberance of freedom. Her father was forced to give chase, following her down the paper street, past a street where people sat at tables, eating cakes.

"Have you seen a small child running and laughing and flapping and dragging coloured paper in her wake?"

Esther told Armando that her father had described that scene so many times to her over the years that she had begun to see herself running along beside him, interrogating the cake eaters with him, chasing herself down. They had finally found her — or rather, *Jackie Lin* had finally found her — trying to climb onto a short pillar in front of a toy store to get at the tin figure of a child not much smaller than herself.

That was the moment she always remembered: he failed to buy her the tin toy, despite all her effort.

Still, she could also see that the only reason he failed to notice the tin toy, much less think of buying it for her, was because he was overwhelmed with relief at having found her. It was not because he was parsimonious or didn't care.

So he had failed in the toy department, but he had passed the greater test.

There would be many more such tests.

Armando still had a blank north wall, just by the entrance to his studio. He decided to throw out his plans for it and devote both upper and lower panels to a vision of Esther's flight over the market stalls of Hanoi.

"But it's my story!" she objected.

"You do not like this idea? It is true I am a thief, but I only steal from those who are higher than me on the ladder of bullshit success. I punch up, not down. You have nothing to fear from me. What if you assisted me? Collaborated with me? What if you had veto power? What if I bent all my considerable skills to your will? What if there was a place down here in the lower right corner where you could sign your name to this wall right alongside mine? Co-creation?"

"Only if we put it in writing," said Esther, who liked the fabricator but did not trust him.

"Very well," said Armando. "We shall put it in writing."

Everyone told me later that while they laboured together on this project, Armando could speak of little else. Ángela particularly regarded this new obsession with an air of disbelief. She laughed to me later about confronting him in the kitchen.

"Suddenly you value collaboration?" she had asked.

"I value this collaboration," said Armando. "Anyway, I have always valued collaboration. I have begged to collaborate with you!"

"Bah," she said. "As I have said before, my necessary condition for a collaborator is that every so often they do something I ask them to do."

"Pah," said Armando. "Anyway, is forgery not collaboration?"

"No," Ángela said. "Forgery is not collaboration. If there is no consent, there is no collaboration."

"And here," Armando declared triumphantly, "there *is* consent. In *writing*, no less."

Ángela was shaking her head. "I don't understand you," she said. "And you are deluded about the practice of forgery as a collaborative act. But," she added, "where this young girl is concerned, you would seem to be both collaborative and chivalrous. This work you have embarked upon is no forgery. I will accept it."

According to Ángela, Armando merely shrugged at her approval and asked if she wanted an espresso. But I suspect he must have beamed with pride.

+++

There were many other things that happened in the house while I was undertaking my solitary commission. Sanam told me later that she had begun to notice little details that portended the emergence of Amir's symptoms. "Like tardigrades with semaphores," she added ruefully. Hannie's shenanigans are best left till later (and anyway I'll confess that even after everything that has happened, I have remained too intimidated to interview her about this period). Finally, the singular strangeness of Jan's work remained hidden from everyone (with the exception of the solitary me).

In short, I believe I have now covered everything that is required for the reader to be able to continue, with one important exception that I hope to attend to now:

In spite of the affection she developed for Armando, confiding in him, collaborating with him, inspired by him, Esther did not let go of her wish to be released from his studio and moved into Sanam's. But, frustratingly, after first promising that he would inquire, her father suddenly expressed the wish that she leave Sanam alone.

He asserted that the calligrapher's work was too esoteric and theistic and theological for the contemplation of a young girl. The constant repetition, in writing, of the phrase *there is no god but god:* honestly, where was the childlike exuberance in that?

She pointed to the new colourful aesthetic. But he said no. She felt he was hiding something and relayed her suspicion to Armando. Armando took the risk of asking her what she thought her father might have been hiding.

To his surprise (and Sanam's and Amir's and Jan's and Ángela's and, eventually, mine), Esther turned to Armando, lowered her voice to the level of whisper, and confided her hunch — nay, her certainty — that this entire kidnapping scheme had

a

purpose

beyond

revenge

and beyond our understanding.

"Yes, but what is it?" asked Armando.

"He won't tell me anything," Esther said. "But I do know that he is looking for a person."

Armando, alarmed to think she could be talking about Ezra: "What do you mean, a person?"

"He is looking for a woman."

Armando, relieved that she was not speaking of Ezra: "What does that have to do with us?"

"I don't know."

"Is this woman an artist?"

"I don't know."

"Is she a forger?"

"I don't know."

Armando, becoming more playful: "Does he think she is one of us? One of us in disguise? Does he believe that I myself, Armando Matamoros, might be this woman, in disguise, despite all appearances?"

"I don't know. Okay, I don't think so."

"Hurray. A different answer."

"It is my strong impression that my father is looking for a woman and you're supposed to help him."

"Me?"

"All of you."

"What is your evidence for that?"

Esther apparently shrugged in the manner of Armando.

"But how is that possible?" he asked. "That we could help him in any way?"

"I don't know. But I do think maybe one of you is already helping him, whether he knows it or not."

"One of who?"

"One of *you*."

"Who among us?"

"The one I'm looking for."

"Who are you looking for?"

"You know who I'm looking for! You all know who I'm looking for!"

"I have no idea who you are looking for!" said Armando, who was a good liar (of course), although it was exhausting to perpetually thwart this instinct in one kid to hone in on another kid in the house, like a beacon.

But the idea that Ezra could be helping Mr. Lin without knowing it? That was absurd. The hostages were actively *hiding* Ezra from Mr. Lin.

Weren't they? Weren't we?

Yes, we were, we definitely were. We were. (We were.)

But when Armando conveyed all this to Sanam, her reply surprised him: she confessed she had recently witnessed something that suggested that perhaps Esther was right: perhaps there was more to the camouflage of Ezra than met the eye. And, more to the point, perhaps Mr. Lin really did have a hidden agenda, beyond revenge and beyond our understanding.

One day, she said, not long after Ezra's move into her studio and Esther's move into Armando's, Mr. Lin had poked his head in to check on Sanam's progress and ask her if she would be willing to take in his daughter sooner than everyone expected. As he looked in, his eye was drawn to some movement against the wall, and, well, Sanam told Armando that yes, this movement could only have been the movement of Ezra.

But instead of tearing the cover off the hostages' gambit, Mr. Lin apparently rushed away with some excitement, mumbling something about "a living wall" or even "life along the wall." Sanam did not hear the whole phrase, but she felt strongly that Mr. Lin had seen evidence of something that excited him, some unspoken theory of art confirmed — a theory that maybe hinted at some larger purpose to our being here, beyond confinement, beyond enforced labour, beyond enriching his collection or educating his daughter. Beyond revenge.

Armando said he understood how this revealed the possibility of a hidden agenda. But, he asked, why did she also think there was more to Ezra's camouflage than met the eye?

Because, said Sanam, the movement that Mr. Lin saw, and that she saw too — movement that could only have been from Ezra — was *halfway up the wall.*

There were no shelf units up there. There were no elk antlers or bear heads or indeed wall mounts of any kind upon which a child might perch. What Mr. Lin had seen was a bird in flight: Mr. Lin saw the wings move; Mr. Lin saw the swoop of the small calligramic body, from right to left, along the wall.

So, before I took my place back in the world of the house, two questions had firmly established themselves among the academy of Ezra-hiding hostages:

1) Did Mr. Lin have a hidden agenda?

2) Was Ezra's camouflage subject to some power that we (or: most of us, *cough cough* Jan Komárek, *cough*) did not understand?

In the meantime, and despite her confessions and conundrums, Esther kept trying to secure a move from Armando to Sanam, in search of the dream she had chased all through the house, elusive and rare, more precious than a parent: a friend. Tin toy come to life.

But she was stuck with Armando. No tin toy. No recourse in sight.

Circumstances changed, however, when a portion of the house collapsed, making it dangerous for anyone at all to spend time in Armando's studio.

PART FIVE

PENTIMENTO

Term (Italian for repentance*) describing a part of
a picture that has been overpainted by the artist but
which has become visible again (often as a ghostly outline)
because the upper layer of pigment has become more
transparent through age.*

39. M A K T 1 E L (who commands the trees)

As I related earlier, I was on my way up to close my window. Since I was not yet apprised of Ezra's relocation, I hesitated by Armando's door, hoping to catch a glimpse of the boy against one of the walls. Ángela slipped by me onto the stairs. I hesitated again half-way up to the second floor. I have always been afraid of lightning, not to mention the thunder that comes with it. I heard a door close above me, I guess it must have been the one to Ángela's bathroom, since her studio door was still open when I arrived on the second floor. I hesitated one more time in the hallway, drawn to the mystery behind Hannie's door and agape at the weather I sensed around and above me, not wishing to ascend under such conditions to the house's highest point.

And then I felt a gust through Ángela's open door and turned.

And so I saw it all: I saw the wide-open front of Ángela's studio, exposed to the elements. I saw, through that wide-open front, a big late-spring rain come, with wind and thunder. And then I saw the big ash tree that stood in front of the house appear to lean forward and peer like a curious giant in through the open wall.

And then, a moment later, the great ash was falling: its primary bough sliced through the wall above the window's opening, landed square on Ángela's studio floor, and then punctured it. I saw it all from the hallway in front of Hannie's studio. When Ángela emerged from her bathroom a moment later, it had all happened, the landscape in front of her had completely changed; and yet she still stepped out, moving into the tree with such bold-ness that I wasn't sure she even noticed the change, accustomed perhaps to the ground always trembling beneath her feet.

And the ground had trembled. The humourious, possibly vengeful house had not put up any kind of a fight against the weight of that bough. And so Ángela's floor collapsed. Above, the bough must have barely missed the sentries' loft. Below, the entire front section of Armando's ground-floor studio was destroyed, with the exception of the big patch of wall where I'd been told he was working on something new, though I did not know yet what it was. And then the entire forward area of the house was filled with the cries of ecstatic blackbirds who came in great numbers seeking shelter from this storm. I could hear them making their rasping calls as they entered the tree, celebrating its fall as they commenced their evening revels in the early afternoon.

Though I still could not begin to guess what Mr. Lin's purpose here might be, beyond simple revenge, I did catch a glimpse, when the tree fell, of the stakes for him and of how he might react if his task were to fail. He ran out through the front door, still clutching his butterfly net, presumably to survey the tree. His daughter followed him, seeking to pull him away from danger. His hair was sticking to his head, his shirt untucked. He must have felt the first responders were going to be here at any moment, bringing his tightly controlled art studio (and our captivity) to an end. Or, perhaps worse, he might have felt that the house was going to collapse into a pile of rubble, leaving his project, whatever it was, abandoned by angels and tardigrades alike, along with all the rest of us.

Well, maybe not tardigrades.

While he was outside, the tree limb lurched again before coming to its final resting place, elbowed into the house. He rushed straight back into Armando's studio to take in the damage even as a bodyguard tried to hold him back. He wept, visibly and openly, sending newly reappeared sentries through the house to check on the status of plumbing, gas, electricity; barking orders over his cellphone to Ella Unton Bride as his daughter screamed at him in Korean. I guessed she was saying that we should all get out of this house, that they should go home, that every one of us should go home, the revealed among us as well as the hidden.

Finally, he pulled himself together and demanded we all meet in the gallery within ten minutes.

For me, this was all but overwhelming. I had only just returned to civilization, and now our little civilization was breaking down.

"We are going to move," he said when we were all gathered. "I have a house here in London. It is quite new: not ideal, but big enough to accommodate all of you."

Esther was nodding her approval. But then:

"No!" shouted Ángela, in chorus with Jan and — of all people — Hannie Van der Roos. Jan shrank back immediately, though, so quickly it was hard to remember he had spoken at all.

Esther did not like this show of resistance. Before any of them could explain their objection, she screamed and ran from the room as I plunged my fingers into my ears. Meanwhile, Hannie and Ángela were looking at each other, trying to gauge which of them should speak first. Until Hannie finally said, "I have no compelling argument; it is simply that I do not wish to be disturbed, currently."

So then Ángela stepped forward. As she began to speak, I saw that Esther had lingered, just beyond the kitchen doorway, and was listening.

"You cannot honestly want to pull me out of here," said Ángela Efrena Quintero, "just as my project is getting underway?"

Mr. Lin was about to respond, but Armando jumped in.

"Oh, so this disaster to my house is all part of your plan, is it?"

"It is."

"Did you plan for the tree falling?"

"No. But I welcome it."

"Oh, is that right?"

"Yes," said Ángela. "That's right."

"Then what will you welcome next?" asked Armando. "Will my house lie in tatters? Will we all be dead? Will you welcome that as part of your plan too?"

"Who can say what will happen next?" said Ángela. "Yes, it's true, I opened up the front of the house to welcome all of nature, and sure, maybe I did not expect a tree to come in. But the tree came in! So let us welcome this big piece of nature into this house and into our hearts."

"Oh, now we must welcome the tree into our hearts!"

"Yes, along with birds and bees and moths. Even before the tree came, I could feel a new power swirling through the house. You cannot claim you have not felt it."

"I have not felt it," said Armando.

"Pshaw," said Ángela. "Of course you have. You have not felt yourself turning into a wild man? Even a little bit? You haven't felt the desire to climb the walls from the first floor to the second?"

"Don't toy with me," said Armando.

"But it suits you, to be toyed with. You should give in to the wild man who is knocking at the door to your heart."

"Pshaw right back at you," said Armando. "My heart does not have a door."

"Others have felt it too, I think," Ángela went on. "We have strange lights and sounds coming from the crack in the door of Hannie Van der Roos's studio. Sanam Haghighi's black scribblings have exploded into an Amazonian rainforest. And here! Look here! Look at her! The pièce de résistance!"

I was so preoccupied, feeling suddenly confused about who was responsible for ushering strangeness into this house — having wondered all this time about Jan's agenda but now being introduced to an apparent conjurer of Nature — that I did not see, for a good five or six seconds, that Ángela Efrena Quintero had whirled around and was gesturing dramatically.

Toward me.

And that the eyes of everyone had swivelled and were looking at me.

My hand went instinctively to my chest in a minor variant of the modest *pudica* pose most famously seen in Botticelli's *Birth of Venus*, but perhaps it would be more accurate to call it the universal *you mean me?* gesture.

"Yes, you!" said Ángela. "Yes, I mean you!" And she turned back and addressed the room again: "This one, Olive, withdrew into her room, fearful as a mouse. We all saw her go. I lifted the roof and allowed the natural world in, and how does she reappear? She has become the bee's knees. Unhunched and flowing, metamorphosed from her cocoon into a beauty!"

(But I was not a beauty. I had not unhunched. I had not meta-morphosed. I had not become a beauty.)

"You cannot honestly be taking credit for this?" asked Mr. Lin, inexplicably not disputing the claim that I had become a beauty.

"I can, I do," said Ángela.

Mr. Lin stepped up and scrutinized me as if I were erected upon a plinth.

"Be that as it may," he concluded, seemingly satisfied by her argument (!), "how can the house itself survive?"

"That is up to you, is it not?" said Ángela. "Nature is a man, a bird, a fox, a gale, a tree. This house is boards and bricks and joists, downspouts and roof tiles."

I cast a furtive glance at Armando, who looked like he might ignite. Ángela saw him too and raised her hand for him to wait. This acknowledgement seemed to tame him for a moment as she went on. "All such things can be fixed. And so you will fix them, Mr. Lin, with your engineers and your masons. My old friend Armando will see his house repaired. But I must insist on keeping the tree limb hanging through my room. I don't intend to abandon it. It is a beautiful destruction, full of possibility."

Gesturing for Ángela to stop, to wait a moment, just a moment, Mr. Lin sat on the floor, overwhelmed. He crossed his legs and closed his eyes.

In the pause that followed, Ella Unton Bride walked into the room, having come into the house without drawing any notice. She was dressed practically in taupe coveralls, as if heading off on an archaeological excursion, albeit with her integral bowtie. She was wearing an ornate cotton mask (presumably to contend with the rising dust) and carried an armful of first-aid kits. She commenced nodding to everyone in greeting, but her eyes fell when she saw Hannie, and then, when she turned to me, her mouth fell open beneath the mask, revealing the tip of her nose, and she dropped everything she was carrying.

So it was true. Was it true? Something was going on. I had somehow arrested the unruffleable, the inscrutable, the plinthian Ella Unton Bride. If ever there was a woman who seemed to stand upon a pedestal, it was she. It was she, not I. Yet she was behaving with me as I might have behaved with her.

And Hannie saw it too, though I couldn't say what she might wish to do with that information.

Mr. Lin maintained his position on the floor.

"Very well, Señora Quintero," he said at last. "We shall stay here. I will do the necessary repairs. I am pleased to see that Ms. Van der Roos does not wish to be disturbed. And as for you, Señora, I suppose I have already made a pledge not to stand in your way. Perhaps something good will come from it."

"Are you saying you believe her?" asked Armando. "With this hogwash about nature and the birds and the bees?"

"Why shouldn't he believe me?" said Ángela. "It is the truth, if you might only cease being an instrument of the patriarchy."

"Fine," said Armando, refusing to counter the insult as Ángela turned to glower at him. "But here is what I have to say. Listen to 'my old friend' Ángela Quintero or do not; pin up her studio, do not pin up her studio; move us out of here or not. You will obviously do what you like, and we are all so soft we will comply."

Mr. Lin shrugged. "You are artists," he said.

"I'm not finished," said Armando. "I am upset about the damage being done to my house, to my beautiful studio, to the flurry of artwork I have managed to create even in these adverse conditions. But, laying all that aside, I have a demand to make: within my broken studio, you must take steps to preserve the undamaged wall that tells the story of your daughter's dash through that old Hanoi market. It's all there, and it is perfect, sublime. We share it, she and I; and I am not ashamed to say it is easily my proudest achievement. So take care of that. You must preserve that."

"Of course," said Mr. Lin.

Ángela was looking at Armando with some confusion, presumably surprised that he would trade all his opposition for this single small assurance. I'll confess it surprised me too: I didn't even know what artwork he was talking about, though I was anxious now to see it.

Mr. Lin paused for a moment as a sentry came to whisper something into his ear.

Then he turned to the rest of us.

"Our water is still running, and we have lost neither gas nor electricity except in the front of the house. Since the only currently endangered parties have asserted their wish to stay, then I have concluded we will stay. To be sure, remaining here is a better outcome for me."

Now Esther, still lingering in the doorway, drew a swift audible breath.

"But why?" she asked. "Why is it better for you here? Why do we stay? What is here? Why is it better for you here?"

We all turned to look at her. Her father said, "It is simply better for me. You need not ask."

"If I did not need to ask, why would I ask?"

"I don't know," said Mr. Lin. "Perhaps to be contrary."

"I ask because I would like to know! I need to know."

"And I have my reasons for keeping this information to myself."

"And what are *those* reasons? If you can't tell me why we are here, then you have to tell me why you can't tell me! Why can you not tell me why we come here every day when we have a beautiful home and everything we need? Why can you not tell me what these artists can do here that they could not do there?"

"Things are already underway here," said Mr. Lin, but Esther interrupted him.

"Ah, yes but what things? What is underway?"

"Please keep your voice down."

"What are you looking for?"

"I cannot tell you. Don't be contrary."

"I'm not being contrary! It's a question! And why do you think you'll find what you're looking for here, even when the house is broken?"

"I can't tell you."

"I want you to tell me."

"It is my own project. It has nothing to do with you."

"Oh!" said Esther.

"It is just my own solitary search. Nothing you need to know."

"It's not solitary! They—" she whirled, pointing her finger at all of us "— are all involved!"

"They know nothing."

"You are the nothing that I need to know," said Esther. "I don't know you at all. Here you are, spending half your fortune on a solitary search with seven blinkered participants and me tagging miserably along. This one has found *beauty* and that one has found salt in a secret light; this one is making a rainforest and that one has discovered how to change words to animals. What does it all achieve for you? What does it achieve altogether? We should do a studio crawl, see what they're all up to, what they all add up to, what they can possibly have in common, how they're helping you with this project you won't tell your daughter about because it is so solitary and just for you, not me, the one who should know you but does not."

"I'm sorry."

This was addressed by Mr. Lin to the rest of us.

"Perhaps," said Esther, coldly, "I need to return to Vietnam and seek out my birth father."

Mr. Lin was looking hurt now, but maintaining his dignity.

"I can't allow you to do that before you come of age—"

"Arrrrrrrrgggggggggggghhhhh!"

Like his daughter, Mr. Lin was beginning to lose his composure.

"All right," said Esther, razor sharp and calm. "We stay here. But it's clear I have to move studios again. And you no longer have an excuse to prevent me going to Sanam."

Before Mr. Lin had a chance to offer a retort to this, his daughter turned to address Sanam herself: "I don't know what you think my relationship is like with my father," she said. "But you can see he keeps one big secret from me, and one day I will find out what it is."

Mr. Lin's eyes widened as Esther maintained her laser focus on Sanam.

"I promise you," she went on, "whatever secrets I might bear witness to inside your studio, I will never reveal them to anyone, ever: not him, not anyone."

After a moment, Sanam gave a small nod.

Mr. Lin sighed. Threw up his hands. Shook his head.

"Very well," he said. "You will move."

Then he addressed the rest of us.

"In jest, my daughter has expressed the wish to embark on what she called a studio crawl. I think, under the circumstances, this might not be a terrible idea."

Oh, I thought. This was a terrible idea.

He went on.

"Given the hard work everyone has done under less than ideal circumstances, and the fright we have all endured this afternoon, I would like to take this opportunity to express my gratitude and, in light of the clearing skies and apparently beautiful weather forecast in the immediate future, to extend an invitation to a party, in one week's time, out in the garden, from where we will commence with this so-called studio crawl, making our way to the top of the house and gradually moving our way down."

The top of the house. They were going to start with me.

"Of course," Mr. Lin added, "anyone who wishes to abstain—"

"I wish to abstain!" I was louder than I expected to be. And I realized I had spoken in chorus. With Hannie. Hannie had spoken in the same moment as me and shouted the same thing: "I wish to abstain."

I looked at her, and she winked at me. I looked away. Looked back at her and she was studying her fingers. Had she winked at me? It didn't make sense; I must have imagined it.

"Fine," said Mr. Lin, with a small nod. "We will begin with the studio of Amir Haghighi."

"I wish to abstain," said Amir. "Just kidding. I most certainly do not wish to abstain. I would be happy to show my work."

It was surprising and funny. But then Amir looked puzzled for a moment, then glanced sadly around and then sauntered out of the room. I recalled my first sight of him earlier, with his badminton racket. There was something wrong with him.

I dismissed the thought. Amir was a man so full of vigour, brimming with youthful energy. How could there ever be anything wrong with him?

I lingered awhile after Mr. Lin took his leave, walking back through the wreckage at the front of the house. I wondered where Ezra was hiding, suspecting (correctly) that he was with Sanam. I wondered if it was Ezra's presence that had changed the nature of Sanam's work from black ink flowing over white walls to a colourful palette of Amazonia. Just as his arrival in my room had changed mine; just as his arrival in Armando's studio had changed Armando's.

Though, where Armando was concerned, it seemed that Esther's arrival had changed his work far more than Ezra's had.

I wondered when I would get to see Armando's project with Esther.

I wondered whether I would get evidence that Hannie had winked at me. I wondered whether I should talk with Jan about his rooftop business. I wondered whether Ángela's falling tree had anything to do with that, or that with the falling tree. Or this business of my so-called beauty. And was there an angel in Hannie's studio or had she merely become a mountaineer?

When she had come down for the meeting, she had not been wearing a harness.

Also, she had abstained from the showing. What was she trying to hide? Evidence of angels?

Was I talking myself into it? Maybe I was.

I suppose I had been provoked by all the talk of beauty to wonder too, suddenly, what might have happened during my eight-hour blackout several weeks before. What if the sink had not been the primary cause of my amnesia? And what if ... what if it had not been me at all who had put those first images on the wall?

Hannie's feet had been an inch or so off the ground. And what of my feet? Could I say for certain that my feet had stayed firmly on the ground for those eight hours?

Were angels a part of nature? I had always thought of them as made-up creatures from made-up religions. But of course nature was not made up. Were religions merely a kind of anthropomorphized view of nature? Or a way for nature to level with us? Over the last three thousand years, say? These are some of the things I wondered and wanted to talk with Jan about. Which is not to say that I could really talk. I was not a talker. Even if I had transformed into "a beauty," I had not also transformed into a talker. And anyway, Jan had disappeared.

Sanam had taken Esther to show around her studio. Armando had gone back into the disaster of his studio, presumably to work toward protecting the only artwork he cared about.

The house did feel wilder somehow. Freer, with so many having spoken their minds without fear of consequences. But was it the tree that had done that? After all, everyone had already been in the backyard, chasing butterflies and playing badminton. Perhaps I was merely overstimulated and overthinking.

I reached down and picked up an ash leaf that had blown all the way here, to the back of the house, presumably from the fallen tree.

The leaf was comprised of seven smaller leaflets that could easily be separated from one another, but fitted together they made a shape that was almost like a feather, with a single leaflet standing solo at the top, pointing somewhere. Tree feather. Delicately serrated leaflets. Dark green on the front. Pale green on the back. I had not studied a leaf since I was a child.

I went upstairs. I caught a glimpse of Ángela again as I passed the open-air tree limb of her studio. There were bees flitting around her. She appeared to be untroubled by them, relaxed and dishevelled, reborn in the wreckage of her room.

This beautiful woman had called me a beauty. Another beautiful woman had appeared to gape before my beauty. But how was I a beauty? I lingered, still holding the ash leaf.

I passed Amir's door. It was open. He was sitting on his chair, which was pulled away from the wall into the middle of this uniquely windowless room. His head was in his hands. I poked my head inside, was about to say something. He ignored me. I withdrew.

Back in my room, I went over the singular strangeness of the day. My reintroduction to society. The falling tree. The declaration of me as a beauty. The rebellion of Esther. The not-rightness of Amir. The possibility of angels.

I looked at the wall. Went and stood by it. Raised my hand, stood on my tiptoes.

The first work I'd done, when I'd been blacked out: it extended several inches above the tips of my fingers.

QED.

I spent a troubled night tormented by the influx of bugs that had come into the house with the tree. Mosquitoes bit me and spiders spun webs in my doorway and there was even a firefly or two. The noises were novel as well: Who knew robins called so loud? Or you might imagine the solo sound of a resonant cricket from a corner of your room, but in this case, it was an orchestra calling from the other side of the house. And how could I ever forget that insistent and deafening toad? A mating call, according to Amir, but he might have been joking.

In short, I was groggy when I arose and disappointed to see I had resumed my habit of sleeping in my day clothes after so many weeks of (I blush to relate) going naked. Perhaps this newly remarked upon beauty was receding.

Descending to the ground floor, I passed Hannie on the stairs. She was looking loose limbed, dishevelled, wearing a weathered black leather jacket with padded shoulders, and she was carrying one plate of eggs and bacon and another with sliced tomatoes and basil, sensual as a still life. One fork on each plate. Two forks then. Her eyes met mine. Her preternatural reserve had vanished. The wrinkles on her face had made room for more wrinkles, ushering in expression. I blushed as I always do before beauty, and she blushed too. My blush was more like the belly of a warty newt. Hers was aurora, like the dawn, like a winter tan.

Two plates. Did angels eat?

And then, just as I was coming into the kitchen, the doorbell rang. Ms. Bride appeared from the front office in the same moment to announce she was seeing police through the window. There followed a few moments of pandemonium. Mr. Lin had only just arrived a few minutes before, in a terrible mood because his daughter had stayed overnight in Sanam's studio and was refusing to see him. It took a few moments for him to recognize the gravity of this new situation. Finally, eschewing subtlety, he told Armando that he would destroy his beloved new mural if there was any funny business. Armando practically laughed in his face as Mr. Lin withdrew into the front office, leaving the Spaniard to assume he was serious and go answer the door.

I poked my head into the hallway from the kitchen and saw a young plainclothes police investigator wearing a black mask stamped with a Scotland Yard logo over his mouth and nose. I considered that perhaps he was merely reporting a neighbourhood anthrax scare. I heard him dismiss Armando's apologies about the fallen tree, remarking that people sometimes go to extraordinary lengths to scare away visitors, especially ones from Scotland Yard, and "especially these days," he added.

Armando was in his yellow housecoat and striped pyjamas. He looked very much at home. When I asked him, years later, why he didn't try to communicate his confinement, he said, "I liked that mural."

"Mr. Lin would not have destroyed it," I said. "You knew that already."

"Well, anyway," he added, "I could already tell this was bigger trouble."

It was certainly trouble. The police officer had brought with him an eight-by-ten photocopy of a sketch. He held it up and asked Armando point blank if he had drawn it.

"That is a photocopy," said Armando.

"I am aware," said the investigator. "I'm asking if you drew the original."

"Ah," said Armando. "You must forgive me. I've yet to have my morning coffee."

He peered at the drawing in the investigator's hand. "What you have there is a drawing of *La maja* by Francesco Goya. Either a preliminary sketch or possibly a study that someone made in a gallery. But look; there is Goya's signature," he said, pointing. "So how could I have drawn it?"

I couldn't help but notice Armando had not said he did not draw it.

"Interesting," said the investigator, "that you should be so familiar with this artwork."

"Everyone is familiar with this artwork," said Armando. "The painting it suggests is one the most famous in the world."

"We'd like you to come down to the station to talk about it. Fill us in on some of the finer points of its fame."

"Right now?"

"Let's schedule something." The investigator was pulling out his phone.

"Sure," said Armando. "There is nothing I like better than to talk about art."

"Don't be modest, Mr. Matamoros. You seem to do so much more than talk about art. How else could you afford this beautiful house? And such an ambitious renovation."

As soon as the investigator took his leave, Mr. Lin came out of the front room and asked Armando if he had drawn the sketch.

"I did draw it," said Armando, grimly, "to entice a commission from somebody. I most certainly did not sign Goya's name to it."

"Who was the somebody?"

Armando shrugged apologetically. "Somebody with money? I try not to look too close."

Once again, he sounded like he was lying through omission.

Within the hour, Mr. Lin, with assistance from Ella Unton Bride, had been able to ascertain that the sketch had been scooped up in a raid on a London organized-crime family known as the Long Fella Syndicate. He zeroed in on the fact that the fake Goya was likely an unwanted bit of ephemera attached to a much larger case, hoping that the investigators would feel encumbered by a minor forgery that had never even been sold. Its single token illegality lay in that telltale Goya signature. Still, they must have felt some responsibility to conduct a follow-up, having sent someone to knock on Armando

Matamoros's London address with a request to come down to Scotland Yard in five days' time. But how had they gotten Armando's name?

Mr. Lin asked Armando to describe the sketch to him, but the Spaniard clammed up and didn't want to talk about it.

"You do understand I am trying to help you," said Mr. Lin.

They were sitting in the rubble of Armando's studio, as Jan and I listened at the door and as carpenters worked around them to secure the structure of the front of the house and pin up the bit of second floor that remained. Above their heads, Ángela was climbing around making a metamorphosis of her space, into what exactly it was hard to say.

Beside them, the precious wall depiction of Esther Lin's flight through the Hanoi market was covered with a huge sheet of plastic. While attempting to eavesdrop on the conversation, I finally got my first look at it. I saw colour and vibrancy and the criss-crossing of black lines through the plastic as through a window being pummelled by rain.

Armando was looking at it himself.

"Yes, I understand," he said. "You are trying to save me. Why, though?"

"I still need you here."

"But I don't think I'm going to do any better than this," said Armando, raising the tarp. He pointed at a small scribbled image of Mr. Lin. "That's you," he said, "running after your little daughter."

"I am aware," said Mr. Lin.

"You should maybe be running after her again, not spending time with me."

"Are you not the least bit concerned about the trouble you're in?"

Armando shrugged. "You cannot help me."

"I can, though. Please describe the sketch."

Armando sighed.

"It makes me look bad. Both as a forger and as an artist."

Mr. Lin threw up his hands. "Your moral code is beyond me."

"All right! All right," said Armando. "If you must know, I tried to rise above my station. I sought to be celebrated as a genius and ended up proving myself a fool. There was a lot of money at play, and I failed."

"I don't understand," said Mr. Lin.

"No," said Armando. "You have not heard the story yet."

We all settled into our listening places. Even Ángela, up above, climbed down the fallen limb to lend an ear. Huddling next to Jan in the hallway, I was nudged by an early memory of nestling by my sister and listening to a radio documentary about Henry Moore being a war artist who made drawings of people sleeping in the tunnels of the London Underground. It occurs to me I still haven't seen those Moore drawings in the world outside my imagination, so this memory is perhaps fitting to how I listened to Armando telling his story to Mr. Lin, describing work that no longer existed in the world.

"Did you see the sketch?" Armando asked Mr. Lin. "No, of course you did not. You were hiding in your office. When I go down to that Scotland Yard, I will ask for the original and point to the smudge I could see in the bottom right corner of the copy, forming a funny sort of palimpsest with the Goya signature."

"Why?" asked Mr. Lin. "What does that smudge represent?"

"Authenticity," said Armando.

It turned out the sketch had once had Armando's signature on it. But it had been rubbed out and replaced with Goya's.

"But why," asked Mr. Lin, "would you ever affix your signature to a piece of work that was destined to be a forgery?"

Armando sighed.

"It wasn't going to be a forgery," he admitted finally. "It was a preliminary sketch, hastily drawn in advance of an audacious original."

It all started, Armando said, when, against all odds, the Long Fella Syndicate acquired the Goya masterpiece known as *La maja desnuda*.

"Surely a forgery," said Mr. Lin.

"No," said Armando. "Let me assure you, for the sake of my tale, that it was the original. I can only guess they had a large sum of money and they needed someplace to put it. Better than keeping a mountain of cash in a barn that might burn down."

"Go on," said Mr. Lin.

"Well, they dispatched one of their guys to talk to me about making a copy of it. I guess they wanted to keep their cake and also to eat their cake. Their guy told me they were going to find a gullible buyer for it in the Asian market, Korea or Japan or someplace. He said that even if their duplicity was revealed, there was very little risk because the collector wouldn't alert the authorities and thus reveal the shame of having been fooled."

"Yes," said Mr. Lin, "I am familiar with this practice."

"Don't I know it," said Armando, gesturing vaguely to his occupied house.

"Indeed, you do," said Mr. Lin. "Perhaps I was the very collector they were planning to mark."

"Yeah," said Armando. "But it never got to that because I said no."

"You did?"

Armando shrugged. "I was in a strange sort of mood that day. They came to my door, unheralded, and I had only just come from an annulment interview. I used to be married, you know!" This last he called out loud to the broader audience of the room, presumably including the overhead Ángela. "Indeed, it was a happy marriage augmented by the fulsome bloom of youth! A marriage that ended without any rancour or bitterness! A marriage that ful—"

"You have made your point," said Mr. Lin, firmly. "Please go on."

After a sigh, a little eye roll and a shake of the head, Armando continued. "I was remembering all the passion and idealism and insane poverty of my university days. So I told their guy, I said, 'Sure, I could copy this priceless painting that you've brought to me, I could do that. But I have a better idea. A more audacious idea.

An idea that could transform me into a legitimate artist and your Long Fella Syndicate into the most spectacular patron of the arts in the history of London.'"

Armando had expected the man to laugh in his face and walk away, but he did not, at least not just yet. So Armando described to him how he had recently made a visit to the Goya Museum in Zaragoza and witnessed something there that had practically unhinged his jaw: a high-quality collection of Goya's *Disasters of War* prints shockingly defaced: fifteen or twenty years before, a pair of English brothers had purchased the ink-and-paper works and replaced the heads of the wretched victims in the prints with big-eared, garishly coloured clown heads and . . . well, more big-eared, garishly coloured clown heads. At that time, fifteen or twenty years before, the vandalism by these brothers created a scandal in the art world, as bad as any forger's ruse discovered. Behold, though, all these many years later, these same defacements had now been embraced by the curators and caretakers of Goya's legacy, who pronounced that such works had allowed the world to look upon the horrible immediacy of the master's hellish vision with fresh eyes.

Armando told this story to the Long Fella rep, and then he said, "Look: you want to make a lot of money? I get that. Here is what I propose: give me the real *maja*, the one you have: the real, priceless Goya *maja desnuda*, and I will outdo those English boys. Sure, they can ruin a few prints, but in all those cases, the copper plates — true source of Goya's genius — remain more or less intact. I, a true Spaniard, will take this singular oil painting, this priceless and original beauty, and bring my own twenty-first-century vision to it."

Armando explained to Mr. Lin how, in his opinion, the *maja desnuda* depicted a frank sexual gaze from the model to a late-eighteenth-century viewer. "But I told that Long Fella guy that I would transform it into someone who shouts, *J'accuse!* and spits in the face of the twenty-first-century viewer!"

"You mean to say," said Mr. Lin, "that you were planning to destroy a singular masterpiece?"

"You've grasped it," said Armando. "The guy did not understand, though, so I sketched it out for him: instead of a naked *maja* or a clothed *maja*, I drew him a sort of werewolf *maja*. I added fur. I covered her nakedness with fur. I added a hint of pointy, canine teeth to her mouth. I surrounded her with a den and took away her divan. The short Long Fella guy wanted to know what it meant. I took the measure of him and crafted an artist's statement for his ear alone. 'I'm so glad you asked,' I said. 'We live in a crap time, a time where teenagers look up to superheroes who wear spandex and zip around the sky, where young men pleasure themselves to cosplayers and cartoons. Two-D doodles as erotic icons, am I right? Goya's famous maja, who used to siren-sing the throng to her naked body like the Greeks to Troy, now waits in vain for a single passing, appreciative glance. Why not, just, do this? It's what the world deserves, leaving you and I and maja to howl at the moon.'"

It seemed that Armando was able to convince the Long Fella representative to agree with him that it was an offence how the young men of the twenty-first century were masturbating to cartoons. And, as every con artist knows, the thing you need to do is get your mark to say yes just once.

"But the guy was still shaking his head, so I doubled down. No, I wasn't going to make a copy of this painting. I told him he shouldn't waste his time with me if that was what he wanted. I revered Goya! So I said to him: 'This painting,' I said, 'sure, it's worth something. Sure. Sure! You can lock it away, sell a knock-off, contribute to its eventual decay and the growing indifference of the general public. Or you can set off a bomb in the middle of the art market and leap from a life of criminality to a grand legitimacy!'"

Mr. Lin was looking at Armando with disbelief. Armando laughed.

"I did not want to work as their forger. What did I have to lose? *Bueno*, the man decided my pitch was above his pay grade. So he took my sketch away, and I believed I would never hear from those stretched-out fellows again.

"But they sent him back. They sent him back with that very painting. The actual Goya *La maja desnuda* was delivered to this very house in the back of a dirty white van. I set it up in this very room. Goya, like a god to me. And in a frenzy of ambition and destruction, I did what I said I would do. I destroyed Goya's poor *maja*, a greater figure in her two dimensions than I have ever been in all my glorious three. That's what I did for those criminals."

"So where is it?" asked Mr. Lin. "I would very much like to see it."

"Yes, me too, Señor Lin. Me too."

Armando paused to collect himself and then went on with his story.

"I worked in a frenzy for three weeks. I transformed our *maja* into the forgotten earth queen of a new age, just as I said I would. In the evenings I watched *Twilight* and other modern monster movies in yonder TV room. Sometimes I fled to the toilet and retched up my guts. I told myself I was seizing the future. 'So this is what it feels like,' I said to myself, 'to be a real artist.'

"The Long Fellas wasted no time with intermediaries. Nor did they spend any time trying to figure out whether they liked the work themselves. Instead, they secured an audience with the curators of the Goya Museum in Zaragoza. A car was dispatched to this address to take me to the airport. They did not bother with invitations, those lengthy fellows.

"Everyone at that museum was shocked and impressed by the work. Fascinating and inspiring, they said. But, they added — laughably, almost as an afterthought — this cannot be the original nude *maja*. The original nude *maja*, they informed us, has hung in the Prado since 1901.

"At first, the gangsters did not believe them. They thought the curators wanted to acquire my defaced painting at a cut rate. They sought to intimidate. Indulging the disbelief of those stretchy fellows, the head curator performed a simple forensic study, scrupulously avoiding my amendments and proving within five minutes that most of the alleged Goya pigments were of a recent vintage in order to finally assert that no, the museum did not want to acquire their painting, that in truth their painting was worth less that the canvas it was painted on or the boards it was stretched over.

"It was a forgery. Ha ha! It was a forgery! The notorious London criminal organization had been fooled by a forgery, and so had I!"

"Satisfying," said Mr. Lin.

"Indeed," said Armando. "Whoever had conned those interminable men had dangled the idea of a gullible Asian collector. But no: they were the marks from the very start, those angry Londoners. They didn't even have the excuse of the original being squirrelled away in a safe somewhere. It had been hanging in a museum the whole time! Ha!

"So then, for a time, they imagined they might blame me. Which took the focus off my more existential failure, albeit in ways I did not appreciate. They were never going to kill me, merely break all my fingers. But cooler heads finally prevailed. And then they attempted to track down the original seller, but the original seller had disappeared into thin air. Of course, they burned the painting. It was worthless, and even more worthless after what I had done to it. So you see you're not the first to burn my work. But they could not very well go sell it in Asia now, could they?

"I was left to ponder my ambitions, to realize I had not really destroyed a great Goya. To rethink the possibility that it would have been an unforgivable act. But you know what really killed me? Even if I had defaced the real *maja*, I would never have one-upped those British boys who had defaced *The Disasters of War*. They had had a world-shaking idea. I had merely tried to steal it. I had been, as always, derivative. If they were standing on the shoulders of giants, what was I doing? Giving everything I had to merely keep hold of their *miembros* without losing my grip.

"Goya is my idol. I don't want to be his defacer. It has always been more honest for an *hombre mediocre* like me to forge and fake and counterfeit. That is the bare truth. So what if I cannot be a great artist? Like the saying goes, Great artists steal. That's not me."

"A forger who says he does not steal," said Jackie Lin. "But I see your point. Though I have long considered that the line about how great artists steal might have been coined with exquisite irony. That it might be a criticism of the very idea of great art. That maybe we should be taking a second look at the so-called 'not great' art of any given period? Find the beauty that has been overlooked, or indeed stolen outright?"

"No," said Armando. "It means what it seems to mean."

But one question had not been answered in Armando's story: Why had the Long Fella Syndicate turned Armando's preliminary sketch into a full-fledged forgery?

It was agreed that Armando would lie low in Jan Komárek's basement studio in case the investigator came around again. The door
to knocking police would be answered by Ella Unton Bride, who
would claim to be working as his art dealer. She came every day   217
with Mr. Lin now, and though we were never allowed to view the
front room, we had the impression they had set up a bed in there
for her in the event she needed to stay overnight.

  All legal considerations aside, it had clearly become more
dangerous for Armando to remain in his ground-floor studio:
with Ángela working around the clock above him, there was a
real fear she might accidentally drop a workbench or a wild pig
on his head. Just the previous evening, she had stubbed her toe
on a twenty-pound sledgehammer forgotten by a workman, had
consequently dragged it to the edge of the hole and dropped it
through. It made a dent in Armando's floor. Luckily no one had
been present.

  So Armando took to brooding in the basement, filling a notebook with new sketches that were more strongly reminiscent
of Goya than of Javier [Redacted]. Jan tried to impress upon
him that this was perhaps not the best idea under the circumstances. But Armando dismissed these concerns. He was sullen
and obsessed.

  Within three days, Mr. Lin secured an invitation to visit Scotland Yard, where he simply told the investigator the truth as he
understood it: that he himself, Mr. Jackie Lin, was a gullible collector who was known for purchasing fakes; that the Long Fella
organization was planning on commissioning a fake for him
to buy; that a talented artist and London resident by the name
of Armando Matamoros had approached them with a different
project, a legitimate if controversial artistic commission that
had thrown them off the scent of their con; that through the

fulfillment of that commission, Señor Matamoros had exposed the Long Fellas' property to be itself a fake; and that the work had been burned before any copy could be made that might fool the buyer that was himself, Mr. Jackie Lin.

He told the investigator that if they examined the artwork closely, they would see that Matamoros had himself signed the sketch and that his signature had been erased.

"Yes, we did know that," the investigator told Mr. Lin. "That's how we identified him as the creator of the sketch."

"Then you must also know," said Mr. Lin, "that a forger would never, ever, put his own name on any artwork destined for the counterfeit market, not at any time."

He also told the police he was grateful to this same artist Matamoros for tripping up the Long Fella Syndicate's designs on him and that he would do anything to take the heat off him. As a show of gratitude, he was willing to make a contribution to a charity of the investigator's choice.

After lightly smacking Mr. Lin on the wrist for offering to bribe an investigator of Scotland Yard, the police decided to drop their scheduled chat with Señor Armando Matamoros. The only thing they wanted to know from Mr. Lin was who his dealer would have been had he made the purchase of the thwarted Goya forgery. This seemed important to them, but when Mr. Lin told them he could not recall for sure whether or not it had been his friend and longtime dealer, Ella Unton Bride, they waved away any concern and let him go.

It might have been a bit surprising to us that they dropped the scheduled chat with Armando, but the matter was clarified a few days later with an announcement in the press that the Police Union Children's Charity had received a busload of cash from an anonymous donor.

It was also true that, during all the time he was dealing with Scotland Yard, Mr. Lin never once saw his daughter, and his daughter never once came out of Sanam's studio when her father was in the house. And that fact was more upsetting to him than a broken house or the near arrest of Armando for allegedly creating a Goya forgery or his reputation as a collector or the threat of our abduction being exposed by an investigation into a London crime syndicate.

And there was also the fact that, unbeknownst to any of us, after Mr. Lin picked up the alleged counterfeit, the police had him tailed all the way back to the Armando Matamoros residence and then planted a stakeout operation half a block away.

Baf.

In the middle of the night. I was hit on the nose by one of my own twisted notes.

I opened my eyes. Moonlight was flooding the room. Still no sentry at the window.

A figure sat cross-legged on the floor, patiently tossing the papers.

"I thought you might feel less startled if my face were situated below your face," said Jan Komárek.

"That's how the bogeyman does it, under the bed," I said.

"What is this bogeyman?"

"Doesn't matter. What do you want?"

"I need your help."

I sat up in my bed.

"Now?"

"Yes."

"Why?"

"Armando Matamoros is in some trouble. I need your help to extricate him from a . . . predicament."

"Why me?"

"Because you care about him and also because you know what I have been up to."

"I do?"

"I imagine you have some idea."

"Well, I have questions."

"There will be time to ask them as we go."

"No, now," I said.

"Very well. I will answer to the best of my ability."

"What were you doing out there on the roof?"

"Conjuring."

"Angels?"

"Yes. And, let me add that, if I have hidden this work from you, as I have hidden it from everyone, then you must forgive me: we conjurers have to be secretive. It was not so long ago we were burned at the stake."

I wondered whether I should ask about Hannie's levitation, opting to come at it from the side: "Have you been successful at summoning an angel?"

"Yes. No. I don't know. More successful than I've been in the basement."

All Hannie questions suddenly shunted to the side: "The basement?"

"There has also been conjuring happening in the basement."

"Not angels."

"Not angels."

"What are you doing it for?"

"I'm not sure I'm at liberty to say."

"So you're doing it for Mr. Lin."

"No less or more than any of us are doing anything for Mr. Lin. But to be truthful, I have been pursuing this work for much of my life. There was a time when we humans knew so little about the workings of the universe that we could imagine it was possible that there were angels just beyond the veil or devils down below the dirt. For my whole life I've tried to imagine that, just so I might see if there was anything we missed before science was torn away from the mysteries of alchemy to become a separate practice."

"So this is your art practice?" I asked.

Jan practically spat with contempt. He raised a crooked finger and wagged it at me. "I don't practise *art*," he barked. "Not in the way any of *you* practise art. I will confess I don't even like art. To me, there is nothing in your images beyond an opportunity to exploit illusion, to use the background of things that are not really there. To me, the world is transformed within our *minds*, not in our doodles. Religious people say that God created the whole world using letters and numbers. The word. Can you imagine what power we would have if we could locate a word or two like that? It was the alphabet that created of the universe, not art. I am attempting to access that kind of power."

I said, "Well, that's interesting. But I have to admit, just as you don't believe in art and you see it as a bunch of doodles, I don't believe in conjuring and I see it as a bunch of babbling. Can you tell me why on earth I should think your magic works?"

"Do not underestimate me," said Jan.

"I don't underestimate you. But hockey is not the same as magic."

He said, "My friend, you have already seen evidence of my magic."

"What evidence?"

"Has it ever occurred to you to wonder how Mr. Lin was able to track you all down? You are all forgers. For every single one of you, the true authorship of your works was hidden behind a veil of space and time, and none of you were ever caught, not even Ángela. So how did he do it? I can tell you how he did it. He brought all your forgeries to me."

I admit I was here at a loss for words.

"I'll give you a moment to get dressed," he said.

I had forgotten. He had come to take me on a quest into the basement — suddenly a far more dubious undertaking, given his stated interests. Anyway, I was already dressed. Old habits die hard.

"Very well, my friend," said Jan. "Come quietly."

And so I followed Jan as we descended through the quiet house, past the closed doors of Amir and Hannie and Ángela's bowing tree, down to the ground floor, where I heard a stirring in Armando's studio, peeked in and saw a pair of carpenters with headlamps working quietly on their knees beside the Esther artwork. I had grabbed some scrap paper as I left, scribbled as we descended, stumbling along and stuffing my pockets with their less-than-coherent messages composed in haste:

Whhy m

passsng anngle dor glow crack there

wallppr glws HUMORUS huse

Jan did not question my scribblings, waiting patiently on the ground floor landing. When I had stuffed the last crumpled paper into my pocket, he opened the door and down we went.

A viscous mist smelling of fresh mud smothered us as we reached the bottom of the stairs. Jan threw an uncharacteristically apologetic look over his shoulder as he led me around a series of folding tables strewn with pebbles, rotting fruit, mouse corpses, sanitary napkins retrieved from the garbage, sealed condoms and other unmentionables, and into a room with a small water tank and furnace.

Here the floor sloped gradually to its cemented centre, but instead of the round drain you might expect to find there, I saw a jagged hole plugged up with the slumped and shirtless body of Armando Matamoros, sunk to the belly, eyes closed, with smoke seeping up through the fissures around him.

He did not look like himself.

"We have to get him out," said Jan Komárek. "But try not to wake him."

"Why not wake him?"

"I don't know," said Jan, lying again. "It's just a feeling. But this is not how the floor looked when I fell asleep an hour ago. So I believe it would really be best to pull him out. You see, I might as well tell you: Señor Matamoros may or may not have been overtaken and possessed by a creature not of this earth . . . or certainly not of the surface of this earth . . ."

"You are saying . . . ?"

"I had made a protective circle of stones. You will see it over there, ringed by a series of divine names. And then a triangle where the demon was meant to appear. You will see he is inside the triangle, where he was never meant to go. So I believe this fool was sniffing around where he should not have been. I do not know why the floor has collapsed. Will you help me or not? Look at him. I fear he may boil like a frog in a pan."

I nodded. In truth, I wanted to run away, fearful of the sinkhole I was about to approach, which had apparently been caused by the drawing of a demonic triangle on the floor. I wanted to go rouse the household. But I did not want to make a scene. Jan bent his small wiry form to take hold of Armando beneath one (suddenly massive-looking) shoulder, tattooed with a black screen-print-style image of a cartoon mouse. On my side, I lifted up the artist's meaty workman's hand and tried to set it safely out of the way before wrapping my two pudgy little arms around the other hefty shoulder.

On Jan Komárek's count of three, we pulled as hard as we could.

Armando did not move. We tried again. His eyes opened, shocking me with a frank gaze that had nothing behind it. Was he possessed, as Jan had implied? Or merely sleepwalking? Who knew what night terror we might inspire in him as we yanked with our grasshopper arms.

Seeing him caught there in the hole made me believe for a frightened moment, within that mass of heady smoke, that he was about to go swirling down into the earth and that whatever power permitted that to happen to him would take me as well. Jan and Armando and me.

Finally the inert body started to shift. The room was filling with the smoke that seeped from below, more of the mud smell that wasn't really so bad, almost an exfoliation and perhaps a balm for my lungs. If it turned out that Mephistopheles was holding on to Armando's feet, the old demon scholar might not be so horrible to witness.

But there was no demon scholar. If this had truly been a tug-of-war, there was no way we pair would have won. Jan Komárek and I finally pulled enough to see Armando's naked hips, his privates, the sight of which nearly led me to flee in terror. But Jan berated me that a life was here at stake, and so I averted my gaze and pulled and pulled, and finally we got the man out of the hole.

The hole turned out to be no more than a small depression. A sinkhole, presumably caused by drainage through a drain cap that wasn't attached to a pipe and therefore didn't lead anywhere except the earth below the cement floor. The mist had dissipated.

When we were both satisfied that there was no gaping hell pit down below — at least not any that we could see — we turned our attention to the man who was looking more like himself.

"What are you doing here?" he said, half asleep but struggling to rise.

"I would ask you the same question," said Jan, unflappable, handing the large man a fitted sheet to cover up with. "You appear to have tried to wash yourself down the drain."

"I don't know, my friend," said Armando.

"You have been sticking your proboscis where it does not belong," said Jan.

"How," said Armando. "Can. Everyone. So. Easily and always. Forget."

"Forget what?" asked Jan.

"My house," mumbled Armando.

"I see," said Jan. "Your house. Must be galling to be occupied and overrun. Still, you are lucky that you yourself have not been occupied and overrun."

"Maybe I have been," said Armando, mustering dignity. "Maybe I have. What time is it?"

"An hour past midnight."

Armando was sitting, slumped like a sullen Roman general in his sheet, looking distracted, but then there was an odd brief buzzing sound, and the next moment his face was up, eyes searching the dank ceiling, and he was sniffing like a large animal. When he spoke again, his voice was wakeful and low; it seemed to resonate below me, through the cement and the earth beneath it. A change in personality. Not Armando. He cocked his head, as if he was trying to roll the round marble of a thought out of a hole and onto the ceramic plate of an otherwise empty head.

"I see," he said, ruminating. "This man makes art. *S'aperse in nuovi amor l'etterno amore.*"

Did he mean Armando? I mouthed the question to Jan, who ignored me and tried to make eye contact with the Spaniard.

"Is that Italian?" he asked. "I had no idea you spoke Italian."

"Translation:" said Armando/Not Armando, carrying on with his languorous train of thought, "'Eternal love opens up into new loves.' Or, to reverse the idea: 'Each new little stupid act of *love* illuminates the *eternal* love of *God.*' And by *love*, of course he meant *art*, that petty preoccupation . . ."

"Oh I see," said Jan, waving a finger in front of Armando's face, watching him closely. "You are granting us a treatise on the famous Dante Alighieri."

Armando/Not Armando did not react. "Art, flitting like a firefly, weaving its way through the night, reminding those who are stuck in darkness of a teeny tiny glimmer of sun . . . I myself have always wondered, down there, whether I could do that. I like to think I could."

Jan was stepping now into the stone circle, gesturing frantically for me to do the same. I was slow on the uptake: this was a conjuring. But was it inadvertent? Or had Jan done it on purpose?

"You mean you want to make art?" asked Jan, now more polite than I'd ever heard him.

Armando/Not Armando, interrupting: "Yes. Make art!" And then bitterly: "To the greater glory of God." He cried out and began to weep, tears streaming down his face.

Jan, patiently, as if to a child: "You feel you have not been blessed with ability?"

Armando/Not Armando: "I'm cursed. Cursed!"

And then he considered again, rolling around the marble in his mind: "Perhaps I have some ability."

Jan: "Ah, I see! You are admiring the storehouse of art in the memory of your host."

Armando/Not Armando: "I will attempt it."

Jan: "Do!"

Armando/Not Armando: "Hand me a sheet of paper."

Jan pulled a crumpled piece of paper out of his pocket, smoothed it out against the floor and then handed it to me (!). Withering under the demonic and the Komárek gaze, I took a few steps toward the sheet-clad silhouette of Armando and did my artless best to fling the paper at him. It slid up into the air toward the ceiling and then the demon snatched it with his left hand, crumpling it again.

"Oh, damn," he said. "Damn."

He tried to smooth the paper against the floor. Then he scooped up what looked like a piece of charcoal and attempted, in one smooth move, to draw a perfect circle.

It did not turn out as well as he had apparently hoped. He was mortified and then enraged.

Demon: "Shit!"

Jan: "No, I accept that! You should feel good about what you have done!"

Demon: "I don't care what you think!"

Jan: "Hear me out: it would have been a perfect circle but for the surface beneath."

Demon: "Pfft."

Jan: "Now you listen to me. It is sublime. An attempt to render the perfection of a circle on a crumpled paper against a rough cement floor, like Giotto di Bondone. I commend you. You have clearly seen the face of God in your time."

The Demon mimicked him. "*In my time*. I see through your flattery. I have no talent! Is this not why I was hurled into hell in the first place?"

And then he threw his head back and howled with rage:

I CAN'T

DRAW

And then, his fit passing as suddenly as it had come, the demon possessing Armando sniffed the air and assumed a manner of distracted contemplation once again.

"I smell honey," he said. "Do you smell honey?"

"No," said Jan. "I have a keen sense of smell, and I do not smell honey."

They both looked at me. With some haste, I shook my head. I did not smell honey.

"I smell honey," said Armando's demon occupier. "It's a fine smell. Earth and life together. It distracts me from the pain of being such a piss-poor artist."

He began to move away from us.

Jan spoke up, declarative: "I called you here," he said, "by mistake. You have no right to occupy this distinguished artist."

The Armando demon paused in his exit and looked back over his shoulder, flashing Jan a look of contempt.

"You don't believe this man is a distinguished artist," he scoffed. "Nobody does. He is derivative and mediocre, too concerned with the regard of others, and alone. But now," he added, "he has my regard. And my gratitude. And my company."

Then he lumbered away toward the stairs, dragging his white sheet into the muddy mist, presumably in search of honey.

Jan turned back to me. "This is Señor Goya's doing, I suspect. Bringing psychic pain to our friend, facilitating a too easy possession by this demon from hell. I will have to remedy it."

"Okay," I said, not wanting to argue, unsure how to feel. Should I be frightened? Armando had not sprouted horns or turned red. And he was obsessing about art. How far could he really be from himself? Maybe he was sleepwalking. Maybe he had regular night terrors.

A wave of fatigue overcame me. I needed to get to my bed. Jan followed as I headed to the stairs.

"I blame myself," he hiss-whispered. "I had believed he was too depressed to get into trouble. Should have known better. We have our work cut out for us in this household, to harbour a demon in our midst. Thank you for your assistance."

He finally left me to make my way.

A light glowed beneath Hannie's door.

As I approached my stairs, I saw a shadow in the dark, crouching low against the wall. I thought, What now? Not Armando's demon again?

But no, the figure was smaller, more lithe and angular. I didn't want to hesitate or show fear, so I continued to walk, heart in my throat, and finally saw that it was Amir, just outside his door, squatting low with his back against the wall, forearms resting over knees, hands hanging limp. He swivelled his head to look up at me.

"Shhh," he said. "Did you notice? I believe Ángela has just taken a lover."

He nodded to the opposite end of the hall, from where I heard nothing.

I said I did not notice. Why did he think Ángela had just taken a lover, in the middle of the night?

"I can always rely on my hearing," he said. "Just came out here to confirm."

We were quiet for a moment, listening. I wondered, not out loud, if perhaps it was Hannie he was sensing.

"Have you ever had one, Olive?"

I stiffened. But then I thought, No, this is my friend, who told me astonishingly personal things about himself within moments of our first meeting; he has the right.

"I . . ."

(found myself thinking only of my admiration, from afar, of the sentry — certainly the most erotic thing I had ever done, though that, of course, does not speak well of me).

". . . no."

"You're not sure?"

"I am sure."

"But you hesitated." His beautiful smile, perfect teeth in the darkness.

"I have not had a lover. But I . . ."

"What?"

"I suppose I want to tell you I have imagined one."

"Ha," said Amir. "Bully for you."

He shifted a bit.

"I can't sleep," he said, serious now, sighing. "There's something roiling inside me. Something not natural. It's nudging my libido, and my libido is answering, yes I will Yes. But to whom? Or to what? It's maddening."

He sighed again. I was not understanding him, and he could tell. He changed the subject.

"I had a great love once," he said. "You often make me think of him because he was Canadian. A Canadian geologist. Six feet tall. Square jaw. Coiffed hair. Could pass through a room full of ayatollahs with no one the wiser. A good thing, too, because the culture that he walked in was a cowboy culture. Broken earth, oil fields, wilderness. Tough guys.

"But he was brave. He pursued little old me. I met him in a club in Manama and then followed him back to Alberta."

I asked him how long they were together.

"Six months. He wanted to marry me, move to permissive Montreal. I felt I was not ready."

"You regret that?"

"No. I was not ready. Perhaps I'm ready now. Or perhaps it's just this strange nudge I'm feeling, or perhaps the petulant grunts I hear from Ángela's beau." He leaned in, mouthed the words without sound, "I think it's Armando."

I made to go past him, up my stairs. But Amir was not quite finished with me yet.

"Do I know this person?"

"Sorry?"

"The lover you have imagined: do I know them? I swear I won't tell."

My embarrassment proved so painful to witness, even in that dark hallway, that he changed the subject again:

"When my Canadian geologist was on site in his home province, he lived in a little trailer that doubled as an office. For the whole six months I was in your country, I never once went in there, but before I left, I gave him a piece of art I had worked on for nearly the whole time: kitschy painting, perfect full-size forgery: dogs playing cards. Ha! He put it on the wall, pride of place. Sent me a photo. That was thrilling to see. I'd also given him a magnifying glass. When you look closely at that painting, you see, behind the dogs and their game, up on the wall, only semi-illuminated in the smoky darkness, a framed image from the *Kama Sutra*, if the *Kama Sutra* were all men."

He was still smiling blissfully toward me, though his eyes were half closed. There seemed to be a little tremor in his shoulders.

"My sentry," I said.

He opened his eyes, not understanding for a moment. Then he knew. Opened his mouth wide with delight. Laughed.

I went up my square spiral stairs, smiling. Darkness and light. And the house: it rumbled all night long.

I awoke in the morning, early this time, feeling uneasy about confessing my fantasy to Amir and queasy about Armando's presumed demonic possession, wondering whether there was something about the house itself that inspired such . . .

The house. How long had we been in this humourious house? The day I'd come out of my exile, just one week before, had felt like maybe early June. Was that possible? Late spring? Almost summer? That would mean we had all been here just over five months.

It was starting to feel like more. Much more. Decades more.

But if that were the case, surely Amir would have painted something we could see on his wall by now, no matter how small.

I recalled with a start that today was the day of the studio crawl. No wonder I was feeling uneasy. Forget about angels and demons: artists were going to be showing their art today. Who knew what hell-hounds would come snarling to the fore? Meaning jealousies and rivalries and insecurities, of course. Hopefully not more bodily possessions.

We were meeting in the garden.

I changed swiftly into fresh clothes and made my way down to the second floor. When I came out of the bathroom, I noticed, just outside Ángela's open door, several discarded animal cages of various sizes. She had been receiving as many as ten shipments a day for most of the previous week, pushing toward the studio-crawl deadline, and now seemed to be adding finishing touches to her interior earthworks project. Inside the transformed and transforming studio, I saw Ángela herself, sitting on a bag of sod and having a conversation through the door of the bathroom with someone I could not see.

I could have sworn I heard her say the word *annulment*.

Looking past her, I saw that she had taken the exposed, torn interior of the tree – pale orange colour – and smeared it with a thick layer of pitch, presumably in an effort to keep it living even as it hung down through her floor like a child-god reaching through a grate to retrieve a ball. I tried not to stare, but alas, it was my only trait, and I finally saw that the interlocutor in the bathroom was Armando, who appeared in the doorway and then, gibbon-like, swung down onto the bough. He was still wearing his fitted sheet, buttocks exposed, Ángela looking down at him through the hole in her floor. I could not tell the expression on her face, as she was turned away, but the stillness with which she regarded him suggested a pleasure that was all in the eyes. Then he swung back up to where she sat and took her by the waist with a force that made her shriek with laughter before they disappeared into the bathroom.

So, possession or no possession, they were no longer quarrelling.

Coming around the corner toward the stairs, I saw Hannie Van der Roos's door shut tight. But then, at the bottom of the stairs, Sanam's was ajar. She was just inside, surrounded by her menagerie of brilliantly coloured Arabic words. I thought for a moment that she was alone, but then I caught a glimpse of some movement by a far wall and saw that Esther was there too, albeit somewhat camouflaged. It looked like Sanam was working Esther into the art. I supposed the girl was not being quite as careful as she might have been, with no one but me to worry about, not her father looming frantic in the doorway. He had yet to arrive. Would be here soon.

I saw enough of the child to make out the trick:

Esther was wearing clothes that blended with the surrounding colours, bold lines and words. Her face was not painted, but all she had to do to hide herself was turn to face the wall and the black of her hair would blend in with the extra-bold weight of Sanam's book hand.

The way she was moving when I saw her, I thought she was trying to mimic the animals . . .

I thought I glimpsed something else too.

If you were a film aficionado in Canada in the late seventies or early eighties and attended a movie theatre showing a cutting-edge animation by the National Film Board, the experience might have been akin to something I saw (or thought I saw) in that moment when I peeked through Sanam's door. A playful, sometimes figurative, sometimes non-figurative animation running along the walls of Sanam's studio: one self-contained jumble of colours and words and solid black lines was being fluid in space and seemed to be pursued across the walls by *another* self-contained jumble of colours and words and solid black lines that was fluid in space: bodies and not-bodies, two-dimensions occasionally busting out into three as they made their chase.

And they were shapeshifting as they went: a cheetah pursuing another cheetah transforming into a squirrel pursuing another squirrel.

One was constantly ahead of the other. The chaser seemed to be blind to the chased, she never seeing him but always intuiting and leaping and arriving too late and giving up and becoming despondent, then hopeful, intuitive, imaginative, and leaping again.

It seemed to me that if the chaser were to ever catch the chased — i.e., if the children were finally to meet — it would make the fall of an ash tree feel like the lesser event.

And then Mr. Lin appeared through the front door looking careworn, anxious. He was accompanied by Ella Unton Bride, who was herself laden down with supplies for the garden party. She dropped a number of bags in the kitchen and then disappeared into the front office while Mr. Lin came straight to Sanam's door, just as I stepped away. But Sanam would not let him in; she never let him in, and he was sworn to respect these boundaries. So, standing outside the door, Mr. Lin placed a paper bag on the floor, pulled a green package out of it and said, presumably to

Esther, "I have here organic cotton candy, natural pink of colour, derived from beets, I believe? It is your favourite. It is so good, even I cannot resist it."

I wanted so badly to look into the studio again to see whether there was any movement against the wall. But alas, I could not. The door was open, but Sanam had dragged her stepladder to the doorway to show she meant business in barring Mr. Lin's entrance. She'd even sat on a step like a sentry, but now kept her head down, presumably in an effort to give the man a bit of privacy for his paternal pleading.

"I am going to eat some," he said. He ate some.

"It is delicious."

No sound from inside the room.

He pulled out another package.

"I have here," he said, "a package of toffees made from tapioca syrup, cane sugar, and natural peppermint oil."

Nothing.

"They are soft and extremely delicious. They have no adverse effects. No meltdown-inducing food colours or any of that dastardly sodium benzoate."

A long pause. He hovered over the bag. There were other confections inside.

Presumably aware of all the listeners around him, Mr. Lin abruptly switched to Korean, speaking earnestly for a few minutes without making reference to the paper bag or its contents.

I don't know what he said, but I'm going to provide a translation anyway.

"I know you think it is a poor father who keeps secrets from his daughter, secrets regarding things that are clearly of great significance to him. How can his daughter be important to him if he keeps something of such significance from her? But his daughter *is* important to him. This is simply a fact. You are important to me. But you must understand the impossibility of my story! You will not believe it. No one can believe it! And yet it remains significant to me. I am not in control of it, and it is hard for a father to reveal any loss of control to his daughter.

"Then again, I seem to have lost control of you. Still, I am simply not yet prepared to tell you all my secrets. But the day will come. You must trust me, the day will come."

He paused and listened, did not attempt to look past Sanam, waited a bit, looked disappointed. He must have imagined his daughter sitting at a table just inside the door.

He switched back to English.

"Today is our garden party. Our so-called studio crawl. This was your idea. Perhaps you could come out for it."

Then he turned, brooding, ignoring me, and headed back down the hall to his front-room office.

PART SIX

PROVENANCE

*The record of the ownership of a work of art.
A complete provenance accounts for the whereabouts
of a work from leaving the artist's studio to the present
day, and the nearer a work's pedigree approaches this
ideal, the more secure its attribution is likely to be.*

Esther Lin did not come to her father's garden party. At least not at first. No one came at first, except for me and Jan Komárek, standing with umbrella drinks beneath the blazing sun of a beautiful day. Everyone else was fashionably late. Not even Ella Unton Bride appeared from the front office. I wondered what sort of work she might be doing in there, besides waiting to answer the door if Scotland Yard came calling for Armando. As a gallery owner and an art dealer, she must have been busy around the clock. I wondered whether she felt compromised by Mr. Lin's failures and fakes. I wondered whether she had been involved in our kidnapping scheme from the beginning. Or whether Mr. Lin had suddenly sprung it upon her and she went along out of longstanding loyalty. There were clearly aspects to it that made her uncomfortable — Hannie's confinement being the principal one. So what was it that kept her on board? Was this her revenge project too?

Dealers are like real estate agents. Where houses are concerned, some are half-eaten by termites, have a foundation full of water or wiring that appears to be grounded but is, in truth, twisted onto knob and tube just behind the drywall. Sometimes the seller isn't even aware of the con; sometimes the seller was themself screwed over by a shady electrician in the past. But, as with art forgery, there's always somebody who's going to know the truth. Not necessarily the homeowner/artist: Ezra didn't know; apparently Hannie didn't know. As for me, I knew, of course, and so did my dealer. My dealer convinced a second dealer, and that second dealer had all the conviction of the true believer: that second dealer was the one who convinced the buyer.

So I wondered: had Ella Unton Bride been involved in Mr. Lin's bad purchases? Had she been that second dealer?

Ella Unton Bride may not have shown her face at the garden party, but the chefs kept her supplied with plates of everything they were putting together for the rest of us: samosas and dev-illed eggs, chicken kebabs, beets and feta on toothpicks, bacon and tomato wraps, garlic shrimp, hamburger sliders, prosciut-to-wrapped cantaloup. There was enough food for fifty people. Perhaps the sentries were going to show up.

Out in the garden, butterflies, four of them, azure blue, were fluttering around like they had been provided, and, of course, maybe they had.

Still, no one came.

"This is awkward," said Mr. Lin finally, to me and Jan. "I will admit it."

"I disagree," said Jan, biting into a devilled egg. "I'm having a wonderful time."

And then Amir walked into the backyard, dressed in his work clothes, and said, "I assume we're starting on the second floor with me? Unless my friend Olive has changed her mind and become willing to show the erotic phantasmagorias she has hinted at so tantalizingly?"

Here I blushed the colour of carthamin, regretting my whole nocturnal exchange with the Persian cad, who stood grinning ear to cursed ear.

"No?" he continued, after an excruciating pause. "I would like to excuse myself, then, so I may go and make my preparations."

Mr. Lin allowed it. Amir took a couple of garlic-shrimp tooth-picks and made his way back into the house.

He passed Hannie Van der Roos, who was coming through the open backyard doors. I half expected her to be on the arm of an angel, but she was alone and had not adorned for the occasion: jeans and the weathered black leather jacket I had seen last week. Just behind her came Ángela and Armando (er — Not Armando?). So now we were almost all met, though Mr. Lin kept an eye on the darkness beyond the sliding door.

Armando was possessed of a big-handed restless energy, hair curly and groomed, wearing a wide-collared shirt. He had finally gotten rid of the sheet, and there was something infectious and infernal hanging about him. But was he really still possessed? He looked like himself, really like his best self: a best self I had never actually seen before, since he had been the host of a hijacked house ever since I'd met him. All the anxiety and discomfort had left him. He was no longer fretting over his Goya failure. Demonic possession was, perhaps, becoming on him.

Ángela, like Amir, was still in her work clothes. She pronounced herself ready for the studio crawl. And then Sanam came, finally, wearing the thaub that had been given to her by Ella Unton Bride. Mr. Lin looked beyond her with hopeful expectation, but she was alone, asking after her brother.

"He is waiting for us upstairs," said Mr. Lin, brushing aside the disappointment and worry etched all over his face. "Perhaps everyone should take a drink and we can make our way?"

And so we went. Inside, through the gallery and the kitchen, down the hall, past Sanam's closed door with its enclosed filial and familial mysteries, up the stairs and down the hall again, coming to a stop at Amir's door.

Amir was sitting inside on his little chair, turned toward the wall. When we arrived, he turned around to perch lightly, facing us, making a performative gesture toward the empty walls.

"You see me in an empty studio," he said. "Ta da."

He took a bow before going on. "No, that's not all there is: I am going to give you a presentation, and the presentation is myself, perhaps just as hard to see as anything I've performed on the wall. You all know I am a miniaturist; you cannot make out any of my work because I have not yet covered enough space for you to see the cumulative effect with your naked eye."

Here he paused and looked pointedly at his sister.

"My time here has made me realize there is much to be done. I worked for most of my life to get good at what I do. I even left behind a great love because he was such a distraction from my work."

I assumed he meant the big, strapping Canadian geologist, and Amir confirmed my suspicion by looking at me significantly, as if to indicate how the temptations of Canadian geologists were somehow my doing. I found myself wondering if this big, strapping Canadian geologist also played hockey.

Amir heaved an outsized comical sigh and carried on.

"But for all that," he shrugged, "I wasted a lot of time on forgeries to make some ready cash. Where did my life go? I believed . . . You know, I really believed I'd eventually be the one who'd bear witness to true winged angels. I believed they'd come on down from their hidden regions to have a drink with a bum like me. I believed they'd sit themselves down beside me at the bar and hand me a cup made from the very clay that fashioned Adam and Eve. Then I would take it and raise it up . . ."

Sanam spoke up. "You're translating that old poet."

"Hafez," said Amir.

"That's just an old fable, Amir."

"Yeah, I believed it though. Except those angels never even revealed themselves to me. Bastards. They've kept their secrets to themselves. My name was not on the lot they drew."

"Don't feel sorry for yourself, brother!"

"Is that the message on your semaphore? Don't feel sorry for myself?"

"Pah!"

I looked over at Sanam. She looked annoyed but also troubled, like she didn't know the right response to her brother's shifting mood. He was playing but also not playing.

"We should try to give up our little war," she said finally. "I can't redo the past."

Amir gave his sister a *never mind* gesture. Then, abruptly, he hopped up onto the chair and performed a soft-shoe dance, surprising in its elegance, on that little square. He finished with a flourish and stepped down, soft as a cat, indicating that his presentation had ended and we should move on. Sanam looked like she wanted to go to Amir's side, but once again he waved her away.

Mr. Lin took his lead, and we turned away from Amir's open door. I felt a flutter of relief that no one was going to suggest heading up my square spiral staircase.

As we headed down the hall, Amir fell in beside me, shuffling, all energy drained from his body, hands hanging limp at his sides like implements he was discarding. I chalked it up to how I would have felt if I'd presented my studio today. He noted my attention and tried to rouse himself, flashing me a swift bright grin that retreated into gloom a moment later. Finally, I threw my foibles over, took his hand in mine and squeezed it as we headed into Ángela's studio, coming into the leafy shadow of her vast hanging bower.

If this scene were a picture you were standing before in a gallery somewhere, you would feel enveloped by the very tree of life: There were birds here, with nests. And there were little garter snakes. Just beyond an enormous beehive was a large spider sitting in the centre of her web, close enough that I imagined the hive and the spider engaging in perpetual struggle. The web was huge and extelligent — that type of braininess that fires through the things you build rather than storing itself inside a cranium. I've always felt I had this sort of intelligence. I imagine a lot of artist types feel this way. I wouldn't say I was otherwise stupid, but I do recall a boy in middle school — in the time before my sister drew a bead on me — who looked at a pretty drawing I'd just made and declared, "I can't believe something like that can come out of someone like you." It has quite honestly remained the single greatest compliment I ever received. How does the dim bulb produce a blinding light? It is a mystery of the universe that could solve any energy crisis you could name.

As for the creatures that might have occupied the cages by Ángela's doorway, I did not see evidence of them, but they must have been here somewhere, tucked into the crevices that conceal them when humans congregate. Or perhaps the cages had never been occupied in the first place and were simply to make us think of the possibilities of what might be there. Artists can be masters of misdirection, like magicians. Still, there was little doubt that Ángela was an artist who had brought a broken tree back to life and was nurturing within it a power to lift the house right off its foundations. Not now, perhaps, not tomorrow. But the tree gave the sense that it was growing and girding itself for a hefty undertaking. Who knew where we would end up.

There was an unfortunate mitigation in all this effect. Ángela had allowed Armando to doodle everywhere, and I was shocked to see that he'd done a lot of damage over the course of a single day of collaboration. The work was not up to any standard one might associate with Armando. He had stripped the bark along the widest section of the trunk and covered it with an array of ugly, thick-lined cartoon bees, using some sort of wood-burning tool that was still there, dangling from a cord. High school shop class–level aesthetics. I could only assume Ángela had allowed this because she hoped his work would come off like street art rippling through her jungle. But the results were horribly out of place, compromising the dignity of the fallen ash like a drunkenly acquired tattoo.

I saw it as evidence that Armando was still possessed by a vain, insecure, untalented demon.

Miraculously, however, Armando/Not Armando's contribution did not destroy the full effect of Ángela's masterpiece. In fact, it seemed as if the Spaniard himself — or his body — dangling playfully from a branch, was meant to augment her artistry: as if Eve had decided to hang back in the garden of Eden with an anthropomorphized serpent and let Adam go off to bungle the world by himself. The serpent's amateurish contribution was, it seemed, a small price to pay.

I noticed that Amir, beside me, was as inspired by the vista as I was. It was energizing him, as art sometimes does, and giving him a second wind. He broke away from me, making to step lightly over the low fence the workmen had set up around the hole in the floor. I think he wanted to hop up onto a bough, to be a part of the scenery somehow, intending to perch there as he sometimes did on a chair.

But he tripped. The toe of his shoe caught the top slat of the fence and his arms flung out into empty air toward the bough. Mere moments earlier, in his studio, he had appeared to defy gravity as he spoke of angels. Now he was falling into the open space between floors.

THE FALL OF THE RED ANGEL -
oil on canvas, Marc Chagall, 1923-47, Private Collection.

He dropped the length of the storey and landed on a pile of books that Armando (the real Armando) had covered with a tarp, barely missing the twenty-pound sledgehammer lying in the middle of the floor.

After a moment of shock, we all rushed back out into the hallway and down the stairs to Armando's studio. Sanam hurled herself ahead, driven to be the first at her brother's side.

But she was not, as it turned out, the first at her brother's side.

I was close to the rear, just behind Hannie, she just behind Mr. Lin, who had been joined in the lower hallway by Ella Unton Bride rushing out of the office. In front of them was Jan Komárek, who was next to Sanam as she came to her fallen brother. I was distracted for a moment, looking up and realizing Ángela had not come downstairs with us. She had rather climbed down into the tree where Armando was still dangling. The demonically pos- sessed Spaniard looked distracted and bored, but Ángela was wide eyed and pale, focused on the fallen man. I looked back and finally saw the small figure kneeling by Amir's side. It looked to me for a moment like some kind of devil out of a Bosch painting, except Amir was conscious and looking up at it, recognizing it. It was only when the mysterious spectre turned its head to look up at us that I recognized him too. I saw the calligraphic characters across his body, nearly transforming him, it seemed, but not really, not at all really, since he had been lured away from the only place where his camouflage succeeded so brilliantly: Sanam's studio.

Mr. Lin stepped forward, ready to sweep Sanam out of the way and confront this young stranger in his house of forgers. Who was this boy?

Amir spoke from the floor: "Gently, Mr. Lin."

And then another voice: "Father, please. Now is not the time."

Esther was behind us all, standing in the hallway, also painted in colourful camouflage. She stepped into the room, walked through us and, practically shoving her father aside, came up to Ezra and held out her hand, nodding for him to take it.

In their prolonged chase, she had finally caught up to him.

"I heard him cry out," Ezra explained to her. "I heard him land. I had to come."

"Thank you," said Amir, enclosing the boy's fingers with a hand whose delicacy I had never noticed before.

But Esther had eyes only for Ezra, with that laser focus I'd always seen in her. "The grownups will help him," she said to him. "Let's go back."

Ezra looked up at her. Through the streaks of coloured paint I saw how thin his face had become, how he'd grown one or perhaps two inches since I first saw him in the doorway seeking a bathroom. I saw how his eyes had become a little sunken, a little sad.

He said, "Do you think he's going to be okay?"

Esther nodded.

Ezra looked back at Amir.

"Come," said Esther. "Let's go back to our game. Let's go back. Let's run through the animals."

"I knew something was chasing me," said Ezra. "Or someone. I didn't know it was you."

"Sometimes you caught up to me, going around, and then it was you chasing me."

"And then I slipped past you and you were chasing me again."

"It was fun. Let's go back."

"But I have the name of God written on me—" said Ezra.

"It's not—" said Amir, trying to reassure, but the girl and boy did not hear him.

"— and I'm a rabbit shooting through the whole animal kingdom, between the legs of zebras, over the backs of alligators and blue whales, bringing a word to the four corners of the room. You too?"

"Me too," said Esther. "Let's go."

Ezra was still hesitant. "But is it not dangerous to play when you have the name of God on you?"

"It's not the name of God," said Sanam, gently. "You needn't worry."

"What is it then?" asked Ezra.

"Merely a stand-in. Just gibberish."

"Let's go back," said Esther gently.

"Will he be all right?" He looked back down at Amir.

"Just come," she said. "Just come. The grownups will take care of him."

The fallen Amir smiled up at the boy, patted his hand and gestured for him to go.

Ezra smiled back at Amir. Then, finally, he took the girl's offered hand and rose to his feet as Sanam knelt down, finally, by her brother's side. Esther led the boy toward the doorway as the rest of us fanned away like courtiers.

As they came into the hallway, Ezra turned, sought out Jan Komárek and said, "I don't know how to thank you. I've felt so free, even if it was a bit solitary. It doesn't feel so solitary anymore. Thanks to you too," he said, looking back to Sanam. And then he looked up into the tree, found Armando and waved, thanking him too.

Armando/Not Armando waved back, looking confused, humbled and proud.

The two children walked down the hall and back into Sanam's studio.

"Am I correct to infer," Mr. Lin asked, turning his attention finally back from his daughter and her friend, "this was the forger of the Charlotte Salomon gouaches?"

Sanam conceded that he was.

"But he is just a boy."

Indeed he was a boy, we all agreed.

"You've been hiding him."

We all acknowledged that we had.

"I had been given such hope," said Mr. Lin, "to catch the occasional glimpse of him inside a painting. But now I'm not so sure. It seems no more than a conjuring trick."

"Why should that be important to you?" asked Sanam.

But Mr. Lin waved away the question. "And my daughter too. Is she in the painting or out of it? And he spoke of the animals as if they were real. Is it real or is it a trick?"

Sanam shrugged. "You will have to ask the children."

Then she turned to Jan Komárek.

"Is it real? Or is it a trick?"

"I agree it's hard to say," said Jan Komárek. "I agree that you will have to ask the children."

"But nobody will allow me to talk to the children," said Mr. Lin.

"I assure you," said Sanam, "you will be allowed to talk to the children."

"How?"

"There is a plan."

"What if I do not agree to this plan?"

"It's your daughter's plan. It is, of course, up to you whether you choose to go along with this plan."

"I will confess," said Mr. Lin, "that one of the qualities I appreciate about forgers over the conventional artist is the priority they place upon wit."

"It's because wit is worthless," murmured Amir.

"And priceless," said Sanam.

Mr. Lin went on. "So here I find myself at the mercy of your *plan*."

"Your daughter's plan," said Sanam. "But good. We will get to your beloved daughter's plan in a moment. First I must attend to my little brother."

Sanam leaned in close to Amir's face and spoke some tender words in Farsi, to which he replied with an expression that hovered between devilish grin and a childlike pout. Then the milk sister turned back to the rest of us and said, "He believes he's hurt his back and his leg. But he thinks, with my help, he'll be able to get up. I'm certain he has a bigger concern, though, I can just tell; but he won't say what it is."

Then Amir turned his head and looked at all of us and said, "*Kheylee ma'zerat mikhaam.* I'm so sorry to have made a scene."

"Why all the sudden humility?" said Sanam. "Truly, brother, you're scaring me."

"Well, you see," he said, "it has come to my attention in the past few weeks that my hand is beginning to shake."

"What?" said Sanam.

Amir smiled, happy to bask in her loving concern. "It's a deep tremor, sister. Bell's palsy or Parkinson's or something of that nature. And so of course now I'm in crisis, thinking of all my ambitions, all the things I've wanted to do, not just upstairs but also in the world, in my life. You have no idea."

Sanam paused for a moment, looking at him.

"What?" he said.

"I do," she said. "I do have an idea. I have always been interested in your projects."

She turned to us. "My brother has always wanted to find a way to crawl into a nutshell and call himself king of infinite space. Even before he found miniaturism, his projects were always of a certain type. I was so often delighted by what he got up to."

"No, you weren't," said Amir, closing his eyes, relishing the attention.

"Once," she said, still to us, "when we were children, he took me up to the roof of our apartment building, in Tehran, in our Behjat Abad neighbourhood, to show me a project he had secretly undertaken: attempting to create the illusion of a reflecting pool for the stars. He had broken down several salvaged refrigerator boxes and littered their sides with hundreds of shiny bottle caps and pull tabs. It was beautiful in the daytime, but he had worked on it at night so he could keep it a secret and also so he could see the sky map he was emulating. Now he said he needed my help because, as a final detail, he wanted it to shine like the stars, but alas it did not: the art he had made in homage to the stars could not be seen by them."

Sanam recalled that she'd not been sure she could help but had felt flattered to be asked. Together they developed a plan to steal a bag of thin candles from a shipment that was dropped weekly in front of a nearby Armenian Catholic chapel-sized building, which was apparently a cathedral. And they'd pulled it off too, the theft: but then they realized they would never have enough matches and that anyway the wind would blow the candles out. Amir was in despair until Sanam made the crucial realization, at long last, and later forgot again and again, that it was enough for her to tell Amir that his creation did not need to be seen at night, that the stars would not see it anyway since they were so far away, and anyway the stars were there in the daytime too, but none of that mattered because the work was beautiful and she loved it.

"You love it?" he had asked.

"I love it," she had replied.

Now he asked, eyes still closed, "You really did love it?"

"I really did love it."

Sanam went on. "That was it. He took my word for it. He takes my word for things. Sometimes, it's true, I can be ungenerous and withhold my word."

She went on with her story. "When we tried to return the unused candles to the church, we got caught! Fortunately, the man who caught us was a member of an Armenian cultural organization who was actively trying to generate interest in a new Boy Scout initiative in their neighbourhood. The upshot," she concluded, "was that Amir had to spend one summer in the late seventies practising a new language, learning the location of Ararat, and struggling with how to tie decent knots.

"He wanted to emulate the stars. He thought the stars were more worthy artists than he. He thought I was a more worthy artist than he. Maybe if I had really encouraged him, not just in that moment but also afterwards, maybe he wouldn't have become an art mimic and ended up here with me. What I did, I'm not sure I ever even considered it art or mimicry or anything. It was just a job. I did it for the money."

"I did it for the money too," said Amir.

"Be that as it may, brother: I will put down my money-making tools and come collaborate with you. I promise you that together we will forge that world you want to make: the one so small, painted on a wall, with everything that exists contained within it."

"But I can't anymore," said Amir. "I think I'm done."

"Yes, you can," said Sanam. "I am going to assist you, so what will it matter if your hand shakes a little from time to time?"

"You don't have the training," said Amir, but his voice now held a hopeful note.

"You will train me," said Sanam.

"You would let me?"

"Why not? I need a new set of limitations. What could be more limiting than my annoying brother always at my shoulder saying, 'Do this, do that'?"

"I don't want to be at your shoulder. I want you to guide me."

"I'm afraid you will have to guide me first."

"With semaphores?" asked Amir.

"Too close for semaphores," said Sanam. "You will guide me

from beside me. We can start right away, but I need for Mr. Lin to see my studio first, finally, and for him to tell a story. I suspect you will not want to miss his story."

"What story?" asked Mr. Lin, who knew what story.

Sanam ignored him. "Do you think you can get up?" she asked Amir.

Amir nodded, eyes still closed. The milk sister took his hand and helped him to his feet. As he leaned into her, she held his head close, speaking into his ear with tones we could not hear, though I could swear I felt the alto resonance of her commitment coming up through the soles of my feet.

I stole a glance at Hannie Van der Roos. She was listening patiently too, just as engaged as the rest of us, giving nothing away.

Then, with her arm around Amir, Sanam moved to leave the room and gestured for us to follow.

We arrived at Sanam's door and saw that Ángela and Armando were coming down the stairs to join us. Ángela stopped to take off her shoes with everyone else. Armando/Not Armando took off his shoes too, didn't bat an eye despite our host's previous ire at being asked to do so in his own house.

255

In the doorway, Sanam turned and asked Mr. Lin to step into the room and find a place to sit on the floor among the menagerie.

"Where is my daughter?" he asked.

"In good time," said Sanam, "she will reveal herself. But she has something to ask of you first."

"She wants me to tell my secret," said Mr. Lin. "My secret story."

He sighed a heavy sigh.

"Yes," said Sanam. "She would like you to tell her the story of why you are here, and what it is that we are doing here."

Another sigh. And then another.

"Well," he said at last, "I find that perhaps you are somehow, against all odds, making headway in your collective task. All of you. We shall see, of course . . . We shall see . . . So then . . . perhaps no harm will come from me telling my tale. Perhaps it is time. But it's not a short tale. Are we prepared for the fact that it is long?"

I looked around. To me, the only relevant answer to that question would be from Amir and Sanam. The milk sister had settled herself on an arrangement of throw pillows. Her brother was reclining beside her, also on pillows, with his head in her lap. They seemed prepared for a long story, so I pronounced myself content.

Mr. Lin moved on to his next preparatory (and perhaps procrastinatory) question:

"Presumably, from his mysterious perch within this room, the young Ezra Coen can hear me as well?"

"I believe he can," said Sanam. "We are all met."

It was true. Even Ella Unton Bride was here. We might well have been back in the front room on the first day. Today, Mr. Lin was far more hesitant than he had been then. More uncertain. When he finally began to tell his story, there was no *adlocutio*, in the manner of Caesar or Napoleon or Ángela demanding an annulment. He barely moved, sitting cross-legged on the floor.

"This story is about a part of my life that may or may not have been . . ." He paused and shrugged bitterly before carrying on. ". . . a fake. But if it was fake — if it was a fake life I am going to tell you about — then I have done you all a dishonour, because that makes me, like you all, an unrepentant counterfeiter. Because I here assert that I would give away all my wealth to have that former fake life of mine back again, keeping only the one person of this world for whom I tell this." Here he raised his voice a touch to ensure his daughter would hear: "The one person in this world whom I dearly love and hope to see again when my story is done.

"But before I begin, since you are all here, I should confess there is one of you who already knows this story. I'm wondering whether that person would mind if I revealed this fact."

After a moment, there was a small "Ahem."

"No," said Jan Komárek. "I don't mind."

Jan: his skills had brought us here. Perhaps I was the only one who knew that. Well, and it had long been clear to me that he was privy to secrets about Mr. Lin's chaebol family. I really don't want to sound smug at this point in the story, but his involvement was not a surprise to me.

Still, by the looks on the faces around the room, it appeared there would have to be an explanation.

"Thank you, Monsieur Komárek," said Mr. Lin. "To the rest of you: I know I have told you I purchased one of his forgeries, but that was an artful lie, alas. That particular piece by Damien Hirst resides in the Artists Rooms collection at the Tate, under lock and key. It has never been faked, a feat that, really, would be impossible. I already knew that, so he never had to fool me with the image that resides in the Matamoros Gallery, which was always just a photo of Monsieur Komárek posing with himself.

"So. A year ago, I made a visit to Prague to purchase a painting by the great Czech artist Josef Čapek — which later turned out to be a fake — and this brought me into the circle of our friend, Jan Komárek. Monsieur Komárek was a magician who wished to mimic the life and career of John Dee, also known as the Queen's Conjurer, famous magus of sixteenth-century England and Bohemia. As part of his research, Monsieur Komárek wished to travel to London and needed a sponsor to get him there.

"I asked Monsieur Komárek just how accomplished a conjurer he was. I told him, among other things, that I was reeling from a catastrophic run of purchasing multiple fakes, including but not limited to each of yours. I didn't know any of you, of course. How could I? Your fakes were signed with the names of other artists. He asked to see these forgeries. I had them sent for. He spent the night in his studio with all your paintings, and in the morning, he had your names, addresses, emails, Facebook pages, Twitter accounts.

"Mind you, he turned out to be much too loyal a Bohemian to ever expose the forger of my Čapek, who was presumably his countryman. And there were others, from my part of the world — Korea, Malaysia, Mainland China, Hong Kong — that proved to be beyond his ken.

"But you: all of you: he found all of you. He said he did it by conjuring an angel who could see the painter hidden behind the painting. An angel who runs down thieves."

Hannie Van der Roos began to protest, but Ella Unton Bride spoke up in just the same moment.

"So that's how you found them," she said and then realized she had spoken out loud, blushed and brought her fingers to her lips, turning away, gesturing for Hannie to carry on.

Hannie, after looking at Ella Unton Bride for a moment, said, "This is just it. I am not a forger. I never hid behind anything.

It has always been a profound insult to me that I should have been placed among this company. Your angel — or at least your conjurer — was wrong."

Glancing quickly at Ella Unton Bride, she added, "And your dealer was remiss to not speak a word in my defence."

Ella Unton Bride was blushing crimson now, looking at her shoes.

"Ms. Unton Bride has suffered too," said Mr. Lin. "As my dealer, she has shared my every shock, my every betrayal. And I will say as well that she did indeed speak in your defence. All your anger and accusation should be directed toward me alone. Not to her, and not to Jan Komárek."

"And so I do," said Hannie. "I do accuse you. I don't know what kind of story might justify our confinement, but this is my life."

"My apologies," said Mr. Lin, hopping up from the floor and giving Hannie a small bow. "You are free to go," he added, "though I would appreciate it very much if you would stay."

Hannie was taken aback. She moved toward the door, surprised and confused by the swiftness of his response.

"But," she said, "I don't understand. Was that the story?"

"No," said Mr. Lin. "That was not the story. A preliminary detail, merely. Would you like to stay to hear the story?"

"I . . ." said Hannie. She looked around at each of us.

"My offer will never be rescinded," said Mr. Lin. "You will be free to go when I finish."

Hannie put her hand up onto the doorframe and studied her fingers. Sighed.

"In that case," she said at last, "I will stay."

"Very well," said Mr. Lin. "Make yourself comfortable. Truly, I should say you will all be free to go. But, as I said to Ms. Van der Roos, I would appreciate it so very much if you would stay."

And so he began.

"My belief, my new belief," Mr. Lin said, settling again on the floor, "as I have watched my child grow, is that with art comes

the creation of the world, organically, spontaneously, serendip-
itously, joyously.

"On the other hand," he continued, "there was a priest named
Henri Breuil who believed that, when humans first painted the
walls of Lascaux, it was for entirely practical reasons: the point,
he thought, was to bring power to the hunters so they could
kill and eat all the bears and bulls and mastodons. This, to Pére
Breuil, was the purpose of prehistoric art and, one might suppose, of all the art that followed in the history of the world. His
theory fascinates me. Art as a means of gaining power over the
world. More like summoning demons than art, don't you think,
Monsieur Komárek?"

Jan smiled his enigmatic eyes-apart smile.

Mr. Lin went on.

"Picture a young man, born in Seoul, during a time when his devastated country was being rebuilt, to a poor but resourceful clan that grew into one of the big families in the south, one of the chaebols that brought our whole country up out of the ashes. This young man was given a cosmopolitan education because of his means and also because of the understanding that he would one day become the heir to a vast fortune, along with its inherent responsibilities. But he grew instead into a man whose first priority was art.

"Imagine him as a young man with his whole life still ahead of him, realizing he is going to enter university in the fall, and so he decides to travel the world for a spell, visiting all the great galleries, first in the East. He visits Hong Kong in the month of April and finds an obscure gallery there, located in a former monastery. Imagine, if you can, that while looking at a painting there, he perceives a figure in the upper right corner, beckoning to him — a young woman with pins like a pair of phoenixes in her hair. She is accompanied by two servant women who follow her every movement and attend to her every whim.

"When he first perceives the beckoning, he thinks it is merely a painted detail to draw his eye. But in the next moment he realizes that no, the woman in the painting is truly gesturing to him. He looks around to see that he is alone in the gallery, then his hand goes instinctively to his chest in the well-known *you mean me?* gesture.

"You must believe what I'm telling you. The woman in the painting: she nods. And now the young man starts to believe he has been given this sudden opportunity because of being in the right place at the right time, and also possibly because his hair is swept back in a certain way. This is how he has caught her eye.

"And so, somehow, he manages to step up, to enter the upper right corner of the frame, and then he journeys down into the body of the painting together with his new companion, accompanied by the two servants, and he remains there for some time. I hesitate to say how long, really, not yet at least. You'll see.

"It was once written, by Leon Battista Alberti — the first artist to ever to set down words about two-point perspective — that there could never be so many stories in a single painting that nine or ten persons could not perform them all in a stage production. The curious thing is that Signore Battista wrote these words down in Latin and published them in Latin. But then, when the time came for him to translate this popular work into his native Italian, he cut that singular assertion. I have often wondered why he did that. I have often wondered what he may have witnessed that could have changed such a view, specifically whether he had experienced what I did: a painting of a courtly staircase within a palace that was big enough within the painting, but in fact featured an entire world stretching out in all directions beyond the limits of the frame: populated by millions of people, with a kingdom and a court, a port city, working men and women, soldiers, rebels, boatmen, sailors, the sea, and the whole great globe, a sky with a moon and stars, a sun that rose and set, allowing for days and weeks and months to go by, as they did for me, all beginning in the arms of the courtly woman who just happened to notice how I had combed my hair that day. Try to apply that to your theories about two-point perspective.

"I see now how I have given the game away by identifying myself as the young man. Oh, but you could have guessed. Still, for the sake of decorum and my own hastening heartbeat, I shall continue in the third person.

"Within that painting, the woman took the young man by the hand and led him into the world beyond the frame: down alleyways and through doors and out along the edges of courtyards, all part of the same single magnificent palace, through clouds of fragrant dust as flower petals blew like snow all around them, up a small staircase into a hallway and a private room for a few precious hours, leaving her two servants standing guard at the sliding door painted with ducks.

"After those lazy, lustful hours were done, as he lay on her bed, nestled in down-filled blankets, he was startled to hear a cannon and then some commotion in the hallways of the palace. He looked out the window at an unfamiliar landscape, though his eye was drawn to billows of red dust rising on the road outside the city gate. To put it bluntly, there was an army coming, led by a rebellious general, signalling the end of one royal dynasty and the beginning of another. Because he did not share a language with his paramour, it took the young man some time to understand that this whole world he was encountering for the first time stood on the precipice of radical change. But he observed with some alarm the haste with which she opened the golden cage of her parrot, brought it to the window and tossed it to the sky. Then she threw some garments into a sandalwood box, stuffed a hundred pieces of jewellery into her bodice, and then — I still shake my head to think of it — she slid open the door and shoved our young man forcefully into the hallway.

"He fell to the ground, only partially dressed in his semi-formal André Kim, and was shocked to hear the crack of a cannon ball hitting a nearby wall.

"He looked up to see the wide-open eyes of the servants, who still stood by the door. One looked away and then down at her feet. But the other held out her hand and nodded for him to take it. He fumbled to find his footing, grasping the servant's hand like a lifebuoy, and together they ran, without looking back, not down the stairs he'd climbed earlier, but up and up and out onto the roof, where she finally let go of his hand and gestured for him to follow, stopping briefly to exchange snatches of information with other running servants, some of them leading children, others holding up their infirm loved ones. The young man followed the woman like a beacon as she led him from one roof to another, leaping over narrow passages and scrabbling up gutters. Occasionally he would glance down from the high path they followed, to see people running willy-nilly on the ground, white flags everywhere. His guide stopped short and pointed into the chaos of the city below until he made out the billowing purple canopy of a carriage rattling its way through a large gate. She made a display to him of her empty hands, then gestured the removal of a crown firmly fixed about her temples, mimed hurling it into the ditch; and then the young man understood that this carriage carried the emperor, who was fleeing the city.

"They continued over the rooftops until they came to the high outer wall of the city. Freedom was there, one long ankle-breaking leap away, assuming the rebellious army would not care to stop a desperate pair heading in the opposite direction of their thrust. The young man wondered about the palatial staircase onto which he had first been beckoned. Would it be destroyed in the fighting? Did he have to return to that place in order to get back to his museum-drifting life of late-twentieth-century Hong Kong?

"He looked to his guide. She was sitting on her heels, looking back at him with hooded eyes that hid some expression she did not yet want to reveal. Why had she saved him? What did she seek in return? She pointed to the field below, the forest beyond, a distant river, mountains. And then she slowly shook her head and spoke for a long time. He didn't understand a word of what she said, but he felt she was speaking of her past life in this city, the time she had spent in the service of that woman of the court, her longing to leave that service, the thrill to the senses that she had now accomplished that, along with the certain knowledge that her life was now over. Her fierce pride in finally, after a lifetime of servitude, taking something that was just for herself. Meaning him: she meant him. She had taken him for herself. With his mysterious clothing and wavy hair. And now they were at the end of the road.

"She rose to her feet, startling the young man as she approached him, placing her hands, one against his chest and the other behind his shoulder blade. And in this firm and gentle way, she drew him to the ground. Reaching into a bag, she pulled out a delicate blanket, presumably stolen from her mistress. Then she bunched up the bag, settled it beneath his head, placed herself beside him, pulled the plain bamboo combs out of her hair, wiped the green paint from her eyebrows and rested her head ever so lightly, so, so lightly, upon his chest. Her hands continued to do their delicate work even as she lay there, pulling the small blanket around them both. She drew up a leg and placed it over his body. She held him after that, like a pillow. And she closed her eyes, resolutely, and went to sleep.

"And, after some moments of wondering what he might do and what would become of them in this strange and violent place, the young man closed his eyes, and he went to sleep too."

After hesitating a few moments to take possession of himself, Mr. Lin went on, once again forgetting he'd been speaking in the third person.

"To understand what happened next, you must imagine that what I've been describing so far has been a painting you're looking at, or perhaps a series of paintings; and so you must also imagine, when I describe what happened when I woke up again, that you are looking at a whole new series of paintings. Do you understand? Perhaps there were hints and details of these other paintings in the one I had first stepped into, foreshadowing what would happen to me, and I had simply not seen them. Perhaps there was smoke off in the distance, or perhaps someone on that grand staircase was pointing and crying out, akin to a figure out of Señor Matamoros's beloved Goya. *The Disasters of War.* Perhaps there were particulars up in the corners, hidden away from the inexperienced eye, such as what you might find in the art of miniature cultivated by our own Amir Haghighi."

Here Mr. Lin tipped an invisible hat to the siblings before carrying on.

"As it was, when I awoke in this servant woman's arms, I felt that the hair had grown on my face. The two of us were stiff and curled up within tufts of wheat sprouts that were poking up through the roof. I assumed it was the same roof we had laid down on, because how could it have been a different roof? Still, my clothes were different than they'd been before: rags, really. Time had passed, albeit in a strange way. What else can you expect from stepping into a painting?

"And she was dressed differently too, also in rags, no longer the formal garments of a servant to the elite. I looked at her, and in the moment before she turned her head to meet my eyes, I saw her gazing at the sky, her eyes following the path of three geese flying toward the south, and I thought to myself: I know this woman now. How have I come to know this woman so well?

"Her name was Lin Xue.

"I was confused at first; my memory was faulty, but my knowledge was sure. I began to sense that it was likely we had been captured after our initial sleep, that we had spent time under the brutal yoke of forced labour. How then were we back here on this roof? Had we escaped again? I looked at my hands, felt the weight of them. They were rough and heavy, padded in layers of callouses that must have taken months to form. My neck was sore, my back thick with brawn. When my guide — whom I no longer thought of as my guide but rather my lady — when my lady touched my back, I felt unfamiliar furrows and ridges meeting her hand, welts that had been raised there and then healed and then raised again. She spoke to me, and I did not understand her. I spoke back in the Korean language of my twentieth-century life. My words were full of love and longing and familiarity. Her eyes widened, tears welled; she did not understand me! But her touch brought a thrill to me. Time had surely left its mark on my heart. It was only my feeble mind that did not recall it.

Lin Xue had not failed to touch me, to love me. I could sense it. Like a hint of perfume triggering a memory. But alas I did not recall it.

"We got to our feet and were able to look farther than our immediate surroundings as the carnage of the city became apparent. The palace we had run from was a shocking ruin, a hollow shell compared to how it had been when I last saw it.

"Just in that moment, I saw a fox chase a rabbit, distant as bugs, up the remnants of the very staircase that had ushered me into this place. Everywhere we looked, we saw white flags flying, stamped with the bold calligraphy of an ideogram shaped like a snarling tiger coiled to spring. I looked at my companion again. She pointed down over the edge of the roof, and I followed the line of her arm, saw a regiment of men armed with lances and swords, swelling through the laneways below us like a flood. Behind them was an even larger swell of prisoners, men in rags like the ones I wore, each man holding a greenish bit between his teeth as he stumbled along. Somehow I knew that the city's preoccupation with this parade of prisoners was what had afforded us the chance to make our escape. There was information in my mind, I just could not locate it in the moments when I remembered who I'd been on the outside of this painting, looking in. But there must have been other times when I was fully present with Lin Xue and could not remember the young man who is now an old man telling this story to you.

"My companion, my saviour, my leader, my guide — my Lin Xue — had seen enough in this last look at the broken city that had been her home. She took me by the hand, and, with the sun overhead, we stepped from the rooftop onto the wall that looked out toward the east. I thought for a moment that we were going to jump. I tell you now: if she had gestured for me to jump, I would have jumped, sure as I sit here before you. But there were rugged flat-topped stones jutting out of the rampart, hidden in plain sight, artfully placed so a climber could cling to the wall and make their way down. And so we descended, slowly, she ahead of me, showing where to put my hand and then my foot, until we finally came to the land below.

"She led me away from the city on a dirt road heading east. We were hungry, and there was no sign anywhere of cooking-fire smoke. Still, though the occupying army's scout patrols passed us from time to time, they paid us no mind, left us alone to make our way. What we must have looked like, to be permitted to walk away from that high wall. We held our hearts in our mouths until we had climbed the slope and entered the shelter of the trees.

"There was another great gap in my memory, and now we were deep in the countryside, had been there for days. No hills anywhere around us. I know it can't be true, but I sometimes believe it was my dear companion who caused time and space to change according to her will, even as she held me steady within her place in the universe.

"We were standing by a river. Xue was negotiating with a boatman. It was early in the evening. He was going to take us downriver. I sensed that this was a chance to move swiftly through a devastated land, to arrive somewhere the war had not touched. Full of hope that a way had been found, we stepped into the boat. The boatman was pushing away from shore. But then he pushed his oar against a bloated body that revealed itself in the weeds. The boatman's oar had gotten caught, and so he wrenched it back and forth and then pulled it out, drawing a torrent of viscera. He was just going to move along. We shouted at him, protesting the desecration of a body. He yelled back at us. Our cries were so basic, so raw, that we might have been speaking the same language.

"The river was running with blood. We demanded that the boatman place us back on shore. He finally did, cursing us before taking his leave. And then Xue enacted a small ritual to honour the dead — collecting a bundle of sticks with which she created the crude outline of an animal in the dirt by the bank.

I understood it was meant to be an image of a sacrifice in place of one we could not make.

"I saw that she was wearing men's clothing now, had been wearing it for quite a while, how long I could not say. Some time had passed, I realized, even since our descent from the wall.

"She finished her ritual. She looked at me, smiled, shrugged. We walked back into the trees. I felt I had understood every word. I loved her. Where did this feeling come from? I would have done anything for her. I would do anything for her. I will do anything for her.

"Another night followed, and a day, and then a week and a month. We still moved through a land devastated by war. We met an old man once, dressed in weeds. Lin Xue gave him some rice gruel, and I was angry with her because I wanted us to survive, I wanted us to thrive, and it didn't matter to me if the land-scape we walked through was empty of living people. I preferred it, even. The gruel was our hope. But I saw by the way she bent kindly toward that man that she wanted a world full of people; she wanted harvest and celebration and kindness. She wanted a society where the elderly could be comforted. I saw by the way she spooned the rice gruel into that old man's mouth that she wanted art and medicine and music and story and community. I was ashamed of how I had felt and proud of her strength. I would follow her always and leave the husk of this old selfishness by the side of the road.

"One day, we came to a decimated town. There had been a thriving market here; nothing remained but fallen fences and weed-covered gardens. An old shrine lay just above, presumably having stood guard over the town for centuries. Cypresses had once stood around the shrine providing shade, but these had recently been hacked down, leaving only stumps and a few hopeful creepers. Still, my companion lingered, and she spoke right out loud to the spirit she believed to be there. She raised her voice in passionate indignation, and I was shocked to realize

I still did not understand a word she said. When she looked back at me, though, and saw my confusion, I could tell she was disappointed but not surprised. This incomprehension had become a regular quirk in my behaviour, to be tolerated. What I would have given — what I would give — to know what it was like when I was fully present, knowing her world, understanding her language. I began to wonder for the first time whether there was a whole other man, a man from Xue's own time, and I was merely a spirit who occasionally, fleetingly, took possession of his being, like an angel come down from the future. Or a demon.

"But then, whom did Lin Xue love? That man? Or me?

"Was I a parasite, a water crawler, skimming along the surface of an ocean fathoms deep? If so, I had not left selfishness behind. I was clinging to another man's love, another man's commitment and strength, jealous of him to whom I clung, desperate to take his place in the full company of this woman who had thrown her fate in with mine. No matter how deeply, magically, I had penetrated this painted world, I was no more than a patron in a museum, not ennobled by the work, merely standing before it in a ridiculous outfit. Or worse: a counterfeiter.

"But can a counterfeiter never have pure intentions? Can a counterfeit never also be legitimate? How can a counterfeiter make themself legitimate?

"Desire and despair grew within me. Up ahead I spotted a crag and a cliff jutting over our path. I saw how by running ahead and doubling back onto the hill, I could easily get up to the summit.

"I thought, desperate, thrilling, hopeful: perhaps I could find a way to tie myself permanently to this place.

"I cried out to my companion, scrabbled up along the path, gesturing wildly back toward her as she turned to look at me, trying to say, 'It's all right. I have an idea. I think I can fix this. We will be together, you'll see!' Trying to convey all that in my own language as I ran. She must have thought I had gone mad. I had gone mad.

"I managed to get to the cliff without much trouble, rushing several hundred metres down the path to a switchback that made a steep climb, then using my fingers to clutch at tufts of grass through the final ascent until I reached the outcropping, seeing Lin Xue come into glorious view below me. I stood high above her, feeling the bright burning of absolute conviction, made one final gesture of confidence, love, devotion, commitment. And then I threw myself off.

"In the next swiftly passing moment, I felt the rush of that mistake, the press of life and squandered joy trying to push up against me with all the strength of feathers as I fell through the air like a stone. And then my body slammed the ground, scattering a pile of rotten bamboo. I felt the shattering of a vertebra in my spine as the blackness rolled down over my eyes.

"When I awoke, it was night. I found myself unable to move, tied to a makeshift litter propped against a rock, surrounded by frost and reed flowers. Xue was crouching beside me, hand on my shoulder, speaking low into my ear as she placed bits of rice gruel and bramble berries in my mouth.

"You might think that, at the very least, my foolish sacrifice had communicated to Xue the certainty of my love, the devout wish for me to be fully, bodily present here. You might think too that my gambit had worked: that I would finally stick to that earth and stay there, hold to it and to the person I knew I loved there, rather than blipping in and out like a radio signal from far away.

"And, perhaps, even, it did work. Perhaps I would have been completely present in that place from that day until the end of my days. Perhaps even my shattered spine would have healed, and perhaps I would have stood again on my two feet, learned the language, bound myself properly to this woman as she had bound herself to me, and gone on living in this beautiful place that was currently suffering under the heel of a rebel's boot; but it would not always be like that. And perhaps we could have done our part to make a better world.

"Alas, my beloved Lin Xue: she had misinterpreted my gesture.

"She was kneeling by me, speaking low, close to my ear, explaining to me, as the tears rolled down her face, what was going to happen. I did not know what she was saying. I did not know what she was going to do. I had a bad feeling about it. I could do nothing to stop it.

"She roused herself, and then she grasped the ropes tied to the bamboo sticks lined up on either side of my head. She turned and hauled these ropes over her shoulders, hoisting me up so my head rested just behind her shoulder blades. And then, as I began to realize the horror of what she was planning for us, she set to walking, down the path, back in the direction of the rebel-held city we had escaped.

"What foolish plan had I begat with my extravagant, self-destructive gesture?

"I began to speak to her. She did not understand me. I told her to stop. You would think such a demand would be clear in any language. She did not stop. She walked, pulling all my weight with the forceful roll of her hips. I begged her to stop. I begged her to turn back. I begged her to leave me there by the side of the road rather than risk walking back into a city that had enslaved her. I became delirious, spinning fantasies where I saw her leaving my crippled body in a cave somewhere deep inside those mountains, with the light of a torch that would burn all through time.

"She did not heed me. Days went by. Weeks. I never once felt the gap of time. Perhaps if I had, the body I occupied like a demon might have been able to communicate the reason for what I had done. But I was caught here, just me. So I kept talking. I babbled about a bootleg cassette I had of Kim Hyun-sik, a young performer I'd seen in Seoul before heading off on my travels. I sang her a song from it. 'I Am the Wind': the words telling of a man soaring so high among the clouds that he cannot be touched.

"She did not stop, though I like to believe she slowed her pace to follow the rhythm of my singing. Perhaps if I had slowed down my rhythm, she might have slowed down more too.

"We passed towns and rivers. Burnt-out granaries. Devastated fields. She walked night and day, through people sleeping in clumps among frost-bitten flowers. Every human being we came across, if moving, was walking in the opposite direction. We entered a copse I thought I recognized and then eventually came out into a widening open road that I did not recognize at all. I understood, as she dragged my litter along, that we had travelled much farther to the east than I had realized and I didn't know the landscape we were moving through.

"I could never see what was in front of us: only the canopy of the trees above and behind, and then only the sky, which carried only birds, scrolling by like the top of an ancient watercolour landscape.

"I saw the city wall as we passed through it. Then we were inside and, for the moment, invisible. There is nothing like the sight of a human labouring under the burden of another human to inspire indifference.

"I was not familiar with the terrain from ground level, remembering only the vista from the rooftops. I could not tell where we were going. But my impotent rubbernecking drew the laughing attention of some men at the roadside who began to amble over. Xue cocked her broad-brimmed hat sideways and affected an ambling squat, taking on the aspect of an elderly woman as she hopped and scuttled along, weaving around these hard-bitten men like so many puddles of beer and mud and urine.

"Then we came to the palace. The one with the staircase. I could not think what was at the top of it. Lin Xue threw her bags down and began to drag me up. What did she think was going to happen? I told her to stop. I told her she did not understand my wishes and desires. I promised I would not be a burden, that I would carry her one day as she was now carrying me. She kept ascending that staircase, bumping and sliding the bamboo shafts of my litter as she made her way up.

"I began to squirm within my bindings. And there it was: my arms could move, my legs could move! In pain but mobile, I raised my head and shouted for Xue to stop. Could she not see that I wanted her to stop? Could she not see that I was on the road to recovery? Why were we here in this terrible place? This city of Chang'an? Safety was to the east, and everyone knew it. But how did I know it? How did I know the name of the city? Chang'an. The city was called Chang'an. I turned inward and saw that there was more to know, more to remember: so, so much more. All the numbers had been filled in, just like that, as I tore at the bindings of my litter. In my gasping, pleading desperation, I was remembering the days, the things I had learned; my brain was brimming with phenomenology. And I was remembering the language: entering, at last, into the inner chambers of knowledge. My foolish gesture of loving self-destruction had not been in vain.

"I began to shout, in the real language — the strange Cantonese dialect of that place — all the information that was coming to me in a torrent: 'This is the city of Chang'an. I know there has been a terrible revolt here. Led by a salt thief named Huang Chao. He drove the emperor from the city. We were captured and enslaved. You, Xue, were so afraid you would be forced into prostitution, but that did not happen because you were a mere servant and that terrible subjugation was reserved for the elite. You and I laboured in menial tasks for petty officials. I shovelled shit in the horse stables and was whipped for my slovenliness until my back grew strong; you worked in kitchens, sometimes told with a laugh that you were mincing and cooking the livers of human beings. Who knew what the truth was? You were groped and mishandled, and we saw each other at the end of long days, when we plotted and planned. At first our talk was all gestures, but then I learned! I learned! The salt thief held the city for a few months and then fled when other governors attacked. But the soldiers of those governors were no better than the rebels, burning more and taking more and whipping more and committing more outrages and falling down drunk in the streets. So the salt thief came back and killed them all. We thought we would root for the government, but in the end we rooted only for ourselves. During the chaos of this second attack, you and I were able to flee the city. We walked a long road, upon which I became disassociated in time and place, as if I were an imperfect angel who did not know how to live always in the present moment. So my memory splintered, scattered across the landscape and could not be recovered until now, until now! It must have been such a chore for you. But I am here! I am here!'

"What I should have said was 'I love you. Don't make me leave you. I love you. Don't make me leave you.'

"Xue had set me down on a wide step in the middle of the staircase. There were sprouts coming up through cracks all around me, holding bits of tattered brocade. Suddenly there was a crush of people there. Men and women. My shouting had drawn them, bringing more shouting, and more. Xue rounded on the crowd, ready to fight them off. I was sitting up, loosening my bindings. I knew I would find my feet. I knew I would stand and fight beside her.

"And then, swift as a dream, I was back in that gallery in Hong Kong."

Mr. Lin looked up at us, tears in his eyes.

"It had all — the whole thing — unfolded over the course of a few minutes, during which time I had stood in reverential contemplation of this painting of the staircase and the woman. Now I looked again and saw only the grand staircase, the still image of the woman on the staircase. She was half turned away, maybe about to look toward the viewer? I did not know, I did not care: her servants kept their backs to me. The servant that mattered, the only woman in the world who mattered, kept her back to me.

A few swift, coloured smudges, that's what she had been reduced to. And there stood I, gargantuan, agape. Desperate for any information I could get, I looked at the inscription.

"Anonymous. Ninth century. China. Tang dynasty."

Mr. Lin paused.

"But now I see I have forgotten again to recuse myself from this story. Well, I wish I'd had such problems when I was with Lin Xue. I certainly never meant to recuse myself from that story with her. She believed I wanted to, but I did not. And here I stand before you on my own two strong, sturdy, old-man legs.

"I have taken her name. The name I have given you is not my family name. I have taken Lin Xue's name: my wife and companion, leader, moral compass and guide. Adopted mother to my adopted daughter, if only they could ever meet. A thousand years apart and more.

"I have tried, so hard, to return to that place. I will tell you how:

"When I became aware, standing in front of that painting, that I was no longer inside it and had been returned to the present, well, what do you think I did? Of course I tried to get back. Imagine that: imagine the sight of a grown man trying to leap into a work of art hanging on a museum wall. How fortunate that it was securely mounted, though I believe I may have done some damage to the substrate. But there were, naturally, security guards, whose job it was to protect the art from unhinged men like me. I was escorted from that place, summarily banished from that museum for life, lucky not to be detained and imprisoned. It would have caused a scandal in my family, and my status would have transformed. I may have welcomed such a demotion at the time, but it would not have been to my benefit in the long term, once I realized that my need to return was a long-term goal.

"I travelled to Xi'an, the city that had once been called Chang'an. I spent a year there looking for my lost Lin Xue's home, which I remembered now, along with the rooftop where we had huddled, the staircase, the grand palace. None of these things were to be found. And again I was thrown from the top steps of art galleries out into the streets, sometimes so violently I nearly broke my back a second time.

"Eventually, I stumbled home, a failure, hair grown long, relishing my ragged appearance: it reminded me of the places I had visited that were etched in my memory if not my body. There was no trace, for example, of scars on my back from all the whippings I had endured in the city of Chang'an."

Mr. Lin hesitated again. "My apologies for this indulgence, but I believe I have to return again to the use of the third person. Otherwise I shall not be able to proceed."

He went on.

"And so the young man — who, I will tell you, no longer felt so young — he spent his life trying to reclaim that lost life, always asking himself: What happened to Lin Xue? What happened *next?* She had been alone in that rebel-racked city. On that staircase, surrounded by shouting people. While it was possible to say that her lower status would keep her safe, one could not really say for how long. This young man could not stop thinking about Lin Xue.

"How was he going to do it? How would he strive to regain that lost time? Why, he became a collector. That's how. Ha. A collector of art.

"But he was instinctively, inexplicably, maddeningly drawn not to anything authentic, but rather to counterfeits. It was surprising how good the fakers were at mimicking the styles of the ninth and tenth centuries of Chinese art. It was an industry, an assembly line practically, the markets flooded with so much ancient-feeling fakery it threw an entire genre of painting into question. Still, his early failures did not deter him. He bought worthless painting after worthless painting, getting burned again and again, bringing deep shame and embarrassment to his family name, experiencing financial ruin, at least within the strict boundaries of his monthly stipend.

"But after one decade of this, and then another decade, and then another, failure transformed him again. Whereas before he had been ready to scorn all the money and power that were his birthright, now he wanted to rise to it, be ready for it. Now he found he needed to move that mountain of power as a distraction from his failure to return to the paradise from which he had been banished.

"He showed up at the office of his father's automotive kingdom — he was a grown man on the latter side of his forties now — and demanded to begin his apprenticeship to power. His father agreed, albeit not in the way he had anticipated: the prodigal son was put to work on the floor of a factory, forced to heed the commands of a cruel foreman.

"This proved a far easier test than his father realized. Automotive factory labour was nothing compared to what he had experienced in Chang'an. And he would always be grateful for the time spent among the workers because he was able to reclaim some semblance of responsibility within himself and fulfill a promise that gave him the great gift of fatherhood to a beautiful daughter. This is a whole other story. My daughter knows this story."

Mr. Lin hesitated, clearly hoping Esther might respond.

After a moment, he went on.

"It was not long before he took over the business, and not long after that that he left his dreams behind and let fatherhood consume him, let himself drift away from the stochastic, granular time that had been uncovered by that artwork in Hong Kong, that had uncovered Lin Xue.

"But, alas, his run as a buyer of fakes did not cease.

"And, perhaps it won't surprise any of you to learn, with each purchase, with each revelation of deceit, he was drawn away from his salutary domestic condition and back to that time when he had stepped into a painting and entered a world and fell in love, with all his heart and soul, all his being — and then was hurled out of that world.

"Was that a fake too? Was this what fate was telling him? If that is what fate was telling him, then why not let him let it go?"

He looked up at us.

"I thought you all might help me. I honestly did. I thought if I could dig down below the roots of all your counterfeits, then perhaps we could create something authentic together. Something as real as Lin Xue is to me. I thought you would recognize the rightness of that without my having to tell you any tall tales.

"But now that I have come to the end my story, I have also come to realize how this whole thing has been just one of my many follies in an effort to reclaim a lost time of youth that was itself nothing but a vain, idle dream.

"I repent. I hereby pledge to turn all thought, all action and all life to the nurturing and the love and the life of my daughter."

Then, still sitting cross-legged on the floor, he placed his face gently into his hands.

We all waited, hardly a breath let out into the room.

And then, we all saw, there was a movement of colour and light against the wall, and there was Mr. Lin's daughter, stepping away from the thicket and moving into three-dimensional space toward her father.

Another figure was there too, forming in her wake. Ezra.

Esther walked, silent as a brushstroke, to her father and placed her hand gently on his shoulder. Mr. Lin looked up, and his hand moved instinctively to cover hers.

And with great tenderness, indeed with an affection I had never seen her express before, Esther drew him to his feet. As he stood, he turned and saw and smiled at Ezra, shrugged charmingly at him, and said, "The last thing I expected to find in this house was a young friend for my daughter. It is really very nice to meet you, Ezra Coen."

Ezra held back and looked on with the rest of us, but then Esther gestured for him to come, so he did. He followed close behind the father and daughter as they stepped through the doorway and down the hall toward the back of the house and out to the garden, in private conference.

The rest of us just stood and watched, following a moment later at a discreet distance, allowing them the time to make their way.

I would like to here assert, before I move on, that I had never quite felt the strangeness of time and the world before, quite in the way I was feeling it now. I don't know how much I should say about this. I can't say I'm very good at self-analysis. Whether Mr. Lin's story was true or not . . . I mean, was the story true? Or not? Could a person reach back in time as easily as looking at a painting on a wall? Whether or not it was true, I was myself changed by it. It cracked me open, especially after he walked away from us, strolling with his beloved daughter. I was left filled with a sort of ache. Of the how-did-we-get-here, where-did-we-come-from, what-are-we-for variety. I wanted company, and so I was open to the company that presented itself to me.

Sanam was holding her brother again around the shoulders, the pair having risen from their pillows, keeping in close conference. Rather than following us outside, the siblings decided to make their way back toward the stairs.

Once we were in the yard, I cast a glance toward Armando, who stood pensive by Ángela's side. She was in no hurry to go anywhere, looking toward the back of the garden where the Lins were walking, but Armando/Not Armando seemed distracted, wide eyed, unfocused. Perhaps there was a thing or two in that story to give a demon pause. Still, I think he also must have been urging Ángela to return with him to her bower. Eventually she seemed to relent, and he looked relieved as they made their way. I suppose the demon, like the toddler, is a creature of routine.

Ella Unton Bride had slipped away as well, presumably back to her front office.

And so there were three of us left at the party. Jan had drifted over to the food table and was scooping up bundles of prosciutto-wrapped melon, leaving me in the company of Hannie Van der Roos.

Hannie, on the precipice of liberation, did not appear to be in any hurry. Still, she seemed so aloof she might well have imagined herself alone. That is, until she turned to me, so unexpectedly I think I might have let out a small gasp. And when she spoke, with her usual inexplicable affection that I did not deserve, there was added a tone of someone who finally felt confident and assured of her status.

"You should know you are not invisible," she said. "I have made less-than-subtle attempts to indicate this fact to you, on more than one occasion, but it never seems to sink in. Which is all to say: I can see you looking at me."

And then she added dryly, "Just in case you were wondering."

I was taken aback. It took me a few moments to recover. Hannie was awaiting a response. I finally came up with:

"I love your work."

Hannie paused for a moment. "I beg your pardon?"

I took a breath and resolved not to stammer:

"I, I, I believed you from the beginning. That you weren't a forger. Because I love your work: Maybe I don't understand it; I don't know whether it's punk or protest or what any of that means, but it reminds me of myself. I, I, I, I feel that you are drawing *me*, urgh . . ." (an involuntary utterance conveying inadequacy). "Not that you are consciously drawing me, of course, but . . . that you understand something about me. And those faces are all staring too, staring at me. Pinned to your chest or . . . or I've glimpsed them too through . . . through your door, occasionally, before you . . . before you turned them all to face the wall . . . which I also saw . . . but I still recall the feeling of their eyes on me. They were like me. Also, do you think the story Mr. Lin just told us is the truth?"

"Yes," said Hannie, "I do think what he told us is the truth. One could say I even have evidence of his truth."

"What evidence?" I asked.

She said, "I want to return to the subject of my work."

"Oh!" I said.

And then she sighed.

"You have disarmed me by blurting out high compliments, like a series of belches after a meal. I am unsettled, I am aflutter. I could slap you or give you a kiss. Very disconcerting." This last she muttered under her breath. She had been looking away from me, but now she took a deep swift breath and looked at my face. For a moment I saw her eye, black pupil swimming in a swirling green nebula, looking right at me, into my eye, which suddenly felt like a single eye, like the cyclops, me, staring back, and her eye was startled and startling.

The stilling of a panicked bird.

Now it was my turn, once again, to be taken aback. "I, I, I don't know," I said. "I don't think of it as a compliment. Who cares about me?"

"Well now," said Hannie. "To be honest, *Who Cares about Me* would be a perfect title for my whole collection."

And then her expression cracked into a moment of levity.

"I would like to see those drawn faces again," I said *bravely*. "I know you keep them sequestered in your room."

"Come then," said Hannie, apprehensive and welcoming. "I'll show you."

"I—" I said.

"I beg your pardon?"

"You mean, to your room?"

"Where else?" She was amused now, enjoying my terror.

"But," I stuttered, "is there not — not — Do you not have a —?"

"Are you coming?" she asked. "Or not?"

PART SEVEN

DYING GAUL

*A celebrated marble statue in the Capitoline Museum, Rome,
showing a wounded warrior supporting himself wearily
on one arm. It is a Roman copy of a Greek work in the
Pergamene style of the late third century* BCE. *The statue
is sometimes called* The Dying Gladiator, *but this is a
misnomer, as the hairstyle and accessories are scrupulously
Gallic. It was first recorded in Rome in 1623 and was soon
famous. After visiting Italy in 1644–5, the diarist John Evelyn
wrote that it was "so much followed by all the rare Artists, as
the many Copies and Statues testifie, now almost dispers'd
through all Europ, both in stone & metall." It was among the
works removed from Italy by Napoleon and was in Paris
from 1798 to 1815. Unlike many once famous antique statues,*
The Dying Gaul *is still admired, particularly for its pathos.*

53. *EPHEMERAE*

And now I was departing the yard with Hannie just as Mr. Lin and Esther were circling back, with Ezra following a few feet behind. The girl turned and gestured, and the boy came forward and took her, once again, by the hand.

And I entered the humourious house, which was far quieter than it had any right to be. I was with Hannie Van der Roos, and we ascended the stairs to her room.

54. RAHMIEL

Upstairs, behind that door, Hannie turned all her pencil, conté and charcoal pieces around, calling the images back from their banishment to face the room. And then she took my hand with a grip that nearly sprained my baby finger and drew me to her bed. I was ~~a virgin and~~ afraid, but I was — oh, what's the word? Consenting. There were not a lot of sensations involved for me other than the sensations of my heart, but she had ointments and tinctures and poppers and devices that strapped around her waist and then pinned me efficiently to the mattress. She was neither too gentle nor too rough, and I was left constantly confronting my sense of my own ugliness and being told it didn't matter. Why was this happening to me? How was I allowing it? Had there been an angel here before, and had I supplanted that angel? Had I supplanted the angel but switched roles so I was the bottom whereas the angel had clearly been the top? Am I using these terms correctly? Hannie was making of me a puppet. I was on my stomach, and as she moved above and behind me, I lifted my face from the dent in the pillow and saw a pair of eyes looking at me from the wall — a scribble in black that looked like it might erode away to pencil filings in a gust of wind — on a face that was long and sad, with a frank expression, resigned to its confinement within a halo of white paper. I felt I had seen this drawing before. Perhaps when Hannie had first arrived at this house with Ella Unton Bride and had dropped her sketchbook.

And then — was I imagining this? — the eyes in the scribble seemed to bulge and then roll up and down. Then they looked past me, as if trying to pretend I wasn't there. Though it was clear from their discomfort that I was.

I was there. Even if Hannie's ecstatically drawn drawings did not want to see me.

Hannie flipped me over again so my eyes were back to pulling in all the bouncing light of the room. More than half the drawings had vague outlines of skulls and other bones beneath the sense of their skin. And they were all looking at me.

I said, "Can we turn the images back toward the wall?"

"Why? Are you the angel of mercy now?"

I did not know what that meant. "No, I just feel as if they are looking at me."

"It should be a simple exercise for you to recognize that it is you, rather, who is looking at them."

"I'm saying they're looking at me."

"But they're not. You are looking at them and seeing yourself."

She ignored my desire to turn the images back to the wall, and we carried on. But the eyes were still tormenting me. First one and then another and another. Hannie flipped me over again and I was back to contemplating the scribbled face with the avoiding eyes that had confronted me, or been confronted by me, before. There was another pair of eyes too, farther along the wall.

Then I saw a thing about the faces that I hadn't noticed before: when she drew them, Hannie had never lifted the pencil. Each face was a single travelling unbroken line, presumably her own technique, developed over decades of struggle and bliss and joy and doubt. That's what style is, yes? Something hard won? Something you must defend with your life? On the other hand, it was so simple, deceptively simple, it reminded me of the life-studies classes I used to love. I loved them because life studies were never art, just exercises, and an unworthy acolyte like me could scrawl a body for an exercise if not for art. These, though, were all far more accomplished than the rough work you do when you only look at the subject in a life-studies class and not your paper. Were they all like this? All the drawings in the room?

I waited for Hannie to flip me over again. She did not. She had straddled my legs and was working a smooth silicone item into me somehow. It felt as big as the world. Still consenting!

I was left with my contemplation of these two drawings with their eyes averted.

I wondered: what would happen if I followed that line in the drawing that was closest to me? It ended, or perhaps began, with a single strand of hair that played above the forehead. I took hold of it, imagined myself as one of Armando's mice on a skateboard, and began to travel along the line as it looped.

But the idea of the cartoon mouse soon left me because, in following Hannie's line, I began to feel something akin to the experience of the line. As if my hand were drawing the line. The line told me that I was standing in a hospital room, visiting and drawing. The person I was visiting and drawing had just looked away from me because she had just asked if she was going to survive this. But she didn't speak words, rather her hands were swooping through the air.

And then I laid aside my pencil and said some words I didn't understand:

*Ja, moeder, en het is net slaaptijd. Ik zal precies hier zijn wanneer je wakker wordt.**

As I spoke, I felt my own hands moving swiftly, communicating something, fingers like sable bristles touching paint to canvas: signing. I was signing. This was what it was like to speak without sound. Painting without colour or paper.

Hannie had said at some point that her mother was deaf.

This was Hannie's mother.

Hannie's mother looked up into my eyes, and I smiled. My warmest, fullest, most loving smile. I wished I had armfuls of children who would smile at her too and fill her up with life and youth, but alas I was childless and did not. I have never wanted children, not in a million years, but I was so sad not to have them in that moment, if only to let them crawl up and put a little weight of life on this good mother.

---

* "Yes, Mother, and it's just bedtime. I'll be right here when you wake up."

Oh, but these were Hannie's thoughts, not mine. Hannie's thoughts while she drew. So much of Hannie was now in me.

Was I doing this? Was this my power? Or was it Hannie's art? Or was it Mr. Lin's story somehow? Or was it the presence in this house of angels and demons? Did Jan succeed in the task Mr. Lin had given him? Or was this another task? Or, finally, was this a joke being played by the humourious house?

Hannie turned me again, and I saw another picture, also drawn with a single line, leaning against a chair by the foot of the bed. I applied the same line-tracing technique, starting with a single strand of errant hair. But as soon as I got down into the features of the face, I realized I had made a terrible mistake.

Because this was an intimate, erotic portrait of the one and only Ms. Ella Unton Bride, suffused with longing, and I was not worthy; this was too private, not for my eyes, or my hand, or the line being traced by my hand . . .

"You cannot do this to me," says the image of Ella Unton Bride. "I am too young, too impressionable, too vulnerable—"

"I love you," say I/Hannie. (I am not worthy to speak these words or to even think them.) "Stay with me," say I/Hannie. "I will give you anything you want," say I.

"I have a reputation to uphold. If it should get out that I am sleeping with a client—"

"I am not a client," say I. "I am slain by your beauty. I am the great lover of the first act of your adult life. I am the famous Ice Queen, melted by you."

"Why the first act?"

"I cannot live forever, my darling darling."

"Are you saying you're old?"

"I am old."

"You're not old!"

"I'm older than you. If you stay with me forever, you'll see me die."

"No."

"Yes!"

"I'll stay with you forever."

"Choosing me is like having a dog—"

"Shush now, I'll stay with you forever."

"— an invitation to pain."

"Shut up!"

"Oh, now you're angry!"

"I am, stop it!"

"Will you stay?"

"I'll stay. Will you die?"

"One day I will die."

"Oh, stop it!"

"But not today."

"Good."

"Good."

"But you're a client . . ."

This was too private. I was not worthy.

When Hannie was finished with me, she saw how wide eyed I was, how vulnerable I'd become. She allowed a bit of lingering, and we lay there curled in the white comforters as the evening of late spring bathed us in its godly light – golden, I mean golden: golden light.

After a few moments had passed like this, she said, "I want you to know that I'm not really like this. The way I've just behaved. You flattered me. It was your fault."

"I accept full responsibility," I said, in a necessary moment of levity of which I remain, to this day, very proud. Like when I had stood before the Somalian immigrant in the roti shop and denigrated the city of Edmonton, Alberta.

But there was another matter, more pressing to me. Casually as I could but with a swift beating heart, I asked, "Why are you here? What did you do to end up on Mr. Lin's list?"

She said, "I stood in a gallery and made some studies of a like-minded artist. A Canadian artist, as it happens, who recently died . . .

"I didn't copy exactly, rather tried to follow the line my own way . . .

"I did not have any desire to keep them, because they were merely studies, you see. I dumped them in the recycling on the way out . . .

"I can't imagine how our Mr. Lin got his hands on them . . .

"I had seen that Ella had an association with Mr. Lin, so I would have thought she would speak in my defence . . .

"The explanation I always tell myself is that his kidnapping project took her by surprise."

These pauses seemed to indicate that Hannie was contemplating, moment to moment, how much she should confide in me.

After another moment, she went on.

"But it's clear that when we arrived here, together, all those months ago, she already knew . . .

"She had kept it from me . . .

"That hurts me more than the confinement itself . . .

"I can work anywhere, of course.

"But when I found myself here, in your company, and before I realized what any of this was all about, she . . .

". . .

". . .

"She turned her back on me. Just like that. As if I had done something to betray her. But I have not betrayed her. I have betrayed no one. I have been betrayed! And the hurt I have felt in all this is beyond description."

She turned toward the wall to conceal the tears in her eyes, but all her drawings looked on in horror and sympathy.

So Ella Unton Bride had left her lover Hannie when she was falsely accused of being a forger. And, however Hannie's studies had gotten into the hands of Mr. Lin, it was clear that Jan's alchemy had merely identified their maker and not their maker's intent. This, I presumed, was why Hannie was so convinced of the truth of Mr. Lin's story. Because he had believed her too. She was, I thought, returning the favour.

"Do you think we owe anything to Mr. Lin?" I asked. "I mean the rest of us?"

Hannie turned and looked me in the eye, as if to say, *Am I not one of you anymore?*

But then we heard the front doorbell.

If there was ever a rarer sound.

Were they coming for Armando?

"Are we going to have to investigate that?" I asked.

"No," she said, placing her hands tenderly over my ears. She had been propped up on an elbow, but then her wispy short hair was all aflutter as she lost her balance.

Now we heard something else. Two voices, from below us. Low, authoritative, commanding, unfamiliar. New. Resonating through the house.

We dressed hastily. I thought I heard a low cry. We opened the studio door. There was a commotion below, so we made our way halfway down, to the landing between floors, and then onto the lower stairs, peering into the front hall.

I felt Hannie stiffen beside me.

Two police officers were inside the house, in the front hallway. As before, they were wearing masks. Perhaps it was a new uniform policy at Scotland Yard. And they were arresting Ella Unton Bride.

She was standing in front of them, same tight white collar as when I first saw her, same bow tie, repeatedly holding out her pale, delicate wrists for handcuffs, as if she were trying to get it done and get out of the house. But the men were not in a rush. One of them was reading a convoluted statement:

"Ella Unton Bride, we are arresting you—"

Behind them, through the open door, I saw the sunset slanting in from the west.

Ella Unton Bride must have sensed the movement on the stairs, because a moment later she turned and her eyes met the eyes of the woman standing beside me. They made a closed circuit and something passed between them.

I heard movement from above. Someone was descending. Armando. He appeared just above us, shirtless, wearing a robe hanging open and large colourful boxers. Ángela was right behind him. She stopped on the landing but Armando/Not Armando kept thumping down, passing us without so much as a glance, arrived on the ground floor, taking in the police officers in the doorway, and then just stood there in the middle of everything with an expression of open curiosity.

"What is the meaning of this?" came a voice just in front of us.

Mr. Lin appeared from the kitchen; behind him, his daughter, and with her, Ezra. I realized they had likely been sitting in the backyard this whole time.

Jan also appeared, from the basement.

Mr. Lin's arrival appeared to pique Armando/Not Armando's curiosity even more. He stepped out of the way, into the doorway of what might be considered his own studio, seeming to want to give the police a clear view of Mr. Lin.

"Ella, why are they arresting you?"

Instead of answering her employer's question, Ella Unton Bride kept her eyes down and thrust her wrists insistently toward the cuffs that had yet to be placed on her.

"Why are you arresting her?" Mr. Lin was addressing the officers now. "I demand to know."

"Sir, if you could just keep back," said the officer.

"I will not," said Mr. Lin, indignant, taking a step forward. "I must insist that you answer me."

Armando/Not Armando was following the back-and-forth with acute interest.

"You should know," Mr. Lin went on, "that I am the one who set up this *abduction*, if we must call it that. And so, for the sake of propriety, you should be arresting me."

Here everyone drew a breath. Armando pointed at Mr. Lin, wagging his finger. "That's true," he said, in a low laughing growl.

Both policemen looked at Mr. Lin, their eyebrows lifting as one. Finally, one of them spoke up.

"Sir, I beg your pardon: nothing of that description has been reported in this neighbourhood. But let me assure you: if you would just give us a moment, we will give your abduction the attention it warrants."

Behind him, the other officer was talking into his radio.

The first turned back to Ella Unton Bride. "Ms. Bride, with a bit of luck perhaps we can wrap this up. As I was saying, we are arresting you on suspicion of collaborating with a known criminal organization in order to sell counterfeit artwork—"

Beside me, Hannie gasped to hear this confirmation.

Mr. Lin spoke up again: "This is unacceptable. I beg your pardon, officer, but Ms. Bride, my associate and friend, has suffered unaccountable losses by association with my failures, both financially and to her professional reputation as a dealer of—"

The officer, visibly colouring in the cheeks above his mask, raised his voice to drown out Mr. Lin as he continued to dictate his convolutions to the woman he was attempting to arrest. "You do not have to say anything. But it may harm your defence if you do not mention when questioned something which you later rely on in court. Anything you do say may be given in evide—"

He kept talking, even as I saw a visibly agitated Armando/Not Armando grumble, "Now you're just being rude, officers."

From the landing behind us, Ángela replied, "Don't concern yourself, my friend; you have your own job to do."

Armando/Not Armando looked up at her with undisguised devotion. "You'll see, *mi amor:* I need to make a good exit."

From the entrance to the kitchen, Mr. Lin tried to retake the centre: "I say again, I really must object."

And then Armando/Not Armando stepped back into the hallway:

"This unlucky art collector really needs to be put out of his misery. He is wasting everybody's time believing they can help him with a problem not of this earth. *I* could have helped him, if he'd only bothered to ask. But he didn't. And now I'm busy."

The demon turned away from the police to address the rest of us.

"Look at you all, standing there with your mouths open. No, you can't help him. Oh, but wait: who's missing? The brother and the sister. Ha! Looks like someone thinks they can help after all: bravely attending to an empyrean task with failing, mortal talent, desolate and diseased."

Now he addressed the police once again. "We have to put a stop to it. How about you handle the arrests down here, while I cut the oxygen to whatever artistic sputtering is getting underway upstairs, simply by taking up this handy dandy hammer, and . . ."

The Armando demon stepped backwards again through the doorway, and I watched with alarm as he picked up the twenty-pound sledgehammer that had been lying in the studio. He swung it casually over his head with one hand and then grabbed the middle of the handle with the other, pivoted from above to the side and smashed the hammerhead through the wall beside the doorway.

"Ah hah!" he said. "That feels good!"

The officers jumped back.

Armando/Not Armando clutched the heavy sledgehammer close to his chest and bolted for the stairs, maneuvering adroitly around Jan and Mr. Lin in the narrow hall and then slipping past Hannie and me as he ascended. He rounded the landing where Ángela stood, pausing briefly to give her a peck on the cheek. His acumen, the joy with which he shifted all that weight, was astonishing.

In the moment that followed, I could hear, in the distance, the sounds of approaching sirens. Not knowing what else to do, I turned and headed up the stairs after Armando, leaving the two shell-shocked (and unarmed) police officers to decide whether to finish their arrest of Ella Unton Bride. Hannie came with me, holding my hand. We passed Ángela, who had not moved.

Upstairs, down the second-floor hallway, we came upon Armando filling the doorway of Amir's studio, looking upset. The sledgehammer was leaning against the wall beside him and he was speaking into the room with sarcastic deference: "Ah, I see you are working."

In the room itself, when it finally came into view, we saw Amir sitting in his chair. He had not altered his focus despite the threat looming in the doorway, but was leaning forward with his nose virtually touching the wall as he worked. I noticed with a shock that, for the first time ever, I could see some small evidence of his work.

"Hello, Armando," he said, finally. "Are you all right?"

Sanam was there too, leaning back in her chair, resting a bare foot comfortably on Amir's shoulder for balance as she drafted in a sketchbook. They were supporting one another in their respective solitudes, creating the impression of a single delicate architectural structure.

Ángela came up behind us, followed soon by Jan.

"Just annoyed by your working," the Armando demon went on. "You have to stop."

"I haven't got a moment to spare," said Amir, not looking up. Contact with his sister gave him a steadiness he did not usually possess.

"It's futile," said Armando/Not Armando. "I've decided to take down this house of mine and build it again. Your work will be for nothing. Please let me in."

"Let you in?" This from Jan. "Why don't you just go in?"

"Huh?" said Armando/Not Armando. "You stay out of this." And back to Amir. "Just let me in."

Jan addressed Amir. "Don't say anything."

I could hear, behind us, the sirens getting louder. There were many of them. Armando was becoming more visibly frustrated by his failure to gain the siblings' full attention. I was becoming concerned for them.

Jan went on. "He cannot enter unless invited, and so—"

"Silly," said Armando, laughing now. "It's not the room I have to be invited into: it's the house, the house, the house. I am already in the house. I own the house!"

"The distinctions are much finer here," said Jan, heroically calm, "as we are all such different people, each one expressive in a unique way, and we've each made a different world in our separate studios. Our rooms are our castles. Think back to when you climbed into Ángela's bower. Did you not ask to come up?"

"He did," said Ángela. "He was so polite! And now you will tell us what is going on, please."

"I am afraid the transformation of your *miláček* into the polite, considerate, if somewhat impulsive and potentially violent man we see before us," said Jan, "is the result of demonic possession."

"*Quelle surprise*," said Amir, continuing his work.

"No," said Ángela.

"Yes," said Jan.

"My Armando is possessed by a demon?"

"Yes."

"Right now?"

"Right now, yes."

"Since when?"

Jan appeared to be counting on his fingers.

"Last night," he said finally.

"So all his solicitousness," said Ángela, "his willingness to listen, his new conviction to do what I ask him —?"

"All the result of possession by a demon," said Jan: "a demon who must be invited into a room."

"Ridiculous," said Armando/Not Armando.

"Why bother with this room?" said Ángela to Armando. "You have a train to catch."

"Yes," said Armando. "But first I need to get into this room."

"What you need to do," said Ángela, "is what you promised me."

"Indeed," said Armando/Not Armando, "and with pleasure. I promised you an annulment. An an nu llll ment an an

NUL ment.

An annulment is just the kind of story I can get behind. You have to tell it; you have to tell it eloquently: but you only have to tell it in order to say it did not happen. Has there ever been a better purpose for story ever? It is the pinnacle of art practice, the annulment: here, look what I made: it is NOT TRUE. And so," he concluded to Ángela, "I will do it. I will procure your annulment. But I have to put an end to this house and its projects first."

"Please don't," said Ángela.

"Oh, but I must. There is nothing that grates at me more than false hope."

"But," said Ángela, "I have invited nature in."

"Then consider this," said the demon, "to be nature's counter-invitation. Come out, come out, come out, come out!"

Then he took up the sledgehammer as we all flung ourselves away, raised it over his head and slammed it into the floor of the hallway.

The house buckled and splintered like poster board, shaking to its foundations as we wondered whether we should flee. Hannie had tears standing in her eyes as I held her hand, but Amir kept working, unconcerned, his studio untouched. And Sanam sat by him, balanced, one foot on his shoulder, curled around her own work and providing congenial company like the elder sibling Amir had always wanted her to be. And Jan kept watching, unflappable, albeit from a safe distance, as the rest of us crowded around him, panicky as a flock of starlings at an intersection.

Jan, to the demon: "I did not conjure you to destroy this house."

Armando/Not Armando snorted. "You did not conjure me at all, with your doodles and your little spells. Let the angels be impressed by all that. *She* conjured me —" pointing to a surprised and head-shaking Ángela "— to her fallen tree temple, with an achievable task."

No, Ángela formed the pout, the *O. No.*

"The woman conjured me. The man let me in when I came knocking. An angel could not do what I've been asked to do.

An angel cannot take possession of a body. Only demons can do that, taking their cue from nature, from her parasites and her viruses. You should know all about that." He was taunting Amir now. "You're sick. You might as well give up."

"Amir may be weakened," said Jan, "but his power is such that it is you who might as well give up."

"Don't tell me what I can and cannot do!" Armando roared at Jan.

"My sentiments exactly," said Amir, working.

Armando spun around and came nose to nose with me.

"May I enter your studio?" he asked, suddenly still, quiet: hovering between menacing and polite.

"Sure?" I said.

Jan smacked himself in the forehead as Armando/Not Armando spun around and barrelled straight up my angular stairs, sledgehammer thudding against the nosings behind him.

"I'm sorry," I said. "I couldn't help myself."

Jan was dismayed. "Why did you not shout 'Privacy!' as you did once so effectively with our host? It would have done the trick."

"I did not conjure him," Ángela interjected. "I would never do that."

"Not knowingly," said Jan.

"Not at all!" said Ángela.

"You did not burn any incense and express any private wishes in that tree of yours?"

"No."

"No unsavoury cauldron ingredients?"

"No!"

We heard a thump from above.

"Did you, by any chance, scribble the words *eras, niras* and *piralla* on a piece of waxed canvas and place it beneath the threshold of his—"

"No!" said Ángela. "No, no no!"

"Well, it would seem you did something. But tell me: did you not pick up on the change of personal aura?"

"I just thought he'd come around to my way of thinking!"

Another thump. The house shook.

"Please do not be offended by my questions," said Jan. "It is frankly embarrassing for me, a professional, to be shown up like this."

We could hear policemen coming up the stairs.

"Maybe," said Jan, looking up, "he won't get through the ceiling."

"That's troubling," I said. "Because I was going to say something about how my floor, um . . ."

"What?"

". . . sags. A bit. In the middle."

A moment later we heard another thump and felt the house shake again, then another thump, and then another. The ceiling of Amir's studio splintered, and, after a decisive assault, Armando crashed through, tumbling after his hammer, and landed on his side in the middle of the room.

We screamed, we hallway witnesses. Sanam nearly lost her balance, but she found it again. Amir kept working, intensely focused, blithely unconcerned.

Armando/Not Armando stood up. He looked a bit surprised to be in the room and was momentarily distracted by the little pieces of crumpled paper fluttering like snowflakes from the hole he'd created in the ceiling. My unfinished art project. I reached out and caught one.

It was one or Ezra's first messages to me:

Hard to tell how much trouble am in, though? can someone advise?

Amir completed a detail, then turned to finally look at Armando. He was wearing a magnifying eyepiece. When he turned to face us, his right eye was four times larger than the left.

"Welcome," he said. "You may have noticed: I invited you in."

"That was my doing!" shouted Armando. And, lifting the hammer again: "I am going to destroy your work."

Amir smiled. "I'm just messing with you," he said. "As I would with my good friend, Armando Matamoros."

Armando's expression changed for a moment, as if put on the back foot by being called a friend.

And then, behind us, the voice of a police officer we hadn't heard before: "Stand aside, we need to speak with Mr. Matamoros. Mr. Matamoros, we have to ask you to come out with your hands up."

But Armando was still looking at the wall, the twenty-pound hammer held aloft. He hesitated, then lowered his arm again, let out a great sigh and said, "I can't do it. I can't shatter your wall. Why can't I—?" And then a massive grin spread across his face. "But I can—" he lifted the hammer again, over his head. Proscribing an elegant, almost slow-motion arc, he smashed the hammer into the floor with such force that it broke through. He worked it out of the broken boards and swung it again, landing the blow a foot or so away from the first. Then he tossed the hammer aside, leapt into the air, both feet, landed hard and, bringing the collective force of his concentrated mass to bear, went through the floor of Amir's studio, crashing down into the TV room. We all rushed forward and peered through the hole to see him hesitate before the work on the walls of the Matamoros Gallery. We thought he would wreak havoc, but he just lingered there for a moment, long enough for us to rush down the stairs. He must have shaken himself free of the gallery's charms, though, because by the time we got to the ground floor he was running again, out of the house, past the broken tree and into the street, ignored by Mr. Lin who was, just at that moment, watching Ella Unton Bride being helped into the back seat of a police car.

And then Armando just kept going, heading past the houses of Olive Road in a boxer-shorted, asymmetrical, attention-grabbing gallop, followed by a posse of officers, some of them jumping into their vehicles and screaming off.

The only piece that did not survive the rout of the TV room was Jan's, which (the reader may recall) was a false fake, or a fake fake: it was only masquerading as a fake so that Jan might be welcome in our company. The fresh white sheet of photographic paper that we found lying in the rubble, which was supposed to be a forged portrait of Damien Hirst posing with a cadaver's disembodied head, and which had earlier revealed itself (at least to me) to be a photo of Jan Komárek posing with a second Jan Komárek, was mysteriously blank, as if never dipped in the fixers or toners of a darkroom. The only way we knew it was Jan's was on account of the fake note in Hirst's fake hand on the back.

None of the other works had been touched.

"Look, that tree's likely fallen because of the emerald ash borer," said one of the firefighters who showed up a few minutes later. I heard him as I was being led out to sit inside an emergency vehicle. "Look, see? It's got all the tell-tell signs."

"Tell*tale* signs," said another firefighter. "And those might be?"

"Woodpeckers. See 'em? And the way the bark is split in places. And witches' brooms down there by them roots."

"Witches' brooms?"

"A.k.a. water sprouts. Little shoots coming up out of the bottom. See 'em?"

"Yeah."

Armando had run away. Ella Unton Bride had been taken away. Everyone else was escorted out of the house by some of the sizeable group of first responders. We were each provided with a blanket, even though it was a warm evening, and installed inside a van.

I noticed, as we entered the wider world, that Hannie Van der Roos retrieved her hand back from mine and shrunk away a bit. Somehow, though, she ended up beside me in the van. With her leather jacket and shock of hair. But we didn't share a glance.

Hannie was private, unknowable. It was what she wanted. Faced with the prospect of showing an intimacy to the public eye, she chose instead to turn her back on it, i.e., me. I understood it; I could not blame her for it. But I knew it was something she had done. She did not turn her back on no one. She turned her back on me.

I was surprised to see Mr. Lin was still with us. I had assumed he would slip away — like his sentries, the few who had remained, who seemed to have made their escape over the roofs of the neighbouring houses. Then again, he had expressed concern for Ella Unton Bride and seemed to want to face the consequences for his actions. But he could not have known that these actions would suddenly include the destruction of a house.

Our regard for him had been so transformed, in this single day, that we spent the whole time in the van discussing how we might say we were all living in the house voluntarily. But he had already told the police he was a kidnapper, and anyway the wrench in that plan was Ezra, a minor, whose absence from the world, despite an unloving parental figure, was a serious matter.

So then we — or some of us, well, primarily Ángela and Sanam — urged Mr. Lin to take his daughter, step out of the van and slip away amid all the chaos.

Mr. Lin just sat there, shivering ever so slightly in his blanket.

"No," he said finally. "I would not wish to take my daughter away from her new friend. I have been remiss in providing her with opportunities to find such friends. I will be remiss no longer."

"But everything was batshit crazy in there," said Sanam. "Surely they won't recall your really very minor confession about being a kidnapper, given everything else that was going on. You could tell them you were having a bad dream; you could tell them you only said it because you were so shocked by—"

"I will tell them," said Mr. Lin, calmly, "that I kidnapped you all with an intent to foster original art projects in a group of counterfeiters. I will not mention any of what Jan Komárek did, although it turns out he has accomplished more than I realized."

"I didn't do anything," said Jan. "At least nothing of consequence if we are barred from continuing to work in this house."

"I will see what I can do about that," said Mr. Lin.

"I'm in the middle of something," said Amir.

"I too am in the middle of something," said Sanam.

"I too," said Hannie.

"Me too," said Ángela.

Almost on cue, a police captain appeared at the open doors of the van, silhouetted by the streetlights. Like all the others, he was wearing a mask over his nose and mouth. He said, "All right now, we've had a look around. I'm going to need someone to explain to me what has happened here."

Mr. Lin waved his hand. "I believe you wish to be speaking with me."

So Mr. Lin spent the night talking to the increasingly befuddled police captain, while the rest of us were put up in a nearby hotel, where we were educated in the finer points of physical distancing. Just as he said he would, Mr. Lin couched the whole project strictly as a revenge project, which proved easy to corroborate since this vision of things covered our beliefs about it for ninety-nine percent of the time we had spent in his company.

Which, by the way, turned out to be five months and twenty-one days, in the middle of a serious global pandemic.

Mr. Lin said he could not account for the extreme behaviour of Armando Matamoros, beyond understanding that it must have been very difficult for the man to allow his house to be taken over. He said he took full responsibility for that and could not comment on the claims being made about a so-called "demonic possession."

He also tried to take full responsibility for the actions of Ella Unton Bride, but all his inquiries, demands and pleas with respect to her were ignored.

And so Mr. Lin was arrested, and so he went through a spectacular media circus of a trial, during which the merits and demerits of forgery were discussed at length.

A great deal of sympathy was expressed for him, in the press and on social media sites, especially after it was revealed, in a parallel trial, that his colleague, longstanding agent and friend, Ella Unton Bride, had betrayed him many times over, setting him up to purchase forgery after forgery and somehow claiming to share in his victimhood even as she was profiting from his losses in cahoots with an organization known as the Long Fella Syndicate.

He became a minor celebrity, while his former colleague gained the notoriety that accrues to photogenic scoundrels.

Ezra Coen's story was mostly shielded from the press, while Hannie Van der Roos, Ezra's fellow innocent,* received a boost to her career.

The rest of us were permitted to fade into obscurity, as individuals if not as the "Unton Group."

The question "What would you forge if you could?" started making the rounds among op-eds and influencers in several disciplines, which was entertaining for a while, until a well-known author managed to turn the tide of public opinion against the practice with a single statement:

In answer to your question: it's kind of weird to think what artist — whose work you admire — you'd like to exploit. If the choice of forgery involved living artists only, it would be impossible for me to name one.

---

* My editor has asked whether this book's title should not be changed to "six forgers" and "two falsely accused." But Ezra has requested that he be numbered among the forgers, ~~presumably to shield the actual perpetrator.~~ I cannot speculate as to his reasons.

I couldn't even conceive of forging the work — music, writing, painting — of a living artist I admire. It's kind of like asking who you'd like to rape, isn't it?

This off-the-cuff remark was said to have destroyed the romance surrounding the institution of forgery for a generation, at least in the UK.

And then we — the posse of art-rapists at the centre of it all — were eventually reminded that we ourselves were victims of a crime: we were asked to give victim-impact statements with respect to Mr. Lin, describing what the ordeal did to us "emotionally, physically, socially, and financially."

I have assembled highlights from each of our statements below.

ÁNGELA EFRENA QUINTERO'S:

Ladies and Gentlemen of the Jury,
I would like to tell a few words concerning the actions of Mr. Jackie Lin. He is a committed and passionate patron of the arts, and he did not harm us. It was his intention, stated many times, to allow several embarrassed counterfeiters to redeem themselves, to atone for their past missteps. He succeeded in this task. While I most emphatically do not consider my past deeds to be missteps — and I will go so far as to assert that anyone who knows my story will agree that my practice required the forger's imprimatur in order to be fully expressed as art — I can see nonetheless how my actions had been personally harmful to Mr. Lin.

Furthermore, I would like to point out that he is an adoptive parent. Anyone who is an adoptive parent should be permitted at least one Get-out-of-Jail-Free card.

Yours with a gesture of solidarity,
Ángela Efrena Quintero

HANNIE VAN DER ROOS'S:

I was falsely accused and held in that house against my will, deliberately maligned and left to the gales of fate by people who had my love, my trust, and my respect.

Upon reflection, however, I realize that I lay the blame for my bitterness fully at the feet of people other than Mr. Lin, who conducted his quixotic undertaking in a manner befitting a gentleman.

It is my sincere hope that the guiltier parties will receive the justice they so richly deserve.

I think it is fair to concede that I shall never forget the time I spent in the company of Mr. Lin: while I would never for a minute deny his guilt in these charges, I find myself contemplating the work I did while living under his conditions. It had a quality that was tied to the place it was made. This fact cannot be denied. And so, if I wish to further investigate that work, I believe it would be prudent for me to make a return.

In short, you may be seeing me again in your United Kingdom.

And so I would like to clearly state the following, for the record:

In the interest of all that is fair and just, I beg the judge to consider clemency for Mr. Jackie Lin.

Sincerely,

Hannie Van der Roos

Amsterdam

SANAM HAGHIGHI'S:

Well, for me, it was never less or more than a studio for the healthy exchange of ideas and of people. Here are some examples of what I found myself doing:

[Here follow eight examples of zoomorphic calligraphy.]

Food was provided that was always magnificent, as good as anything served at the Villa Lena in Tuscany. As a bonus, I got to patch up my relationship with my brother, following a long-standing feud. So I have no complaints. In fact, I would like to take this opportunity to thank Mr. Lin for organizing the whole thing.

AMIR HAGHIGHI's:

I loved it too. Like my sister. We consulted each other about our statements. We consult each other about everything now. This is entirely because of what happened. You see, we were estranged before, I mean in a terrible way. Your heart would break if you heard the story. She tells me I am not permitted to relate it here. But that is only because she never takes my ideas seriously. It is the cross for a younger brother to bear. But I shall bear it! What's more, my sister had once limited her considerable skills to calligraphy just because she did not want to see any grown man walk into a room and then try to walk around a horse someone had painted and hung on the wall. These were her concerns before. Now she has discovered zoomorphic calligraphy, which she applies to every figurative image under the sun, and has also taken up a miniaturist practice alongside my own. In truth, I could not be happier.

Also, I have acquired the legal means to purchase the house. This can be done when a building is in dire need of repair and its owner — in this case, the missing Armando Matamoros — is indisposed. I will buy the building then, and that will give me the legal means to restore it to its former standing, after which I will invite all the participants to return to the work they were conducting there, if they wish to do so. I would like to invite Mr. Lin at that time too, but he won't be able to come if he is in prison.

Yours,

Amir Haghighi

Artist, miniaturist, raconteur, wit

Dollis Hill

JAN KOMÁREK'S:

To Whom It May Concern:

As you will plainly see, my English writing is very good, beyond anything you might expect to see from a citizen of Bohemia. And it is on this very subject of English that I wish to post certain remarks, specifically regarding its potential for calling up demons. To wit, I fear for all your safety in utilizing this language, this English, which has been proven (by me) to contain traces of heretofore hidden or at least undefined necromantic elements that should be of serious concern to the UK justice system and beyond, including but not limited to schoolteachers, writers for the BBC, and literary scholars.

Most conjurers employ a language known as Enochian, which hearkens back to the sixteenth century. But our understanding of this Enochian language is limited to the bombastic stylings of angels who have been forced to appear against their will; it is a language that is meant to make us fall to our knees and tremble. As such, it is hardly ideal for the nuances of communication.

Your English is a bastard language, the opposite of pure. And so, over the centuries, it has picked up traces of every other language under the sun. It is colonizer and virus and mimic. So on one fine day while sitting in my Golden Lane studio on the castle grounds in Prague, I asked myself: what if English had also picked up traces of Enochian? What if, in fact, it contains more Enochian than the known vocabulary of Enochian itself? That would explain a lot, I think.

I am aware that this is supposed to be a statement about Mr. Lin, but I feel I must take this opportunity to warn you all, on behalf of myself and all citizens of Prague — in the tradition of mysticism and alchemy for which we have long been known — to be careful. I suggest you consider adopting a new language to call your own. May I suggest Bavarian, Navajo or Yiddish. You may also wish to advise your former colonies through official channels so they will treat your message with the dread seriousness it warrants. Where the incremental bastardization of your English is concerned, you simply do not know what you are dealing with. I plan to return to my country and advise the relevant authorities to use their influence in restoring German or even, God forgive me, Russian, as the second most prevalent language in the Czech Republic, rather than your English, which has grown there like a weed in the years since Václav Havel was first elected president in 1989.

Please tread carefully.

By the way, I write this here because I credit Mr. Lin for allowing me to conduct significant research in arriving at these conclusions, under the auspices of "making art."

Yours sincerely,

Jan Komárek

EZRA COEN'S:

I was never held against my will. My fellow art forgers (because I was an art forger too) worried about my safety, but it was clear to me that I could have broken the perimeter and escaped at any time. I was too curious, though, and then they drew me into their little family, and then I had to stay. And so I stayed, right up until the last days when I made a friend who I think it is safe to say will be a lifelong friend, like the friendship between Boris Pasternak and Marina Tsvetaeva or the friendship between Barack and Michelle Obama. My friend is Mr. Lin's daughter. Please forgive him and let him go. A girl needs her father.

Yours,

Ezra Coen

MINE:

I can say *mine* now. This is a credit to Mr. Lin.

was unable to make a victim impact statement, as he was still on the run and highly indisposed throughout this entire period, ultimately coming face to face in the Sistine Chapel, about a year later, with an exorcist who had travelled by footmobile directly from his own residence in the Vatican.

The possessed Armando had climbed up onto a section of scaffolding erected behind the altar to restore a damaged section of *The Last Judgment* and was pointing at the ceiling, making lewd comments about the finger of Adam and the finger of God. He complained to the exorcist that "when you've seen one painted figure by Michelangelo you've seen them all," that "the Vatican should have taken El Greco up on his offer to repaint," that "the ceiling looked so much better back in the days when it was a simple blue painted with gold stars, before that hack got his mitts on it. But it's always, always on to the next thing, isn't it, Michi? Yes, it is. A muscular naked God hopping from panel to panel. Tasteless."

Just before the exorcist began zapping him with prayerful invocations, Armando's demon — apparently still thinking about the problem of concealing Ezra Coen — added that it would be "impossible for anyone to hide out in any of these frescoes except *The Last Judgment*. And why would anyone want to do that? I'd rather be caught by that savvy old art collector than get stuck here in a permanent state of getting judged by God. Ugh!"

And then, as if to illustrate his point, he tried to climb off the scaffold and into *The Last Judgement*, scraping at the paint with his fingernails.

As it turns out, the exorcism was a complete success, and a sheepish Armando Matamoros was taken into Italian custody. The UK government demanded his extradition, but the Italian government argued that his defacement of the Sistine Chapel was a far more serious matter than the damage he had done to his own London house, even if the latter charges did include resisting arrest.

Armando was lucky to get his trial in Italy, where he was given a famous lawyer whose fee was paid by the Vatican itself. Since the defence of demonic possession held far more sway in that country than in the UK, Armando ultimately won an acquittal, albeit after several months, and the Vatican won the news cycle for more consecutive days than at any time since an anonymous cleric penned reports from the second ecumenical council for *The New Yorker* magazine in the mid-1960s, thus allowing Armando to achieve a quantum of revenge against Condé Nast for kicking off his spectacular run of personal humiliations.

Finally, due to the Vatican's continued influence over his case, and after several years of earnest negotiation, the UK eventually granted Armando a full pardon for his actions in the house on Olive Road (along with another alleged incident inside the Chunnel that necessitated the eastbound Eurostar train to come to a stop for a full thirty minutes).

Armando was finally a free man. And his house was free too. Amir's repairs had been financed by Mr. Lin, so he was able to restore it to its former owner without any accumulated debt.

Still, I imagine Armando's victim statement would have been substantively different depending on whether it had been made by himself or the demon. If the man himself had been able to do it, I suspect it likely would have weighed heavily against the rest of ours.

As things stood, Mr. Lin was given a sentence of eight months.

PART EIGHT

EX-VOTO

(*Latin:* from a vow.) *A painting or other work of art made as an offering to God in gratitude for a personal favour or blessing or in the hope of receiving some miraculous benefit.*

Years went by. Vaccines were implemented, failed, were implemented again, and eventually became a part of life. Francisco Goya's importance was reaffirmed for a new generation, not via artistic defacement but rather climate activism: two protesters, a man and a woman, entered the Prado and glued hands to both *majas*. The young man chose the *vestida* and the young woman the *desnuda*, each showing regard for the works by pressing their hands against the frames rather than the paintings themselves.

There was also, during this time, a massive theft of intellectual property, arguably the biggest in history. It was perpetrated by the programmers of a series of AI image generators with engaging names like DALL-E and Stable Diffusion, who purloined the uploaded work of every artist in the world, both amateur and professional — yours, your doctor's, your daughter's, Leonardo da Vinci's, Henry Darger's, Ai Weiwei's — absorbed it, digested it, and then belched it out again, in various recombinations, eliciting gasps of wonder from all the same people whose pockets had been picked and then erased altogether. Earthworks were safe, the output of those who — like Ángela Quintero and her beloved father — created ephemeral experiences that could never be uploaded. Protest art was safe: DALL-E could never mimic Hannie Van der Roos pinning a hastily drawn portrait to her chest to stare down those who would snatch her up and imprison her. I suppose every tactile artwork was safe. But the theft was real.

As for me, I gave up my forgery practice and got a job in the coat-check department of the Art Gallery of Ontario. The hours were good, the benefits were decent, no one was going to kick me out of this job or otherwise accuse me quite accurately of being ethically subpar. I could pay compliments to the truffula trees that came out of the kindergarten workshops in the lower level.

And my basement apartment was within walking distance of the museum and also within walking distance of the best dim sum in the country.

I continued the habit of doing my own work, and I liked to do it, and I considered it important, but I thought of it only as a private matter: I did not show it, at least not in the conventional sense, or sell it. I just did it for myself, secretly, in all the bathroom stalls of Toronto.

One day, I received a surprising letter:

My dearest O,

You were in my dream the other night. I was at a small exhibition of my work at a fancy dealer's house, and the other artists showing in the next room were all supposed to be impressive, but it felt very unimpressive and meaningless to me. I hadn't invited anyone because I didn't want to have to be nice. But you showed up, and I was so happy to see you.

We were in the suburbs of a city I did not know. You didn't mind that it was boring. You were full of determination and happiness having just got back from a trip to somewhere or other. It was lovely to see how you had grown into yourself. I have always rooted for you.

You tossed me a coin, a big silver one that had some black wear in it. "You should go there," you said. I studied the coin. It seemed very old, but lighter than I expected, so I briefly wondered whether it was a fake. You went to leave, but then you realized you were wearing my leather jacket. You looked down and pulled out a coin from my pocket. But I still had the coin you gave me. You were happy about that. I think you left on a moped.

It all made me think you had picked up more from our house necromancer than I ever realized. I wonder if you know he has changed his name to Pan? Pan Komárek, he's called now: the Grand Wizard of Prague, with a golem as a bodyguard.

You are likely unaware that I have taken up residence in the Dollis Hill house for the last several years, along with Amir, Sanam and Ángela Efrena Quintero. There was work I needed to finish there.

I tell you all this because you will be receiving an invitation soon to an exhibition here. We have had to wait, to ensure that Mr. Lin would be able to attend—there were some concerns around his travel due to matters of health—and also that Armando would not be arrested if he tried to come into the country.

But it is finally happening, and I am very much looking forward to closing this chapter of my life.

And also to seeing you, if you can make it.

Specifically I would like to show you my latest work.

Perhaps you will arrive on your moped.

The letter was not signed, but I knew who it came from. The next day, I received Amir's invitation, which was simply an old newspaper photo of the destroyed house and the word *Come!* along with a date three months hence, and a time.

And then, about a week later, I received another letter, this one from Mr. Jackie Lin, which had another letter enclosed within it — not a copy either, I couldn't help but notice, but rather the original.

Dear Ms. Willowes,

I have perhaps been remiss in not bringing this letter to your attention earlier. I will confess I did not know what to make of it for the longest time. Recently, however, I have found cause to revisit its claims and discovered I had misplaced my incredulity.

I think you will find my reasons for sending it to be self-explanatory.

Yours,
Jackie Lin

I examined the letter. Across the fold someone had written *resignation letter* in blue ink. I could see the letter itself had been handwritten as well. The paper had yellowed a bit, possessing a brittleness that gave it the feel of a rare and precious thing.

I opened it with trembling hands.

Dear Mr. Lin,

I am aware that I signed a contract with you that said I would work for the whole time of your project, but I hope that, once you have read through my explanation, you will be satisfied that I cannot in good conscience carry on.

Early one evening — maybe it was an evening, I can't remember when exactly except to say that it was not long after the artist I was guarding — her name is Olive — had been confined to her studio and was taking all her meals in there. Anyway, she had just fallen down and was in a compromised position, and I was trying to figure out whether I should seek assistance for her while at the same time granting the privacy that was her due.

In that moment, I was approached by a person walking across the rooftop. My assumption was that you had sent this person, sir, because this person was not one of the residents of the household, and more to the point, this person was shining like a big light bulb and did not give me time to figure out the trick. I'm sorry I keep writing "this person," sir, I just don't know how to describe them in a way you will understand. Perhaps the less said the better.

They came up to me, sir, and they said they had a favour to ask of me, although it didn't sound like a favour to me. It sounded like a command.

They instructed me to assist the artist I was watching over. They said she needed me to be a footstool, at the very least, and an artist's assistant otherwise. They reminded me that another sentry had been instructed by you to assist an artist on the other side of the house with the retrieval of bird eggs and stuff like that.

Anyway, I said I'd do it. By this point, sir, I honestly thought I had fallen asleep and was dreaming.

I went in there, and, for several pretty intense hours, I, for lack of a better word, collaborated with the artist — I think I already said her name was Olive — on a project. I assisted her. I don't know how else to put it. And we did other things too.

Sir, you have been a fair employer to me, but I have to go. I feel embarrassed by what happened. But I also would not change it. Still, I have to go. To be perfectly honest, I have to go and find out if I can do this thing myself. I read somewhere once that there is no magic in the world, there is only what you make. I want to try that.

I hope I have made it clear that I was always only doing my job as I understood it. Please be assured I will always honour the terms of our NDA.

I took off in a bit of a hurry, though, and I left some books. I am enclosing a PO box address. I wonder if you can forward them.

I also wonder, if the day ever comes that you communicate with your charges, if you could tell Ms. Olive thank you. It was an honour and a privilege. It was an education. I hope she didn't regret it. I didn't regret it.

Yours sincerely,
Jason Lange, sentry

I must have read that letter a thousand times. I knew I would never see the sentry again, but I found myself recalling him with a new fondness and finally began to understand the feeling of thrill that had passed over me whenever I had thought about him before.

I had so many questions, not the least of which was how Mr. Lin came to "misplace his incredulity" about the sentry's letter.

About Jason's letter.

The name did not feel like news to me. Jason. It felt rather like the uncovering of a distant memory.

Jason implied in his letter that we had done other things. Things that he did not regret and that he hoped I did not regret.

What other things had we done?

I found fits and snatches of him began to surface in my memory: kind eyes . . . a gesture he made toward the wall . . . that I should lean against the wall . . . him kneeling . . . Oh! How could I have suppressed that? How could I regret that?

I remembered now my fingers laced within his hair like silk.

He had implied — *Jason* had implied — that he was going to learn to be an artist. I hoped — how I hoped — that would turn into a real thing. How I hope. It is one joy to be an artist; it is a whole other to engender the desire in another person.

60. *A B D A L* (*"the substitutes"*)

I took the Heathrow Express downtown, bought an Oyster card (the first one had long since expired due to a change in design) and took the underground to Willesden Green Station. Came up just after one p.m. into a windy overcast day and stopped for a sandwich in the location that had once served me a roti. The roti place had closed down during the Covid-19 pandemic. I recalled the conversation with the server from Somalia and how I had cast aspersions on Edmonton, Alberta. My sister had lived at that time in Edmonton, Alberta. I am aware that is no excuse. These days she lives in Ottawa, my nation's capital, and I stand ready to dump all over Ottawa, if given a chance, and stand in defence of Edmonton, Alberta, which city did survive my opprobrium, and my sister.

So, then I walked out onto Walm Lane or Walm Line, I still can't remember which it is, walked up and left and up and left, found myself approaching a Victorian-style house that had undergone serious renovation. For one thing, it had a tree growing into its second floor. Otherwise, it looked as good as new, standing like an exclamation mark on this residential street that was as quiet as a mole in a hollow tree of Gladstone Park.

And there were a man and a woman out in front of the house, and they were screaming and waving as I approached.

Amir and Sanam had come out to greet me.

How did Amir look? He had aged, of course. And his Parkinson's was taking its toll. But his eyebrows were funny and white, as if singed by their proximity to the light decussating from his eyes. It was wonderful to see him.

Sanam looked older as well and had not misplaced any of her style or vitality or warmth. There was something different about her though, and I realized after a few moments that it was the first time I had ever seen her without a headscarf. I very nearly asked her about it, but then she picked up a burlap sack that was lying at her feet. "We collected these for you," she said. I had no idea what was inside. Opened it up to see all my bits of scribbled paper.

"Some of them blew away," she said. "Some of them were balled up in old blobs of paint. There is a lot of wear and tear. But we got as many as we could."

Then she took me by the arm as Amir turned and led us past the base of the ash tree and into the house, turning immediately into the front room, where everything had begun. It was bare walled and empty except for the pair of club chairs and the old couch, all of which had been reupholstered, and its once-shattered window was bright and clean.

I was late to the party. Jan (now Pan?) was there, dressed in a weathered tuxedo with a bow tie instead of his usual cravat, I thought perhaps in tribute to the absent (but apparently no longer incarcerated) Ella Unton Bride.

He gave me a small nod just as he settled cross-legged on a pentagram-patterned floor cushion he seemed to have brought for the occasion.

And Ángela was there, in her detonating antlerite, though Armando, sitting by her, perched on the arm of her chair, gave no sign of detonation. They wore rings — presumably married? — and both rose to greet me, distracting me from the sight of Hannie by the window, who gave me a light nod. Inscrutability trumped intimacy every time. Still, I cherished the letter she had sent me. I remembered the moment her hand reached fearful for mine as Armando's demon rampaged through the house, and I forgave her.

Of course, I loved her. I don't know if that is obvious or not. She was a mystery to me, beyond understanding. But I loved her.

She stood by the window, pensive in a spiderweb shawl, looking out.

I wished I had arrived on a moped.

There was a tall young man there too, whom I could not place at first until I realized it was Ezra Coen. He was sitting on the couch having a conversation in Korean with a young woman: Esther Lin.

They had arrived together, having flown in from Seoul that morning.

Esther looked strong and confident, a young woman doted upon by the elderly man who had brought her up, who had devoted every waking hour since his release to her happiness and well-being, to the exclusion of every other ambition.

Mr. Lin, beside her, was perched on the portable leather strap that slung across his walker, presumably a constant companion now.

"It's been a while since I've spent any length of time in this house," Armando said for everyone's benefit, after granting me a big warm bear hug. "It is calling up some disquieting memories."

"If it's any consolation," said Sanam, "your demon was clearly an art connoisseur."

"I'm afraid he was more than a connoisseur in the end," said Armando. "Some of my exploits under his influence have not been accounted for. And I seem to have a lot more money. Lately, I have begun to recall that I may have travelled to Barcelona and that, during my time there, I may have undertaken a forgery of Picasso's *Guernica*."

We all gasped.

"I seem to recall that I had the help of some shady operators and was paid handsomely once the switch was made."

"But ..." said Jan, "I had thought your demon's whole problem was that he was a poor artist?"

Armando shrugged. "He must have improved. And he left a scrawled note telling why he was interested in Picasso."

He produced a large freezer bag with a paper inside it.

"His choice of ink has a very bad odour. Señor Komárek would surely approve."

"May I see it?" asked Jan.

Armando handed the artifact to Jan, who opened the seal, gave a little sniff, nodded with satisfaction, produced a magnifying glass from somewhere and began to examine the writing: "It reads, 'That bald Spaniard wanted to paint like a child because children always copy each other and nobody cares.'"

"You see?" said Armando. "He thought Picasso would approve of his forgery. I don't know whether it's good or bad, but I can't shake the memory that it replaced the real one. I really don't know whether I should speak out or just let sleeping doodles lie. If I speak out, I suspect there will be some unpleasant people showing up at my door in the night."

"By all means," Jan spoke up from behind his magnifying glass, "let the sleeping doodles lie."

We all agreed that the fake *Guernica* should shelter in place, though this might not speak well of us.

As everyone was discussing this revelation, Jan beckoned for me to lean in, whispering that the demon had also secured the annulment of Armando's first marriage. "He had no compunctions about getting certain things done," he added. "And Ángela was able to successfully realize her Oaxacan wedding earthwork at the Templo de Santo Domingo de Guzmán. So she was wise,

I suppose, to summon him." His eyes narrowed. "If indeed it was she who conjured him."

So Jan was still smarting from being shown up by Ángela in the conjuring of demons. I assumed he was sharing this with me because I was the one who knew best not to underestimate him. I didn't know how to respond, reached out and gave his shoulder a gentle squeeze, which gesture he seemed to accept.

Once we were all settled in, pleasantries exchanged and some
of our sins further discussed, Amir stood and beckoned us to
follow him.

The hallway, it was somehow only now revealed, was full
of Sanam's zoomorphic calligraphy, wordplay animals rushing
headlong out of her dining-room studio. We looked closer. The
calligrams weren't rendered in gibberish anymore. They were
telling a story. Not in Arabic either, but rather her native Farsi.
Not exactly the story I've just written here, since of course it was
from Sanam's point of view. But it was the story, told in bold, simple strokes, about how we all came to be in this house. Sanam
took the time to read out bits and pieces to us in translation. She
didn't need to, though, because each word was also a picture, and
the pictures told the story too.

Just outside the door to her studio I saw a depiction of the
moment I had first arrived at the house, interrupting an argument between her and her brother.

"You did not believe you were an artist," said Sanam to me,
taking my arm, "even though you held the invitation in your
hand! But look here."

I looked. On the wall in front of me, lightly rendered as image
and text, was a small woman in a state of undress, rendered taste-
fully, holding a paint brush in one hand and charcoal in the other,
marking up the wall in front of her.

"Is that — ?" I asked.

"That's you."

"I'm not sure anymore that I was always by myself," I said.

"Whatever do you mean?" asked Sanam.

"Never mind," I said.

Still, I had questions. How did Sanam come to know about
my state of undress? Was it just assumed that we worked this

way? Had I written about it in my crumpled notes? Had she read my crumpled notes?

Nearby, Jan Komárek was perusing another set of calligrams in the hallway, hands clasped behind his back, a wide smile spreading across his eyes. I looked where he was reading and saw what appeared to be the fanning of a flip book showing a boy rolling out of a deck chair in the shadow of an umbrella and then leaping into the air, sprouting wings and taking flight.

So Ezra's tale was getting told too.

The story progressed down the hall, swirled up toward the ceiling, entered Armando's studio, climbed down again toward the floor, and then nestled in rings around the spot where Amir had fallen from the upper floor.

Then, when we were all gathered there inside Armando's old broken studio, we looked up and saw, above our heads, a lush forest canopy, beyond anything Ángela had achieved when the broken bough had first clung to life in the wake of the ash tree's fall. Here the animals were no longer syllables in flight; rather there were real creatures, crying and mewling and chirping and howling and scurrying and barking and biting and sometimes dropping little chewed fruit pits and bones at our feet, where they scattered among others half-buried in the dirt that crept up around the toes of our shoes.

"With Jan's help, we filled the basement with soil," said Amir. "Plugged up that demon portal. I suppose it was all for the best in the end, Señor Armando. As with many things touched by the infernal, the portal of that basement drain infused the soil with decay and made it fertile."

Armando looked embarrassed as Amir continued. "I have had a chance these past few years to think about Mr. Lin and the task he laid at our feet. What a serious disruption of our lives that time was. And yet, I think I am secure in saying we've all forgiven him. Why is that? Because we realized that, if he had come to each of us, simply told his story and asked us to help him with his task, we would have listened with our mouths open. And if we had believed his story, we would have gone further; we would have helped him. As humans, as artists, even of the counterfeit caste. But it is also more than likely that none of us would have believed him at all."

I recalled again the email I had received from Ella Unton Bride, the roti restaurant, my first approach to the house. Would I have believed his story if he had told me then? Probably not.

"Anyway," said Amir, "as you will see, we have, in our time here, come to a better understanding of the task that has been asked of us."

He led us upstairs. Mr. Lin made his way slowly, pausing on the landing, buoyed between Esther and Ezra, as Sanam carried the walker.

Upstairs, as Amir came to Hannie's studio, Hannie herself, quite unexpectedly, took over the tour.

She opened the door, itself a remarkable act (at least to me), and we all stepped inside. I felt a pang of jealousy for losing my one-time privilege in this regard. Right away, I saw that there was no bed anymore. Where did she sleep?

Having divined my question, Hannie said, "I sleep upstairs now, perched at the top of the house, the former room of our gentle Olive here. This studio," she gestured, "is strictly for work."

There were hundreds of canvases of all shapes and sizes. They were all turned to face the wall.

"I beg your pardons," said Hannie. "I leave them like this sometimes, when I . . ."

She stepped toward the wall, turned one around. It was a drawing, in black acrylic and charcoal, of an aged man regarding me with a patient, resigned expression on his face.

I thought for a moment his eyes might swivel to look away from me, but they did not.

I wondered whether I should help Hannie with the task of turning all these works around to face us, but then she stopped and addressed us once more.

"I am usually one to express loathing for the institution of the artist's statement. But I find, today, that I have no other recourse. Otherwise I don't know how I could broach this subject. So here goes:

"There have been angels here. Oh, it sounds silly, but it's true. I don't believe there are any angels here just now, at this moment, but over time, there have been a few. More than a few. For a long time, there was only one, and I believe you will soon learn how that one lent a hand, first to Olive here, briefly, before anyone else, though she did not tell any of us about this angelic assistance."

"Because it was second hand," I murmured, thinking of my sentry being approached by the person who glowed like a light bulb. "And anyway, I didn't know," I said a little louder. "I had hit my head."

Hannie nodded, thoughtfully, seeming to believe me, and then went on.

"Then, after that brief encounter with Olive, the angel came to me and sat while I did their portrait, for a lengthy period of time. Days and days."

I blushed, did my best to conceal it. Hannie could have her angel. I had my sentry. She could have her days and days. I had my eight precious hours. I looked around quickly to see whether anyone had noticed my little storm of emotions and found myself sharing a glance with Mr. Lin. For a moment I thought I might faint, but I saw my secret was safe with him.

"And then, later," Hannie continued, "all the rest of them sat for me as well. I had the great honour to have them as my subjects."

She turned back to the wall and revealed a small charcoal drawing on canvas. It was of a beautiful young person of indeterminate gender. I found myself recalling the vision of Hannie's feet rising from the ground. Remembered suddenly, too, my sentry, Jason, my hands in his hair. And I wonder, even now, was Hannie not telling the whole story of the time she spent with that first angel?

"As is often the case when you are a subject sitting for a portrait," Hannie went on, "you get to talking. And so these angels spoke to me. I learned some of their secrets, I mean, at least their secrets with respect to me. From that first angel I learned quotidian things, like how they had come to the assistance of Olive. Later, much later, after many portraits, I came to learn how they viewed what had happened to our own Mr. Lin and why they had come to take such a great interest in him."

Now she sighed and looked again at Amir and Sanam, slightly uncomfortable with her assigned task.

"Well . . . how to begin? First I came to learn how — and this is important — angels have no past or future. They experience only an eternal present.

"For humans, on the other hand — we humans — we parade through the world *ad una ad una*, as Dante had it. For us, things happen one by one. Good things, bad things. And we get to create things, little things, detail by detail, within this vast cosmos of creation. We get to create all these new little loves in our lives and with our lives. Like the time, for example, our friend Amir Haghighi here tried to recreate a sky full of stars on his Tehran rooftop. The stars smiled down on that, I'm sure they did. Or, if I may, the angels smiled down on that.

"Sometimes, one of our little artistic concoctions gets caught up in an eddy that pulls it into the swirl of all creation. I don't know why this is the case, and the angel did not explain. They simply stated it as fact. I asked, Was it due to a brilliant brushstroke or did it come down to simple luck? They did not seem to understand the question. But I can tell you what it means for us:

"Whenever that little catch happens — the little swirling into the big — the vast host of heavenly angels will pause in their ceaseless motion, and then they will feel — and revel in the feeling of — what it's like to live in that single moment. The experience doesn't have to happen in the instant the brushstroke is made; rather it is akin to any one of us standing in a gallery and becoming overwhelmed by a detail. Except these are angels: for the angels, this little catch distracts from their usual preoccupation with keeping perpetually in front of the face of God. I'm not sure what they meant by *God* in this statement. I'm not sure it's the same as what I think of when a human being says the word *god*.

"Really the pause is hardly noticeable, only a moment: a mere yoctosecond, a rather small unit of time. It can even happen at a time when a painting is alone, unremarked and unnoticed. You'd be surprised at the amount of time a work of art spends alone. In which case the sudden magnifying focus of — well, the

most conservative estimate is just over three hundred million —
angels, on a single painting, in that moment, will have no human
consequences.

"But from time to time, this brief catch and sweep of some
piece of art into the dance of all creation happens in front of
an observing human eye. It could be the artist's own eye, and
indeed it has sometimes been so, but it is not necessarily so.
In fact it could happen to any little person, any old passerby:
an aficionado; a connoisseur. When the angels have a human witness to share in their moment of breathless appreciation, that
pause extends for even longer, in fact everything just comes
to a halt while the whole heavenly host rushes to the window
to peek through the blinds and take a look at the wonder that
unfolds. If you were to be that person, that passerby, this is what
would happen to you: you would find yourself abiding by the
angels' rules of existence rather than your own. One moment
you would be looking at a brushstroke on the canvas and then,
in the next, you would find yourself there, living inside the world
of that brushstroke. I say a brushstroke, but of course it could
be a doodle or an etching or a *remarque* or a linocut. I asked
what the possibilities were for non-figurative art, but the angel
was silent on the subject. Perhaps Armando's demon could have
told us, since the fallen angels take notice too. They may lack
specific details as to when and how and who or even why — such
is the fullness of their darkness — but they still feel the blip in
the surface of creation.

"I confess I find myself curious about the possibilities of
angelic attention on non-figurative art: I wouldn't mind stepping into a canvas by one of the abstract expressionists, say, just
to see what that would be like. But I must leave that curiosity
aside, at least for the moment, since that would not be relevant
to our story, which goes like this:

"Some years ago, when our erstwhile kidnapper and host, now
friend, Mr. Lin, stood in front of a painting in a former monastery

in the city of Hong Kong, he was drawn into the eddy, pulled out of his point in time and — experiencing the angelic rules of existence, not his own — zeroed in on the love of a single person: a woman, a leader, a servant, a guide, seemingly only a few strokes of pigment on silk, yet there she was. That journey changed him. How could it not change him? His experience of love inside that anonymous creation became a star in the vast firmament of eternal love, adorning the sky above our heads.

"And so, when Mr. Lin decided that he would not let that moment go — and why should he have? Who would ever want to let that moment go? — it became especially diverting to a cheering section beyond the veil such as our world has never seen, where a trillion translucent fingers pulled down the slats in the blinds to get a closer look at this gentleman and his quest.

"Now, as it happens, Mr. Lin began to intuit this seraphic interest, especially once he saw that his more mediocre attempts to recreate his experience through acquisition and ownership were met with failure and humiliation. This is not at all to say that there were angelic hands at work in his failures. Bad luck can happen to anyone. The fraud and exploitation of Ms. Ella Unton Bride, it would seem, can happen to anyone. I can assert this fact from personal experience."

Hannie paused to allow her personal shadow to pass.

"But Mr. Lin eventually made the intuitive leap of deciding to secure the services of a somewhat ham-fisted semi-amateur mage, our very own Jan Komárek, who must forgive my characterization of his abilities in light of the fact that he has, in turn, oft expressed only the slightest regard for our work, doodlers that we are."

Here Hannie paused and allowed Jan the opportunity to answer. The magician merely gave his head a slight nod.

"Monsieur Komárek proved to be skilled enough in his craft to pull an angel through one of their own routless slats and into this very house.

"When that angel sat for me, it was like the loosening of a spigot. They were the vanguard. After them came many others. All wanting their portraits drawn. I found it was important to employ a style I had long practised without quite knowing why: I could never allow my hand to rise from the paper or the canvas. In order to prevent it from trembling as I drew.

"So, you will see."

She turned over drawing after drawing, canvas after canvas. They weren't at all like the first. A collection of spirited geriatrics paraded into our view, many of them peering through sets of blinds, concealing and revealing, rendering them shy and in hiding or sometimes giving them an attitude of peep-show voyeurism.

Were these the angels? They seemed to be the residents of a long-term care facility.

Some of the drawings were life-size to a human. Others were small, no bigger than a bedside clock. It took Hannie a good twenty minutes to reveal them all to us. And we were so enraptured no one lifted a finger to help.

When she was done, the full effect was of an audience of elderly LTC occupants sitting on the inside of a window visit while visitors outside were performing a play.

We were the performers. Ours was the play. They were here to look at us.

After a time, Amir said, "Are we ready for the next?"

+++

As we filed out of the room, I sensed Hannie sidle up beside me, felt her fingers interlace with mine.

"Did you like them?" she whispered.

I turned, crimson-faced, and kissed her lightly on the cheek.

I have thought long and hard on this and have concluded that it was the first kiss I had granted anyone in my living memory.

64. *SURIA*
TUTRECHIAL
TUTRUSIAI
ZORTEK
MUFGAR
ASHRULYAI
SABRIEL
ZAHABRIEL
TANDAL
SHOKAD
HUZIA
DEHEBORYN
ADRIRION
KHABIEL
TASHRIEL
NAHURIEL
JEKUSIEL
TUFIEL
NAHARIEL
MASKIEL
SHOEL
SHEVIEL
TAGRIEL
MASPIEL
SAHRIEL
ARFIEL
SHAHARIEL
SAKRIEL
RAGIEL
SEHIBIEL
SHEBURIEL

RETSUTSIEL
SHALMIAL
SAVLIAL
HARHAZIAL
HADRIAL
BEZRIAL
PACHDIAL
GVURTIAL
KZUIAL
SHCHITIIAL
SHTUKIAL
ARVIAL
KFIAL
ANFIAL
TECHIAL
UZIAL
GMIAL
GAMRIAL
SEFRIAL
GARFIAL
GRIAL
DRIAL
PALTRIAL
RUMIAL
KATMIAL
GEHEGIAL
ARSABRSBIAL
EGRUMIAL
PARZIAL
MACHKIAL

Just before we arrived at Amir's door, he turned and said, "Let me remind you what Hannie said: we have been assisted in our project. But I personally have also been assisted."

He went on: "The demon who highjacked our friend Armando was correct when he said no angel can take possession of a human body the way a demon can. You will scour the record in vain if you wish to see an example of that. Angels have bodies of their own."

I immediately thought of Linda Blair, her head spinning around, her body scuttling backwards down the stairs. I immediately thought of, well, yes, I thought of Warren Beatty — not an angel — his soul entering the body of a dead quarterback like a hand slipping into a discarded glove. He was a simple man in need of a body, assisted by an angel. Presumably the angel couldn't hold the body for him, the timing of Warren's entrance had to be exactly right, if I remember correctly. Were these stories relevant? They were just made up.

Remarkably, I had allowed my attention to drift, missing the beginning of the next part of what Amir said. "— inson's disease, taking medication to loosen my stiffening limbs. But none has taken possession of me. Rather, I have separate ones taking charge of individual muscles and bones. They're good at it too. I have separate angels guiding each of my metacarpals and my phalanges, my radius and my ulna. I have separate ones guiding my forearms and my upper arms and my elbows. I even have them pulling and pushing on my shoulder blades, which sometimes gives me the sensation of having wings. Six angels help me void my bowels, and somehow they make it seem like a pleasure. And then there is the single powerhouse who holds me up by my hips from behind. I call this angel Simon because I cannot pronounce his real name. I can't even turn my head to look at him, and so I find myself imagining he is a human personal care worker. Such people are angels in their own right, no? Finally, I speak to you with clear enunciation only because of those who work my cheeks and my mouth and my jaw. They all listen closely to the whispers of my will. But I do not possess them, and they do not possess me. You might assume the sensation is like I'm crawling with ants, but let me assure you: to have the hands of many angels on your body is almost worth the price of Parkinson's. How grateful I am for them.

"And I'm grateful, too, that they also took up brushes of their own and assisted in the workshop. You are just about to see the fruits of all our labour."

65. *BEN NEZ* ("hawk")

Then we came to the doorway of Amir's studio and were greeted by, well . . .

338
We saw that the siblings and their angelic assistants had covered every wall with a pattern of paintings so small, so tightly knit, so *miniature*, that it seemed, to the human eye, as if all the light entering the room was pulled into it and not let out again.

In other words, the walls looked as black as can be imagined. As black as the pigment known as Vantablack. Blacker. As black as the cluster of vertically aligned carbon nanotubes that were discovered at the Massachusetts Institute of Technology to be the blackest black.

"Fascinating," said Jan Komárek.

But the rest of us were shocked. The room did not extend a welcoming hand, not by any means. Awe-inspiring but not welcoming. Why would anyone want to walk into that?

"This is not how I pictured things would go," mumbled Armando.

"Let me assure you," said Amir, "light may not easily come and go from this room. But I can come and go, and so can you. And so can Mr. Lin, if he so chooses."

"I don't understand," said Mr. Lin. "What is this all about?"

I looked at him. He appeared elderly, frail: clutching his walker with his daughter and Ezra Coen hovering on either side, ready to catch him if he tumbled.

"There," said Amir, venturing into the room like a slightly tremorous man dancing in front of the cosmos. He pointed to a spot about a foot above and just to the left of the room's north corner: "Right over here, you will find an *exact* replica, or rather a miniature replica, or, I suppose, since we are all friends here, a *forgery*, of the very painting in that Hong Kong monastery gallery that drew you in, Mr. Lin."

He turned back to us and flashed his I'm-not-being-too-serious smile.

"Wonders, yes? One may point out the obvious and say that although Mr. Lin was banished for life from visiting it, I was not, and neither was Sanam. And so we travelled to that place many times, made many studies; and here it is, complete, if writ very small.

"Hannie told us earlier that inspiration is a fickle demon and artmaking can only intersect with the cosmos so often, and so it is entirely possible that this has all been for nothing. But I am sure in this: we have gotten the approval of forces that have no memory, that exist in the eternal present, and that came to our aid. We've all done the best we can, and so can only respond to our possible failure by saying that the work brought pleasure and was worth every plank's length we sanded and nailed together."

Esther Lin spoke up. "But if the miniature of my father's painting is where you say it is, then what is covering the remaining walls?"

"Ah," said Amir. "Your approach to life has been an inspiration to us all, Ms. Lin. As a child of three, you led your father on a chase through the Hanoi market, all the goods of the world whirring by the two of you as you ran.

"Ultimately you were in search of a toy that hung behind the windowpane of a store.

"For the sake of Mr. Lin, we have here conspired to create just such a market again: a market of possibilities this time; a market of potential lives; such a market that will make the angels press so hard against their windowpane that it will threaten to push loose from its frame and send them falling a billion storeys into the tumult and the fray.

"Mr. Lin will, I hope, be able to step into that little painting, take his love by the hand, lead her out again, and then, rather than lingering here, step directly into a different painting: this second painting a place where they can be safe, in which they will be able to live in harmony with the world around them and in peace.

"When he makes his first entry, where will he find himself? Will he be the same young man he was before? I think so. I hope so. But will he find himself where he left off in the story? As if he's placed a bookmark there and leapt back in? Will he be climbing out of his back-broken litter? Then he must move quickly, be strong and focused in the centre of that whirlwind: stretch out his hand as she once did for him, let her take it and then get back here!

"Or will he rather be holding the hand of the lady who first drew him in? And if that's the case, our witnessing angels will thrill to see, no doubt, how he will turn away from the noblewoman the moment he arrives, bow to one of her shocked servants, kneel before that servant, take her by the hand and draw her away from there before a single hair on her head is harmed. Did she not choose to take this man for herself without knowing a thing about him? She has the same will, the same moral compass, the same fierce intelligence, the same instincts. Hardship did not create those qualities. Anyway, she's had a lifetime of hardship already. Get her out of there!

"I don't know which it will be.

"Once back here, though, they have been provided a whole world to choose from, in miniature: a series of subjects and locations from every tradition of pastoral and bucolic painting that has ever existed in the history of the world."

We looked and saw only the absence of light.

"And we have taken the liberty of providing a pair of carved walking sticks."

Here he turned to address Mr. Lin alone.

"There are times in history when our aspirations as artists can rise no higher than to be able to say, simply, we are at your service. This is such a time. Please do not let the darkness fool you. It's all so beautiful in there that the light simply does not want to come out. So tread lightly, sir. Do not stumble down the road to legend, for these are your dreams, and also mine, and all of ours, if I may speak for the assembled company."

We all gave our assent that indeed he could.

And so Amir concluded, "God speed you, and good luck. The angels at their windows are widening their eyes."

What can I tell you about what I saw next?

If I told you now that Mr. Lin turned, taking his hands off his walker and lifting them up to embrace his daughter,

and then to embrace the man beside his daughter, after which he spoke to him for a long time, *sotto voce*, wagging his finger,

and then embraced each of us in turn,

and then embraced his daughter again and then stepped away from her and gave her a little salute, and she gave a little salute back.

And then he nodded to Amir, who held out the pair of rustic walking sticks.

And then stepped away from his walker,

took hold of the walking sticks,

and ventured into the carbon-nanotube room,

and stepped into a painting that he presumably saw,

actually shrinking down and popping into it,

like a jumping flea.

And then, if I told you that he reappeared a moment later, youthful and vibrant and holding a woman by the hand,

and that they emerged full size,

covered in dust,

dressed in rags,

and smelling of both love and death,

disappeared again

into another section of the wall,

certainly a place where Mr. Lin would be able to find his bearings,

just like Amir said,

for when we are strangers in a strange land,

we need to take hold of something familiar or we are lost,

and there needs to be a choice,

a multiplicity of choice,
this goes for us if we are
devils
or angels
or counterfeiters
or Ezras and others coming up a walk . . .
If I described all these wonders to you now,
would you believe me?

THESE ACKNOWLEDGMENTS
CONTAIN SPOILERS

I cannot stress enough the delicacy and detailed eye that was brought to my little winter's tale by freelance editor Liz Johnston. From suggesting the inclusion of floor plans, to gently asking after the fate of Olive's considerate sentry when I had lost my nerve on following through with him, to assuaging my hesitancy re the novel's pandemic setting by pointing out that my denouement evokes an LTC window visit, she was witty and exacting with her challenges and eloquent in her support. It was fortunate for me that Kelsey Attard engaged her services on my behalf.

Thanks to: Dr. David Sutton, Mani Haghighi, Maggie Helwig, Alan Gasser, Daniel Mroz, Elizabeth Rucker, Davoud Magidian, Bill Barclay, Christine McNair, Anita Dolman, Everett Dixon, Jean Yoon, Jiri Cizek, Erin Brubacher, Kate Cayley, Catherine Cooper, Alana Wilcox, Coach House Books and the Ontario Arts Council.

Angel names were mostly found in *The Dictionary of Angels,* by Gustav Davidson, The Free Press, 1967.

The eight epigraphic definitions are drawn from the *The Oxford Dictionary of Art,* edited by Ian Chilvers, Harold Osborne, and Dennis Farr (1994). Every effort has been made to contact their heirs and obtain permission for the use of this material.

Sanam mouths the words of a tenth-century poem by Roudaki when Hannie forbids entrance to her studio. Here is the poem, translated by the Iran Chamber Society. Every effort has been made to contact this organization and obtain permission for the use of this material:

> Muliyon laps and glitters, and calls me,
> And my beloved ane calls me.
> The river sand of the Amu is at my feet like silk.
> Hard ford and green hills calls me.
> Up there foam reaches the knees of horses,
> Up there Jeykhun is crying: they call me.

Later, Amir and Sanam have an argument about which sibling is more worthy of being visited by angels. Within their argument, they each quote fragments of a fourteenth-century poem by Hafez. Amir quotes from the poem again during the studio crawl. Here is the poem in its entirety, translated into English by Mani Haghighi:

> Saw angels at the bar last night, knocking down the door,
> Saw them knead Adam's mud with wine.
> Down from the region of concealment
> to have a drink with a bum like me!
> Heavens just couldn't bear to keep their secrets,
> And so there it was, my name on the lot they drew.
> Forget the Seventy-Two Nations' War:
> Groping for truth, they stumbled down the road to legend.
> Thank God Peace was declared between He and I,
> Now dancing sufis are just guzzling that thanksgiving wine.
> The flame that makes the candle smile? That's not a 'Fire'—
> A Fire is what charred down the field of moths!
> No one can rip the veil off the face of truth like me!
> I'm the one who combs the tress of truth with my pen!

I learned about the notorious practice of copying an original and selling it on the Asian market from the article "How to Make a Fake," by Clive Thompson in New York Magazine, May 20, 2004, about dealer Ely Sakhai.

Lyrics from Kim Hyun-sik's "I Am the Wind" were translated for me by Jean Yoon.

Spanish bits were confirmed for me by my multilingual brother, Everett Dixon.

The oversized declarations by Armando's demon are rendered in the Toronto Subway font, designed by David Vereschagin for Quadrat.

The "well-known author" quoted on pages 305–306 is Andre Alexis, who kindly answered this question posed by me.

The statement the demonically possessed Armando makes in the Sistine Chapel, that "when you've seen one painted figure of Michelangelo you've seen them all" is a paraphrase of a translation of an actual quote from a contemporary critic, Lodovico Dolce, found in Michelangelo: Divine Draftsman and Designer by Carmen C. Bambach et al.

The sentry's letter contains a quote from the artist Tamara de Lempicka: "There are no miracles. There is only what you make."

Thanks to Amiel Gladstone for holding on to the working drafts for me during the pandemic.

Love and thanks above all to Kat, my partner in everything; and to Ava, our spectacular child.

SEAN DIXON grew up in a family of 12, including his 8 siblings, parents and a grandmother, through several Ontario towns, predisposing him to tell stories about groups of people thrown together in common cause. His debut novel, *The Girls Who Saw Everything*, was named one of *Quill & Quire*'s best of the year. His previous books include *The Many Revenges of Kip Flynn*, *The Feathered Cloak*, along with the plays *Orphan Song* and the Governor General's Award nominated *A God In Need of Help*. A recent children's picture book, *The Family Tree*, was inspired by his experience of creating a family through adoption with his wife, the documentarian Kat Cizek.